THE *SPIES* IN JIMMY'S PLACE

A SUSPENSE NOVEL

MICHAEL MAYO

CAVEL PRESS

Kenmore, WA

CAMEL PRESS

A Camel Press book published by Epicenter Press

Epicenter Press
6524 NE 181st St. Suite 2
Kenmore, WA 98028.
www.Epicenterpress.com
www.Coffeetownpress.com
www.Camelpress.com

For more information go to: www.epicenterpress.com
www.mike-mayo.com

ISBN: 9781684923083 (trade paper)
ISBN: 9781684923090 (ebook)
LOC: 2024952540

For Marcia

And

Jan Harrison

Foreword

Like the other novels in the Jimmy Quinn series, this one is fiction based on fact, specifically, the events that followed the arrest of Bruno Richard Hauptmann. The details of news reports, police actions, and weather are real. So was the explosive polnol.

See the Author's Notes to differentiate the real, the invented, and the repositioned.

Chapter One

WEDNESDAY, SEPTEMBER 19, 1934

"We got him, the son of a bitch that snatched the Lindbergh kid. He's a kraut who lives up in the Bronx, name's Hauptmann, Bruno Richard Hauptmann. I was in on the stakeout."

The words were like an electric current running up through my shoes to my fingertips. It had been two and a half years since the Crime of the Century. The guy telling me they solved it was Detective William Ellis, a cop I had a working relationship with. We were in the Second Precinct Station House which is usually quiet on a weekday afternoon. That's why I was there. On the third Wednesday of every month, I delivered an envelope to a Captain that Meyer Lansky kept on the payroll.

The building was down on Greenwich Street by the El. You see, the Second wasn't like most Station Houses. When they built it, they thought that Reds might try to bomb it or take it over, so they put the building off a courtyard that ran between Greenwich and Washington Streets with heavy gates on both ends. Like I said, every time I'd been there, nothing worth speaking of was going on. I'd go inside, talk to the Desk Sergeant if it was a guy I knew, and then find the Captain, retire to somewhere private and slip him his "honorarium," as he called it. But that Wednesday, the courtyard was packed with cops, uniforms, plain clothes detectives, even some brass, and civilians. First, I thought maybe there was some kind of ceremony, handing out a commendation or medal, but no, this wasn't a celebration. They were all talking in low voices. I asked the kid at the gate what it was. He said, "I dunno but it's something important. Phones been ringing for more than an hour."

I went in and edged through the crowd to the officers' locker room upstairs. That's where Ellis spotted me and gave me the news.

He muttered, "Schwarzkopf's gonna question him, but everybody wants to be in on this. Hell, they're saying Hoover came up from Washington. He's around here someplace. We got the guy through the money—the gold certificate business with the serial numbers."

I was about to ask him what he was talking about when things got louder on the other side of the room. Somebody yelled to clear a path through and that electric charge I'd felt seemed to flow through the crowd. Guys pushed against us as they made way. Ellis was tall enough to see over them. I muscled through using my stick to make room. After lifting kegs and cases for years, I'm stronger than you'd expect of a guy my size. I got to the front as they went past, hustling Hauptmann to an interrogation room in back. He was a sharp-faced little guy with a sweaty, sick look. He wore a dark gray double-breasted suit, blue shirt, old tan hat, and blue and gray striped silk tie. He was cuffed and braced by three big bulls crowded around him. Schwarzkopf was right with them in his sharp New Jersey state cop uniform with the breeches. Another tight-faced guy with a better suit and a hat pulled down tight to his ears hurried to keep up with Schwarzkopf. I made him for a Bureau man. They pushed their way through without saying anything.

I'm not sure what I'd been expecting. Truth is, from the beginning I figured somebody who committed the Crime of the Century would be more threatening, but this was just a regular guy. You passed him on a sidewalk, you wouldn't even notice him. Then I thought about it and remembered that's how you want to look when you're up to something. Hell, I learned that when I was ten years old. Shouldn't need to remind myself.

I spent another twenty minutes looking for my Captain. More men were crowding in and by then the place was so jammed up, I gave it up for a bad job. The Second being that crowded, the Captain wouldn't check in and I'd have to explain that to Lansky. I had to go uptown to his apartment anyway, because he wanted to see me about something else. Didn't say what it was, only that it was important and needed to be face to face. But it was too early. I had an hour to kill and it was my day to open, so I caught a cab to Jimmy's Place.

I got there right before three. We didn't open until four, so I spent some time tidying up the joint before the first customers came in. They were a couple of guys I didn't know and they took a two-top. The same with the next four who walked through the door. I was drawing their beers and trying to figure how I could casually spread the news, when I saw a familiar smiling face. Franz Voss.

Thus it began.

Voss stepped up to the bar and put his foot on the rail. I was already making his drink. He opened his cigarette case, took one out, and asked how life was treating me.

"They caught him, the guy who kidnapped the Lindbergh baby. He's a kraut."

He forgot about his smoke and stared straight at me. "What? I haven't heard anything about it on the radio."

"The press doesn't know about it yet. They got him this morning. He's being booked at the Second Precinct House. I just came from there. They say Hoover's up from Washington."

Voss frowned. "You're sure the man is German."

"That's what a cop I know told me. Said he's from the Bronx. First word is they caught him with one of the ransom bills."

Still frowning, Voss shook his head and muttered to himself something about "complicating things." Then he tossed back his drink, dropped a couple of bills on the bar, and said, "I'm afraid I don't have time to talk, Jimmy. I'll see you soon," before he hurried back out the door.

• • •

I laid eyes on Franz Voss for the first time a week or so after I bought the place. That would have been late 1928 or early 1929. Call it five years past. A slow Wednesday, about four thirty. No customers. I was polishing glasses. Fat Joe Beddoes was at his seat near the front door. A gent came in and spoke to Fat Joe like he knew him, even shook his hand. Fat Joe actually smiled, something you didn't see often. The gent gave his hat to the girl who was working the coat room and took a few moments to look the place over as he approached the bar. The first thing I noticed about him was his suit. Bespoke. Savile Row, I thought. Fit him perfectly. The suit was a navy three-piece with a faint pattern to the weave. Bright yellow tie. Polished black brogans. The Brooks Brothers I was wearing looked shabby by comparison. He was not much taller than me with pale skin, bone-white hair neither short nor long, and a quick smile.

He perched on a bar stool across from me and said, "I heard this place had changed hands. The last time I was here, Carl Spinoza owned it. Good to see that Fat Joe's still here. I've been told that you have the finest selection of spirits in the city, and I suspect that you are the owner."

I nodded. "Jimmy Quinn. There may be bars in some of the hotels that have more brands than we do, and they may have bartenders who will put together screwier cocktails, but I'll stack my inventory up against anyone. What can I get for you?"

He eyed the bottles behind me and pointed at the top shelf. "Is that really Teeling?" One of the better Irish whiskies.

"Everything you see up there is the McCoy, except the King's Ransom Scotch. I wouldn't carry it but a lot of my customers won't drink anything else." Since the first days of Prohibition, King's Ransom had been doctored with things I didn't want to think about, but it wasn't expensive and some guys developed a taste for it.

"Let me have the Teeling then, a double. Two cubes. You do have cubes, don't you, not shaved or crushed?"

I fished out two ice cubes from the bin and showed them to him. He approved. I poured a couple of generous tots into a short glass and set it on a coaster in front of him. He held it up to the light and appreciated the color. "I like to give it just a few seconds to cool to the proper temperature. Two solid, completely frozen cubes is all that you need to chill the whiskey without diluting it, as cracked or shaved ice will do. Two cubes is perfection. If you look closely, you can see how the pale amber whiskey and the small amount of water from the melting ice swirl and commingle around the cubes. Beautiful." He took a long sip and closed his eyes in appreciation. *Commingle*? I thought I knew what it meant, but I'd have to look it up to be sure.

He put the glass down and stuck his hand across the bar. "Franz Voss, Mr. Quinn, pleased to make your acquaintance."

"What do you do, Mr. Voss?"

"Nothing in particular. I dabble in the market. Sometimes I help people turn money into more money, you know how it goes. How did you come to take this place over from Carl? I ask because you appear to be rather young. One doesn't see many neighborhood bars that carry this kind of merchandize."

"It was a matter of timing. I came into an inheritance when Carl was ready to retire."

"If I'm not asking you to give away a trade secret, how are you able to deal in quality goods like this?"

"I know some people."

"Is this your first business?"

"Yes."

"You're charging what, three or four times more than other places in this part of town?"

I shrugged and nodded.

"And that is at least part of the reason you and I are the only ones here. I'll do all I can to keep you in business and the riff raff out."

We both laughed at that, and the rest of the conversation was the same. He flattered me, showing a genuine interest in what it was like to run a ginmill. At the time, I was nineteen, twenty years old. Not many grown men wanted to know what I thought about anything. That's the way it was with him. He'd be in, always early in the afternoon, a couple of times a week, then he'd disappear for months. I looked forward to talking with him and was always happy to see him.

That first afternoon, he drained his whiskey, pulled a thin gold watch out of his vest pocket and said, "Oh, no, late again. I must go but we'll be seeing more of each other, I'm sure."

When he opened his coat and fished his wallet out of his breast pocket, I saw the label. Davies & Son. It was Savile Row, all right.

He was wearing it the night I shot him.

Chapter Two

When Frenchy and Marie Therese came in, I took a cab to Central Park West and went into the lobby of the Majestic apartment building. After talking to Lansky on the house phone, the guy at the desk sent me up to the third floor. I knocked and let myself in. The big apartment overlooked the park. It was warm enough that the windows were open and you could see out over the trees.

Lansky came out of his office in the library. He frowned when he saw the envelope in my hand. "What went wrong?"

"Your Captain likes to meet on the QT at the Second Precinct House. The place was packed this afternoon. Ellis says they caught the guy who kidnapped the Lindbergh kid and brought him there for questioning. I saw him."

Lansky's eyes opened wide. The news hit him like it hit me. "Anybody we know?"

I shook my head. "Ellis said he's a kraut from Brooklyn named Hauptmann. Didn't look much like a kraut to me. Just a regular joe."

I held out the envelope. "If the Captain was there, I couldn't find him."

Lansky waved it off. "Keep it until he calls me. You think it's really the guy?"

"I don't know any of the particulars, but the cops were acting like it. Schwarzkopf was there, and there was another guy, looked like he was from the Bureau of Investigation. Ellis said Hoover came up from Washington. I didn't see him."

"That bastard!" Lansky's face twisted at the name of the man who was giving him so much trouble. He blamed Hoover for listening in on his telephone lines. Lansky, as they say, kept his business under his hat in the best of times, but with the cops snooping in so many different ways, he didn't use a telephone for anything. With the end of Prohibition, you'd have thought the cops and the Bureau would have backed off, but ever since La Guardia had been elected Mayor and started booting the Tammany guys, they'd got serious about "good government." They were even about to install a new Police Commissioner who promised to clean up the department. At the time, I didn't take it seriously, but you never know.

Lansky had seen the end of Prohibition coming and before it happened, he was setting up a casino in Saratoga with Joe Adonis and Frank Costello. It was a classy carpet joint. Like selling alcohol had been, it was illegal but most people thought it was fine, and it was aimed at the society crowd from the city who went up to the races in August. As long as the local politicians were paid off and jobs were created for their friends and the local farmers got contracts for milk, meat, and vegetables, everybody was happy. Everybody made money.

But Lansky had other things on his mind. "Don't worry about that Captain. He's small change," he said and that strange day got even stranger.

"I need to use your place tomorrow. Longy and I are meeting some important people. We've got to work out the details of some business that's turning out to be trickier than it ought to be. Sometime in the morning before you open."

Longy was Longy Zwillman, the boss of the important rackets in New Jersey. Over the years, I'd transported booze, pinball machines, and this and that for him. Him and Lansky got along because they went out of their way not to get in each other's business.

"Ten o'clock too early? What is it?" I couldn't think of anything those two would be working on together that would need me.

Lansky shrugged with a curious little smile. "It's hard to describe. It involves a rabbi, a judge, and those goddamned Nazis."

"What the hell?"

"Yeah, I know. Like I say, hard to describe."

Stranger and stranger still.

Chapter Three

The truth is I didn't have to work for Meyer Lansky, but I'd been dealing with him since I was a kid. If I stopped without a reason, it would look funny to people. And right then, I didn't want to do anything that looked funny.

About four months before they nabbed Hauptmann, my beautiful and larcenous girlfriend Connie Nix went to Paris. While she was there, a couple of millionaires tried to kill me. Three times. I've already told the story, so I won't go into it again, but it wasn't completely finished. With the help of some associates and Connie when she got back, I persuaded the millionaires not to try to kill me again. We persuaded them permanently. Three other men died that night, and in the process, we stole about a hundred thousand dollars and as many crates of expensive liquor and wine as we could load onto Frenchy's truck.

You don't walk away from something like that, killing a couple of powerful millionaires. At the time we did it, they had borrowed or stolen the hundred grand from the companies they owned, so it was to everyone's benefit for them to have passed away quietly from natural causes. At home. That's what you read in the papers a few days later. As for the other guys, nobody cared about them, and the cops were able to claim there'd been a falling out among thieves.

But even if the cops weren't looking for us, that kind of killing does something to you. I'd been in tough situations before, where I'd shot guys and guys shot at me, and I'd been beat up more often than I like to remember. But that time was more of a nightmare than anything I'd done. It got to Connie even more.

A couple of weeks after it, I woke as the sun was coming up, around five, maybe. We were in my third-floor rooms at the Chelsea. The blackout curtains were open and Connie was sitting in an armchair facing the window looking down at West Twenty-third Street. It was already a warm morning but she had a blanket wrapped around her. I got out of bed and sat on the floor next to her.

Without looking away from the window, she said, "Do you ever think about the people you shot, the ones you killed?"

That was a question I'd half expected but didn't want to hear. "Yeah, sometimes."

"Does it bother you?"

I started to say no like I was some kind of tough guy, but that was a lie. "Every time. Mostly at first, but I've never shot anybody who wasn't trying to kill me or threatening somebody else." That last part wasn't completely true but it was true enough to answer her question.

She turned her head and looked at me. "I shot two men."

"They were trying to kill you. Don't forget that."

"You've said that before, and I know it's true, but I still see their faces." Her voice sounded raw, quavering like she was about to cry.

"When I was twelve years old, me and Walter Spencer, your old boss, and Oh Boy Oliver went out with some other guys to hijack a shipment of booze straight off the boat down in New Jersey. It was late at night on a sandy road in the middle of a bunch of pine trees. We ambushed them, but they had as many guns and clubs as we had, I guess. Maybe more. I shot two of 'em. Oh Boy shot one, a guy who was coming right at me. I didn't see what Spence did, not all of it, but he was in the thick of things, and he'd been in the war, so I guess it was easier for him. But, yeah, I still think of it sometimes, usually when I smell a pine tree, and I still get a little sick to my stomach. Then I remember that everybody who was there that night, meaning us and the guys who got hijacked, each one of us knew what he getting into. He knew he was breaking the law and he was hoping to make a lot of money. It was the same with you and me that night."

She looked at me. "You were twelve?"

"It was different then. I don't know how to explain it."

"But that's not like what we did."

"Maybe it is and maybe it's not, but don't forget they killed other people, too, men and women. And when it mattered, we were better prepared."

That morning in the Chelsea, she didn't believe me. I knew her well enough to understand that, and I didn't press her on it because I knew

I couldn't make her feel any better. I also knew it had changed her, just like going to Paris had changed her. I think Connie got over the horror of that night by focusing on the money. There was a lot of it stored in the basement of Jimmy's Place. It became a problem to solve and she has a good mind for things like that. The first thing was figuring out where we could put the cash without doing anything out of the ordinary or anything that looked funny.

Chapter Four

It was past three when I got back to Jimmy's Place. It's on the bottom floor of a brownstone, a few steps down from the sidewalk. The Cruzon Grill is upstairs. My place is narrow and long and not nearly as dark as it used to be. I started remodeling before Prohibition ended and paid out serious money to get the permit and license applications I needed, and to get moved to the front of the line. I figured that if I was going to turn a successful speakeasy—or "speak" in the parlance of the day—into a successful legal bar, I needed to be open as quick as I could after they repealed Prohibition. Some places closed down for months. Not mine.

Being legal turned out to be a hell of a lot more complicated than I thought. My lawyer Jacobson told me I had to hire an accountant to take care of taxes. He knew a guy. Then I had to have a bank account for the business. For years I'd been padding the pay envelopes of my two beat cops, Norris and Mahan, to keep an eye on the place. After Repeal, I made arrangements for them to drive one of us to the night deposit of the Corn Exchange Bank on nights we knew we'd be busy.

We refinished the mahogany bar that runs down the right side and put in mirrors and small lights that gave the room a warmer feeling. Reupholstered the booths. Put in new padded bar stools and were still replacing the older chairs and two-tops and four-tops. New fixtures in the bathrooms, too. Had coasters, napkins, and matchboxes made up with 'Jimmy's Place' on them. As much as I complained while I was paying for all that, I had to admit that it worked. Like most speaks, mine served a fair number of women but they were almost always there with a husband or boyfriend. Once we were legal, and put up a classy green canvas awning outside, we started attracting younger women in groups. You see, during Prohibition, it was common knowledge that both crooks and cops were welcome in my place and that nobody was allowed to bring a gun. That might have made some ladies think that it wasn't the sort of establishment where they'd feel comfortable.

After I bought the building in 1928, it took a while for word to get about that we were dealing in the good stuff. Once it did, business was fine. Then came the Crash, and we struggled along with everybody else. Frenchy and Marie Therese Reneau came with the place. They'd been there since it opened and knew all there was to know about the day-to-day running of it. Frenchy's a big man who spends most of his time behind the bar where he is a master of his trade. He's about twice the size of Marie Therese. She is a soft touch who collects strays. She does it so well and so often that she's been responsible for more than half of the waitresses who have worked at the place since I've owned it.

Fat Joe Beddoes also came with the deal. He was a thick-necked slugger who worked the door and kept the right people out during Prohibition. Since Repeal, he'd been sitting by the door and pretending that it's work or drinking with some of the guys he palled around with. I don't think I ever heard him speak without him saying either "fuck" or "shit." Quick to ask for an advance on his pay, sucked down as much free beer as he could, and left a half hour early unless I told him not to.

Arch Malloy's a wiry old Mick with a soup strainer mustache and an opinion about everything—a "well informed opinion," he'll tell you and Arch is always happy to talk. He's traveled all over the world and he reads constantly. He wound up working for me after he got fired as a guard in a warehouse that was owned by the first Nazis I met. The Nazis and me, we did not get along, but that's another story I've told before.

Now Lansky had something to do with those bullying bastards. I had a feeling his being involved would be difficult. I didn't know the half of it.

Arch, Frenchy, and Marie Therese were in on the heist. Fat Joe overcharged us for a couple of riot guns but didn't know anything about what we did with them. I didn't trust him anyway. On one of the first nights the money was there, the five of us stayed after we closed and talked it through. We agreed that there would be no big spending for a year. Connie had measured the cash and decided that each share, or most of it, would fit inside a large safety deposit box. I volunteered to scout out banks that looked like they weren't in danger of folding, not immediately, at least. I didn't want to rent another box under my own name, and I didn't think they should. I told them, I'd figured a way to get around that. They were interested. I went to work on it.

That Wednesday, Fat Joe grunted at me when I came in. I made a quick count of customers. Fourteen. Not good, not bad, a typical Wednesday. Arch, Frenchy, and Marie Therese were behind the bar. They didn't need me. I asked if Connie had come in. Marie Therese said she was in my office. I went up the back stairs.

Connie was at my desk with a pencil between her teeth and account books in front of her. The safe was open. So was the cashbox. She was working with the doctored receipts she was creating to account for the recent increase in our sales. A dance band was playing on the radio and she moved her head to the music. She was so intent on her work and the music that she didn't hear the door open. Her head snapped up when she noticed me, and her hand went straight toward the .25 automatic in the open drawer on her right.

I took off my coat. "Has there been anything on the radio about it?"

"Anything on the radio about what?"

I guess they were still keeping it under wraps. "They caught the guy who kidnapped the Lindbergh baby. I was down at the Second Precinct this afternoon when they brought him in. I saw him."

It hit her as hard as it hit Lansky, and she reacted the same. Her eyes got wide and she said, "Is it anybody you know?"

"No. Detective Ellis was there. He told me the guy's a kraut from Brooklyn. Name's Hauptmann. But nothing on the radio or in the late edition papers? They must want to sweat him as hard as they can before the word gets out."

"What were you doing at the Second Precinct?"

"Lansky." That was all I needed to say. "And, he wants to use this place tomorrow morning for a meeting with Longy Zwillman."

She made a face trying to remember the name. "From New Jersey?" I nodded. "Why here?"

"The Bureau's been bugging Lansky's phones and hanging around outside most of the places he uses for business. Him and Longy know they can talk here without being overheard. Tell Vittorio I'll come in early and make coffee."

Vittorio ran the Cruzon Grill on the top two floors of the building.

I stuck a finger between the slats of the Venetian blinds on the window that looks down on the bar. "We're filling up. If you've got more to do with the books, stay here. It's not that busy."

She closed the cashbox and the account books and put them in the safe. "I've done enough of this for now."

"Anything else?"

"Yes," she said with a smile that probably meant I was in trouble. "You got two telephone calls this afternoon. One was from," she read a slip of paper, "Petey Beck."

"Good, about time he got it done."

"And the second was from Daphne Prewitt, your old girlfriend."

Oh, hell. "Did you talk to her? What did she say?"

"Marie Therese took the calls. Here's the numbers."

I turned the telephone around, unhooked the earpiece and dialed Beck. No answer. The same with Daphne. Connie watched me, still smiling that funny little smile. I figured if I said anything about Daphne, she'd give me the business so I waited her out while she locked the safe.

Before we left to go downstairs, she checked herself in the mirror, added a little color to her lips and brushed her shiny black hair. Trying to sound like it meant nothing, she said, "What do you think she wants?"

That, I could answer honestly. "I have no idea. I have not spoken to her in… what? More than a year."

I couldn't tell whether Connie believed me. Figure, probably not.

That night, Connie and Marie Therese waited tables. I stayed behind the bar with Frenchy and Arch. A few minutes later, one of our regulars came in. I poured a double shot of good rye as soon as I saw him. After he'd had his first long soul-restoring drink, he asked how I was doing. I told him I had it on good authority that they'd caught the guy who kidnapped the Lindbergh baby. Sweating him down at the Second Precinct. Probably read about it in the papers tomorrow. Connie was saying the same thing to her customers. Within minutes, the bar was buzzing with it, and a normal Wednesday night changed. People started talking about where they'd been when they heard about the kidnapping… how they knew somebody who knew somebody who said… how it was all a hoax, that hadn't been the real baby they found. Still, there was nothing on the radio. Around eleven, another guy came in and said he'd heard the same thing someplace else, and that started it up again.

If you don't remember the particulars, one night in March of 1932, somebody climbed a ladder to a second-story window of the Lindbergh house out in the middle of New Jersey. He stole the baby son of the most famous man in the world and left a ransom note on the bed. "Lucky" Lindy paid a ransom and he and his wife waited and waited. Nothing. A few months later in May, a colored man found the little body in a shallow grave in the woods not five miles from the house. It was clear from the decomposition that the guy who took him killed the kid that first night.

Then the story slowly went away. You'd see pieces in the paper saying that the cops were sure they knew a gang of five men and a woman had taken kid, but nothing would come of it. About a year later, the fall of '33, the New Jersey and New York cops turned it over to the Bureau of Investigation. After that, you might see the kidnapping mentioned in a story about the various flying trips that the Lindberghs took, but that was all. Until that afternoon.

We closed before two, and Connie and I walked back to the Chelsea. She waited until I was in bed with a brandy and she was down to her silk slip. She poured a short one for herself and slid into bed beside me. "Seriously, what does she want? Daphne."

At one time, Daphne Prewitt was the prettiest and most popular blonde who worked for Polly Adler. She looked enough like Fay Wray that she was offered the lead in a blue movie version of *King Kong*. That didn't pan out, but not long after it, she became a kept woman.

"I told you she's got a Wall Street sugar daddy who set her up in a little house down in the Village. Last time I talked to her, she was worried that he was getting her into some kind financial scheme that wasn't completely legal. She didn't understand it, but he told her to dress really conservatively and not wear makeup and then go to different brokerage houses at certain times, find certain guys by name, and then buy 'instruments.' Even if she didn't know what was going on, she could tell that the young guys who were selling her these 'instruments,' whatever they were, knew that something wasn't kosher. But whatever the game was, she was getting big cashier's checks delivered by messengers. She was talking about thousands of dollars. She wanted to know how much I'd charge her to figure out what was going on. I told her ten percent, but that was the end of it. And that was a year ago."

I started to go on but remembered something else. "You know, the last time I saw Daphne, it was in the bar, and she was talking to you."

Connie ignored that. "When she was at Polly's, did you ever…"

"As a gentleman, I can't—"

"Gentleman, my ass! You couldn't afford her." She put our glasses on the bedside table and rolled over on top of me. I helped her with her slip. "Call her tomorrow," she said. "I want to know what she wants."

Chapter Five

Thursday morning, I was up by eight, a ridiculous hour. Showered and strapped on my brace. I chose a grayish blue double-breasted from Finchley, light blue striped shirt, and a silvery silk tie. I stopped at a newsstand and picked up all the morning papers. The big story was the still-unsolved hijacking of a mail truck two months ago in Chicago. Nothing about the kidnapping. They'd really locked down the lid on this guy. I walked around the block to Twenty-Second Street and let myself in through the front door. When I got up to my office, I could hear the sounds of guys moving in the kitchen above me. I went up the stairs, had an egg sandwich, and told them I'd need a coffee service for two later.

Back at my desk, I tuned the radio to WNYC where I was likely to hear news, not music, and went over Connie's count from the night before. When I put my estimate of our real take against the numbers Connie had recorded, it looked like she bumped us up about twenty percent. We still had more cash in the place than I was comfortable with, but I hoped to talk to Petey Beck and take care of that. I found his number tucked into the edge of the blotter and dialed. Again, nothing.

When I'd finished, I went down to the cellar to make certain nobody was there. Then I unlocked the front door and busied myself spiffing the place up. Lansky walked in at quarter after ten and did a small doubletake. It had been a couple of years since he'd been there. "What did you do to the place? The awning's a nice touch."

"Things changed with Repeal. Now that everybody's selling good booze, I've got to build up my business in the neighborhood. So far, we're doing fine. You want coffee?"

He said yes. I called up to the kitchen and had them send it down in the dumbwaiter. Meyer sat down at the four-top where I'd spread out the newspapers and read. He'd got to the sports pages where the Giants had extended their lead over the Cards when Longy Zwillman shouldered through the front door. He was a tall, thick, barrel-chested guy with a big nose and wavy hair that he kept carefully combed. Like Lansky, he was wearing an expensive black suit, and like Lansky he did a doubletake when he got a look at the place. The last time he'd been there was years before and he was squiring Jean Harlow around.

"When did you get so high-hat, Quinn? Hello, Meyer."

They nodded to each other. Lansky said, "Yesterday, Jimmy told me they got the guy who kidnapped the Lindbergh baby, but there's nothing about it in the papers. They're really sweating the bastard."

Longy looked at me. "Is that straight?"

I explained that I was at the Second Precinct on other business when they brought him in, and that it was crammed with cops.

"Was Schwarzkopf there?" he asked. I nodded.

"About goddamn time," he muttered around his cigar. "You know I actually offered a reward for the guy that did it when the kidnapping happened. Troopers were pulling over too many of my trucks. A couple of guys showed up, claimed they knew who it was, but they were trying to con me. The bastards. They didn't con anybody after that."

"Gentlemen, if you'd like anything else, the bar is open."

Meyer shook his head. Longy said he'd take a cognac with his coffee. I got the bottle of Delamain down from the top shelf, poured a generous snifter and left the bottle on the table. "Some guys are working in the kitchen on the top floor. I've checked the cellar. Nobody's there, but if you'd like to look at it yourself… I'll be in my office if you need anything."

I've learned that it's good to be careful around guys as powerful as Lansky and Longy. Things are just different with them. For instance, Meyer didn't ask if he could use my place for the meeting. He told me. But you can't bow and scrape to them, either. You do that, they'll walk all over you, and that's not good for business. The Delamain was a small investment.

They talked for thirty, forty minutes. I was going through the *Gotham Comet* when Meyer came in and said, "I need to do this again on Sunday morning. There'll be three of us, and make sure the place looks good. I'm going to have important guests."

Later when I went downstairs to clean up, I saw that Longy had had two more knocks, maybe three of the Delamain. Must have been a serious conversation.

Chapter Six

I tried to telephone Daphne Prewitt again that afternoon. Still nothing. Petey Beck called at five and said he'd be in that evening.

Back in June, when we decided to stash our money in safety deposit boxes, I said I'd scout around to find banks that looked safe. That was easy enough. But any bank we'd want to deal with would demand identification, and we didn't plan to use our real names. If there was a way to slip around that bit of business, I didn't know it. I did know how to find phony papers, assuming the guy was still in business and hadn't been locked up. Petey Beck was said to be the second-best counterfeiter and forger in the city, and if you didn't believe it, he'd tell you himself, leaving out the 'second-.'

He worked for a printing company down on Beekman Street near the newspaper offices on Park Row. I didn't know the name or the address, but I remembered that it was on a corner and Beekman was a short street. As a sideline, Petey could produce just about any kind of official document you might happen to need. He'd been a customer since Carl Spinoza owned the joint. Now, Carl was the one who let everybody know that both cops and gang guys were welcome. That's why Petey drank there. It was a good place to pick up some after-hours business. But I hadn't seen him in more than a year, so I was waiting outside the building where he worked one afternoon around five. I stayed on the other side of the street. He didn't leave with the first big group of men in coveralls who came out of double doors on the cross street. They kept hitting the sidewalk for another half hour. Petey came out the front door with a couple of other guys, the three of them in suits and carrying briefcases. He was an older, balding, stoop-shouldered jamoke who wore wire-rimmed glasses. He fired up a cigarette as soon as he was out of the building. They headed toward a subway station. I gimped ahead of them. Petey saw me and stopped when I crossed the street. He told the other two to go on. I asked if there was someplace close where we could talk. He knew a bar.

It was an older place on the second floor of a building that didn't have an elevator. They hadn't redecorated and it probably looked like it did in 1920—pressed tin ceiling, electric fixtures in the gaslights, cracked tile floor, spittoons by the bar. That time of the afternoon, it was filling up. All men, mostly working men, no women. We took a booth that had some privacy. When the waiter came over, I asked Petey what he wanted. "I remember your drink was Scotch, King's Ransom, right?"

"If you're buying, make it Dewars."

"Two Dewars with ice."

After the waiter left, I leaned forward toward Petey and said, "I've got work. You interested?"

"As long as it's not too complicated. I'm about to throw in on a big job, a really, big job with Romeo Forlini."

That might have been true, but I didn't buy it. Word was about that Forlini had been behind the $500,000 mail robbery in Chicago. I noticed then that Petey's long thin fingers were twisted with arthritis. I'd served him often enough at the bar to know that his hands hadn't looked like that before.

"I need five New York Operator's Licenses, three for men, two for women, and five proof of residence documents, utility bills or leases with the same information on those. Keep them in the city."

"That's easy enough." He smiled. "What else?"

The waiter came back with the drinks. I didn't say anything until he'd left. The scotch had been watered down.

"What do you need to put on the licenses?" I asked.

"Just the basics. Name and address, date of birth, color, sex, weight, height, eye color, hair color." He blinked behind the glasses.

"You better write this down."

He took out a business envelope, and slowly unscrewed the top off a fountain pen.

"For the first woman, her name is Simone Patterson. Let's give her an address in Washington Square. Born on April 1, 1915. White. Female. A hundred and ten pounds, five foot three, eyes brown, hair black." That was Connie.

"The second woman is Jeanette Martin. She can be in Washington Square, too."

He interrupted. "The same apartment building?"

I hadn't thought about that. This was for Marie Therese. Did it matter? Maybe. "No, make it Brooklyn. Jeannette was born in 1894. White. Female. A hundred and fifteen pounds. Five foot two, eyes hazel, hair blonde."

"The first guy is James Doyle. He lives in Tudor City. Born on January 5, 1910. White. Male. A hundred and fifty pounds, five foot four, eyes black, hair black." That was me.

For Frenchy I said, "The second guy is Paul Martin, same address as Jeanette. Born 1890. White. Male Two hundred and ten pounds. Five foot eleven, eyes brown, hair brown."

"The third guy," Arch, "is Dylan O'Doyle. He lives down on West Thirteenth Street. Born 1881. White. Male. A hundred and forty pounds. Five foot six, eyes brown, hair gray."

He put the pen away and fired up another smoke. "How soon?"

"Next week. How much?"

He pretended to think. "Fifty apiece."

"Two fifty? Hell, I can get these made for a tenth of that."

He sniffed. "You get crap for a tenth of that and you know it. Don't try to jew me down. Half now and half when I'm finished." He was trying to sound tough, but I could tell that he needed the money, or maybe he needed to show himself he could still do the work.

We went back and forth until we'd finished the weak drinks. Then we settled on two hundred, fifty now and one fifty upon completion and approval. Plus a double shot of real Dewars at my place. After that, nothing. A week, my ass. Six months later, he calls and says he's got the material.

I was at my table in back when Beck came in that night. Frenchy and Marie Therese knew who he was and what he did from the days when he was a regular. He was surprised by the changes we'd made, too. He looked around the place until he saw me and hurried to the table. Before he sat down, I knew he was trouble. He had a twitchy smile and he kept looking around like he was afraid somebody was sneaking up behind him.

Arch came over to the table. He knew about the deal I'd done with Beck. "Is this the gentleman you were telling me about, the one you were expecting?" he said. Beck glanced at him and looked away quickly.

"He'll have a double Dewar's on ice."

As soon as Arch was out of earshot, Beck lit a cigarette and said, "It's going to cost you more."

I stared at him and didn't say anything. He worried his smoke until Arch brought his drink. He was getting more uncomfortable so I stayed quiet. The truth is, I figured he try something. I grabbed my stick and nodded toward the stairs. He followed.

In my office, I made a small show of taking off my suit jacket, hanging it up, and sitting behind my desk. Beck sat opposite and drained his drink. He fumbled for another smoke and looked for an ashtray.

"Not here. Not in my office."

He put the pack back in his shirt pocket and squirmed in the chair. "Look, it's hard to get to some of these things now. It's not like it used to be. I mean, the licenses were easy, but the lease agreements took more work, and you got to—"

"Do you have them?"

"What?"

"The licenses and the leases. Five of each. What we agreed on. Do you have them with you?"

He tried to hide his nervousness, and I knew he was about to pull something. He took an envelope out of his coat pocket. "Here's the papers for the women."

I reached across the desk and took the envelope from him. The operator's licenses were simple white cards that had been hand stamped in blue ink by the New York State Department of Motor Vehicles. The personal information had been filled in by hand and he'd left the signature line blank. The leases were complete forms filled out on a typewriter. Simone in Washington Square was on Waverly Place. The Brooklyn address was on Clark Street.

Beck said, "Those are real lease agreements. You can see where the sheets of carbon paper were attached."

"Where are the other three?"

Still trying to look smart, he said, "They're safe, but like I said, expenses have gone up. It's not as easy to get the forms and the right stamps. That's why it took me so l0ng. I knew you wouldn't want second rate work, so for me to cover my nut here, I think it's only fair to ask for another hundred for the rest."

I stared at him without blinking until Beck squirmed in the chair and reached for his cigarettes. After a time, he shrugged and pulled another envelope out of his pocket. "Hell, Quinn, you can't blame a guy for trying."

He had the operator's licenses for Frenchy, Arch, and me, but no leases. For now, Frenchy could stash his money with Marie Therese's, but that didn't help Arch.

"You're still short."

"Don't worry. They'll be ready soon. Maybe tomorrow or the next day. A week at most."

"What happened? Is this big deal you're working with Romeo Forlini taking up all your time?"

"You better believe it. Every night after work. If you knew what we're up to, you'd sell your mother to get in on it. This is gonna be my last job. I'll be able to retire in Florida when it's over."

"Sure you will."

"I don't suppose you could see your way clear to giving me a hundred for the licenses, just to tide me over while I work on those leases. Maybe hurry things along…." I didn't say anything. He shrugged. "Yeah, I thought so." He got up to leave.

"Listen to me." I didn't say anything else until he stopped and looked at me. "If you don't deliver the leases in a week, I will find you."

Chapter Seven

LINDBERGH RANSOM RECEIVER SEIZED;
$13,750 FOUND AT HIS EAST BRONX HOME;
THE MYSTERY SOLVED, POLICE DECLARE

That was the headline in the *Times* Friday morning, and the stories made it clear there was no doubt that Hauptmann did it. The picture they ran had been taken at the Precinct House Thursday. Same suit, same tie, same handcuffs. There were four long stories about the guy and how they caught him. I read every word.

Detective Ellis had been right. It was the money that got him. Two years before, when the kidnapping and ransom demand happened, the government was about to go off the gold standard. I didn't know what that really meant, but for regular people, the important thing was that they were going to take gold certificate bills out of circulation and replace them with a different design. The gold certificates had a round yellow seal on one side that was hard to miss. Somebody had the good idea to use those for the ransom money and to list the serial numbers. After they found the baby's body, they told banks to be on the lookout for the bills, and they were able to trace some of them to bank deposits from stores, theaters and the like. Two years on, the old gold bills were still good but it was illegal to horde them. By then everybody had forgot about the kidnapping, so the cops spread a story that counterfeiters were passing bogus gold certificates and merchants should take note of any they handled. They told service stations to write down license plate numbers if drivers paid with gold certificates.

The bills had started showing up days after the kidnapping but nobody paid any attention to a guy paying for something with small denomination cash. Then just a few weeks ago, bigger bills, tens and twenties, started appearing. A guy bought a pair of expensive shoes in Fordham with a twenty from the ransom money, and the cops got a description of him.

Then a week ago, Hauptmann drove his Dodge to a Warner-Quinlan station up on Lexington Avenue in the Bronx. He asked for five gallons of premium and paid the ninety-eight-cent charge with a ten spot gold certificate. When the day manager, one Walter Lyle by name, made change, he mentioned to the driver that you didn't see many of the gold certificates these days. Hauptmann allowed as how he had a hundred of them at home. Lyle wrote down the license plate number on the ten spot and put it in the register. It went in with the rest of the weekend receipts for deposit at the Corn Exchange Bank where they counted it on Monday morning. The bank called the feds, and the feds called the New York and New Jersey cops. The locals went to the Warner-Quinlan station and talked to Lyle. He remembered that the guy was German. That fit with what the cops already knew. Other bills from the ransom money had been showing up in Yorkville and the Wakefield section of the Bronx, both places popular with the krauts. People remembered the guy passing the banknotes being in his mid-thirties, blond, German accent.

It didn't take them long to trace the license plate number to Hauptmann. Not leaving much to chance, seventy-five cops staked him out for the rest of Monday and Tuesday. When they pinched him after he left his house on Wednesday morning, he had another twenty from the ransom money folded in his vest pocket.

He claimed to know nothing about the Lindbergh kidnapping. He was just a simple carpenter, a gentleman, retired now after hitting it big on Wall Street. They took him back to his house where they found the Fordham shoes in his closet. After that he clammed up. They took him down to the Second Precinct and brought in a taxi driver who'd been in on one of the only face-to-face contacts anybody had with him right after the kidnapping. The cabbie fingered Hauptmann straightaway, no question. But the other guy who'd been involved in the ransom negotiations, a crackpot by the name of John Condon, decided to withhold a complete identification. Even then, he had a reputation as a grandstanding prima donna who'd do anything to see his name in the papers. Truth is, that's how he got involved in the first place.

A day or so after the kidnapping, Condon wrote a letter to a local paper volunteering to be a middleman between Lindbergh and the kidnappers.

Hauptmann wrote back to him accepting the offer, and Condon did the face-to-face negotiating. He was the one who delivered the ransom. But on Wednesday afternoon at the precinct, Condon made a big show out of picking Hauptmann and three other guys out of a line-up, then questioning Hauptmann and talking to him so quietly nobody could hear them. And after all that, he said he couldn't be sure.

While all that was going on, back up in the Bronx the cops were tearing apart Hauptmann's garage. First, they found $10,000.00 in a dirty oil can on a shelf. Tens and twenties wrapped in a newspaper from September, 1932, six months after the kidnapping. They pulled up the floor planking and came up with more money wrapped in more newspapers from September, 1932.

Hauptmann tried to explain it by saying that after he'd made a pile on the stock market and he collected gold certificates because he thought Roosevelt was going to ruin the economy.

When the cops talked to the neighbors, they learned that Hauptmann had fought for the Kaiser as a machine gunner in the Saxon regiment during the Great War. In 1923, Hauptmann stowed away on an ocean liner and snuck into the city. He had a wife, a German woman named Anna, and a ten-month-old baby boy. Said to play a decent game of low-stakes pinochle. As I'd noticed, he dressed well but not fancy. Nothing unusual about his house but he did have a new $400.00 radio set. And the new shoes. He was a hunter and the cops found a pile of raw furs in his place. Hauptmann said he traded them with his partner, a guy named Fisch.

Toward the end of the last story I read in the *Times*, I came across one of those details that hit home. A woman whose husband ran a neighborhood delicatessen said Mrs. Hauptmann had been a customer for about two years and usually paid with a ten or twenty.

"About a year ago her husband came in. He seemed to have taken over the family shopping. One day he gave me a $10 bill and I looked at it, the way you look at all big bills when you own a place like this. But he didn't seem to like it. Neither he nor Mrs. Hauptmann came into the store after that."

Yeah, handling money is always more complicated than you think it's going to be.

That Friday night, Frenchy and I worked behind the bar. Marie Therese was selling cigarettes and cigars out of the coat room because a new girl I'd just hired didn't show up. Arch and Connie waited on the tables and booths. By five, we were filling up and everybody in the place was talking about Bruno Hauptmann. Rumors of an arrest had been getting about on Thursday and it had been announced on the radio late in the day, but after people saw it in the papers, nothing else mattered. Some of the regulars from Wednesday knew that I'd seen the guy, so I was fielding a lot of questions. How tall was he? What did he look like? Nobody asked what I was doing at the Station House, so I didn't have to come up with a story, and I tried not to make too much of it. Sometimes it's nice being the center of attention. Other times, no.

By nine o'clock Petey Beck hadn't shown up with the papers he'd promised. Figured. Things were still busy when Arch edged up to the bar and motioned for me to come over. "A young blonde just took a table. I'm almost certain she's been in before when we were involved with the actress and the moving picture business."

I moved to a spot where I could see that side of the room. It was Daphne, all right. I held up a hand. She nodded.

"She'll have the Chablis and she'll probably want to talk to me." I pulled an open bottle out of the ice and poured a glass. Arch smoothed his mustache with his thumb, put the glass on a tray, and carefully draped a clean napkin over his arm.

"Name's Daphne Prewitt," I said. "How much do you know about her?"

"Enough, I imagine. Connie gave me her particulars." Arch winked and waded into the crowd. He delivered the wine with a small bow and a flourish, and he said something that made Daphne smile.

She still looked terrific. Somebody told me that Robert Benchley said she was the prettiest girl he'd ever seen at Polly Adler's. She was Charlie Luciano's favorite, too. She wore her blonde hair unfashionably long. Like all of Polly's best girls, she could dress herself to the nines for a nightclub opening or a society soirée. Or she could stroll around Polly's wearing high heels and a smile and make herself comfortable on a John's lap. That Friday night, she had on what looked to be a nicely fitted skirt, blouse, and jacket, with her hair done up and a small, tilted hat.

I went back to work but tried to keep an eye on her. A few minutes later, I saw Connie had taken a seat at her table. Looked like they had a lot to say to each other.

But we were so busy that Connie couldn't stay at Daphne's table for too long. Customers kept coming in. It was turning into one of the busiest

Friday nights we'd had in months. By eleven, the place had got so noisy and smokey that I didn't catch the first sounds of the fight, and it started at a six-top right across from me. I heard a loud, aggressive man's voice and saw the guys at the bar turning to look behind them. Then the crowd pressed toward them. I hurried around to the leaf at the far end of the bar, ducked under it, and shouldered my way into the thick crowd.

Two good-sized younger guys, maybe in their twenties, were just squaring off. Both had taken off their coats and pulled their ties loose. Their sweaty faces were red from alcohol and anger. One had his fists up. The other one, taller, was waving a finger in the first one's face and yelling. There were four other guys at the table. They were part of argument the other two were having, and they were talking and yelling at each other, but they were hanging back, not getting between the first two. The tall guy said something like "because he's German." The other one slapped the waving finger away.

By then it sounded like everybody in the place was yelling. I was close enough to jam myself between them but before I could push them apart, they went after each other. Without my stick I couldn't do anything useful and got clipped on an ear and took a couple of decent shots to the ribs for my efforts. Other guys must have been piling in by then because I was getting shoved from all sides, and it took everything I had to stay on my feet. I can't say how long it was before Frenchy and Fat Joe made their way through the crowd, but by the time things calmed down, Frenchy had a headlock around one of the belligerents, and Fat Joe was leading the other one toward the front door.

I couldn't understand what they were saying, but the four that were left still seemed to be arguing about the same thing that started the fight. I told them to settle up with Arch and take care of their friends outside. When Frenchy came back, he asked if I wanted him to try to call patrolmen Norris and Mahan.

"You think they're going to continue to mix it up on the street?"

Fat Joe came over, looking for a beer. I asked him the same thing. "Are those two guys going to cause any trouble outside?"

"Shit no, they just had a little disagreement that got out of hand."

Things had calmed down by then. Daphne was gone and two guys were sitting at her table. The next time Connie got close enough to talk, I asked her what they'd said.

She frowned. "It's hard to… I can't… Look, I'll tell you after we close. It's not what you think. At least, I think it's not what you think."

Anything I said in answer to that would have been wrong, so I kept my mouth shut and waited. We stayed busy, so busy I didn't worry about Daphne, and we didn't close until two o'clock Saturday morning. Maybe the news about Hauptmann made people want to be where they could talk and talking made them thirsty.

It was the best Friday night we'd had in months.

By the time we got back to the Chelsea, both of us were whipped. Connie said no to a cognac. I poured a tot and took off my tie. "Tell me what Daphne said."

Connie unbuttoned her blouse. "She's worried about her boyfriend."

"Is this the same boyfriend she had before? His name is… I know it but I can't remember it. Howard?"

She took a sip of my cognac. "Harold. She says he has come up with a new idea that's 'better than the last one' and that scares her."

Chapter Eight

Connie slept in on Saturday but I got up around noon. I stopped at a newsstand and bought the morning papers and the Friday evening papers. I went to work through the alley so I could check the heavy back gate. From time to time, guys tried to get over or through it, and lately, that happened more often on late weekend nights. The gate was fine. I got coffee from the kitchen of the Cruzon Grill and took it downstairs to a two-top. Arch was behind the bar. He already had one customer.

I spread the newspapers on my table and the one beside it. Fifteen hundred people had died in a typhoon in Japan, but the big stories were all about Bruno Hauptmann, filling in the details. The headlines read: **New Jersey Prepares Murder Charge**. *Foley To Seek Indictment*. **Extradition Is Put Off**. *New Clue In Handwriting*. **Past Bared By Inquiry**, and *Science Used in Search*.

As the papers put it, back in '32, two days after the ransom was paid, the first twenty dollar gold certificate showed up at the East River Savings Bank. The feds printed up thousands of copies of a book that listed the serial numbers of the ransom bills, fifty thousand bucks. A couple of weeks later, the cops went around to the banks to see if the tellers were using the books. They found most of them down in the bottom of drawers. Then they decided to give more of the books to the Federal Reserve district branches, and to put extra girls on duty to do nothing but check for ransom bills.

During those two years, about five thousand turned up at stores near stops on the Lexington Avenue subway line. And they noticed something unusual about the bills. They'd been folded in a particular way—once lengthwise, and then doubled twice, to make a compact little square that a guy could tuck into a vest pocket or watch pocket.

They sent those bills to the city toxicologist. He found that the money had a musty smell, like it had been buried or kept wrapped up away from air. He also found "glycerine esters" that made him think the guy who had the bills was a mechanic, maybe a machinist or a carpenter who sharpened his own tools. One of the ransom notes had included a drawing and instructions including dimensions for making a wooden box to hold the money.

After I read that, I got out my pen and notebook. I opened it to a fresh page and wrote, *toxicologist* and *glycerine esters* to look up later. I figured there would be more to come.

The cops found some shopkeepers who remembered the guy well enough to describe him. They said he looked like a dressed-up working man. Had prominent cheekbones, flat cheeks, cold blue eyes, sharp thin nose, and an unmistakable German accent. That was Hauptmann, all right.

They had given the ransom notes to a psychiatrist who said the writer was methodical, probably German or Teutonic. When they looked into Hauptmann's past, they found that he came from Germany where he had two prior arrests. He'd been locked up for breaking into a mayor's house and stealing goods worth a thousand marks. For that, he was sentenced to a five year stretch, sprung after four for good behavior. After that, he stowed away on a liner from Bremen to New York. They caught him on board the ship and immigration deported him. It didn't take. A few weeks later, in 1923, he was back.

When they asked him again how he came to have thirteen thousand bucks in his garage, Hauptmann changed his story about Roosevelt and the economy. He said the money had been given to him for safekeeping by his fur-trading friend Isador Fisch, while Fisch went to Germany. Fisch couldn't back him up on that because Fisch died while he was there. The truth was, Hauptmann said, he didn't even know it was money that he was keeping until three weeks ago.

The papers also published facsimiles of two of the thirteen ransom notes he wrote to show the similarities with two of the crummy handwriting samples he'd given them at the Second Precinct. One of them was a postcard that read, in capital letters:

MR. CHAS. LINBERG,
YOUR BABY IS SAFE BUT HE IS NOT
USING NO MEDICINES. HE IS EATING
PORK CHOP, PORK AND BEANS JUST WHAT
WE EAT. JUST FOLLOW OUR DIRECTION
AND HAVE ONE HUNDRED THOUSAND
BUCKS READY IN VERY SHORT TIME
THATS JUST WHAT WE NEED
YOURS, B.H.

Did he really sign the card with his initials? I know it sounds unbelievable but I know guys did things that were even dumber. What didn't make any sense to me then was why he was sticking to such a weak story or changing it to make it even weaker.

By the time I'd finished all the papers, my word list included *modicum, stolid, canvass,* and *fortnightly.* I closed my notebook and slipped it back into my breast pocket.

As I was folding up the papers, the guy at the bar stood up and walked, with a noticeable limp, to my table. I'd seen the face before but I couldn't place it until I noticed how his hat was pulled down square on his head. It was the Bureau man who'd been with Hauptmann at the Second Precinct. First thing I thought was, *Does he know we killed a couple of millionaires?* Then I realized, no. He wouldn't be here by himself if he knew anything about that. He flipped open his wallet to show a small brass shield.

"Mr. Quinn, Leo Turcot, Bureau of Investigation. I need a word. May I sit?"

I nodded and tried like hell not to let on how rattled I was. Turcot was medium height, a hundred and fifty pounds, tops, thick through the chest and shoulders. Nice three-piece worsted suit. Snug shirt collar, tightly knotted tie. Sharp crease in his trousers. He put his hat on the table and I saw that he had receding brown hair, cut short. He lit a cigarette.

"You were in the crowd at the Second Precinct, and I see by these papers that you're following the Lindbergh case. Fascinating, isn't it?"

What the hell was this guy doing here?

"I've been working on something else, but Director Hoover brought me in when he learned that Hauptmann is German. I've spent some time there and speak the language, but the truth is the boss wants to make sure that the Bureau gets some credit for solving the kidnapping, whether we deserve it or not. You understand, he has to make sure that his budget is increased every year and that means keeping our name in the papers."

As he spoke, he smiled and leaned forward with his forearms on the table, fingers loosely laced. Like we were two pals sitting around shooting the breeze, even if he was doing all the talking. He had an accent that I couldn't place.

"Not that I haven't been able to help. We had Hauptmann copying paragraphs from newspapers all night on Wednesday and got them to our Crime Laboratory and the documents examiner at Treasury. I was with them on Thursday morning when we found the money in the garage. There really hadn't been any doubt before then, but after we found so much of the cash in one place, that sealed it. He did it on his own. There is no second man, unless Condon, who delivered the ransom, was in on it, and I'm sure he wasn't."

The Bureau man leaned back in his chair and gestured more broadly. "Our Bruno would never throw in with a blabbermouth showboat like Condon. No, Hauptmann realized from the beginning that he had to have an intermediary—something you have had some experience with, I'm told—between him and Lindbergh, and he could see that the old man wouldn't be a threat to him."

He paused, waiting to see how I'd react to his knowing that I worked both sides of the street. That didn't bother me. Dozens of New York cops knew I was a go-between. It was no secret. I tried not to show anything until I knew where all this was leading and what he wanted from me.

"After Condon went through his act of 'holding his identification in abeyance for the present,' they sidetracked him to another room to cool his heels. I kept him company. He expected me to try to browbeat an identification out of him, but I did the opposite. I let him take the lead and he told me more than he thought he did. He really wanted to know the details you've been reading here." Turcot tapped the newspaper stories.

"He asked if Hauptmann had confessed. Had we found the money. Why were we detaining him. Would Hauptmann's accomplices come after him. I didn't answer any of those but when he asked if he was under arrest, I had to tell him I had orders to keep him there. He threatened to leave then but said he had too much respect for Director Hoover to do that."

He leaned forward again. "Here's something you haven't seen in the papers yet. You read that Hauptmann broke into a mayor's house in Germany?"

I nodded. "It was a second-story job. He used a ladder. They'd also nailed him on another set of burglaries and that's why he took it on the lam to America."

Took it on the lam? Why was he talking like that? Sounded like he wanted me to believe he knew what things were like on my side of the law.

"We've two solid witnesses in New Jersey," Turcot said, "who can place him near the Lindbergh house before the kidnapping in his car, a '29 Dodge, with pieces of a ladder in the back seat. The cashier at the Loew's Sheridan down in the Village, a Mrs. Cecile Barr, identified him, too. She was brought in because a five-dollar ransom bill was found in the Loew's Sheridan deposit that was left in a bank's night deposit box a year ago. When she was questioned at the time, Mrs. Barr remembered how rudely the man had tossed the folded bill under the ticket window, and when the New York police checked the stubs, they found that one missing. Hauptmann didn't go to the movie. He bought a fifty-cent ticket to get rid of that big bill.

"You'll read all of that in the next day or so, and judging by all these papers, you're very interested in the case. Why is that?"

"Everybody's interested."

"Everybody doesn't read for an hour and a half. Or take notes," he said.

So, he'd noticed that. I still didn't want to say anything more than I had to.

"Look, I know you don't make a habit of talking to officers of the law, and I want to assure you that I have no interest in your business. I'm here because I've led some of the most productive investigations anyone at the Bureau has attempted. That being the case, Mr. Hoover is about to entrust me with another. It will be important, and your fine establishment is part of it."

He stood, put on his hat, and smiled. "Don't worry, we'll get along fine. You have my word on it."

Chapter Nine

As soon as the Bureau man was gone, Arch came around from behind the bar. "What in the hell was that all about?"

"You heard him?" I asked. Arch nodded. "When did he come in?"

"A few minutes before you. I told him we weren't ready to open. He said that he didn't care. He'd heard this was one of the best bars in the city and wanted to take a look at it. We talked a bit. He introduced himself without mentioning that he was the *Garda*. Told me he'd lived in Dublin, and said enough about the place that I could tell he knew it. After a time, it seemed impolite not to ask if he wanted a drink, and he asked for Polish vodka!"

"Vodka? Nobody but Reds order vodka."

"Precisely, and damn few Reds work for the Bureau, not that I knew that when he ordered it. I said that we don't get much call for it. He said he was born in Poland and he'd have the Russian potato juice if that was all we had."

"How'd he take it?" I asked.

"On ice. He said we should store it that way, keep a bottle buried in the ice chest along with cold glasses. One other thing, all the time we were talking, he was keeping an eye on you in the mirror behind the bar. Asked if you were the owner."

"What else?"

Arch thought for a few seconds. "Said he'd come back to the city for work, and he'd been told this place had been a speakeasy, and that we'd gotten one of the first licenses in this part of the city after Repeal. He assumed from that the owner must be well connected, and I may have bragged on you more than I should've, explaining how Jimmy's Place was known for having the best selection, even during Prohibition, and so we had always welcomed a rich panoply of customers from many walks of life."

Panoply, another word for the notebook.

"Did I hear him say this place is going to be a part of an important investigation?"

"That's what the man said when he finally got around to it. He was more interested in buttering me up, spilling details about Hauptmann that haven't been published yet."

Arch sat opposite me. "You figure he was trying to persuade you to go along with this vague investigation?"

"He said he spent some time with Condon, and he made it sound like he was trying to worm information out of the old guy without giving him the third degree."

"Just as he was doing with you."

"And he was trying to impress me with what a hotshot investigator he is. But it doesn't figure that he has any business here."

Arch leaned across the table and lowered his voice. "Could there be any federal involvement with our most recent enterprise? From the other side. Perhaps in gathering all that pelf, the two miscreant millionaires broke some regulation that was beyond the purview of local officials and the federal authorities are now looking into it."

Miscreant? Purview? "What do I know from federal banking laws?"

"And if it were anything like that," Arch said, "I can't believe he'd tip his hand by coming in and announcing himself."

"Whatever he's up to, I don't like it one goddamned bit."

We hashed it out for a few more minutes until the early evening crowd wandered in.

Saturday was Saturday. We almost always did good business and that one was no exception. One interesting thing did happen and two things didn't happen. The first thing that didn't happen was Petey Beck not showing up. Figure he lied when he said the papers were ready and now he was having trouble finishing the work. The second thing that didn't happen was Fat Joe not coming in to work. It was nothing for him to come in an hour or two late, and then bitch when I docked his pay. That had been happening a lot since Repeal, but he always told me when he wasn't going to be there. Go figure.

The interesting thing that happened was Daphne Prewitt showing up again. After the fight and the commotion that went along with it the night before, she made a quiet exit. About ten or so, I was handling an order of six drinks, when I glanced toward the front door and saw that Daphne was back. She'd just come in. She was wearing another well-cut suit, simple double-breasted coat and skirt that suited her. Connie went straight over, led her to a two-top in back near the stairs and sat with her.

It was hard to concentrate on my drink orders and watch the two of them. They talked for some time before Connie got up and came to the bar. Arch was working that end. He must have been watching them, too, because he had the good Chablis ready. He and Connie talked for a few seconds, then he opened the leaf and took the wine back to the two-top. Daphne gave him a big smile and patted the chair beside her. Arch sat.

Whatever was going on with those three, coming on top of the Bureau man's strange conversation made me worried and angry. Things were happening that I didn't understand and I couldn't predict or control. Add scared to worried and angry. And, when I realized that Sunday was only a few hours away, I remembered that I had to have the place cleaned up in the morning for Lansky and his important guests.

The next time I looked over to Daphne's table, she was gone. I caught Connie's attention and motioned her over to the bar.

"What's going on?"

Connie had a small wouldn't-you-like-to-know smile on her face. "She had to leave, but she told me what she needs to talk to you about. I'll tell you later."

We were so busy for the rest of the night, I didn't have time to think about Daphne or the Bureau man. After we closed and the others were cleaning up, I got the last of the cash out of the register and took it up to my office and added it to the rest of the day's take. The rough count was about what I expected. I sorted the bills by denomination and when I put them in the safe, I got a pistol from the back of the bottom shelf, a snub-nosed Colt .38. Checked to make sure there was an empty chamber beneath the hammer, and even as I slipped it into my coat pocket, I knew it was a foolish thing to do. Whatever was going on, it wasn't likely a revolver would be much good.

As we were walking back to the Chelsea, Connie could tell that something was up.

"What's the matter with you?" she said. "Your head's swiveling around like an owl."

"Yeah, I guess I'm a little jumpy. Did Arch tell you about the guy who came in before we opened today?"

"The Bureau man, yeah. He said he didn't really understand and you'd explain it."

"The name's Leo Turcot. I saw him when they brought Hauptmann in. He comes in this afternoon and tells Arch he's been working in the city and he's heard that Jimmy's Place is one of the best bars in town. Asks for vodka and—"

"Vodka! Only Reds drink vodka."

"Says he was born in Poland and wants Polish vodka but he'll take the Russian. Then he engages Arch in conversation, which is not exactly the most difficult thing in the world to do. When he sees that I'm folding up my papers, he comes over and introduces himself, says he remembered me from the Second. Sees from all the papers I'm interested in the kidnapping and Hauptmann, so he bends my ear providing a few more details. As he's leaving, he says he's working on an investigation that involves Jimmy's Place."

She stopped on the sidewalk and grabbed my arm. "An investigation? What the hell's going on, Jimmy? Do you think he knows…"

"No, I thought the same thing and so did Arch, but the way Turcot said it, whatever this investigation is, it involves the place, not me."

"I'm not sure I buy that."

"Me neither."

We didn't say anything else until we got to my rooms. I could tell she was still as worried as I was. She looked more worried when she saw me put the .38 in the drawer of the bedside table. I poured two tots of the good cognac and pulled off my tie.

"Tell me about Daphne. Looked like you two had quite a little tête-á-tête." So did Daphne and Arch, I thought.

Connie turned toward the wardrobe and unbuttoned her dress. I couldn't see her face, but when she spoke, I could tell she was leading up to something. "We didn't really have a chance to talk. I mean it was so noisy and smokey and she really didn't want anyone to listen in on us, so she was careful."

Connie hung up the dress, shimmied out of her slip and toed her shoes off. I sat and watched. You see, while Connie was in Paris, she bought half a dozen outfits that were designed for her by a couturier—that's a guy who designs clothes. They didn't look like the clothes you saw on other women in New York then. Most women's dresses came down almost to their ankles. Connie's were just below her knees. There was even a suit with trousers. The fabrics were softer, and they fit her perfectly. If she wore them when we went out, people noticed, particularly women. She'd always got more than her share of attention from men, no matter what she was wearing.

Her Paris outfits were too expensive to wear to work, but after she had them, she didn't want to go back to what she'd been wearing before. She couldn't find anything she liked in the big department stores, so she hunted out smaller dress shops. She brought her designer clothes to the women who ran those shops and got them to make things that were similar. Shorter, more closely fitted skirts, blouses and knit tops that flattered her, small simple hats. When she wore those clothes at work, every woman who came into the place asked her about them, and men paid even more attention than they had before. So, did I.

Connie took a small sip of her cognac and walked behind me. "Daphne thinks that her paramour, Harold, is about to get himself into some trouble and she's not sure what she should do." She leaned over me, pulled off my tie, and turned off the floor lamp. "If you don't get undressed, you're not going to get a back rub."

The offer of a back rub meant that she was about to ask me for something and she wanted to be sure the answer was yes.

"When you put it that way…" I stripped down and got in bed.

Connie sat on the back of my thighs and went to work on my shoulders. "The problem is Daphne doesn't really know what he does, and he's told her not to ask about his business. She has a telephone number for him but she's only supposed to use it for an emergency. His house and his wife are on Long Island, but she thinks he has another apartment in the city."

"Thinks but doesn't know?" I turned my head so I could see her.

"That's right." She reached back to unhook her brassiere, pulled off her panties, and dug her fists into the small of my back.

"What does she want me to do?"

"Daphne wants someone to follow him, when he leaves her place and find out where he goes and what he's up to."

"Someone meaning me."

Connie ran the heels of her hands along my spine to the nape of my neck, and stretched out on my back. She murmured into my ear, "Arch has volunteered since you're so busy with other things."

"It couldn't be that you don't want me to be spending time with a beautiful, willing blonde."

She lifted up enough for me to roll over without losing contact, and then settled back down. "That's true, but it's more true that Arch wants to spend time with a beautiful, willing blonde."

"I don't doubt that." I slid my hands down her back and coaxed her up to straddle me.

Connie whispered into my ear, "Your doing it wouldn't fit with my plans." Then she started to wrestle with me the way I liked, and I rolled on top of her and didn't think to ask what she meant by 'my doing it wouldn't fit with her plans.' *What plans?*

Chapter Ten

I've never understood how people can get up on Sunday morning. For somebody who runs a bar, it's just nuts. But there I was, at nine o'clock, unlocking the front door of Jimmy's Place for Meyer Lansky. The morning papers I hadn't read were waiting for me in my office. I made coffee in the Cruzon kitchen and had a service for three set up on a four-top at the back when the front door opened.

Lansky was wearing one of his better suits, a black three-piece. He paced and smoked even more than he normally did until he saw that he was lighting a Pall Mall while one was still resting on the ashtray. Then he stubbed both of them out and put the pack back in his jacket pocket. I'd never seen him acting like that, so I figured we were waiting on a couple of big cheeses. They showed up a little before ten. Lansky was sitting at the four-top when we heard a knock on the door. He straightened his tie and told me to answer. Two men were outside, both in suits and light topcoats. I was right. As cheeses go in New York, they were about as big as you'd find.

I recognized the first man, Nathan Perlman. He was a Republican lawyer who'd been a congressman. You'd read in the papers how Mayor LaGuardia was appointing him to this commission or that committee. He'd worked hard to get Prohibition repealed, damn him. He was a plump-faced, barrel-bellied gent who appreciated a good meal and a good drink. He'd raised a glass in my place once or twice, back when it was hard to find good whiskey anywhere else in that part of the city. He'd just been appointed to a judgeship and I'd heard that he could go from jovial fat man to cold-eyed hardass without missing a beat.

The second man was taller and broader through the shoulders. He had black hair that he wore long and combed straight back from his stern, craggy face. I recognized him, too. Even a goy like myself knew that Rabbi

Stephen Wise was one of the most influential Jews in the city. I read in the papers that he was trying to get Jews into Palestine, and he palled around with the likes of Professor Einstein.

As they stepped in, Judge Perlman said, "Mr. Lansky, do you know Rabbi Wise?"

"Only by reputation."

"I want to impress the seriousness of this matter on you, so it's important that you understand it has the rabbi's approval."

Wise said, "I doubt Mr. Lansky worries about my approval."

I knew Lansky had arguments in his family about religion, and didn't go along with their ideas. But he smiled at the rabbi and motioned the two men toward the table. He motioned me toward the stairs. I went up to my office and sat near the little window that looks down on the bar. Before Lansky arrived, I'd cracked it open and turned the blinds so I could hear and see. If he was going to use my place to meet with a couple of guys who were so important they made him nervous, well, I figured I should know something of what they were up to. Let's just say I let my natural curiosity get the best of me. Since I didn't even know who they were until I saw them, I didn't know what to expect them to talk about. Not what I heard, that's for sure.

They were there for more than an hour. Judge Perlman did most of the talking. I could tell from the beginning that they were putting a soft sell on Lansky because what they were asking him to do made them uncomfortable.

Perlman said, "Mr. Lansky I understand a man like yourself may not follow politics, but it must have come to your attention what the Nazis in Germany are doing to our people. It's been bad since this madman Hitler took over and it's getting worse. Now some of them are trying to do the same things here in America. Here in New York. We have to stop them."

I won't try to write down everything they said, but it boiled down to this. The American Nazis had been organizing for years, first as the Friends of New Germany. I knew about those guys. Now they were calling themselves the Silver Shirts and the White Shirts and there were other outfits that seemed to identify themselves by the color of their clothes. There were enough of them that they held meetings openly, and they were staging rallies. They were also harassing Jews.

Perlman said they couldn't depend on the cops. "Too many on the police force appear to share their ideas, or they think that if we simply ignore them, they will go away. Some men I thought were our friends try to tell me not to worry, it can't happen in America. They're wrong."

Lansky agreed and asked, "What can I do? What help can I offer?"

The rabbi and the judge went into the last part of their pitch.

"The Nazis have to know that if they use or threaten violence against Jews, they will be met with violence. I believe you know Jews who would not hesitate to deal with these thugs on their own terms and are capable of doing so effectively."

Lansky was as careful as the other two. "Yes, I do know Jews, tough Jews, who are experienced at such things, and we can remove anyone who threatens us. Give me names and I'll see to it they never bother anyone again."

Both men immediately said, "No!"

"There must be no killing," said the rabbi.

"We cannot be party to that. No killing, none." the judge said. Yeah, they couldn't get their hands too dirty. "But broken arms and legs, a few cracked heads, missing teeth, those are acceptable, even commendatory, and we want to make sure everyone knows about it. Do you think your tough Jews can accomplish what we wish with that much restraint?"

Lansky let the question hang for a moment before he said yes.

The judge and the rabbi smiled at each other. The judge said that of course, they'd see that these men were properly compensated for their efforts, but Lansky raised his hands and said, "No! Absolutely not." He'd been waiting for that.

"I share your sympathies for what's happening to our people in Europe and so do the men who will be helping me… helping us. We don't want to be paid." He paused again to give them a moment to think about what that meant. If they agreed, they owed Lansky.

"I will ask two things. First, if anyone is arrested and charged, can we expect some assistance?"

The judge nodded his head. Lansky went on, "Both of you have some influence with the Jewish press. If there are any arrests, don't let them make us look too bad. I don't want my wife or my father to read anything that would embarrass them."

"That we can do. But these Nazis do not announce many of their meetings and rallies outside of their own neighborhoods. Can you arrange for your men to be there on short notice."

Lansky waved that away. "Don't worry about it. Walter Winchell lives in my building. He gets information about this kind of thing every week. We talk."

He paused long enough for them to know what he was about to say was important. "And one more thing." The judge and the rabbi looked worried for the first time. "It happens that Longy Zwillman and I were discussing something similar just a few days ago. The Nazis are also organizing in Newark and he intends to let them know they are not welcome. I will pass along your no-killing rule if you can promise him the same treatment, if his men are arrested."

Big smiles on all three faces. I guess the meeting had gone better than any of them expected.

As Lansky showed them to the door, I eased the window down, closed the Venetian blinds, and moved behind my desk. A few minutes later he came in, looking pleased with himself, and why not? A big shot judge and rabbi were about to owe him a couple of favors.

"Impressive visitors," I said.

"An intriguing conversation. Listen, I need you to move some things over to New Jersey, to Longy's place. They're at the garage on Broome Street, but I've got to be careful. The goddamn cops are watching me and I can't be sure that the Bureau isn't listening in on my telephones, even at the apartment."

"How much stuff? I've got a Ford coupe and Frenchy's flatbed truck."

"It will fit in the trunk of the Ford."

"When?"

"One night next week, probably."

"What is it? Do I need to worry about being stopped by the Jersey cops?"

"If the wrong guy pulled you over, you might have trouble explaining it, but mention Longy's name and you'll be fine."

Chapter Eleven

The news about Hauptmann was thin beer that Sunday. The idea that his pal, the late Isidor Fisch, had anything to do with it was looking even weaker. Hauptmann said he was holding the fourteen grand for Fisch when Fisch had been living in a $3.50 a week room before he decamped to the Fatherland. The German cops volunteered to dig up Fisch's body, and that screwball Condon allowed as how Fisch had been poisoned. The old man would say anything to keep his name in the papers.

A con in the Ohio state pen claimed that Hauptmann had been writing to him about the kidnapping before it happened. Nobody bought that. The cops said that they had a suspected accomplice, a woman, under surveillance, but the papers didn't add any details, so it figured there wasn't much to the story. They were just gassing. The handwriting expert swore that he "could give the most positive expert opinion" that Hauptmann wrote all the ransom notes. Mrs. Hauptmann continued to say that her Bruno was completely innocent. The cops up in the Bronx sweated him all day Saturday, and Col. Lindbergh was flying back from California.

I can't say why I became so nuts that I had to learn all the new details as they were revealed about Hauptmann each day. A big story like that, everybody follows it, but I went overboard. The way I met Connie because of the kidnapping had something to do with it, but there was more to it. I've broken just about all your major laws, most of the big ones more than once. I've done some things that were wrong, and a few things that I'm sorry about. But all of them had to do with other guys, usually guys who were trying to do the same things I was doing, and we knew the risks we were taking. We'd decided to engage in something that somebody had declared to be illegal at that time. Buying a drink, placing a bet, what have you.

You get into a business like that, you know that the cops—some of them, anyway—are going to try to stop you and arrest you. Other guys who're engaged in the same business, they're going to try to stop you, too. They're going to do whatever they need to do. Rob you, beat you, shoot you, and you've got to be ready to do the same to them, and you want to do it first.

That day I saw Hauptmann, I knew he was guilty. I've been around guys like him my whole life—cons, grifters, hustlers, cheap yeggs and big-time thieves. Guys who never pass up a chance to grab an easy dollar without thinking about how they'll get away. Would they do what Hauptmann did? Kill a kid intentionally? Plan out a job, knowing that you're going to murder an infant, I still can't figure that. And that is exactly what Bruno Hauptmann did.

From the moment he started thinking about the kidnapping, he knew he was going to kill that boy. Now, some people say he did it by accident. They claim that he must have dropped the kid when the ladder broke as he was hurrying down. No, he climbed that ladder to the second floor, opened the window, and the first thing he did was clamp his big hand over the kid's mouth. He had to keep him quiet. Couldn't risk any noise. He knew the longer he kept the kid, the more danger he was in. He yanked the kid out of bed, climbed back down and left the ladder. He ran across muddy ground, got into his car and drove a few miles away. Couldn't have taken him more than ten, twenty minutes. Sometime in there, he killed the kid and stripped off the boy's clothes to use as proof he had him. Hauptmann parked near some woods, crept a few yards away from the road, pushed some dirt and leaves off the ground, scratched a short shallow hole, and put the body in it. Given how careful his planning was, he'd already cased the spot where he was going to hide the body.

I remember thinking right after it happened that I hoped there was a woman involved because if it was just one or two guys, they wouldn't keep the kid alive. A lot of people thought that. I'm not saying that a woman couldn't have been just as ruthless, but the kid would've had a better chance if a woman was there. And the more they found out about how Hauptmann operated, there was nothing that pointed to anybody else, not even his patsy, the late Mr. Fisch.

Chapter Twelve

Monday morning, six o'clock, still dark outside, somebody was knocking on the door. I tried not to believe what I was hearing but it didn't stop. Connie rolled over and dragged the pillow over her head. I pulled on a pair of pants. It was Tommy, the nightman, looking worried.

"Mr. Quinn, you've got to come downstairs right away. It's Officer Mahan."

Oh, hell, I thought, this is what I pay him for. "Tell him I'm on the way."

I found shirt and shoes, grabbed the stick. No time for the brace. Connie burrowed deeper under the covers. I gimped down the stairs, leaning heavily on the rail. Hell of a way to start the week, unsteady and confused. It was about to get worse.

Mahan was a fireplug of a guy, a little taller than me, thick through the neck and shoulders. He looked grimmer than Tommy.

"What's going on?"

He muttered, "Come with me," and headed for the front door. His patrol car was double parked in front of the building. He got behind the wheel. Not wanting to look like I was being taken in, I sat next to him. He drove east, moving quickly but not making any more noise than he had to. He turned right on Seventh Avenue and right again at Twenty-Second Street. Stopped in front of my place. In the light of the headlamps, I could see that my expensive new green canvas awning was ripped and sagging down at one corner. Some son of a bitch had torn it and bent the metal poles that held it up. There was movement under it, by the door. Figured it was Norris, Mahan's partner. Mahan got out of the car and ducked under the awning. I hurried behind him.

By then the sky was turning gray. You could make out dark shapes but no detail. Something was down on the landing against the door. Mahan said, "Where's the goddamn ambulance. They should've been here by now."

"Try the radio again."

Another set of lights swung onto the street and a long ambulance braked to a stop behind Mahan's car. With the extra light, I could see two people in robes and pajamas standing on the stoop of the brownstone across the street. I wondered how long they'd been there, watching what was going on. Two guys in white opened the back door of the ambulance, pulled out a stretcher and told me to get out of the way as they went down the steps. They switched on their flash lamps, and I saw a bloody body sprawled facing the door. In the harsh white light, I could make out the shape of twisted legs, and arms wrapped around a head, all of it splotched with dull red blood and what looked like black dirt. Too big to be a woman, maybe.

One of the guys from the ambulance said, "Any signs of life?"

"Thought I felt a pulse in his neck when we got here," Norris said.

The ambulance guys tried to open the stretcher next to the body, but there wasn't room on the landing. Norris and Mahan got out of the way and trained their flash lamps down on the landing. The ambulance guys leaned the stretcher on the steps and then tried to lift the thick body away from my door. I still couldn't tell anything about it. The bigger ambulance guy got his hands under the arms and pulled it up. As he did, a loud nasty liquid squish came out of the body along with a foul smell of shit and something worse. It was enough to make me back away. Mahan and Norris gagged and pulled out handkerchiefs to cover their noses. It even got to the ambulance guys.

They managed the body onto the stretcher, strapped it down and then maneuvered it back up to the sidewalk where we could see it. I still couldn't tell much. The clothes were covered in some kind of black sticky-looking mud and rusty red caked blood. So were the arms that covered the face, and the stench was about as bad as anything I ever smelled. One ambulance guy pulled out a stethoscope and the other pulled at the body's arms to get them away from the face.

After a few seconds, the first one said, "I've got a weak heartbeat."

The second one reached for the man's head. "There's something in his mouth. He can't breathe. Give me some light."

Mahan pointed his lamp at the guy's face. More of the black stuff covered the eyes. The nose had been pulped and the lips were stretched wide, crammed full of the black stuff. The ambulance guy felt carefully with gloved fingers, pulling at the stuff in the guy's mouth. It came loose in a couple of clumps. The mouth and jaw stayed open.

Without saying another word, the attendants took two corners of the stretcher. Mahan and Norris grabbed the other two, and they carried him back to the open door of the ambulance. They backed it up to Seventh Avenue and headed to Bellevue. As soon as they were gone, Norris went across the street and talked to the people on the stoop. I asked Mahan what happened.

"Around five o'clock, one of these good citizens," He pointed with his thumb, "called in to the station and said there was a disturbance at your place. Men fighting in the street. Station radioed us. Were you open that late?"

"On a slow Sunday? Hell, no. Shut the doors around midnight."

"Did you recognize the guy? Was he a customer?"

"I couldn't tell you anything about him. What was that black stuff that was all over him?"

"Smelled like it might have been tar or asphalt."

Norris came back, frowning. "The neighbors, Mr. and Mrs. Casny, said they were woken up around five by loud noises in the street. Their bedroom faces the street on the second floor and they had their windows open. Mr. Casny said he couldn't really see anything on account of the trees, so he went downstairs. He said there had been trouble with your joint before. Everybody knows it's run by a gangster. Looked through the glass in the front door and saw at least four men beating another man, and one of them was hitting him with a wooden bucket. Their car, a long black four-door he thinks, was in the middle of the street with the doors open, blocking his view of whatever was happening. It went on for several minutes and was still going on when he called the station. By the time he came back to the door, the car had left. That's it. No make or plate on the car. No physical descriptions of any of the parties involved. They didn't know there was a guy down there until we showed up."

Mahan said, "Nothing happened last night that could've led to this?"

"No, like I said, a slow Sunday. Had a little dust up Friday, but it was nothing."

"Then it was just your bad luck that he wound up in your doorway. Looks like those other guys were chasing him in their car and caught up with him here. Maybe he thought he could get inside."

By then, there was enough light to get a good look at the damage. Norris said, "Damn shame about your awning. It was a nice awning. Classy."

Expensive, too. "O.K., what's next? Do you need me for anything else?"

"If he dies without identification, we may need you to come in, but not now. Sorry to bother you so early, but we figured… you know."

Yeah.

After they left, there was no point in trying to go back to sleep, so I decided to clean up. The awning was ruined. We might be able to use part of the frame but the canvas would have to be replaced. The blood and dirt, or whatever it was, had made a mess of the landing. I unlocked the front door. Found bucket, mop, brushes, and soap, and set to work. It would only get harder to clean if I left it alone.

Twenty minutes later, I was still at it. I heard footsteps and saw Leo Turcot, the Bureau man, hurrying toward me on the sidewalk. He frowned when he got close enough to see what I was doing. "What happened here?"

"A guy got himself beat up."

"Who?"

"Can't say. The goons who worked him over did a hell of a job. Covered him with dirt or something. Couldn't really see his face. People across the street say it was four guys in a car."

"Damnation, they know. The local police have been here?"

"Yeah, and an ambulance. What're you talking—'they know'?"

Turcot ignored me and looked around, first across the street, then at the wet doorway I was mopping, and then at the sidewalk. "An ambulance," he muttered to himself. "Bellevue?"

I said yes. He ran back toward Seventh Avenue to hail a cab.

Chapter Thirteen

That Monday morning while I was scrubbing blood off my front door, Arch Malloy was having coffee with Daphne Prewitt in her little house down on Gay Street. It's in the Village, one block long between Christopher and Waverly with a dogleg at the Christopher Street end. Daphne opened the door. She was wearing a peach-colored silk robe, Arch told me later. Her hair was nicely done up, and she was wearing makeup, not a lot but enough to let him know she'd put an effort into how she looked, and a touch of perfume that he'd never smelled before. Arch didn't tell me what he was wearing.

Daphne's house was small, two stories with the bedroom upstairs. She had good furniture, an expensive radio and phonograph, and a calico cat named Andrew. She took Arch's hat and offered him brandy with the coffee. He said no and sat in a chintz armchair. Daphne and Andrew took the loveseat.

"As I understand it," Arch said, "you suspect that your 'paramour' Harold is up to no good."

"Yes." She leaned across the coffee table between them to pour two cups, letting her robe slide open. Arch said she knew what she was doing. They both understood sex was something that might happen.

The rest of the conversation was either a dance or the first round of a prize fight, depending on how you looked at it. They were taking a measure of each other, trying to decide how honest they had to be.

"What is Harold's full name?"

"Henninger, Harold Henninger."

"Do you have a photograph? No? What does he look like?"

"He's about six feet tall, light, brown hair, blue eyes. I wouldn't call him skinny or fat, he's large—that's the first thing you notice about him.

Athletic, plays golf, tennis, and squash. Champion middleweight at Yale. He was going to be part of the Olympic Yachting Team two years ago, but there was some disagreement between him and the team captain. They haven't spoken since."

"Where does he work?"

"He's a partner at Dickinson and Dean Securities, but he doesn't actually go to work anymore. He doesn't need to. When I've asked him anything about money, he waves it off and tells me not to worry, he's got more than enough for anything we need, anything I want. A car, a trip to Spain, anything. That's not why I'm so worried. It's the other things he does with money." She scratched Andrew behind his ears.

"Jimmy told me that Henninger involved you with some sort of transactions where you purchased and sold 'instruments,' which you did not understand, and then you saw an immediate profit on them. How much have you made?"

"Almost thirteen thousand dollars, but Harold said we had to stop more than a year ago."

"You still don't know exactly what you were doing or why you had to stop?"

"No. Harold just said that too many people were doing it and it was too risky."

"But when you began, he told you it was completely legal."

She nodded. "I knew that wasn't true but I went along with it."

"Of course, the money was too good. What's happening now?"

Daphne sat back and took a deep breath, tightening the silk over her chest. "It started about a month ago. We were having dinner at Keen's." Andrew made an irritated growl and jumped down from the love seat. "It's one of his favorite places."

"Keen's? I take it then that Harold doesn't feel he has to hide your relationship."

"No, it would be different if his wife ever came into the city but she hates it. His son is living in Philadelphia. If he thought there was a chance that one of them would see us together, we wouldn't go out because it would embarrass them. But it's different in the upper crust. People would talk if he didn't have an attractive companion." She smiled and cocked an eyebrow.

"And you certainly are that. But back to that night at Keen's."

"Harold noticed a man he knew who was coming in. We were getting ready to order when he said, 'That's Mark Bridges. Haven't seen him in years,' and he stood up and waved him over."

"This man Bridges, describe him."

"About Harold's age. Very well dressed, obviously prosperous, and his companion was a young woman, much younger and, well, obvious." Daphne said with a catty edge.

"They shook hands warmly. Harold put an arm around his shoulders and spoke to him so softly that I couldn't hear what they were saying, but I could see Bridges' face. They talked for what seemed like a long time and something Harold said made Bridges pleased and excited. Then Harold produced a card from a card case and gave it to him. He said this was his private number and Bridges should call him, but not from the bank."

She took an engraved cream-colored card from the pocket of her robe and handed it to Arch. Thick cardboard. Expensive.

"I know Harold's habits. I know the brand of his underwear, what kind of Scotch he drinks, what he sounds like when he gargles, how he sleeps on his right side until he rolls over on his back and snores. But until that night, I had not seen this card."

Art flicked the edge of it. "And how did you come by it."

"He left the card case in his vest pocket that night."

The only thing on the card was a telephone number. RHinlander 4-3340.

Daphne said, "That's not the number of his house on Long Island, and it's not where he works, or where he doesn't work, I suppose. I think, no, I'm sure that he has another place here in the city, an apartment or house."

"And what do you make of that? When it comes to pillow talk, is he open or do you think he's hiding this place from you?"

"He's hiding it, all right. With Harold, there's always something cooking behind the scenes, but that same night when we were in bed, Harold mentioned that he'd found another investment opportunity. He tried to sound casual but he tried too hard."

"A girl can always tell," Arch said, smiling.

"Of course," she said, smiling back. "Harold said it was still in the preliminary stages. That's what he and Bridges had been discussing. He said it looked to him like this was going to be an incredible deal, one that would be too good to pass up. If I remembered any wealthy men from my time at Polly's who'd be interested in something out of the ordinary, he'd like to know their names. He even suggested that I might want to put 'our' thirteen thousand in it. If it panned out, he would have to limit the number of investors, so I'd want to get in soon."

That's when Arch knew what was up. "It's a confidence game."

"And Harold's the perfect man to pull it off. In the financial world he has a reputation as a genius, the golden touch. And he can be incredibly persuasive. When he wants to, he can talk anybody into anything."

He must be, Arch thought, to lure such a beautiful bird into this gilded cage and to keep her here. "What do you plan to do?"

"I don't know and that scares me. With Harold I'm never sure. Does he want me to bring in pigeons, or am I a mark, too? In the game we ran before, I was the one taking the risks. Harold always said I wasn't but I knew I was and so did the young guys I was dealing with at the brokerage houses. Something wasn't jake about that business and they were nervous. And Harold never put his name on a piece of paper. It was all me, and those thirteen G's are sitting in a bank account in my name."

Arch said, "You're certainly in a quandary. What do you want me to do?"

The way she smiled, Arch knew that she'd been waiting for him to say that. "First, I want to know if Harold has another place, wherever this Rhinelander number is, probably. I think if you're able to follow him when he leaves here, you'd probably find it."

Arch agreed. "Does he have a regular schedule with you?"

"No, unless he stays overnight, he's never here in the morning. He telephones if we're meeting for dinner or drinks. He spent Saturday night here and left late Sunday. If he's going to come over tonight, he might call, but he probably wouldn't."

Arch said, "It shouldn't be difficult to follow him then. But, as you said, you want to know exactly what kind of con he is proposing and whether you are to be a victim or beneficiary of it."

It took her a second to figure what 'beneficiary' meant the way he put it, but then she nodded her head. "And let's take this one step further. Once we know what Harold intends your role is to be, you have to decide whether you're going to stay here or take your thirteen Gs and say goodbye to New York."

Daphne gnawed on her thumb knuckle. Arch asked if Harold kept any personal items at her house.

"Just toiletries and a few clothes."

"Let's take a look. They're upstairs, I assume. After you."

Again, she gave him a funny look and led the way. He told me later that she thought he just wanted to follow her up the stairs to watch her rear, and so she gave it that extra little twitch, which he found most attractive.

The second-floor seemed larger than the first, with a double bed, wardrobe, and vanity, bathroom in the back. The aroma of perfumes, soaps, and lotions was strong and, to Arch, pleasant. Daphne opened the wardrobe. "His things are on this side," she said, and pushed dresses on hangers away so Arch could see that Harold had a narrow space on a shelf for a pair of slip-on shoes, folded sweater, flannel slacks, underwear, and sleeveless undershirt, all with British labels. In the bathroom, a toothbrush, shaving kit and mug. More Brit imports.

"Is this the way it's been since you and he entered your arrangement? Did he ever keep more things here?"

"Hmm? At first, he did, I suppose, but the wardrobe isn't that large. He bought most of my dresses and outfits. I'm supposed to look my best whenever we go out."

"What I'm really asking is if he has given you any hints that he's planning to move on. I'm sure you're sensitive to signs of loss of interest and you know how to deal with them."

Daphne gave him another funny look. "Maybe you really are as smart as Connie says."

"Be that as it may, this does sound like an intriguing situation with a number of possible outcomes. I think I'll take that brandy now."

Back downstairs, Daphne opened the liquor cabinet. Poured Calvados. She handed Arch the glass and stretched her legs out on the love seat.

"We almost always go out to dinner on Tuesday night. Harold stays until Wednesday morning. He usually leaves around eleven."

"Which way does he go? To Christopher Street or Waverly?"

"Waverly. He either taxis uptown or calls his driver."

"All right. I'll be here Wednesday morning. There's just one more detail," Arch said. "What's in it for me?"

"Well," she stretched the word out. "We don't know exactly what Harold is up to yet, but once we do, I'm sure someone as sharp as yourself will come up with a way to separate some of that cash."

Arch was tempted, 'more sorely tempted than I have ever been in my long and temptation-filled life,' he said later. 'I wanted to say to her, 'Darling, the one thing I don't need is your money. I've just been part of a monumental knockover that has me more flush than I have ever been. No, I'm doing this simply for lust and adventure.' But he didn't say that. Daphne was the last person he'd tell about what we'd done.

Instead, he said, "We can't assume that there is any cash to be had. Who knows, perhaps you've misjudged Harold and he is planning to donate his profits to the Little Sisters of the Poor, and we will see nothing more. You, however, have already profited handsomely from your relationship with Harold. What can you do to maintain my interest? I'm sure you have some ideas."

She fluttered her long eyelashes. "I have ideas you have never imagined, even in your most sinful dreams, but we're not going to explore them this morning. Why don't we keep our negotiations open?"

"For now, that's agreeable, but I am not a man of infinite patience and I'm not some horny young buck you can lead around by the prick. However, I am sufficiently intrigued to want to know more. You say Harold is likely to come over tomorrow and you will go out to dinner. Is there a place nearby that you like?"

"Four Trees, down on Sheridan Square. I like it more than Harold does. The food's terrific but it's not expensive or fashionable."

"Can you persuade him to go there tomorrow? Around nine?"

She nodded.

He put his hat on. "We'll talk on Wednesday."

Chapter Fourteen

I hosed down the front door and mopped up as much of the water as I could. I was putting the cleaning stuff away when Arch came in and asked what happened to the awning.

"Neighbors across the street say that around five this morning, some guys in a car beat up another guy. Beat him bad. They chased him down to the front door and knocked the pole down and that tore the awning. The bastards. Maybe the guy thought he could get in, I don't know. He was covered in some kind of black stuff."

"What? Anybody we know?"

"No, he was so bad his face was pulped, and there was the black stuff. And, get this, an hour or so later, Turcot, the Bureau man, shows up. When I tell him about it and that an ambulance took the guy away, he acts like he knows something, but before I can ask him, he turns around and runs off."

"Curiouser and curiouser. Nothing good can come of this."

"Ain't that the truth. Having a federal cop say there's something going on in my place is the last thing I need."

"He certainly complicates the situation."

My stomach growled and I realized I'd been up for hours and hadn't had breakfast. "Did'ya eat yet? No? Let's go up to the kitchen."

The Cruzon Grill was closed for lunch on Mondays. Arch made coffee while I sliced a loaf of French bread in half, buttered it and put it in the oven. Diced a stick of salami into a frying pan. When it began to sizzle, I threw in four eggs, salt, and pepper, and hashed it all together. Arch had bought the morning papers, so I dished up the eggs and bread, and we read the latest Hauptmann news as we ate.

The Lindberghs were flying back from California in their little

Monocoupe airplane. The October Bronx Grand Jury was about to be sworn in. It would be chosen from a list of 5o businessmen whose names and addresses were published. Twenty-three of them would be paid three dollars a day to serve on it and indict our boy Bruno. Nobody seemed to doubt that the Jersey cops and the feds would dig up enough evidence to extradite him for trial.

Hauptmann was being kept in a cell by himself in a Bronx jail. He declined newspapers and magazines and the services of a barber. His wife still claimed he was innocent. She also denied her husband was a Nazi and said that Fisch was a Jew. In a new version of the money story, Mrs. Hauptmann remembered that Bruno told her the late Isadore Fisch gave him some satchels and a box for safekeeping while he, Fisch, was in Germany. Bruno put it on the top shelf of a closet and forgot about it until a recent rain leaked in the closet and he got the stuff out. Imagine his surprise at finding all that money.

In April of '32, right after he got his mitts on the ransom, Hauptmann quit his job at Great National Millwork and Lumber. The wood from the homemade ladder he left at the Lindberghs' house was similar to lumber sold there. At the same time, he opened a brokerage account in his wife's maiden name at Steiner, Rouse and Company with ten grand. One year of Hauptmann's stock transactions came to $264,000. That sounded like a lot to me but, according to the papers, that just meant he'd done a lot of transactions, not that he had that much cash. What did I know from stock trading? But Hauptmann still had a credit balance of $4,500.

When we'd finished, Arch poured more coffee. "I've spent an interesting morning with the delightful Miss Daphne Prewitt."

"What's her story?"

"It looks like her lover Harold Henninger is about to become involved in some kind of confidence game. He wants her to be part of it. She's not sure what she wants to do."

"But you're going to help her?"

"Possibly. I hope to watch the two lovebirds at a restaurant in the Village tomorrow night and take a better measure of the man. After that, we'll see."

"You just want to get Daphne in the sack."

"Of course, I do. Beyond the obvious attributes of her face and figure, which she made sure I got a few glimpses of, there's the fact that she was one of Polly Adler's most sought-after temptresses. Something tells me that she is practiced in pleasures of the flesh that rival those of the dusky beauties of the Orient."

"And so you want time off tomorrow."

"In a word, yes."

We cleaned up the kitchen. Arch said he had an idea that had something to do with Daphne and left. It was about noon by then. Connie ought to be getting up. I'd locked up and was walking back to the Chelsea when I saw Leo Turcot, his hat still jammed tight on his head, getting out of cab on Seventh. He was pissed off. "We have to talk. Now."

We went back to Jimmy's Place and sat at the bar. I asked if he wanted a drink. He said no. Then, "Why did you tell me that you didn't know the man who was beaten up last night?"

"Because I don't. His face was too dirty and bloody and swollen, and the light was from flash lamps."

"By the time I'd gotten to Bellevue, they had him in the emergency room and they'd washed his face. I know him. So do you. His name's Josef Bruder."

"I don't know any Josef Bruder," I said but I had a feeling I knew what he was talking about.

"He is—or was—your bouncer and lookout man."

"Fat Joe? He's dead?" That didn't make any sense to me.

Turcot said, "Yes, he didn't survive, and it was no accident. He was supposed to meet me here this morning."

"Meet you? What—"

A heavy fist pounded the door hard and a familiar voice yelled, "Open up, goddammit." Detective William Ellis, last seen at the Second Precinct House.

I unlocked the door. Ellis rushed past me and went straight to Turcot, still yelling in his face. "What the hell do you think you're doing horning in on an active investigation?"

Ellis was half a head taller but the Bureau man stood up to him. Didn't flinch. "Calm down, detective. This has nothing to do with anything you're working."

"You arrogant bastards think you can waltz in here and do whatever the hell you want but you're nothing but college boy lawyers who act like they know everything. No wonder they don't let you have guns."

That got a reaction. "I'm not a college boy. I'm not a lawyer. I don't need a gun to deal with anything the Bureau asks me to do, and that includes big city cops on the take."

Ellis was ready to slug him, but this wasn't getting us anywhere. "Ellis," I said, "he's telling me that Fat Joe Beddoes is dead. Somebody killed him out front this morning."

Ellis did a doubletake.

Turcot looked at both of us. "Josef Bruder, known to you as Fat Joe Beddoes, has been working for me for the past four months."

"What're you talking about?"

"He's been a spy. Since he started with me, he's been a double agent. It got him killed."

Chapter Fifteen

"That's just nuts," I said. "Fat Joe Beddoes couldn't be a spy any more than he could fly to the moon."

It hadn't sunk in yet that Fat Joe was dead. I still didn't really believe it. "Look, are you sure about all this? I mean, even though somebody worked him over and covered him with that black stuff, how could I not recognize him?"

Turcot said, "I've seen other cases like this, not exactly like this but close enough. The doctors had declared him deceased when I got to the hospital, and they'd cleaned him up. The 'black stuff' is bitumen..." He saw the blank look on both our faces. "Asphalt. The witnesses and the patrolmen got it wrong. He wasn't chased here. They tortured him somewhere else. Then they put him in the trunk of their car and brought him back to send a message to me."

Ellis said, "Who's they?"

Turcot cut his eyes between Ellis and me. "Nazis. American Nazis."

Ellis said, "Are you talking about those guys who hold the rallies, the Silver Legion, Silver Shirts, something like that?"

"No, those clowns are just a sideshow. The men and women I'm hunting have nothing to do with them. They're gathering information for the Fatherland. Germany is putting together a wide-ranging espionage operation. Cells are at work in Washington, Philadelphia, San Diego, Newport News, Montreal, and, of course, New York. They have agents in every major shipyard, armament factory and arsenal. They want blueprints of airplanes, ships, bomb sights, anything and everything that we will use against them when the next war comes and believe me, it is coming."

"Wait a minute," I said. "I thought your job was interviewing Hauptmann and helping them find the ransom money."

"I've been on the kidnapping since President Roosevelt ordered the Bureau to do all it could and Director Hoover created the 'Lindbergh squad,' but until last week, the trail had grown cold. For the past eleven months I've also been assigned to the spy ring because I'm fluent in German and several other European languages. That's also why they brought me in to get handwriting samples from Hauptmann."

I said to Ellis, "You know anything about this?"

"Never heard of it and until I see some proof, I'm not sure I buy it, whatever the Justice Department says."

"Whether you buy it or not, you're both going to help me stop them."

"Don't bet on it," Ellis said.

Turcot shrugged. "Your boss will be hearing from my boss. And as for Quinn, he's not the patriotic type but he can't let word get about that someone killed one of his people and he didn't do anything about it."

"Maybe so, but I'm still not sure I believe Fat Joe is dead on your word."

Ellis said, "No, he's right. Fat Joe's gone. Mahan called me when he saw this guy at the hospital. Said I ought to know a Bureau man was poking his nose in our business."

He gave Turcot a hard look that didn't bother Turcot. "I didn't think we were close enough for Bruder to be in any danger. He knew the risks he was taking, and he knew the situation took a turn we didn't expect a month ago."

"What situation? You say Fat Joe was a 'double agent.' What's that?"

"Bruder was recruited by one of your customers. Ignatz Griebl."

"Dr. Griebl's a spy?" Griebl was a prissy little guy who wore big round specs. He dropped in every week or two and always had a big blonde on his arm. They both drank schnapps. Always took a booth and played with each other under the table.

Turcot said, "The woman he comes in here with is his mistress, Katherina Moog, Kate. They're setting up a honey trap for an Army Colonel who's the commanding officer at Fort Totten. Trying to find out when the anti-aircraft guns are going to be removed and what they're going to be replaced with."

Ellis saw that I didn't understand. "A honey trap is when she gets pillow talk from him when they're in the sack."

Turcot said. "They use the McAlpin Hotel."

The McAlpin was a few blocks north on Broadway. Nice older place.

Good restaurant. Ernie Golden and his orchestra broadcast from there every Saturday night. The idea that spies were working there was nuts, like Fat Joe being a spy.

"We're not worrying about that now. We know how to stop it, but something else has come up. Bruder told me that Griebl was worried because Berlin was sending in a new man to evaluate his operation, and this man is with the SS."

"What's that?"

"The *Schutzstaffel*. SS. The Protection Squad. They answer directly to Hitler and everyone, even the most dedicated Nazis are afraid of them. With good reason. Bruder didn't know who the new man was but said he was going to meet him. I told him to be careful, but before his meeting, I was reassigned to deal with Hauptmann."

He turned to Ellis. "This is officially a murder investigation now. Is it yours?"

"Yes."

"This morning, you thought that Bruder was beaten to death by some drunken friends that he'd pissed off, just like he pissed off everybody, right? Now you know there's more to it. I can help you. Come with me to Bruder's apartment. I've got a key."

Chapter Sixteen

After Ellis and Turcot left, I went up to my office and called the sign company that made the awning. They said they'd send a guy over, but he probably wouldn't get to us until Tuesday. I hung up and got cash out of the safe to start the evening. As I was counting, the telephone rang. It was Moe Sedway from Lansky's garage. Still worrying about people listening in, he said, "The spark plugs and parts you ordered are ready."

I said I'd be there later and sorted the bills for Frenchy and Marie Therese. They were opening. I walked back to the Chelsea and found Connie getting ready for work. It took a long time to explain everything that had happened since I left before dawn. After I finished, she had the same kind of confused reaction I had. She didn't really like Fat Joe—nobody did—but, dammit, he was one of us. And she had a hard time buying Turcot's story about him being a spy. But not Griebl.

"I've known there was something wrong with that four-eyed bastard since the first day he came in with his bosom buddy. They sit there in their booth and she's unbuttoned his fly before their first schnapps gets to the table. She makes this revolting kissy face when she takes out his pocket square and unfolds it. Then under the table it goes and she's giving him a little handy dandy workout. Do they think they're fooling anybody?"

"I doubt it. They've noticed how you only touch her empty glass with your fingertips."

"She doesn't wash her hands."

"Turcot says her name's Moog, Kate Moog. She's probably a Nazi spy too, what'da'ya expect?"

"We shouldn't be joking," Connie said. "Fat Joe's dead."

"That's not all. Arch came by. He's helping Daphne Prewitt."

"I know all about that."

From Arch or Daphne, I wondered.

"And that's still not all. I've got more business with Lansky. I'm going over to his garage and pick up something that Longy Zwillman needs in Newark. It shouldn't take long. I'm just the deliveryman."

Fat chance.

I took a long shower trying to wash away the morning. It didn't help. I still saw Fat Joe's mashed up face and battered body. I strapped on my brace, found khaki pants, work shirt, brown woven tie, cracked leather jacket, work gloves, and an old fedora. I was about to drop my knucks into my pocket but stopped. Knucks were illegal in New Jersey and could get me arrested. Same with a pistol. I'd have to get by with my stick. I walked over to the parking garage on Ninth where I kept a Ford coupe and drove across town.

During Prohibition, Lansky spent a lot of his time at his garage down on the Lower East Side. He liked to work on cars, and he used the place to repair the trucks and cars we used to move booze. Even though his real business was in casinos after Repeal, he kept the garage. From time to time, it was useful. Moe Sedway ran it. He was waiting by an open service bay. I backed in and he rolled the door down behind me. We were the only ones in the place. Moe was a short, moon-faced guy with a receding hairline and a taste for flashy suits and monogramed silk shirts. He went back with Lansky almost as far as I did.

I opened the trunk of the Ford. "What've you got?"

He pulled a paint-stained drop cloth off a small crate. "A couple of cops brought this by early this morning."

The crate was made of unfinished pine boards. It was about two and a half feet wide, a foot deep and maybe eight inches tall, held together with nails. Rope handles at each end. 'NYPD' stenciled on top. Moe said, "I got curious and pried it open." He lifted the top away. I saw excelsior packed around dull black metal cylinders lying on their side. Twelve of them. They were about the size of a can of beans with a smaller cylinder and a split ring at the top.

"What are they?"

Moe held up the lid he'd pried off and showed me the other side. A label was glued to it with instructions for arming and using tear gas grenades. "What the hell?"

Moe shrugged. "I dunno. He wants you should take 'em to Nat Arno's gym in Newark. You know where that is?"

"Yeah. It's been a while since I was there." Eight, ten years—when I was moving juke boxes, pinball machines and slots for Longy. I thought as Moe and I looked at the grenades, it's one thing to haul illegal machines around New Jersey when Longie has the state cops in his pocket. I might have a hard time explaining how I came to have a trunkful of New York Police Department weapons.

Moe said, "Probably illegal to transport grenades across state lines. Better drive careful, and I got this for you." He tossed me a thick sealed envelope. "Lansky said you'd know what it was for."

He put the lid back on the crate and we stashed it and the drop cloth in my trunk. Moe rolled up the bay door. I drove west to the Holland Tunnel, paid my fifty-cent toll and went under the river. Signs said the Pulaski Skyway would take me into Newark. It had been open about a year and I hadn't used it. Eventually it got me into the city and I found my way to the gym near Hillside. In those days, if you drove from the Lower East Side of New York to the Third Ward of Newark, it was like you hadn't gone anywhere. Both of them were Jewish neighborhoods with lots of small storefronts, shops, and horse-drawn carts selling everything you could think of. You still saw the big draft horses in other parts of New York, but there were more of them on those streets.

It was late afternoon by the time I got there. Nat Arno had boxed professionally as a lightweight. For a while, he was a contender and he retired with a winning record and brains that hadn't been scrambled. That's when he went to work for Longy out of a boxing gym that he opened. I knew who Nat was but we'd never done any work together. The gym was underneath a bakery. I parked on the street and found the door to his place off to one side. There were three practice rings and a lot of equipment I didn't recognize. A couple of guys smacking the big bag and the speed bag paid no attention to me. The good smell of the bakery did nothing for the stink of the gym. Another guy had his feet up on a desk in the corner. He wore suit, vest and tie. A fat cigar stuck out of the corner of his mouth. On the wall behind him was a faded poster of the same guy, several years before in boxing trunks and gloves. He was billed as "Nat Arno, Newark's Fighting Hebrew."

He put his feet down as I walked over and introduced myself. "I've got the stuff for Longy out in my car. Want me to bring it in?"

Arno stood up. He was a little taller than me and thicker around the middle than he was in the poster, but he still had a fighter's big rounded shoulders, and his biceps strained his shirtsleeves. "Jimmy Quinn. You got a place across the river, don't cha? Work with Lansky and Charlie Lucky. And you were with Rothstein, right? How did that come about?"

"Woman who raised me, Mother Moon, she owned the building I lived in. Everybody who lived there worked. She hired me out to A. R. as a runner. I took to it."

"What was he like?"

"I was just a kid, so I didn't really understand a lot of his business. I guess the main thing I remember is the way everybody else wanted to be with him. He always seemed to be in charge, whatever he was doing, and there were always guys needing to talk to him, wanting to tap into his bankroll."

I could've said a lot more about A. R., but that seemed to satisfy Arno and I didn't know him well enough to tell him how things were at the end. He put on his suitcoat and hat and said, "Let's take a look. No need to bring 'em in here."

He followed me out. I unlocked the trunk and propped it open. We stood close together to keep anyone on the sidewalk from getting curious. I pushed back the drop cloth and took the lid off the crate. Arno picked up two of the grenades and said, "Twelve? That's more than we need tonight."

He put the two grenades into his coat pockets and handed me two more. "Here, take these. We're going down to Springfield Avenue. You drive. Take your next right."

The grenades were heavy in my jacket pockets as I locked the trunk. We eased out into the evening traffic, and I asked Arno what was going on.

"We're going to kick some Nazi ass. These bastards have been making a lot of noise but now they've gone too far. They've been pasting up flyers on utility poles and walls saying 'German Destiny Will Not Be Fulfilled Until Jewish Blood Runs In The Streets of Newark,' shit like that. Then they march around in their damn uniforms in their brown shirts with their swastika armbands and they pretend to be drilling in city parks. And they think we're going to roll over and take it. Not tonight. Stay straight here."

By then, we were on Springfield Avenue, heading toward the Passaic River and Irvington, the German neighborhood. We weren't moving much faster than we could walk. The street and the sidewalks were crowded with most of the traffic headed in the same direction we were going. You got the feeling everybody was expecting something to happen.

"We've got a problem here in Third Ward. The older, established guys who have already made it think we should leave the kraut bastards alone. They say the government won't let them treat us like they do in Germany. But the government's letting them march and wear their uniforms and put up those flyers. Somebody's gotta stop 'em. Longy asked me and Abie Bain to put together a few guys who know how to use their fists to show them that we're not going to roll over."

Abie Bain was another boxer, a bigger guy with a huge jaw who fought middle- and light-heavyweight.

"Abie and the other guys are already there. Go on up another block and pull over where you find a space."

We couldn't have driven much farther. Just ahead on our right was a large brick building with a shoulder-to-shoulder crowd in front of it. Arno said it was the hall where they were meeting. There was a wide cross street on the other side of the building, and people were milling around in the intersection, paying no attention to traffic.

I parked. We got out and I gimped along on my stick, having trouble keeping up with Arno. He stopped where five guys were standing next to a big LaSalle Phaeton with the top down. I recognized Bain, and the others had the same hard-faced look about them. I heard Bain mutter "they're already in there," as the others crowded around Arno. They huddled there for a few minutes. The way they gestured and pointed, it figured they were going over what they'd been planning to do. Arno said something and pointed at me over his shoulder with his thumb. They turned and looked at me. Their expressions didn't change.

There were three cop cars down the street, and I could see more uniforms in the crowd as a streetcar passed through and turned at the cross street. I tried to spot the blue caps. Stopped counting at twenty, and I could see that one cop standing on the running board of a car was signaling the others with hand gestures. Four guys in brown shirts and black ties stood shoulder to shoulder at the doors of the meeting hall. They frowned at the restless crowd milling around in front of them. I can't judge crowd size but I'd say there were more than two hundred people in the intersection, mostly guys, a few women, no kids. The cops were worried, too. Something was up, and they wanted to be in control. I should've brought the knucks.

Arno talked some more. Then the five sluggers spread apart and made their way through the crowd toward the front of the big brick building. Arno said, "This way," and we went on down the sidewalk to a small hardware store. An older guy with a nail apron wrapped around his stomach, the owner I guessed, greeted Arno and they ducked through the door. They came back right away with a wooden extension ladder. Arno pulled some bills out of his pocket, but the older guy shook his head.

Arno turned the foot of the ladder toward me. "Can you handle this with your…" He waved at my stick.

I hoisted my end onto my shoulder and said, "Which way?"

He picked up his end and we eased through the sidewalk crowd past several storefronts. When we got to the corner of the big brick meeting hall, Arno turned down a cobbled alley that I hadn't noticed. As we walked beside the building, the ground sloped down. The cobbles were broken and uneven, so I was even slower than usual with the ladder on my shoulder. The alley ended at a fenced-in yard overgrown with weeds and filled with rusted car parts, bald tires and garbage cans. There was a wide half-open window about twelve feet above us in the middle of the wall. Through it I could see a red flag or banner with a white circle and part of a twisted cross in the middle, and I heard music and men's voices singing Happy Birthday. The singing ended with cheers. Then what sounded like a small band with horns stumbled into the first notes of The Star-Spangled Banner.

Nat said, "Quick, while they're still making that racket." He raised his end of the ladder as I pulled the rope to extend it. When we had it about halfway up, we stopped and moved to one side. Nat found a chunk of cinderblock to put under one leg of the ladder to level it against the wall, and we pulled it the rest of the way up, so that the top was above the open window and on the left side of it. Nat climbed up until his head was just at the bottom corner of the window. He craned his neck to peek in past the edge of the banner.

After a few seconds, he hugged the ladder with his left hand and tugged a tear gas grenade out of his coat pocket with his right. Still holding tight to the ladder, he pulled the split ring out, then tossed the grenade through window with an awkward sidearm. As it left his hand, a metal clip popped open and gas began to hiss out of it. Quick as he could, Nat yanked the other grenade out of his left pocket. It caught on the fabric. He ripped the coat getting it out and pulled the ring. Instead of sidearming it, he stuck his hand through the window by the banner and let it drop. By then, the guys inside were making a lot of noise.

Nat looked down and motioned me to toss him another one. I did. He caught it easily but before he could throw it, a guy who'd been blinded by the gas ripped the banner aside and stuck his head out the window to get some air. Nat smacked him in the kisser with the grenade, lobbed it in, and backed down the ladder fast. He ran back up the alley. I gimped along after him. By the time I got back to the street, everything had changed. The intersection was full of people yelling. They were fighting or trying to get away from the guys who were fighting.

It looked like a dozen or more guys in brown shirts had made it out of the meeting hall and more were pushing through the doors. Nat's sluggers were working on the first guys with sawed off bats, wrapped lead pipes, crowbars, and anything else that would do damage. Two big private buses had stopped on the other side of the intersection and more guys in brown shirts were piling out. Nat pointed to them. "Reinforcements from New York. We didn't expect that." He said it with a smile and shouldered his way into the crowd. By then, more guys were pouring out of the meeting hall to join in the fight and more people were running away.

The street was so crowded by then that I went back to my Ford and stood on the running board so I could see what was going on. The cops in the crowd seemed to be going after anybody who was fighting, both Jews and Nazis. The cop I'd seen who looked to be in charge was gone. As I watched, a bunch of the biggest New York Nazis linked arms and charged forward in a V-shaped flying wedge. That's what they called it in football, and it worked. They went straight to the meeting hall. The Nazis outnumbered Nat's guys but Nat's guys outclassed them. These were trained fighters. They hit other guys every day and got hit hard every day. Makes a difference. A bully in a brown shirt thinks he can throw his weight around but when he gets a crowbar across his face, he pauses. A fighter punches right back.

It got a lot louder as they mixed it up and that's when the cops decided to put a stop to everything. They had their own gas grenades. Two of them went off and the intersection cleared out PDQ. I got a little whiff of it and that was enough to have me coughing and gagging and reaching for a handkerchief. That also meant it was time for me to get out.

I was about to step down from the running board when a voice I knew cut through the loud babble of the mob, a prissy German voice saying, "*der verdammte Jude Arno*." I heard him but I couldn't see him. Ignatz Griebl, the Nazi who recruited Fat Joe Beddoes to be a spy.

Chapter Seventeen

I was halfway through the Holland Tunnel before I remembered I had a grenade in my pocket. And seven more in the trunk. Damn. What the hell was I supposed to do with them? By then, it was past nine. Moe might still be at Lansky's garage and I was close, so I went there. No luck. It was locked tight. I drove back to the West Side and thought about stopping at my place, but Frenchy would have his truck parked in our loading area off the alley, and I didn't want to leave the Ford and a trunk full of explosives on the street. So, I drove back to the garage on Ninth and put the grenade back in the crate before I locked the trunk and went back to work. It was almost eleven.

As I walked the long blocks, I tried to figure everything that had happened since I'd been woken up before dawn. Seeing the guy beaten bloody and left in front of my place. Then the guy turns out to be Fat Joe and Fat Joe's dead and Fat Joe is really Josef Bruder. And he's working as a spy for Dr. Griebl, but Fat Joe is really a double spy working for the Bureau man Turcot. And then Griebl shows up at the Nazi rally. And Arch is going to shadow Daphne's sugar daddy hoping that he, Arch, can slip into the sack with Daphne. At least that last part made sense.

I let myself into the loading area and went in through the back door. Not being dressed for work and having missed dinner, I went up the stairs to the kitchen of the Cruzon Grill. I told the guys to fix me a hamburger and fried potatoes and bring it down to my office. Then I thought about it again and told them to make that two burgers. In the office, I hung up my coat and hat and cracked the venetian blinds to check on business. Even for Monday, it was slow. I called the phone behind the bar. Frenchy answered. I told him I was back and asked him to tell Connie to bring up two glasses of red wine, whatever he had open. A few minutes later, she bumped the door open with her hip and put the wine on the coffee table in front of the divan. She looked terrific.

She was wearing a plain white blouse that had been altered so that it fit more closely. Her black skirt had been shortened to come just below her knees, and she'd taken to wearing her black hair up and held with a couple of long red lacquered hair pins. She wrinkled her nose and said, "What is that smell? Ammonia? Vinegar?"

"Tear gas," I said and realized there was still a little of it on me. She looked at me like I was nuts. I explained, "Lansky arranged to get some tear gas grenades from the cops so Longy Zwillman's guys could drive a bunch of Nazis out of a hall where they were having a meeting and give them what-for in the street. I delivered the grenades. Helped out a little. And there's this…"

I pulled Lansky's envelope out of my hip pocket and opened it. A lot of tens and twenties. "Put half of this in tonight's take and half in tomorrow's or spread it over three nights if that makes the books look better."

When I dropped the envelope on the desk, the bills spilled out. Connie picked up the cash and whistled low through her teeth. It was more than I thought. "Damn, Jimmy, who did you kill?"

"Nobody recently. Just this and that for Lansky."

"A lot of this and a lot of that."

"It adds up. Did'ya eat? They're bringing down a couple of hamburgers."

"I'm not really hungry," she said, and sat at my desk to count the money.

She hadn't finished when there was a tap on the door. A tall, long-haired young guy in a food-spattered white chef's jacket brought in two covered plates and set them on the coffee table in front of the divan. When he took off the domes, the smells of grilled meat and fried potatoes filled the office, and my stomach growled. As the guy turned to leave, he stopped and said, "Mademoiselle Connie."

She frowned, irritated, and looked up. Then she smiled. "Phillipe, you're here. I thought you weren't going to start until next week."

She ran around from behind the desk and hugged the big bastard. What the hell?

"When Chef learned that I had given notice, he flew into a rage, just as Anthony said he would and forever banished me from his kitchen."

Hearing the name Anthony and the tall guy's French accent, I started to figure what was going on. Assistant Concierge Anthony.

Connie finally let go of him and said, "Jimmy, you remember at the—"

"At the Pierre Hotel, this is the sous chef, right?" I've already told the story, but the important part is that for a week we had to hole up in a big suite at the Pierre. Not a bad place. If you ever have to lay low in New York for a few days, I recommend it. While we were there, Connie, who'd just got back from Paris, told the kitchen to prepare some of the things she learned about over there. Most of it, I'd never had before, and I still remember the smell and the taste of the first bite of chicken cooked with garlic and wine. And this was the guy who'd cooked it. I'd heard the name but hadn't seen him.

Connie said, "I tried to describe some things Philippe made to Vittorio, but I just couldn't get it across. Then I explained that we'd had them at the Pierre. Vittorio suggested I invite Phillipe to the Cruzon kitchen and he could show them how to do it. Once Phillipe saw this kitchen and Vittorio started talking…"

"Vittorio offered him a job. Great. The place'll be packed every night." I took a better look at the guy. Taller than I thought at first, and young. Maybe eighteen, same as Connie. Loose-jointed. Bony wrists sticking out of too-short sleeves.

"There's a little more to it than that," Connie said, and the way she looked, it figured there was a lot more to it. "But the important thing is that you're here. Does your mother know yet?"

"Non, but I have written to her, like you said."

Connie motioned for him to lean down and whispered to him. He smiled and whispered to her.

"Good," she said. "I'll see you tomorrow."

He said, "I can't tell you how much this means to me. Thank you again, and to you, Monsieur Jimmy." He kissed her on both cheeks and left.

I'd heard French people do that to each other all the time, but I still didn't like it. Not that I was jealous. Connie could get chummy with anybody she happened to meet if the circumstances were right.

She forgot that she wasn't hungry and sat beside me on the divan. "This is going to be so good for him. I knew he and Vittorio would understand each other, because Chef Marcel at the Pierre treated Philippe like some kind of slave. But Philippe's mother told him he had to expect that in his first job, so he was afraid to leave. I managed to talk him into it. Things are starting to fall into place."

I might have asked her what she meant by '*things falling into place*,' but by then I was tucking into the hamburger. The kid had not lost his touch. The potatoes had been cut thinner than you usually got them and it tasted like he'd put more salt on them.

Between bites, she said, "This is what they eat every day in Paris. Everybody, not just the rich people who stay at the Pierre. On every street, there're cafés where you could order a meal like this for a few francs."

Chapter Eighteen

There wasn't much I didn't already know about the Lindbergh case in the papers on Tuesday, and I scanned them without getting as involved as I had been for the last week. I couldn't stop thinking about Fat Joe. Nothing that the Bureau man said about him made sense to me when I thought about the mug I'd known for five years. My Fat Joe Beddoes was an ugly, lazy, mean-tempered bastard who enjoyed hitting guys who couldn't hit back, and drinking beer and cheap gin. During Prohibition he'd been good at sitting by the door and sizing up strange customers to keep out any law enforcement that might try to shut us down. When fights broke out, he made sure that me or Frenchy or Arch had stepped in before he got off his big butt. The only guys I'd ever seen him being friendly with were lowlifes like vice cops who were the worst crooked cops in the city. Other crooked cops hated them. But Fat Joe'd shown up for work just about every day. Until recently, I realized. For the past few months, he had been missing more than a few days. When I asked him about it, he mumbled something about being hung over, and I left it at that. Detective Ellis and Turcot said they were going to search his apartment. I wondered if they'd found anything. Then I thought, hell, I don't even know where he lived. Somewhere in the Bronx, maybe. I knew he took the I.R.T. to work and back.

The guy from the sign company showed up just after noon with a new aluminum frame and leg for the awning. He said it would take them a week to make up a new one with our name on it, but he was able to stitch up the torn canvas up with green twine. Better than nothing.

I was getting ready to open when Arch came in and reminded me that he'd be taking time off that night. "I told you that Daphne and her sugar daddy are going out to dinner at a local place down in the Village. I'd like to get a look at the man, so I plan to be there when they arrive. I've spent the morning educating myself about him, and I have to admit that I'm intrigued. Look at this."

He took two newspaper clippings out of his pocket and handed them to me. The first one was a fuzzy photograph of a smiling man wearing a dark blazer, white slacks and white shoes, and a billed white cap. He was standing on the deck of a boat behind a big steering wheel. The second was the same man, younger in boxing trunks and gloves, posing for the camera with his fists up. In both pictures he had a wide smile and a big, jutting jaw.

"That's our man," he said. "Harold Henninger. Like so many of those well-heeled Wall Street bastards, he got a head start by being born into a wealthy family with all the right business and social connections. The man has never wanted for anything. He is fifty-seven years old. Yale man. His wife Victoria, who bears an unfortunate resemblance to the late monarch herself, is one of those terrifying clubwomen who's involved in dozens of noble causes. After delivering their son Harold, Jr., she lost interest in Harold, Sr. They've lived apart for many years. If they have appeared together in public, none of the newspaper society writers know of it, and they really don't care. Henninger is boring. When I hinted at his arrangement with Daphne, they yawned.

"I hear a different story when I talk to the financial writers. The first thing they tell me is that Henninger has a reputation as something of a genius whose predictions almost always come true. The second thing they tell me is that he has a deep hatred of John D. Rockefeller which he'll share with anyone who'll listen. He doesn't like Jews, either, but he's not so public about that and among his set it's not at all remarkable. A couple of the older writers say that his reputation for brilliance is overblown. The man is so charming personally that everyone forgets his mistakes, they say. I'll have to learn more about that. If nothing else, he was not involved in any of the double dealings that went on at most of the banks before the Crash. At least, it appears so. He has never been accused of any financial misdeeds. I'm not sure what, if anything, that means."

He took back the newspaper pictures. "If they follow their usual schedule, they'll finish dinner around ten o'clock and then repair to her cozy little place. Harold will stay the night, enjoying the delightful Miss Daphne, damn his eyes. When he leaves tomorrow morning, I will follow."

At eight-thirty that night, Arch was sitting at a two-top at the Four Trees restaurant. As Village beaneries go, it was on the quiet side. I mean, there were screwy places down there where you had to slide down a chute to get in or where they tried to make it look like you were on a pirate ship and the waiters and waitresses wore eye patches. The Four Trees just had a plank floor, rough unpainted wooden walls, and four fake trees with cardboard bark and paper leaves. That time of evening, it was filling up. Arch was nursing a whiskey and reading the *Daily News* when Daphne and Henninger came in.

He strode into the place with the comfortable confidence of a man who knew he could buy it if he wanted it. The maître 'd knew it, too, and waved them through the crowd of people waiting for a table. He tucked a menu under his arm and led them to a table near the front window and the fireplace. Henninger had a drinker's rosy cheeks and schnoz, and his face had been darkened by the sun, a yachtsman's tan. He kept a big paw on the nape of Daphne's neck as they crossed the room. The maître 'd put the menu on the table at the better seat and pulled Daphne's chair out for her. They made an attractive couple, Arch told me later. At six feet Harold and his jaw towered over her, but when she was dolled up with that golden blonde hair and a dress that showed off her figure, Daphne got most of the attention.

Henninger ordered drinks and the maître 'd scurried to the bar. Harold pulled a silver cigarette case from the breast pocket of his coat. He opened it and offered it to Daphne. They both took smokes. He fired them up with a silver lighter. Daphne said something that made him smile. The waiter brought their drinks, a martini for Daphne, Manhattan for him. Such an awful waste of good bourbon. He ordered for both of them, giving the waiter detailed instructions. The waiter hurried away and returned quickly with an ice bucket and a bottle of sauterne, "one of the sweet ones," according to Arch. The waiter opened it for Harold, who gulped down his Manhattan. Daphne ordered another martini.

Until the meal came, they seemed to talk comfortably, though Arch couldn't hear what they were saying. He could see their posture as they sat. He had a full view of Harold and saw Daphne in profile. No arguing or disagreement, nothing serious, either. It was more a "what did you do this afternoon" talk. Then the food arrived. Fish for her, liver and kidneys for him.

As he watched the man eat, Arch understood what some of the financial writers said about him. Henninger was one of those men who had a combination of size, wealth, and self-assurance that made some guys fall in line behind him without thinking. Other guys would get their hackles up and answer "hell, no" to anything he said.

Chapter Nineteen

While Arch was watching Henninger and Daphne, Frenchy and I were behind the bar. Connie hadn't come in yet. It was a normal Tuesday, business better than Monday but not much. Sometime after six, Dr. Griebl came in by himself and looking worried, blinking behind his big round glasses. He was dressed in his usual plain black suit, black tie, and white pocket square but without the buxom blonde. He went to the booth where they usually sat but he got up before Connie could take a drink order and walked to the bar.

I had the bottle in my hand before he said, "Schnapps." Gave him a generous pour in a short glass. He knocked it back and asked for another.

"Tell me, where is your man Josef that I usually see at the door?" No question that was the voice I heard in Newark.

How to play it? "It looks like he got into a fight after we closed Sunday night. He was beat up pretty bad. Some neighbors saw it. Told the cops some guys in a car did it. Fat Joe died at the hospital."

Griebl's eyes got wide behind the big glasses. "That is impossible. Do the police have any suspects?"

"Not that I know of. Fat Joe worked here for a long time but he kept to himself. Outside of work, nobody really knew him." I was trying to keep Griebl interested without giving anything away. It still seemed more than a little crazy that he could be a spy, and even crazier that he'd try to make Fat Joe a spy. But if it was true, it might not hurt to put on a little pressure.

"I can tell you this." I leaned across the bar and lowered my voice. "Since it happened here, right out front, they called me and I came over. Yeah, I saw him and I gotta tell you, I don't know I've ever seen anybody been beat that bad. And somehow, maybe when Fat Joe was trying to get away from them, he must've fell in some hot asphalt. The stuff was all over him."

Griebl's face went pale when I said that last part. He gulped, threw a dollar on the bar and bolted out the front door, leaving most of his second schnapps.

Frenchy said, "What was all that about?"

I said I'd tell him later, took off my apron, grabbed my coat, stick, and hat, and followed Griebl. As I figured, he turned east, toward Sixth where he hailed a cab going uptown. It took a couple of minutes for me flag down another one. I told him to take me to the Hotel McAlpin. We stopped at the hotel's 34th Street entrance. Griebl was out of the cab and paying his driver. I gave my guy a buck, probably the biggest tip he got that night, and followed the doctor inside.

Griebl hurried down a long entrance hall toward the lobby. As I followed, I felt like I'd been there before, but I couldn't pin down whatever I was remembering. If you'd asked me, I'd've said I'd never been inside the place, even though it was so close. The lobby was one of those grand rooms with a high ceiling, heavy glass chandeliers, marble floor, and a balcony on two sides. About half full. Griebl went past the long registration desk to an alcove with a Dutch door. The guy working there gave Griebl the key to his room. Then the guy said something, reached into the back of the alcove, and handed the doctor a small white envelope. Griebl ripped it open, read the message and stuffed it into his coat pocket. He turned and went into a crowd waiting at the bank of elevators.

I thought about trying to figure which floor he was going to, like they do in movies, but not with that many people around him. I turned to leave and saw Leo Turcot, the Bureau man, standing right behind me, smiling a cocky little smile. Oh, hell.

"Didn't expect to see you here," he said. "Let me buy you a drink."

We crossed the lobby to a set of stairs leading down to the basement and the Marine Grill. I'd heard it was an unusual place and it lived up to the billing. It had tiled columns and a vaulted tiled ceiling, sort of like the Oyster Bar in Grand Central Terminal, but the ceiling was a lot lower and the tiles weren't white. They were different dark colors and patterns. The room made me feel like I was deep underground and the ceiling was pressing down. Didn't bother the other customers. The place was doing a great Tuesday business. Most of the tables were full. The bar was not as busy. Turcot and I took a two-top in an empty corner. When the waiter came over, he said vodka on ice. I asked for Teeling with two cubes. They didn't have Teeling. I said any Irish would do.

After the waiter left, Turcot said, "Do you believe me now?"

"About what?"

He took out a cigarette and tapped it on his thumbnail to tamp down the tobacco before he lit it. "About Josef Bruder and Dr. Griebl. Don't try to tell me that you just wandered into the McAlpin. I suspect that Griebl came to your place earlier this evening and asked about Bruder. You told him Bruder's dead and that surprised him. He probably left in a hurry. Since I mentioned this hotel, you followed him here."

I didn't say anything.

"The McAlpin was the headquarters of German Intelligence in New York before the Great War, and they never really left. It's perfect for them, you see. It's a big place, biggest in the world when it was built. Very easy for them to go unnoticed here."

I tried as hard as I could to keep a poker face, but it rattled me that Turcot knew as much as he did. The man always seemed to be one or two steps ahead of me. Did he know about Griebl and Newark? I decided to ignore what he said and what he might know.

"Did you and Ellis toss Fat Joe's place like you said? Where'd he live?"

"Edgecombe Avenue, near 155th."

That was the north part of Harlem, up by the Polo Grounds.

"How did Griebl react when you told him Bruder was dead?" I didn't answer, trying to come up with a lie he'd buy. The waiter brought the drinks and I used that to stall for another few seconds. Finally, he said, "Don't make this difficult. We can continue at my office."

He took a polite drink. I took a big drink.

"O.K., you got it right. The doctor came in by himself. He looked worried and at first, I thought he was expecting his big blonde. But he came to the bar and asked where 'Josef' was. When I told him what happened, it surprised him, and when I got to the part about the asphalt, he threw down a buck for two schnapps and made himself scarce."

"As expected," Turcot muttered. "He's starting to understand how dangerous his position is. It's time to work him."

Turcot took a leather-bound notebook out of his pocket and wrote something short in it. "Yesterday I told you that Griebl had recruited Josef Bruder into his organization. I surveilled several of their meetings and identified most of the members. Some, I knew, were true believers. I'd have no chance persuading them to help me, but Bruder was different.

He was simply angry at the changes he saw going on around him every day. He was particularly upset by Negro families who are moving into his neighborhood and into his building. One of them, a young man, apparently tried to get Bruder to join the Community Party."

I couldn't help but laugh.

"Exactly. Bruder was as upset by communists and Jews as he was about Negroes. Two members of the Silver Legion are regular customers at your establishment. At their urging, Bruder attended a couple of meetings and liked what he heard. He also liked the beer they served. Two meetings is not enough to fully indoctrinate a man and so I knew that if I could explain to him what the Nazis' real goals were, he could be persuaded to work against them."

"In a pig's ass you 'explained' anything. How much money did you promise him?"

The Bureau man shrugged. "Enough."

"Explain it to me, then. What do these guys want?"

"The Silver Legion and the other 'shirt' organizations are nothing more than a distraction. Griebl and his people know that a war is coming. Not next month and not next year and maybe not the year after, but it is coming. Right now, most Americans don't want to believe it, and the ones who do see that it could happen, the isolationists, they want to keep us out of it. That's what the Germans want too—a neutral America. We've forgotten what we learned about the Germans in the last war. We don't understand them and what they're going to do."

"I still don't see what that has to do with Fat Joe."

"Griebl is dealing with a new man, an operative who's been sent over from Germany. I told you that yesterday. Griebl is a capable spymaster, but he is mostly passive, cautious. He works behind the scenes, picking up little bits of information where he can, poking at the edges. But this new man from the SS is ruthless. If he thought there was any chance that Bruder was a double agent, he would order his death without a moment's hesitation. That, I think, is exactly what he did. I can't prove it now, but I will. We will."

I didn't say anything. No point in telling him that I didn't cooperate with cops I don't know, and I wasn't sure how much trouble a federal agent could make for me.

Turcot said, "I've done this kind of work before. Usually, it has involved Reds in unions trying to sabotage key military projects. I've done it often enough to know what it feels like when something big is about to happen. They're going to meetings and rallies and speeches. They have long political discussions in bars. They're making all the noise you expect to hear, and then it quiets down because something more important is in the works. That's what's happening with Griebl now. He has received marching orders from Berlin, and now he's frightened. You saw that tonight when he learned that Bruder had been murdered. You and I won't have any trouble bringing him in."

"You and me? I'm not going to help you."

"Not now." Turcot smiled. "But when the time comes, you will. And don't be surprised when they come after you."

"What're you talking? Coming after me how?"

He gave me a long expressionless look. I had the feeling he was trying to decide if he should say something, something important. But all he said was, "You'll know when it happens."

It was after ten when I got back to my place. Business might have picked up while I was gone. Behind the bar, I shed my coat and put on my apron. Frenchy and Connie wanted to know why I'd taken a powder. Connie knew about Griebl and she'd filled Frenchy and Marie Therese in on what the Bureau man said. I told them that it was too complicated to explain then. We'd talk after we closed. Arch showed up around midnight. After the last customer left, we locked the front door and cleaned up. I told everybody to pour what they wanted. Then I went upstairs to the kitchen to make sure that nobody was up there and the Cruzon Grill was empty. It was.

Back downstairs, I found that Arch had broken into the stash of illegal booze that we'd taken from the millionaires and opened a bottle of the hundred-year-old Croizet Cognac. He'd poured six snifters. I was about to ask what was going on when it hit me. Monday had been too crazy. There hadn't been time to do anything. The five of us raised our glasses to the sixth.

We toasted in a ragged chorus, "To Fat Joe."

Marie Therese said, "He claimed he was always nice to his mother."

Frenchy said, "If he told me that once, he told me a thousand times, and it was always a lie."

Connie thought for a second or two. "There has to be something good to say about him."

"He was a son of a bitch," I said, "but he was our son of a bitch." And it pissed me off that they'd made a point of killing him in front of my place. And there was the green canvas awning.

Arch said, "I didn't know him as long as the rest of you, so I did not dislike him as much, but I can say that day in and day out, he was one of the most irritating individuals I have ever encountered. As the Bard put it, 'Nothing in his life became him like the leaving of it.'"

Chapter Twenty

Late Wednesday morning, Arch was waiting on Waverly Place near Daphne's house when Henninger came out. Arch didn't have a plan until a black Cadillac with a chauffeur approached on Sixth and parked at the curb. Daphne said Henninger's driver sometimes picked him up. Arch figured there was a better than average chance that the Caddy was waiting for his guy. He trotted over to Sixth and flagged down a metered cab heading north. He got in the back seat and said, "This is going to be a little unusual. Look in your mirror. Do you see the big Caddy parked behind you?"

The cabbie, an older guy, leaned to check the mirror. "Sure."

"Circle around the block and come up behind him. Double park if you have to. In a few minutes a man will get in the Caddy. I want you to follow him."

"Your money, pal." He said it like he did that sort of thing every day. The cab made three quick rights to get back to Sixth. By then, the Caddy was gone.

"Oh, hell, you've lost him."

"No, I haven't. He's turning on Ninth," the cabbie said, still deadpan. "You wanna drive this heap?"

They went north and east through slow midday traffic to East 56th Street where the Caddy turned toward the river. It slowed and stopped, blocking the street in front of one of the apartment buildings on Sutton Place. The high rent district. The chauffeur hurried out and opened the back door. As Henninger got out, a liveried doorman held open the front door of the building. Henninger paid no attention to either of them as he strode inside. The chauffeur got back in the Caddy, rolled ahead a few yards and turned at the entrance to a private parking garage.

The cabbie said, "What now?"

Arch was trying to get a better look at the front of garage and the apartment building. "Go on around the block. I want to see it again."

"Okey doke. You wanna tell me what you're up to?" Now he sounded like he was interested.

Arch thought, why not. "The gentleman we've been following, and I use the term 'gentleman' with some reservation, has an extremely attractive mistress, a kept woman. She suspects he is up to something that involves shady financial dealings, possibly a confidence game of some kind. She has already been part of an ill-defined scheme that resulted in more than ten thousand dollars currently deposited in an account that she may or may not be able to plunder. You begin to see the problem. She wants to know what he is planning. So do I. I also want to take her to bed."

"You got a shot with her?"

"D'you think I'd be doing this if I didn't? Here, slow down."

The apartment building was five stories tall and not particularly wide. It shared one wall with the larger building beside it. Might have been part of the second building, Arch thought. That one had double doors and a polished metal plaque beside them that read: EAST RIVER YACHT CLUB.

Arch asked the cabbie, "Are you familiar enough with this neighborhood to recommend a good bar?"

The cabbie said, "You're kidding, right? P. J. Clarke's is around the corner."

"Excellent. Let me out there and tell me something. Did the other driver know he was being followed?"

"Nah, too much traffic and we was never that close."

Arch gave the hack two bucks for a ninety-cent fare and hoofed it back to Sutton Place. He spent an hour walking the blocks between First Avenue and the river. The neighborhood could have been the Village with more money. A lot more money. It had that feeling of being separated from the rest of the city and the river made it sound different. Narrow streets, iron fences painted black, slender maple trees, flower boxes, stoops and sidewalks swept clean, a couple of small parks. There were two big apartment buildings facing the river with storefronts on the streetside. Farther north, it was brownstones. On the other side of the East River Club from Harold's apartment building, there was a narrow walkway between the club and the garage. It ended at a tall fence. Through it, Arch could see a wide fenced terrace that ran from the back of the club to the river's edge and a dock with a dozen or more boats, some with tall masts. That close, the wind off the river carried the smells of salt, decayed vegetation, and diesel exhaust.

When he thought he'd seen enough, Arch walked back toward First and stopped in the first bar he came to. Like a lot of the joints in that neighborhood, it was new, and the barkeep was young, too young for his purposes. He left straightaway. He didn't even go inside the next bar he passed. He found what he needed in a place called the Brewery. It looked like it had been a speak before Repeal. He took a seat at the end of the bar away from the other customers. There weren't many. He put two five-spots on the bar where the bartender could see them. He was a plump, balding guy about Arch's age with a round, pink, cleanly, shaven face.

"I'll have a pint," Arch said, "and a few moments of your time, if I may."

"Certainly." He drew a careful pint.

"The name's Malloy, and you are?"

"Collins." By his accent, a countryman.

"Are you, perhaps, the owner?"

"Partner and employee. I live with the owner. She and I have an arrangement."

"Are you familiar with the neighborhood then, specifically with the East River Yacht Club?"

"The neighborhood, yes. The club, I don't know as well as I'd like to. What do you need?"

"Anything you can tell me. I know this delightful part of the city by reputation only. If a pint would help your recollection, please join me."

Collins checked the modest crowd. Nobody needed anything. He drew another pint and said that the club had only been open for a year or so. "It was supposed to be an answer to the River Club of New York. That's the grand building a few blocks south. It's a place for Vanderbilts, Roosevelts, Astors and their ilk. The East River Club may not be that exclusive but, as they say, if you have to ask how expensive it is to join, you can't afford it. However, if you're needing a dock for your yacht, it's just the club for you. And unlike the River Club, it's only for gentlemen. The apartments are smaller, too. I've heard that many of them are pied-à-terre."

"But you don't see many of the residents."

Collins shook his head. "They go to the new places."

"Then I don't suppose you've ever encountered a gentleman by the name of Harold Henninger."

Collins perked up. "I can't say it's the same man but we have had a customer who's come in twice while I was on duty. Big, strapping fellow. Impressive jaw, brown hair, face burned by the sun. He's worn a blue blazer, white duck pants and the little billed captain's cap. He's been with a beautiful blonde, and both times I could tell that they'd already had several drinks. The only reason I think it might be him is that she called him 'Harold.'"

"It doesn't sound like him, but how do they act? First, describe her."

"Bottle blonde, almost silver. She's on the short side, very well put together. Caters to him, and he almost always has a hand on her. Around her waist, on the back of her neck, rubbing an arm, that sort of thing. The last time he was here, it was a Sunday afternoon, I think, and he and the young lady had been out on the water. They had that windburned look. He was engaging some of my regulars in conversation. I couldn't tell you what they were saying but he seemed to have three or four of them very interested in whatever it was."

Arch shook his head. "No, that can't be my man. This is an insurance matter involving an accident and a claim that was filed more than a year ago. How I wish they'd give me a case that involved a beautiful silver blonde." The last thing he wanted was for Henninger to hear that someone was interested in him. The question now was whether the blonde was Daphne or was Henninger keeping another woman?

Chapter Twenty-One

On Wednesday, the cops released the ransom letters Hauptmann had sent to the Lindberghs two years ago. They even printed a facsimile of the first notes in the papers. The man's handwriting was even worse than mine, and I'm more or less self-taught. There were fifteen notes. He left the first one the night he took the kid, the last one after he got the money. Over and over, he warned Lindbergh not to talk to the police and he told him that the kid was safe and being cared for. To read the notes on the page of the newspaper, knowing that he'd written them after he'd bashed in the boy's head made it even worse. That was one cold-blooded bastard. But not everybody saw it that way.

In the middle of the second page of the *Times*. The headline read:

ARREST BELITTLED
IN A NAZI PAPER

BERLIN. Sept. 25 –The West
German Beobachter, the leading
Nazi newspaper in Western Germany, writes today under the title
"Lindbergh Tomtom," as follows:
"That the kidnapper of the Lindbergh baby has been found after
two years is not exactly a great ac-
complishment, but that does not
matter to American propagandists.
The entire world press is full of long
reports about the arrest and every-

thing connected therewith. Regular Edgar Wallace novels fill the cables. America is again in everybody's mouth. The world is given the impression that American tragedies are to be put before all others.

"But that is not all. American sensationalism over a wrong object had other consequences.

"The fact that the criminal comes from Germany is being utilized for an anti-German campaign of vast proportions. The part of the foreign press hostile to us nobly competes with the émigré press, especially in the Saar territory, in constantly emphasizing through big banner headlines that the perpetrator is German. Here again the saying holds that 'There's method in madness.' Of course every German will regret that a member of the German people is guilty of the deed. But every sensible person will consider it insane to make the whole people responsible for the crime of a single person.

"Suppose the criminal had been a Jew. Would that have been emphasized just as much? Certainly not. For in that case all the psychoanalysts and philanthropists in the world would have united to make of the criminal an honorable man. But since he is German, the occasion is welcomed to hang some-

thing on the German people in an
externally harmless form."

I read it twice and then I read it again. Remembering what Turcot said about not understanding the Germans, I thought that Lansky and his guys knew what they were doing. The krauts were a thin-skinned bunch and they were ready to blame the Jews for anything they didn't like. Better hold onto the tear gas grenades.

I was behind the bar getting things ready early in the afternoon when Franz Voss came through the front door. The new hat check girl wasn't in yet, so he dropped his Panama on the bar and perched on a stool. "What happened to your awning?"

I got the Teeling from the top shelf and two intact cubes from the freezer. By then I'd told so many people about Fat Joe it was like singing a song I'd memorized, but when I finished, I remembered the first evening that Voss came in. He'd known Fat Joe from the time Carl Spinoza owned the place, and I could tell that hearing about the death hit him hard.

"I don't believe it," he said. "I know he wasn't exactly the nicest man in the city, but he was one of those New York characters you couldn't imagine ever dying."

I poured the Teeling over the cubes, and he held it up to the light. "Join me," he said. Pour one for yourself and we'll toast Joe. You know, I saw him fight once or twice."

I raised my glass. "Here or professionally."

"In a ring. Some club up in the Bronx, I think. He wasn't very good but he could take a lot of punishment. They said it was impossible to knock him down."

"From what the witness said—guy across the street—it took a lot of 'em."

"Do they have any idea what went on?"

"No, but he did have a talent for pissing people off."

Voss laughed, "God, yes. I heard him rail against Reds, kikes, wops, spades, greaseballs, Chinks, he didn't care for any of them. That was the world he came from."

The papers I'd been reading were still on the bar. I started to clean them off, but he picked up the *Times*. "What do you think of this Hauptmann business? They certainly make it sound like there is no doubt the man was responsible."

"He keeps trying to explain the money but none of it washes. The only question is whether there's a second guy. From the beginning I figured it for at least two, but not now."

Voss said, "I was out of the country when the kidnapping happened, but I remember how amazing the news was and how quickly it became the only thing people were talking about."

"I was here. An old friend who was living in New Jersey not too far from the Lindberghs asked me to come out there and stay at his place. He wanted me to, I don't know, to 'guard' his wife and baby son because he had to leave on business." I didn't mention that the business was bringing in a plane filled with German drugs from Mexico. "Remember how shocked everybody was that the son of the most famous man in the world could be snatched, and, hell, if it could happen to him, it could happen to anybody. That's what my friend thought, and his wife, jeez, she was terrified. It was a crazy time. Something like that happens, it changes everything."

"Indeed." He tapped the *Times* article about the Nazi newspaper. "What about this?"

Not thinking about what the Bureau man told me about spies, I said, "I don't know. Since back in the Great War, there's been a lot of people who got no use for krauts, just like some people got no use for Jews. Me, I know good krauts and bad krauts, good Jews and bad Jews."

"But it's said in certain circles that you have worked closely with several of the more important Yids, including the Big Brain himself."

"It's no secret and that's where this Nazi paper gets it wrong. If it was a Jew that snatched and murdered the kid, they'd come down as hard on him as they are on Hauptmann. It's not who the guy is that's important, it's what he did."

Voss finished his Teeling and gestured for a second. "There's no arguing with that, but at the same time, the Germans have a point. They're trying to rebuild their country and every time it looks like they're making progress, someone tries to stop them."

I got a clean glass and made him a second drink. "Thinking about what you just said about your friend in New Jersey after the kidnapping—a year ago, I was in Berlin the night that the Reds tried to burn down the Reichstag. Do you remember that?"

"Sure, it was on the front page."

"It hit the Germans really hard. Elections were coming up. Everyone was talking about politics and who was ahead, and then these Communist traitors tried to burn down the heart of the government. When a thing like that happens, it changes everything. It was meant to stop the election but it united the people in a way that I hadn't seen before."

"Wasn't there something later about the Nazis being behind it?"

"Nonsense. Why would Hitler try to sabotage an election he was about to win easily? No, there was no question but that it was the Reds, the same sort of Reds who bombed Wall Street."

"I remember that, all right. I was just a kid but if I'd been a few blocks closer, I wouldn't be here now."

"Then you understand. There's only one way to deal with those people. They see mass murder as a political tool and they won't hesitate to use it. That's why the Germans shut down the Communist and Socialist newspapers after the fire, and that's why all of their leaders got out of the country as fast as they could."

He had a short sip of Teeling. "I don't want to sound like I'm standing on soapbox and I'm certainly no follower of Herr Hitler but I've seen what these fanatics are capable of. They've got to be stopped."

He took that thin gold watch out of his vest pocket. "Good, I've got time for another. I know I shouldn't, but I owe it to Joe. That's as good an excuse as any, I suppose. How the hell did we get off on politics and Reds, anyway?"

"I believe it was Hauptmann and the German papers and the way nothing is working for them."

"Exactly, but that's their problem, not ours, and we're drinking to Joseph. Please, join me in another."

I poured another short shot for myself, but by then, more customers were coming in. As I took orders, Voss picked up the *Times*. The next time I looked his way, he was engaged with a couple of other guys. Around four, he tipped his Panama to me and left a big tip.

Chapter Twenty-Two

We had fights in Jimmy's Place. Every joint like mine does, but we didn't have them often. I mean, it wasn't one of those bars that guys go to if they're looking for something to fight about. At my place, when two guys went after each other, it was almost always about a woman and everyone involved, men and women, had had more than a few. From time to time other customers would get in on the action but we always tried to shut it down as quick as we could and turn it over to our patrolmen. Most times, unless we were really crowded, you could hear a fight coming. Raised voices, chest-thumping, commotion, chairs scraped across the floor. If you could get to them before the first push or punch, you could stop it right there. Slip between them, keep them separated. I was good at that part, being small enough to snake through a thick crowd and strong enough to push two drunks apart. I wasn't good at stopping things once they started swinging. Frenchy was big enough to handle average-sized guys. When Fat Joe saw fit to roust his fat butt off his seat by the door, he could crack heads but he usually waited until guys had punched themselves out and were less likely to do anything to him. He was big enough to grab two guys by the collar and drag them both up to the sidewalk.

That's the way I liked to handle it. Get the guys outside, keep them quiet so they don't disturb the neighbors, and turn them over to the cops so an honest saloonkeeper can go about his business.

What happened that Wednesday evening wasn't like any other fight we ever had. When we talked about it later, we guessed that the guys came in over a thirty-minute period, sometime around eight. Arch wasn't there. He was working on his business with Daphne Prewitt. Frenchy and I were behind the bar. Marie Therese and Connie were waiting the tables and booths. There was a new girl in the coat room. Again, as we tried to piece it together after the fact, there were four of them. They didn't come in together. All young, younger than thirty anyway. White. In shirtsleeves. No hats. It was a warm evening. Didn't check anything in the coat room. They spaced themselves evenly. One at the bar, and one at a two-top in back. Two in one of the middle booths. They all ordered bottles of beer. At the time, nobody thought it was unusual.

The first thing I noticed was when the guy at the bar tilted his head back and drained his beer. He turned and glanced at his pal at the two-top. They nodded to each other The first one swiveled around on his stool and raised his bottle. I was stepping toward him, ready to pull another bottle from the ice, when the guy at the two-top threw his bottle at Frenchy's head. Frenchy was less than ten feet away, waiting on another customer and never saw it. The bottle didn't shatter when it hit him. It broke into a few pieces and sliced open his scalp. Frenchy cursed and turned to see what had happened.

The guy at the bar threw his bottle at the mirror behind me. Starred the mirror and broke a couple of bottles on the second shelf. Then he kicked back his stool and vaulted over the bar. I remember how his lips were pulled back from his teeth as he swung at me. I tried to duck away but his fist smacked my forehead hard enough to get my attention.

A few years before then, when I was a teenager running booze and pinball machines and such, I ran into situations where guys tried to punch me or club me, so I got used to being hit. I had to expect it. Part of the job. So, when this mug tagged me, I came right back at him, pushing in close, keeping my elbows in and punching at his gut. He was still going for my head, swinging his fists wide and connecting. He was nearly a foot taller so I crouched and hit him in the balls as fast and hard as I could. That slowed him down. He staggered back, clutching his crotch and breaking more bottles and glasses. I was able to fish my knucks out of my pocket and got him once in the face before the other guy came over the bar. He knocked me into the first guy and the three of us wound up on the floor. Both of them went after me.

While that was going on, the other guys busted up the place. They yelled at the customers to get out. Turned over tables, broke chairs, slashed the padded booths with knives or razors. Frenchy tried to get the other guy off of me but one of the thugs came over the bar and went after him. Frenchy was able to get at the .44 hogleg he kept on a nail under the bar.

He grabbed it by the barrel and smashed the guy's face. One of the bastards threw a chair and shattered the mirror behind the bar and a couple hundred dollars' worth of booze.

What they did with Connie and Marie Therese was worse or better, depending on how you look at it. As soon as it started, two of the thugs grabbed Connie and Marie Therese and got them in bear hugs from behind. The women had enough experience putting drunks in their place that they fought back, biting arms, stomping feet. For that, their clothes were torn and they got groped. The new girl in the coat room wisely slammed the top of the Dutch door closed as soon as the rough stuff started. They didn't bother her.

How long did it take? Five minutes? Ten?

While it was going on, the thugs were yelling at each other. I couldn't understand anything they were saying. After a time, one of them yelled, "Let's go!" and they broke off. The thug that was on top me ground my face into the floor, and rasped, "Jew lover." He stepped on my back as he went over the bar. Then they were gone. When I got to my feet, I could hear sirens. I ducked under the leaf in the bar and was just beginning to see how much damage they'd done when one of them kicked open the front door and lobbed in a gas grenade. I could tell it was smaller than the ones I had, and round, about the size of a baseball. Yellow green fumes hissed out. Without thinking, I gimped over and kicked at it with my good leg. I managed to roll it out onto the landing before I fell on my ass. Frenchy slammed the door shut to keep any more of the gas from coming in, but we were all coughing and crying, trying not to breathe in any more. It doesn't take much.

For a few seconds or minutes—I don't know how long it was—we stared at each other. Adrenaline and anger were still buzzing through me and it felt like air in the room was vibrating. Finally, Connie said, "What the hell was that?" Frenchy and Marie Therese shrugged. The new girl peeked out of the coat room and ran out the front door. I never saw her again.

"I'll explain this later when we've got time."

Connie grabbed my shoulders. "Does it have anything to do with you going to Newark on Monday?"

"The Nazi rally?" Frenchy said. I heard sirens approaching.

"It might, but don't say anything to the cops. As far as we know, this was just a fight that got out of hand."

Marie Therese pointed to the slashed cushions and the shattered furniture. "They'll know it was more than that."

"Yeah, but we're not going to tell them anything. I'm going to take care of it."

That's when I started to understand and the anger burned so hot I had to force it down. I make mistakes when I'm angry. Sometimes I remember that. Those guys were the needle-dicked Nazis who killed Fat Joe. Now they'd torn up my place. Getting back at them wouldn't be easy but I knew how to begin.

Mahan and Norris were the first to arrive. When they saw how bad it was, they called their station on my telephone and more patrolmen showed up. Frenchy took the worst of it. The bottle had cut his scalp around his hairline, and he had a mouse under one eye. So did I, and my ribs were already starting to ache. My suit pants were torn at the knee and it was bleeding from the broken glass on the floor. Marie Therese and Connie got the first aid kit, cleaned my knee, and put some mercurochrome on Frenchy's cut. He yelled louder than he did when the thugs were on him. They taped some gauze to his head and then Marie Therese made him drive his truck over to the emergency room at Bellevue. She went with him. Connie and I stuck to the story. Some guys got to arguing. We didn't know what it was about or who started it, but a fight like you see in one of those Western moving pictures broke out.

I was going over it for the third or fourth time when Detective Ellis showed up, over dressed as usual. Silver clip on his collar, stick pin on his lapel, Glen Plaid summer weight he'd gotten on the arm, and the haberdasher had probably been glad to be rid of it. Connie was separating the useable stock from the broken stuff behind the bar and sweeping up the broken glass. Ellis listened to Mahan for a few minutes before he came over to me.

"Just a fight that got out of hand," he said, not buying it.

"That's right."

"We'll talk about this in your office."

We went upstairs. I sat behind my desk. He went to my bar, poured gin for himself and opened the empty ice bucket.

"Call down for some ice."

I shook my head.

"Dammit, I hate warm gin," he said and gulped it down. He sprawled on the divan. "What really happened."

"Last Friday, we had a fight here. Just a couple of guys, part of a party of six. We broke it up. Soon as we got them outside, they settled down. No need to call Mahan and Norris. Another group came in tonight. Might have been some of the same guys, I'm not sure. They were young, some of 'em were blond, I dunno. It broke out fast. They were going after each other and then Frenchy and me when we tried to stop it. Couple of 'em grabbed Connie and Marie Therese. Rest of the customers scattered."

"And that's all you know."

"That's all I know."

"It couldn't have had anything to do with Abe Attell's thugs beating up Nazi thugs in Newark."

"I ain't been to Newark in I don't know when."

"What about the grenade? Anybody ever use tear gas in this place before?"

"I don't know about that. It happened at the end when they were all piling outta here. It was almost like it fell out of some guy's pocket as he was leaving. Christ, that stuff stinks. It's gonna be hard as hell to get the smell of it out of everything. Any of the neighbors see anything? Say anything?"

"Not yet." He waited for me to say something else. I didn't. Finally, "And that's it? That's all you've got?"

"That's it."

"Then just between you and me and the wall, that goddamn Bureau man Turcot probably already knows about this and he's not going to buy that lame story. He's still up my ass, and he's gonna be up your ass, too."

About the time the first beer bottle was being thrown my place, Arch was knocking on Daphne Prewitt's door down on Gay Street. He'd called that afternoon and she said that if Harold hadn't shown up by nine o'clock, he wasn't going be there. Arch called again at nine and she told him to come over.

He noticed right away that she'd cleaned. No dust on polished tabletops. Empty ashtrays. No newspapers or magazines. A dry smell of sandalwood coming from a candle. Glassware, ice and bottles carefully arranged. Daphne was wearing an off-white short sleeved blouse and skirt. Her blonde hair was loose and she was barefoot. She asked what he was drinking. He said whiskey. Andrew the cat looked at him from the back of the loveseat. Arch sat in the chair facing him and thought at first that Daphne had made sure her place was spiffed up for him, and maybe that meant she'd like to offer some extra inducements later. But then he realized, no, that's not it. She keeps it spotless whenever Harold might show up. He comes over and sees that his kept woman isn't keeping the place up, he's not going to keep her for long.

She handed Arch a Scotch and elegantly tucked her legs under herself on the loveseat. Sipped white wine from an open bottle of good Chablis that had barely been touched. She sat straight, expectant, eager to hear what he had to say. Andrew climbed down to her lap. She pushed him off.

"I was waiting nearby when Henninger came out this morning. His driver took him uptown to Sutton Place, a nice neighborhood, to be sure, though it lacks the louche languor you have here in the Village. He got out at the East River Yacht Club. He may have an apartment there, and probably a boat."

She leaned forward, looking at him without blinking. "Yes, he has a yacht, more than one, I think."

"Have you ever been on it?"

"No."

"A barman at an older establishment that's not far from that address said that a man named Harold whose description matches your Harold had been there with a young blonde. It was a Sunday. The fellow was wearing one of those silly little captain's hats. Both of them were sun and wind burned, like they'd spent the day on the water."

Daphne shrugged. "With Harold, there's always other women. He knows I don't want to hear about them, so he doesn't say anything and I don't ask. But, you know something, the telephone number on Harold's card, it's a Rhinelander exchange. That's Sutton Place."

"Really?" Arch was impressed.

"You think Polly's girls don't know where their best clients hang their hats."

"I suppose so. What can you tell me about this East River Club?"

"Nothing, Harold's never mentioned it."

"Apparently it's new, and meant for gentlemen of Henninger's ilk who can't get into the River Club of New York."

"I can't believe there's a club in this city that's too rich for Harold's blood."

"This place caters to Vanderbilts, Rockefellers, and Roosevelts."

She sniffed. "That explains it. Cornelius hates Harold, and Harold wouldn't have anything to do with a place that's associated with the Rockefellers. Did you learn anything else?"

"No, I didn't really see him do anything, but I may have an idea for what we could do next."

Chapter Twenty-Three

We taped a "Closed for Repairs—Open Soon" sign on the front door and made the first pass at cleaning up. I did a quick inventory of broken tables, chairs, and bottles. Connie went upstairs to the kitchen. Vittorio told her they hadn't heard anything in the restaurant. The thugs had managed to bust up my place without disturbing any of his customers. But somebody on the street heard them and called the cops. Thick walls. It was around midnight when we locked up. I called for a cab to take us back to the Chelsea. We didn't say anything until we were in my rooms.

Connie went straight to the good brandy. "What does this have to do with you and Lansky's guys and Newark?" She sounded serious and handed me a short tot.

"Maybe nothing," I said but I didn't believe it. "One of them called me a 'Jew lover,' but it's no secret that I've worked with Rothstein and Lansky and, hell, lots of other Jews for a long time.'"

Connie downed her brandy, unbuttoned her blouse and stripped off her skirt. "The bastard who grabbed me licked my ear. I've got to take a shower before I do anything else." She reached around to unhook her brassiere.

"Later," I said, and wrapped my arms around her stomach.

"No." She wrenched away from me and spat out the words, "I can smell him on me and I still want to kill him."

Probably better to wait.

While she was showering, I realized she didn't know everything she needed to know. I had to tell her. I took off my clothes and saw that the slacks I'd been wearing were ruined, and I tried to work through it. When she came out, I poured two more tots and had an extra pillow behind my back. She shimmied into the pale blue slip she slept in, sipped her tot, and sat on the bed beside me.

"The other night, I told you a little bit about Newark."

She pushed her pillows back and shifted over on one hip to face me.

"But I didn't tell you everything. You see, the big shot Jews are taking these Nazis seriously. Remember I said that Lansky used the place for a quiet morning meeting."

"No, but go ahead."

"That meeting was with Judge Nathan Perlman and Rabbi Stephen Wise."

Her eyes got wide. "Those are big shot Jews, all right."

"They want Lansky and Longy to get their guys to bust up Nazi rallies wherever they can, but they made a real point about their guys not killing anybody. They can do anything else but they can't kill anyone. From what I saw in Newark, it's not that hard for them. The Jews are boxers, strike breakers, sluggers—guys who bust heads for a living. These Nazis are big-talking bullies who like to throw their weight around against anybody who's smaller and weaker. That's what we saw tonight. They made sure we weren't ready for them. Did you have any idea they were planning something before they did it?"

She shook her head. "Nothing. They'd been giving me the eye and trying to flirt clumsily but that happens every night."

And who could blame them, I thought, as a shoulder strap slipped down.

"Then there's the Bureau guy, Turcot. Last night before you came in, that creepy bastard Ignatz Griebl dropped by. By himself. The blonde who gives him the rub-and-tug under the table wasn't with him. He asked where Fat Joe was. I told him the story and he was out of there like a shot. Turcot told me before that Griebl works out the Hotel McAlpin."

"Up on 34th."

"Right. So, I decide to follow Griebl, just to see if Turcot is on the level, and sure enough, Griebl goes to the McAlpin. I see him pick up a message and then Turcot shows up and invites me to sit down for a friendly drink. Friendly, my ass."

"Wait," Connie said, "Did Turcot follow you from our place?"

"No, I think he'd been waiting for Griebl, and when he saw me, he figured what had happened and told me so. I hate to admit it, but the son of a bitch is a damn good detective."

She hitched a little closer and messed with the strap, distracting me.

"Then Turcot tells me that Griebl recruited Fat Joe to join this Silver Legion Silver Shirts, silver something, even though Fat Joe wasn't really a true believer. After that Turcot got Fat Joe to rat out Griebl's spies. Probably offered to pay him. But the point Turcot was making is the same one that Judge Pearlman and Rabbi Wise are making. The Krauts are preparing for war. They know it's coming and they want us to think it's not coming. But Turcot says there's another German here who's Griebl's boss. This guy works for something called the SS and this guy figured that Fat Joe was a double spy and that's why he killed him. Turcot doesn't know who this guy is and he wants me to help find him."

She looked at me for a long time before she said anything. "Damn, Jimmy, what have you got us involved in? What are you going to do?"

"Before tonight, I'd say nothing. It's not my fight. With Fat Joe, they probably figured out he was double-crossing them and they beat him up and killed him. He knew that could happen and he took the risk. But when they come in and bust up our place and go after you and Marie Therese, hell, they're not going to get away with that."

She finished her brandy, moved over next to me and put her head on my shoulder. "Right. *Our place.*"

I thought about that for a time before I shifted around and moved a couple of pillows. I reached down to the hem of the pale blue slip and tugged it up. "I think you need a backrub." She raised her arms to make it easier to get the slip off and stretched out face down.

"Yeah, a back rub," she said into the pillow. "That's exactly what I need."

'*Our place.*' Did I say that?

Chapter Twenty-Four

I was up early Thursday. First thing, I called the glazier who'd done some of the remodeling work for us before. He said it might not be as bad as I thought. The mirror was in sections, and they were a standard size, not custom. He might be able to replace them that afternoon. Then I called the upholsterer who'd done the booths. He wouldn't be able to get to me for a week, at least, so I called the awning guy and told him about the slashed cushions. He said he had some special tape that would probably make them usable for a while. What color was the cloth? He'd try to match it.

Three chairs and three barstools were beyond repair, and we still had some of the old furniture in the basement, so maybe we could make do for seating. I spent the rest of the morning sweeping, vacuuming, and washing down shelves. That's when I saw that they'd damaged the walls. We'd need to patch plaster and repaint. The glazier and the awning guy showed up around two. Leo Turcot was right behind them, still tightly buttoned up. Figure he knew exactly what happened last night. He surveyed the damage, taking in everything they'd done. Then he said we needed to talk and held up a manila folder.

I told the other two guys I'd be upstairs if they needed me and led Turcot to my office. From what Detective Ellis said the night before, I'd been expecting the Bureau man, and so I'd straightened up and stashed everything. Cash, ledgers, and guns were locked in the safe. The last thing I wanted was a federal cop that close to my business. I sat behind the desk. He surveyed the room carefully, just like he did downstairs, like he was memorizing it. Starting with my desk and chair, the safe, the liquor cabinet, the Caucasian carpet, the leather chair, the divan, and table. He even went to the window behind the divan and lifted a slat of the Venetian blind to look down into the bar. After he'd taken it all in, he sat in the leather chair across from me.

I still wasn't sure how to handle him but decided that making nice might pay off. "What can I offer you? Something to drink? I've got vodka or the kitchen can send down coffee."

"Coffee."

I picked up the earpiece of the telephone and spoke to the kitchen.

He put the folder on my desk and said, "When we talked Tuesday night at the McAlpin, I told you they'd be coming after you. Do you believe me now?"

He opened the folder and handed me a short stack of 8x10 photographs. "Are these the men who were here last night? Some of the faces are hard to make out. We had to enlarge them considerably, but you'll recognize at least one of them."

The pictures had been taken outside on a sunny day. The first was of a group of men standing on a narrow street made of Belgian block. You could see part of a large black car next to them. Older model, long hood. The photographer had been on the other side of the street. The men were smoking and talking to each other under El tracks with steel girders above them. There was a "To Let" sign in the window of the storefront behind them. I counted five of them in the first picture. The other pictures were enlargements of their faces. Fat Joe was one of them. I went through those slowly, then gave one back to the Bureau man.

"I can't be sure about most of them, but this is the bastard who coldcocked me. The others were probably here but I couldn't swear to it."

Turcot nodded, like he'd expected me to say that. "That's Florian Hoffmeister. He would have been the leader. Detective Ellis says you claim it was a fight that got out of hand but he doesn't believe that. I think it's more likely they came in separately, sat apart from each other and when Hoffmeister gave the signal, they attacked you, drove the patrons out and inflicted as much damage as they could in a short time. Is that accurate?"

One of Vittorio's cooks knocked on the door and brought in a coffee service. He poured and left. Turcot took his with milk.

"Who are these guys? Where'd you take this picture?"

"Pearl Street, just south of Fulton. Besides Bruder and Hoffmeister, the others are Melvin Richter, Lars Grambo, and Anton White. Hoffmeister and White are veterans. Richter is Army Reserve. They're Americans, mostly children of German immigrants. They think that what's happening in Germany ought to be happening here."

"You know how to find them?"

"All in good time, Quinn."

"Why did they bust up my place?"

The Bureau man made me sweat before he smiled and answered. "Maybe because they thought they'd have an easier time with you than they would at Nat Arno's gymnasium."

Oh, hell, he knew about Newark. I didn't say anything.

"Given Arno's situation, I'm assuming that Zwillman didn't have the gas grenades and so he asked Moe Sedway for help because of his connections at the New York police department and you brought them over."

"O.K., yeah, I was the middleman. And these are the guys who killed Fat Joe."

"Probably. Almost certainly. Almost. That's where you come in. As I told you on Tuesday, you're going to help me put the screws to—"

"The hell you say." That got me steamed and I had to hold back the anger. "I don't rat anybody to the cops. I'm taking a chance letting you in my place."

He said, "Simmer down, Quinn," and that made me even angrier. "I'm not asking you to turn on your 'associates.' I want you to help me catch the men who killed your man Josef Bruder and vandalized your establishment. Forget about not working with cops, you know that if you don't do something, they will come after you again, right?"

I had to nod. "And so you're going to help me find out who is now giving Griebl his orders. That's the man who ordered Josef's death. Here's what I want…"

He rattled off something about arranged meetings but I wasn't listening. If I was going to do anything with this guy, it was going to be on my terms. Sure as hell, I didn't want him looking over my shoulder, I had too many things to hide. And I had some ideas of my own. So I waited until he stopped talking and said, "O.K., I'm your man."

It might have surprised him that I agreed so quick. "Excellent, first you'll come down to the Bureau offices and we'll—"

"Not a chance. You want to talk to me, you come here and don't bring anybody with you."

"All right. For now, we'll do it your way. I still need authorization to run an operation like this but that's a formality."

"Fine. Get it."

We went round and round for a few more minutes. He said I'd have to sign an agreement to give testimony to a grand jury before he could get started. I lied and said, sure I'll sign once we get closer to actually doing something. Before he left, he said I could keep the pictures. I put the folder and the pictures in my safe and started thinking about things I might be able to do.

I went downstairs and found that the glazier had replaced three mirror panels. They looked fine but he didn't have any of the special glass we used for the shelving. Then I saw that the little spotlights in the ceiling and on the walls had been damaged. They were the ones that gave the bottles of booze that inviting drink-me glow. I'd need an electrician to fix those. The awning guy's tape didn't come close to matching the colors of the upholstery. It looked like exactly what it was, a quick cheap fix. The glazier was sure he could have new shelves and brackets by Monday. The awning guy said his cousin's brother-in-law could be there tomorrow and replace the padding and the upholstery. If he could find the guy, and he'd want twenty up front. I said yes to the glazier and told the awning guy I'd think about it.

By then it was midafternoon. Marie Therese and Frenchy would be there soon. I put out a few bottles and turned the lights on to the middle level we used during the day so I could see how bad things were. The more I looked around, the worse it got. Less than a year before, we'd remodeled the place. Refinished the bar and the floor, reupholstered the booths, replaced chairs, tables, and stools with top grade items. Until last night, the place still looked and felt new. Now it looked like a crummy joint run by a gangster who didn't know shit about what he was doing. I couldn't reopen like that, and it made me mad all over again to realize it.

Frenchy and Marie Therese got there around three. He had a big bandage that covered part of his right ear. Arch and Connie came in, heads together, already talking about something else. When Arch got a good look at the damage, he said, "Sweet Jesus, these bastards have really got it in for you, haven't they."

"No more than I've got it in for them, and I know who they are."

I told them most of what the bureau man told me. Then we spent the rest of the afternoon going over the room item by item and making a list of what needed to be done. While we were doing that, customers were knocking at the door from time to time. Regulars could see us moving around inside and wanted to know what was going on. I explained to the first couple of guys that things had got out of hand and we'd reopen soon. Connie put more cardboard over the window in the door and we didn't answer after that.

When we finished the inventory of destruction, it was two pages long and at least a grand. There were still a lot of guys looking for work, so it figured, I could find people who'd do the jobs, and the things that needed to be replaced weren't hard to find. But get the painters in first. Frenchy said he'd stayed in touch with some of the guys who did the work a year ago. He'd call them right away. The longer I looked at the list and thought about what it meant, the madder I got. Connie noticed and asked me when I ate. I had to think.

"Breakfast."

"Then you can't make any decisions now. I'm going to get the kitchen to fix something for us. Don't drink any booze either. Stick to water until I get back. I'm serious. There's something else we've got to think about, and I guess it involves all of us. Arch'll explain it."

"After I visit the cellar," he said.

Three waiters came down the back stairs from the kitchen. They put a white tablecloth on a six-top and set places for five. One of them tossed lettuce in a big white bowl with dressing he poured from a stoppered bottle. A few minutes later, we heard the dumbwaiter rumble. Philippe, Connie's tall friend from the Pierre, came bouncing down the stairs. He opened the dumbwaiter and put two large trays of covered platters on the bar. They smelled great.

"Connie said you need something quickly. The potatoes lyonnaise are part of tonight's special. The bread is still warm and the steak is something that Vittorio may put on the menu. It's an inexpensive cut, not as tender as some but it is… *trés savoureux*… very flavorful with the marinade I use. And it cooks quickly. I hope you like it."

He took the dome off one of the platters and the smells filled the room. There were two thick flat steaks on it. Philippe produced a chef's knife, gave it a few licks on a steel, and set to work with practiced speed. Arch and Connie came back with dusty bottles of French wine. In short order, corks were pulled and plates were served and we dug in. After the first bites, Frenchy and Marie Therese started yakking away to Philippe in French about how good everything was. They were right.

It was one of those meals that I still remember in detail. It wasn't just the food—the kid was right, it was *trés savoureux*—all of it, the steak, the potatoes, the bread, even the lettuce with the vinegar dressing, all strong simple tastes. But there was the anger I couldn't get rid of. It made everything sharper stronger. Anger at the damage they'd done to my place and my friends and to Fat Joe. And my anger at the goddamn Nazis was mixed up with the news about that cold-blooded bastard Hauptmann. I can bring all of it back when I think of that night. What we did next was an even bigger part of it.

After we finished, the other four cleared. I stayed at the table, thoughts of what Turcot told me and what Lansky and the rabbi and the judge were up to got mixed together and I knew that I couldn't do anything about them. Something had to change. Could I make it change? Connie opened another bottle of wine and poured. When the others were back, I said, "I need to tell you a little more about what's been going on."

Then I explained it without mentioning Lansky's name. About Newark, the judge and the rabbi. The Bureau man and Fat Joe being a spy for Griebl and then a spy against Griebl. They had as much trouble understanding that part as I did. The McAlpin Hotel. Griebl's unknown German boss from the SS, whatever that was. And now the Bureau man wanted me to work for him, and to agree to testify before a grand jury. They started laughing as soon as I said that.

"Yeah, I know."

Frenchy stopped laughing first. "And he believed it when you said you would?"

"Yeah." And that got them laughing again.

Finally, Arch said, "What are you going to do?"

"I think I'm going to poke around the McAlpin. See what's going on there."

"As it happens," Arch said, "I am involved in something unusual myself."

Frenchy said, "I bet it has something to do with that blonde dish, Daphne."

"Indeed, it does and it may also involve a large sum of money. That side of it has yet to be fully clarified. I should know more in a day or so, and if things develop as I anticipate, Connie will be helping me."

I looked at her and raised my eyebrows. *What's this?* She mouthed, "*Later.*"

"The gent who has been taking care of Daphne's expenses has already used her in a shady scheme that was almost certainly improper if not illegal, and now he is about to embark on another venture. We don't know what it is yet but with Connie's help we will find out."

"Enough of this talk," Marie Therese said. "Let's not forget the job that's right in front of us. Reopening,"

"PDQ," I said.

We took a cab back to the Chelsea around midnight. Again, I kept my hand on the pistol in my coat pocket. I was a little pixilated from the booze and the wine, and the nutty ideas I had were still mixing it up in my head when we got to my rooms. After I locked the door, I said, "All right, what's going on with you and Arch? And Daphne?"

"For now, just a little advice on a new wardrobe, but if things play out the way Arch thinks they might, I'll pretend to be his concubine."

She saw that I didn't know the word. "Kept woman. Now, what are you talking about? '*Poke around the McAlpin?*' That's your plan?"

"There's more to it than that. Let me explain." I did.

Connie listened. She stopped me and made me go back and explain a couple of things in more detail. When I finished, she said, "Well, it's not something I'd have thought of, but you might learn something. We can call the hotel tomorrow and get things started. The first thing you need to do is talk to David and Bernard."

"Who are David and Bernard?"

"They live on four. I'll introduce you tomorrow."

Chapter Twenty-Five

About two o'clock Friday, Connie and I walked up one flight of stairs. She knocked on the door of 402 and opened it without waiting for an answer. A man inside said something that sounded like a garbled "Come in." He was standing on a stepladder and pinning a shiny tinfoil tiara on a giant papier mâché head with hair that looked like it was made of orange yarn. He had the pins clenched between his lips and he worked quickly, sticking them into the yarn. He was bald and barefoot and he wore paint-spattered white bib overalls and a sleeveless undershirt. Maybe 30, about six feet tall but it was hard to tell with the stepladder.

He said, "Hello, Connie," then louder, "Bernard, Connie's here and she finally brought her gangster."

It was a big room, bigger than the main room in my place, anyway, with a wide passageway to another room. It smelled strongly of paint and overlooked 23rd Street. All the windows and curtains were open, letting in a lot of light. These were work rooms, no conventional furniture. Instead, there were four tables, two about the size of card tables with drop clothes under them and two longer. The giant head with orange yarn hair was on one of the card tables. The walls were filled with drawings of landscapes and costumes thumbtacked to bulletin boards. One of the long tables was covered with a set of more than a dozen model train cars and engines.

"David and Bernard are designers," Connie said. "They do Broadway shows, costumes and make up, museum exhibits, department store windows. Things like that."

The second man, Bernard, I guessed, came in from the other room. He had short brown hair and a bushy beard. He wore a blue smock that was too big for him. He was shorter and thicker than David and he was trying to clean his paint-stained hands with a rag that smelled of turpentine. He looked familiar.

I said, "Bacardi, lime, splash of soda over ice." He came in occasionally with a woman who was either his girlfriend or his wife. She was Seagram's and Seven.

"Yes, indeed. Bernard Perez. I'd shake hands, but… That's David Dunst with his pet head. You know you're supposed to make the little girls ask their mothers to buy the doll, not terrify them."

David got down from the stepladder. "I know but once I get the shape right, and we move the finished product onto the throne at the back, it'll be fine."

"Macy's window?" Connie asked.

"Lord & Taylor, but not the big one. The eyes still aren't right."

I looked at the bulletin board and saw a couple of photographs. I recognized them as two of the big balloons from the Macy's parade, Felix the Cat and Eddie Cantor. They were pretty scary, too. Bernard said, "We helped with those. Still don't like Cantor's legs."

Connie said, "Their good stuff is in the other room, but we don't have time for that now. Sorry, gents, but this is not a social visit. Jimmy wants to hire you."

They got interested at the word 'hire.'

"Jimmy needs a disguise. He wants to go to a hotel where he'll be around people who have seen him in Jimmy's Place, but they can't recognize him. He wants to find out what they're doing."

"And he wishes to pass among them incognito and unnoticed," said David. *Incognito?* He padded over on his bare feet and bent down to look at my face closely. "You said a hotel, will he be outside?" He moved around to look at my profile.

"Probably not."

Bernard came over and both of them circled me as they asked Connie questions like I wasn't there.

"How well do they know him?"

"There's two groups, one couple and four guys," Connie said. "The couple comes in from time to time. The others…"

"The others are the goddamn thugs who busted up my place."

"Then they don't know him so well that they'd immediately recognize his walk. Will he have to disguise his voice?"

"Doubt I'll talk much."

They muttered to themselves for a time, then, "Is he going to be a guest of the hotel?"

"Yeah, and I might try to look like I'm on the staff, too. Not sure."

David said, "Then, he'll need two different characters. His size is a challenge but it can also be useful. We could go young. Remember the teenaged tennis player in, oh, what was the name of it, from the Schubert, two years ago?"

"*Beebee's Boyfriend*. Terrible show but Brooks said the costumes were 'engaging.'"

"And we've still got the flannels. They're the right size."

They palavered some more. Then Bernard said, "If they know you from your bar, when they think of you, they see someone well dressed who always stands straight with his shoulders squared. You don't slouch and you move purposefully. Behind the bar, you know where things are and you don't waste energy. Your voice isn't particularly loud and you don't have an accent that sounds unusual in the city. Now, the cane, that is a problem. As I remember, you don't use it behind the bar and I know I've seen you waiting tables without it. Will you have it with you?"

I hadn't thought of that. The idea of going without it was like being naked. When I didn't answer, Connie said, "He'll need it, but he could be without it for a time if he had to."

Bernard said, "I've got an idea to work around it." He found a pad of paper and started drawing. "The first thing is the clothes. You can't wear a well-tailored suit. It needs to be too big and cheap. Second, the posture. Lean forward, scuff your feet when you walk. Be hesitant. David, take his measurements. I think we've got something else that will fit with only a few alterations."

He finished with a flourish and turned the pad around. "How about this?"

It was a pencil sketch of an old man in a baggy suit, uncombed gray hair, mustache, glasses. He had a cane in each hand.

"I have the wig. I'll tell you before we go any farther it's not cheap. Good wigs, wigs that actually fool people into thinking it's real, are expensive. They're expensive because they are made with real human hair. How soon do you need this?"

"Monday."

They looked at each other. Both shrugged. David said, "We can do a rush job if we agree on a price."

I took two twenties and a ten out of my wallet. "If it's more, I'm good for it."

David scooped up the bills. "Come around Sunday afternoon. We'll have everything you need."

Chapter Twenty-Six

It was a little after three when we got back to the bar. Painters were at work. Marie Therese had found the guy who did the job before. He said he could match the colors and sent a crew over. She locked up the alcohol and stayed around to supervise. Arch was with her. I asked him to come up to the office with me and Connie and explained what we were planning. He said he could lend a hand but he had other things to do. "I'm meeting Daphne later at her place."

Connie turned to him and said, "Is it time for me to get involved?" *What the hell did that mean?*

"I think so. We may be too early, but it might be advantageous for you to join us. If nothing else, you bring a different perspective."

She nodded and I said, "What are you talking about?"

"I told you. Daphne asked if I'd help and I said I would. Arch agrees." I didn't remember her saying that. "We still don't know what her Harold is up to. I'm curious and, don't forget, there may be money in it for us."

Arch said, "We'd be meeting here if we were open. We just need to sit down and talk about what to do next."

"And now to the business at hand," Connie said. She pulled a chair over close to the telephone and dialed. As it rang, she held the earpiece out so Arch and I could hear.

"Hotel McAlpin switchboard. How may I direct your call?" You could hear other operators' voices behind the woman who answered.

"Reservations."

"One moment, please."

"This is the Reservations Desk. Mr. Frederick speaking."

"This is Mrs. Witherspoon at Klein and Day. Our client, Professor Patterson, is arriving on Tuesday to testify later in the week. He specifically requested that we put him up at the McAlpin. We'll need your finest suite for a week to ten days, beginning Tuesday. What do you have?"

"Let me see what's available…"

"And we will also want a car from the hotel to meet the *Olympic* at the Cunard-White Star pier on West 14th. The exact time of its arrival hasn't been announced. We expect it to be in the evening, but I trust you can check that detail and have a suitable car there for him." Her voice was quick, crisp. Giving orders, not asking for anything.

"Of course. Now…, yes. Let me check on our suites. I believe, yes, the Herald Suite is free. Now, we'll need—"

"How large is it, how many rooms?"

"Normally, it is a three-room suite but it can be enlarged to four or even five rooms if necessary." He sounded insulted that she'd asked.

"Four will be sufficient. Now, Professor Patterson's secretary will be accompanying him, and she will need a room."

"Of course. The sixth floor is for women only."

"Very well and make that one of the better rooms or a suite. I'm sure they will incur incidental expenses during their stay. I'll send a man around within the hour with two hundred dollars to secure the rooms."

"Excuse me, I did not catch your name."

"Mrs. Witherspoon, with Klein and Day. Thank you, Mr. Frederick." She hung up and smiled.

"Professor Patterson has a secretary," I said.

She shrugged. "It might be useful."

I got four fifties out of the cashbox in the safe and sealed them in an envelope. Connie addressed it, "Mr. Frederick. Professor Patterson reservation. Herald Suite, Oct. 2 through Oct. 9" She gave it to Arch. We figured that since Arch had not waited on Dr. Griebl and his doxy, and he hadn't been there when the thugs hit us, it was less likely he'd run into anyone at the McAlpin who'd recognize him.

Arch said he'd see Connie at Daphne's around six and left. She went downstairs to help Marie Therese supervise the painters. I could have joined them but I knew I couldn't add anything, so I closed the cashbox and put it back in the safe. I started to lock it but stopped and reached down to the back shelf. That's where I kept any pistols that happened to have come my way. You see, from the time I ran Mother Moon's target range when I was a kid, I've been most comfortable with the .38 Detective

Special or Banker's Special with a two-inch barrel. They're both small revolvers. They fit my hand and they're easy enough to slip into a suitcoat pocket without calling attention to themselves.

But if a guy was on the lookout for a telltale bulge, he'd notice a revolver. An automatic would be better, and at that time, I happened to have three. There was the .25 that Connie liked to keep at hand in the desk when she was counting the day's take. I also had a couple of .32s in the safe, a Spanish Ruby and a German Walther. The kraut gun was the better pistol, so I took it apart, cleaned it, oiled it, and reloaded. Then I gathered up two days of newspapers for the Hauptmann news I'd missed.

I went downstairs and told Connie if she needed me, I'd be on the roof.

On a breezy Friday afternoon, the roof of the Chelsea Hotel is one of the most agreeable places in the city. Some of the top floor apartments open onto it. Most of us got to it through a heavy metal door at the top of the stairs. Outside, people have put out potted plants and trees. They've strung tarps, and set up umbrellas, rocking chairs and lounges, even a couple of swings and hammocks. I found a chair on the north side of the building where I could see the pointy top of the Chrysler Building behind the Empire State. Took off my coat, loosened my tie and settled back to learn what had happened with our man Bruno.

The day before, Thursday, they'd indicted him in the Bronx for extortion. The New Jersey Attorney General said they'd take their time bringing kidnapping charges against him. For now, they'd let the Bronx work out the extortion beef. J. Edgar Hoover said he was sure that more accomplices were still at large and they would "swiftly" be brought to justice. Horse shit.

They'd also found more of the ransom money in the garage, $840.00 and a little automatic hidden in a rafter. The carpenter had carved out five openings in a section of rafter to hold rolled up bills and a .25 caliber pistol. They also found more money in bank and brokerage accounts and mortgages. Other articles had been saying that Hauptmann broke down and cried in jail. The D.A. said no, that wasn't true. Hauptmann was still holding onto his "sullen determined composure and stolidity."

I wrote *stolidity* in my notebook under *incognito*.

The Friday papers said they were testing the lumber from the building to see if it had anything to do with the homemade ladder he'd used to climb to the kid's window. And to make sure they didn't miss anything, they leveled the garage. Took it apart board by board and dug up the foundation.

When I saw that, I put down the papers and let everything I'd learned about Hauptmann sink in. Why did I have to read every detail of the case in the papers? The answer came to me that afternoon on the roof. It was on account of when it happened and where it happened. You see, at the time, I had owned Jimmy's Place for about three years, and I wasn't really sure that's what I wanted to do with my life. Hell, I was 19 years old, I didn't know any damn thing. I'd fallen into buying the bar almost by accident. Still didn't understand the business.

Then on Tuesday, March 2, 1932, Bruno Hauptmann stole the Lindbergh kid in Hopewell, New Jersey. Thirty miles from Hopewell in Valley Green, New Jersey, Connie was working as a maid for Catherine Pennyweight. My old friend, fellow bootlegger, and car thief Walter Spencer had married Mrs. Pennyweight's beautiful daughter, Flora. They'd just had a baby and Flora was certain that the kidnapper was coming after their little boy next. To keep the family from being ruined financially, Spence had to fly down to Mexico. The thought of him leaving was enough to send Flora into a screaming fit. The only way Spence and Mrs. Pennyweight could calm her down was for me, with my overblown reputation as a gunman, to come out to Valley Green and protect her. As it turned out, they needed protecting. Things got bloody before it was over and Connie decided she'd rather work for me. That changed everything. She took to my business like she'd been born into it. We took to each other and when I realized that she was learning more than I knew, I had to keep up with her.

What I'm getting at is that if Bruno Hauptmann hadn't done what he did at that time, everything in my life would be different. I wouldn't have met Connie. That's what I was thinking as I went through the last of the stories about him in the *Times*. Now he was in jail and would be for the rest of his life, and I was sitting on the roof on a pretty Friday afternoon, and trying to figure what I had to do to get my place back open.

I put down the papers and opened my notebook. Drew a line under "stolidity" and started a list of things I had to do.

Chapter Twenty-Seven

I had six items on the list when David showed up on the roof.

"There you are. Connie said I'd find you up here. One of the wigs is ready if you'd like to try it."

We went down to his place on the fourth floor and through the passageway to the second room. Racks and boxes of clothes filled up about half the floorspace. Posters of plays I didn't know, all of them covered with autographs, were tacked to the walls. David pointed to a barber's chair and told me to sit. He raised it with the foot pump until I was at the right height for him. He brushed my hair straight back, then stretched a silk cap over my head to hold my hair in place and adjusted it.

"Connie can help you with this but you'll be able to do it by yourself easily enough. Now, this," he showed me a wig of gray hair sticking up in every direction, "this was for a revue that had Professor Einstein singing a song that explained his theories. It was every bit as bad as you imagine, but the rug may be just the ticket."

He held it near my hairline when he put it on and pulled at the back to get it in place. Then he did something at the back to tighten it. "Here, feel these straps. That's how you adjust it there and you pull on these little tabs here on the sides to finish it. Now the mustache."

He opened a small pot of glue that smelled funny and dabbed it on my lip with a little brush. "When you're putting this on, start in the middle here, right under your nose. You know what this is called, this place right here?" He tapped the middle of my lip with the brush. "It's the philtrum. You can look it up."

"I will. With an *f* or *ph*?"

"*Ph*. You work outward from there. Not too much." He brushed more of the glue on both sides of my lip to the corners of my mouth. "Now we let it dry just a bit while we get this." He carefully picked up something fuzzy with his fingertips and leaned in close. It was a few inches long and almost transparent. He used the edge of a narrow comb with long teeth to attach it to my philtrum. Kind of tickled. He ran the teeth of the comb under the whiskers and pressed on my lip, working outward.

"What you want to do with this is to apply pressure to the lace backing, not the hair. It will mat down and look bad if you do. The wig is human hair but the mustache isn't. Whiskers aren't the same as the hair on your head. You really can't reuse it, either, so I'll give you three, if you think that's enough. More if you need them. You'll need some of this spirit gum to attach it, and I've got something else here to clean it off after you take off the mustache. You can use soap and water or olive oil, but this works better." He stepped back and frowned. Then he picked up something on a counter behind me. It was a brush or crayon, some kind of makeup, that he worked into my eyebrows. He used something else on my forehead, cheeks, and throat.

"This is making you look older. What we do for stage and moving pictures is all wrong for what you want. I'm just slightly emphasizing the lines in your face so that the first thing somebody assumes when he looks at you is that you're in your fifties. If you run into anybody who really knows you, he's not likely to be fooled, but Connie says you're not really worried about that…"

He went on for another few minutes, talking to himself and moving from one side to the other while my eyes were trying to follow him. Finally, he said, "This is good enough for now. Voila!" and turned the chair around to a mirror.

The face I saw then isn't much different from what I see every morning now. I don't have a mustache and I keep my hair combed and it's more silver than gray. But that day, it surprised me so much that I pushed back in the barber's chair.

David said, "We've got a suit. It's not ready yet but it will be by Tuesday. Now, try these." He handed me a pair of metal-rimmed glasses. I put them on and the world looked curved at the edges, but with the specs, the phiz in the mirror looked even less like me. "Don't worry about distortion. On stage we either use frames without lenses or clear glass, but you're going to be dealing with people face to face and they'll notice both of those. The lenses must have some curvature. And here's the last part. Stand up." He hit the release and the chair hissed down.

I was still trying deal with the old man who looked back at me, and the thought came to me, *That's what I'll look like in a coffin. If I'm lucky.*

"Here. Try this." David gave me a metal cane with a vertical strut above the handle and a curved piece that fit around your forearm. I'd seen them before, used by guys who lost a leg in the Great War. "This is from another show that should have played longer than it did but theater-goers don't want to be reminded about some things. What I'm thinking is that anyone who knows you is used to seeing you with your cane. You're 'Jimmy the Stick,' after all. No offense, I hope."

"Can't argue with the truth." I slipped my arm into the curved piece tested my weight on the stick. It was an inch or two too long. That might be helpful.

"But Bernard says you stand straight when you walk. You don't depend on your cane to support your weight. With this, you'll lean more heavily on it. That will change your posture and you can exaggerate your limp. Put it together with a shapeless suit, either a beaten-up hat, or no hat—better still, and nobody is going to look at you and see Jimmy Quinn, stylish proprietor of the finest bar on the West Side."

About an hour and a half later, Connie unlocked the door to our room. I was in an armchair with the *Times* held up in front of me. She dropped her bag on the table, took off her beret and fluffed out her hair. I put down the paper. Didn't say anything. "I've been talking with Daphne and Arch," she said, not looking at me. "*Listening* to Daphne and Arch is more like it, and they are—what the hell?"

I still had on the wig and glasses and old guy makeup. It worked.

She came over and studied David's work. "This is amazing."

"But the wig is damned hot and the mustache itches. Let me get this stuff off and we'll go over to see how the painting's going. Get something to eat. Tell me about Arch and Daphne while I'm cleaning up."

The wig and the silk cap came off easily. The mustache did not. I used some of David's stuff to remove the spirit gum and scrubbed off the makeup at the sink. I brushed my hair back the way it belonged and reknotted my tie. There was the real Jimmy Quinn looking back at me.

Chapter Twenty-Eight

It was a clear warm evening, so we walked back to the bar. I kept one hand in my jacket pocket with the pistol and we paid close attention to guys we passed on the sidewalk.

"I sat down with Arch and Daphne for about an hour," Connie said. "You've been to her house, haven't you?"

"The place down on Gay Street? Just once, a couple of years ago. Lots of chintz. And a cat."

"Andrew. He's a sweetheart. It's a cute little place she has. Cozy or cramped, depending on her mood." Easy to understand. "The house isn't the problem. Well, it's part of the problem but not the whole problem and it's something she wants to fix. Like her relationship with Harold, it's not easy to describe."

"Harold? The sugar daddy?" She said yes.

As we rounded the corner onto Twenty-Second Street, I saw that Vittorio had about a dozen people on the stoop of the Cruzon Grill waiting to get in. Good for him on a Friday night. I'd be full too, if I was open. The painter's truck was gone but there was a plain Chevy Suburban Carryall parked at the curb. Inside we found Marie Therese and Frenchy and an electrician. Looked like the painters had patched all of the holes and gouges in the walls and done some work with rollers. Marie Therese had described the kind of lighting we had behind the bar and this guy said he could do that again or he could add some more of the indirect fixtures behind the bar. That would soften the light and make the ceiling look higher. And he could put in more lights under the bar where we did the real work. I asked for an estimate. He made quick measurements of the room and the bar. We talked about prices and schedule. Then he agreed to write up a formal estimate with drawings. He could bring it by tomorrow. Marie Therese and

Frenchy said the painters were coming back tomorrow morning. They'd be there to supervise. I locked the front door after the electrician left.

Frenchy's truck was parked in the loading area behind the place. While Connie went upstairs to see about getting some dinner, I went out with Frenchy and Marie Therese to unlock the heavy gate to the alley and close it behind them. While I was there, I checked to make sure nothing had been moved or changed, no trash cans left where they could be used to get over the fence or the gate. Made sure the locks on the gate and the steel doors that led to the cellar were tight. Then I went up the back stairs to the kitchen of the Cruzon Grill.

The place was as busy as I'd ever seen it. Goddammit, I thought, my place should be this busy, too. Cooks, waiters, and busboys were yakking at each other and passing plates back and forth. Connie waved me over from the little table in the corner. She was talking to Vittorio and her tall friend Philippe. I edged through the crowd. Most of those guys knew I was the landlord and they didn't mind my being there as long as I didn't get in the way.

Connie said, "Vittorio can pull a two-top out of storage and make room for us in the dining room, but I told him no. We just need a quick bite and a place where we can talk." Philippe nodded and left.

"And something to drink."

"Of course." Vittorio snapped his fingers, barked an order to someone, and hurried off. Seconds later, a guy appeared with a bottle of red, two glasses, a long loaf of warm bread and a pot of soft butter. He poured. Connie and I ripped the bread apart with our hands.

She said, "You know Arch has been keeping an eye on this guy Harold. His last name's Henninger. According to Daphne and Arch, everybody on Wall Street thinks he's some kind of financial genius. Arch spied on them while they were having dinner at a place in the Village and on Wednesday, he followed Henninger up to Sutton Place. Looks like he has an apartment at the East River Yacht Club. Arch went up there yesterday morning waiting for Harold to come out again but he didn't see him."

"And the reason Arch is doing this," I said, "is because Daphne thinks that Henninger is up to something illegal, like he probably was a couple of years ago, right?"

"Yes," Connie talked through a mouthful of bread. "Damn, this is good. Daphne said that one night at another restaurant, Harold saw an old friend. They talked for some time and later Harold told Daphne that he was trying to get this man to go into some kind of 'investment opportunity' that wasn't for everyone. It was meant for the 'adventurous' or something like that. He wants her in on it, and he said that if she knew anyone while she was working at Polly's who fit that 'adventurous' description, Harold would like to meet him."

She stopped talking when Philippe showed up with two big plates of salad. Lettuce, black olives, green beans, capers, and anchovies with some kind of mustard and vinegar dressing. We didn't talk much until we were soaking up the dregs of the dressing in the last of the bread.

"How well do you know Daphne," she asked. She must have seen something in my face because she said, "No, I don't mean it like that. So, how well do you know her?"

"To explain that, you've got to understand that I knew Polly Adler before she got into the business. But once she got set up with her first house, I was in and out on a regular basis because I worked for Rothstein. You see, whenever those goddamn vice cops raided a place and took the madam and the girls down to Magistrate's Court, the women would have to pay off everybody in sight to get out. When that happened, they always knew they could go to A. R. for a quick loan. I collected a lot of their installment payments. A. R. sent me because I was a kid. If he sent any of the regular guys who worked for him, they'd be there all afternoon or night. The girls who worked for Polly knew I was her friend and so they played nice with me. Can't say I didn't enjoy the attention." I smiled, thinking about those days.

Connie noticed. "Yeah, I'll bet you did."

"By the time Daphne came to Polly's, A. R. had been dead for a few years. I met her because Polly had something she wanted me to deliver to Meyer Lansky. What it was, I cannot say. She knew she couldn't contact him by telephone because the Bureau might be listening in. So she called me and told me to come over and pick up an envelope."

Polly got along better with Lansky than any of the other gang guys and almost all of them were regular customers of hers. Lansky wasn't. As long as I knew him, he never talked about girlfriends or hookers the way the other guys did. Then after he got married, his first son had cerebral palsy and that changed him. He and Polly respected each other professionally, and I think she got along with him for the same reason I did. The three of us were short and smart.

"I'd heard Polly had a new girl who was a real knockout, and, well, you know that's what Daphne is. Of course, she had a nice trim figure and blonde hair and that something that a lot of guys say they're looking for—call it innocent, unspoiled, fresh. Daphne had it in spades because she worked on it. Polly gave her a few acting and makeup tips to make the most of what she had. She managed to hold onto it, too, and not many can do that. Polly made sure she met Charlie Luciano right out of the gate, and he took up a lot of her time. Harold must have met her around then and invited her to set up housekeeping. I didn't see her again until that business with Miss Wray."

That was the time when Fay Wray came to New York for the world premiere of *King Kong* and some guys tried to put the touch on her with dirty pictures that looked like they'd been shot on the movie set. It wasn't her but the studio was still willing to buy the guys off and I was the go-between. There's more to it but I've told the story before.

"You ask how well I know Daphne, I guess that's it. What do you think of her?"

Connie had another bite of bread and a sip of wine before she answered. "When I first met her, I was a little bit starstruck. I'd only been in the city for a year or so and everything still seemed glamorous, and she was an exotic creature—nothing like the women who worked in the houses on Clinton Street in Napa where I grew up. I saw them sometimes in the afternoon when they were lounging out on the porch. I wasn't supposed to be there, of course, but sometimes my older sister wanted to walk that way after school. She was fascinated. I was scared, not just that mother would find out what we'd done but the women, I don't know how to describe them. They were sickly pale and sloppy-looking, nothing like Daphne."

"Ain't that the truth."

"She hasn't said it in so many words, but I think she knows that one way or another she and Harold aren't going to be together for much longer. She's still young and pretty but there's always another girl who's younger and prettier. For now though, she has a man who will give her anything she wants. But she's worried."

"About what?"

"She says that Harold is changing. What bothers her most is that lately, he doesn't care about money. It means nothing to him. He wastes it. He buys something expensive and if it doesn't work, he doesn't care. Doesn't try to get it fixed or replaced or returned. He just throws it away. When she mentions that she needs something, say… a new hat, he opens his wallet and gives her a hundred dollars."

When she said that, it reminded me of A. R. at the end, the way he bragged to anyone who'd listen that he wasn't good for his markers. It was bad enough to welch in private but to tell everybody about it like you were proud. Nobody understood that.

"What are you going to do then?"

"Arch and I are going to have dinner with them tomorrow night. Maybe you should join us."

"What the hell are you talking about?"

She explained.

Chapter Twenty-Nine

I spent most of Saturday waiting for the electrician. The painters got there early and finished by the middle of the afternoon. Marie Therese said they did good work and had them repaint the bathrooms even though they didn't need it. I went to my office. Finished the list of things I'd need and called Detective Ellis. I didn't expect him to be there but he answered. I told him he needed to see me.

"Are you open yet?"

"No, but if you can get here before six, I'll give you a drink."

"Maybe, don't count on it. What is it?"

I didn't say anything. He knew that meant I didn't want to talk over the telephone, so he said alright and hung up. I knew I should call Turcot, the Bureau man, but talking to him would be difficult and I didn't want to do it. So I looked at my list some more. Added some things, crossed out some things, and realized that what I was thinking about doing at the Hotel McAlpin wasn't even half-baked. Maybe quarter-baked, not even as baked as what Connie and Arch were contemplating. But, hell, even that was better than sitting around waiting for the next Nazi thug to come through the door.

Marie Therese and Frenchy left when the painters finished. I went downstairs and unlocked the liquor, figuring there was a chance I'd have company before the afternoon was over. Ordered coffee from the kitchen and spread out the papers to find out what Hauptmann had been up to overnight. Turned out he'd hidden a big spoon from his breakfast tray and tried to sharpen it into a shank. His cell was solid steel so the guards couldn't see what he was up to, but the kitchen noticed the missing spoon right away and let the guards know. Hauptmann said, 'Spoon? What spoon? I didn't have no spoon.' They moved him into another cell, strip searched him, and found the pieces of the spoon in the basin and crapper drains. From then on, Bruno would be eating off paper plates with paper fork and spoon.

A federal "wood technologist" said there was no question that the wood the ladder was made of came from a lumber yard where Hauptmann had worked in the Bronx. Figure there was more to come from him. The New York cops had sent a detective to Germany to look into Bruno's background. The detective interviewed one of Hauptmann's school pals, and visited the prison in Bautzen where he'd done time. Then while Hauptmann's mother was away, the German cops got a locksmith to pop the front door and the detective went through the place "from garret to cellar." Didn't find anything. His next stop was talking to friends of the late Isidor Fisch, Bruno's fall guy. While those pieces were fitting together like a jigsaw puzzle, Hauptmann, through his lawyer, did the smart thing and clammed up. He didn't do anything, he didn't know anything, he didn't see how any grand jury could indict him, he just wanted to go back to his beloved wife and son.

The Bureau man showed up late in the afternoon. He ignored the closed sign on the unlocked door and strolled in. Took a moment to examine the damages and the repair work and sat across from me at a two-top. He noticed that I was in shirtsleeves so he tried to act human by taking off his hat, unbuttoning his collar and loosening his tie. Even tried to smile.

"They're keeping us busy with Hauptmann's house and garage," he said. "I don't have the authorization I need yet, but I will by Monday, Tuesday at the latest. Here's what I've got in mind—"

I interrupted, "You said Griebl works out of the Hotel McAlpin. Where? Which rooms? Does he live there or does he keep an office?"

Turcot narrowed his eyes, pissed off that I was asking him questions, not answering. "We don't need to go into that now."

"Humor me. You've been after this guy for months, years, right? You must know something about what he's up to there."

I could almost hear the gears turning as he weighed how much to tell me. "All right, it can't hurt. The McAlpin has three wings. Essentially, it's three separate buildings. Griebl has an obstetrics office in B-477. What are you up to?"

"What else can you tell me about the thugs who busted up my place? Are they likely to show up at the McAlpin?"

"It's possible. Now, look, you are not going to do anything yet. First, I get authorization, which is guaranteed, then we spell out in writing what your duties are going to be and your signed agreement to testify when the time comes."

I pretended to hesitate. "I've got to admit that testifying anywhere is not something I've ever thought about doing, but if that's what it takes to nail those guys, I guess I will."

He patted the table, like he was giving me a pat on the head. "Good. If you just do this my way, we'll get along fine. Not only will you get the justice that Josef deserves, but you'll also be serving your country."

I nodded like I was agreeing. He bought it.

"Tell me more about those guys in the picture. They killed Fat Joe."

"We don't have proof of that."

"A bunch of big guys in a big car brought him here and killed him. We've got a witness. You took a picture of this bunch of big guys standing next to a big car."

"Don't make this personal, Quinn."

"My reasons are my business. They don't have anything to do with you. We'll agree on what you're asking me to do, right? I won't screw around with it. Beyond that, don't ask me any questions."

He thought on that for a long time before he slowly nodded his head. "I'll go along with you for now, but I'm not foolish enough to trust you—understand that. The minute you step out of line, I will make your life and your business extremely difficult. Don't doubt that I can do it."

It was time to step back. Let him end it on that note. "Sure. Get your authorization and we'll go to work. You know where to find me."

He gave me a look as he buttoned his collar and tightened his tie. I could tell he was still figuring how much he could trust me, and I figured he was smart enough and experienced enough to know that he couldn't. But as long as he thought he could use me, I could string him along.

It was beginning to get dark when the electrician finally showed up. Said he'd been called to another rush job and I was ready to tell him to forget it until he showed me his estimate. He'd done drawings that were as detailed as blueprints. He mentioned other bars and nightclubs, all places I knew, and claimed he could make the same kind of lighting effects they had. Like he said yesterday, he could make the ceiling look higher with hidden lights, and he could change the lighting in the hall to the restrooms. Not too bright to reveal too much and not so dark it was spooky toward the back. I asked what he drank. He said Scotch, King's Ransom. I poured two and we discussed what he'd said, how much he wanted for the work, and what he'd be willing to do for the amount I wanted to pay. I wanted a firm date when he'd be finished with an agreement that knocked ten bucks off the bill for every day he went over. He wrote that out in longhand on the back of the last page of his estimate. We both signed it. I poured him another drink and went up to my office to write a check.

When I came back downstairs, I found Detective Ellis making himself at home behind the bar. The electrician looked worried as I handed him the check. "It's o.k." I said. "He's a cop."

The electrician left. I took my untouched drink over to the bar and sat on a stool across from Ellis. "You look terrible."

He smelled of sweat and dirt, and his suit looked like it had gone through a wringer. When he took his hat off, his hair stuck to his head. "Spent the morning sorting through lumber in the goddamn kraut's garage. Every stick of it is going over to New Jersey."

"Yeah, I read about that in the papers."

He reached into the freezer with his dirty mitt, scooped ice into a short glass and poured a double shot of my best gin over it. Gulped it down and poured a second. "What the hell do you want?"

"Was the Bureau man with you at Hauptmann's house?" I needed to give the gin a few minutes to work its way into his system before we got down to the serious stuff.

Ellis snorted, "Strutting around and giving orders. Asshole."

"Papers made it sound like there's a mob of cops and people driving by."

"Constant parade of rubberneckers." He drank some more. "Oh, hell, this hits the spot."

"Have another," I said.

He did. Then he came around the bar and sat on a stool. "What do you need?"

"I shouldn't be asking you this. Yeah, you've got better connections than the mayor, but the more I think on this, the more I think, it would be too tough for you. The payoff is good but I'll have to figure out another way to do it. It's one of those situations where the less you know, the better."

"Come on, Quinn, don't try to shit a shitter."

"I'm not. Look, I'm involved in… what? An investment situation. I'm involved in an investment situation where I've got some inside information that might put a nice piece of change in my pocket. But before I commit to anything, I need to know more about it and to do that I've got to play an angle."

Mixing the chance of easy money with the gin was working. "Go on," he said.

"You know the house dick at the McAlpin hotel." It wasn't a question. Ellis was on close terms with the house detectives at all the big midtown hotels, swapping information and helping to keep some activities out of the press.

"There's three at the McAlpin."

"But one's the boss."

He nodded. "Right. Bob Sallie. Retired detective first, good man."

He was a good man, all right. I'd delivered regular payoffs to him from Rothstein for years. This was somebody we could work with. "How well do you know him?"

"He's a few years older than me, we worked a few cases together. I can't say we were ever asshole buddies but I've always been glad to see him."

"I need some items that he can provide. I'm willing to pay, but he doesn't know me." If he remembered me at all, I'd be that little Mick kid who showed up every other week. "He'd say no if I approached him, but he'll listen to you. I'll give you two hundred dollars. You cut the best deal you can for yourself."

He took another slug of gin. Good. "What 'items' are you talking about?"

I handed Ellis my list and an envelope of cash. "He asks what they're for, tell him it's kind of a joke. For an officer's wedding and a bachelor party. I need them by Monday."

Chapter Thirty

The Divan Parisiene was one of those quiet overpriced places over on the East Side where older gents who could afford it showed off their young girlfriends to other older gents who could afford it. The floor-carpet was thick, the waiters were silent, and the little booths looked comfortable. The light from the wall fixtures was a flattering amber. It made the girlfriends look even better and it didn't hurt the old gents either. Maybe I could get my electrician to give me that. At eight o'clock on a Saturday night, the joint was close to full. I told the hat-check girl I'd hold onto my lid. The maître d' was ready to say it would be impossible to seat me until I slipped him a buck and said I was meeting someone at the bar. He gave my suit the onceover. It was a dove grey double breasted, not new but well-fitted. It would do. He raised a hand and a waiter appeared to guide me through double doors on one side of the dining room. I followed him, walking carefully without my stick, and took a two-top just inside the doors where I could see most of the restaurant.

I ordered Teeling on ice and opened the early edition of the Sunday *Times* for the latest on Bruno. The D.A. claimed to have a surprise new witness, a woman, who had damning testimony about Hauptmann, and three alienists were planning to peek into his brain. About twenty minutes later, Daphne and Harold Henninger came in.

He was a big man. That was the first thing you noticed about him, his size. Make him a 48 Long. Second thing was how darkly tanned his face and hands were. He wore a baggy tweed suit. Tie loose. The maître 'd tried to lead them through the tables, but Henninger stopped when he saw an old guy he knew, one of the gents with a little lambkin. He clapped the guy on his shoulder with a meaty paw, acting like he was being friendly, but you could tell from the guy's face he wasn't. Henninger said something I couldn't hear, likely asking for an introduction, and gave the lambkin the eye. It embarrassed her and she looked down at her plate until Harold put a finger under her chin and raised her head to make her look at him. As far away as I was, I could see her blush. Daphne acted like nothing was happening. Guess it wasn't anything she hadn't seen before. Harold gave the old gent's shoulder a painful squeeze and off they went to their table.

They sat at a four-top where Harold could see most of the room. Ordered Manhattan and Martini and a bottle of good French bubbles. He fired up a cigarette and smoked steadily for the rest of the time I was there.

One Teeling later, Connie and Arch came in. She looked terrific in one of her Paris outfits, another matching blouse and skirt that ended just below the knee. She was also wearing her purple beret and she had an orchid tucked behind her ear. You could hear the level of the hushed conversations drop as she and Arch walked to their table and everybody watched them. I was used to that. It happened whenever we went out and she was dolled up. I was not used to watching her walking with another guy, even if it was Arch. Didn't care for it. Connie paid no attention to anyone else in the room. Just held Arch's arm and laughed at something he said. He was wearing an old suit I'd never seen. I learned later it had a Savile Row label and he and Connie found it at a second-hand store on Canal Street. Arch sat heavily and sprawled in his chair at another four-top, acting like he'd already had three or four drinks. Henninger hadn't taken his eyes off Connie since he first spotted her. As soon as she sat, he raised a hand and snapped his fingers for the maître 'd. Impatient fellow, this Harold.

So far, it was all going according to the plan. The night before, Henninger told Daphne to make a reservation at the Parisiene. She told Arch. Arch made a reservation. Daphne had seen Connie's Paris *couture* and knew that Harold would notice her.

The maître 'd hurried over to Henninger's table and leaned down. Harold asked him who the gent with the soup strainer mustache was. The maître 'd said the reservation was for a Mr. Middleford. That's when Daphne whispered to Harold, "I know him." About then, Arch glanced over and pretended to notice Daphne. His eyes widened just a little. A quick little smile twitched behind the mustache, and his nod to her was so slight only Henninger noticed it. Then Daphne and him began an intense quiet conversation over their entrees, her doing most of the talking and Henninger sneaking glances at Connie.

Daphne was telling him that Arch had been a customer at Polly's. He was a Brit, and she had hoped she'd never see him again. Why, Harold asked, did he hurt you? No, but he did like to spank girls. She didn't mind it but it was just that he had so much money he could do whatever he wanted. Some of the girls said there were other things and they didn't want to go with him, but Polly said they had to. You wouldn't know it to look at the shabby way he dresses but he's loaded and nobody knows where it came from. None of Polly's gangster crowd knew him, so it wasn't booze or drugs or policy, and those guys didn't give him any trouble either. Henninger pushed away his dinner plate, lit a cigarette, and stared at Connie and Arch, paying no attention to Daphne or anything else. Just like Daphne said he would.

Arch made a show or ordering for Connie. After the waiter left, he told her it was working. She nodded and turned in her chair so her back was mostly toward Henninger. He squirmed and twisted in his chair and smoked while they ate. Arch made eye contact with him once or twice but kept his attention on Connie. When Henninger saw that they were close to finishing, he called the maître 'd over again.

A few minutes later, coffee for four arrived at Arch and Connie's table. Henninger walked over quickly, pulled out a chair and sat across from Arch. "Don't mean to barge in Middleford, but I'd be happy to buy you an after-dinner drink. I'm Harold Henninger." He said it like Arch was supposed to be impressed. "I believe you know my companion."

He stuck out his paw to shake. Arch gave him a flat cool stare and ignored it. Connie pointed to her empty wine glass and a waiter appeared at her elbow to pour. She sipped and looked at the rest of the room. Arch turned to Daphne and smiled. "Nice to see you again, Daphne. I can't tell you how disappointed I was when I learned you'd left. It appears you're doing well with the presumptuous Mr. Hellinger."

Harold didn't mind his name being wrong. "And this young lady is?"

"Enjoying her dinner, or at least she was. Excuse me." Connie stood, smoothed her dress over her thighs and strolled slowly to the restrooms. Henninger and every other guy in the joint watched her.

A hallway along the back of the bar led to the restrooms. From the bar, you could get to them through saloon doors. I saw her go past, waited a while, then walked back that way. You couldn't see their tables from there. When Connie came out, she kissed me quick and hard, and said, "This is the tricky part."

While Connie was gone, Arch said, "Now that I think of it, you do look familiar. We must have crossed paths at Polly's."

Henninger said, "It's a curious little game we play, pretending to ignore our shared experience. I mean we haven't done anything we're ashamed of."

"Speak for yourself."

Henninger laughed, "Well, yes, I suppose so, but society tries to enforce so many rules around an act that's simply pleasurable for all parties concerned. Seems silly to be embarrassed about it, yet so many are. Have you been there recently?"

"It's been some time since my last visit," Arch said. "I've been traveling."

"Business or pleasure?"

"Both. Let's just say the business has been pleasurable and profitable. Now I'm hoping to enjoy a few weeks with Miss Constable, and perhaps, finally, to buy a place here."

"And what is your business?"

Arch waved his hand. "Anything that interests me."

Henninger leaned forward. "Can you give me some examples?"

"No, I don't know you well enough."

Connie came back to the table. Arch stood and stumbled as he tried to hold her chair. She hissed, "I told you you shouldn't have had that last one."

"Nonsense, I'm fine and Hellinger has ordered a round of port for the table."

Connie said, "No, it's Henninger, not Hellinger."

"Of course, of course. I'm terrible with names. Sorry about that, old sport."

One corner of Henninger's mouth twitched when Connie said his name. "Thank you," he said. "And this Daphne, Daphne Prewitt."

The women did the pleased-to-meet-you business with Arch still pretending he'd had more than the glass of burgundy he drank with dinner. When Daphne gave her the signal, Connie waved for the check and said, "It's time for us to go, darling. We've got to meet the man from the real estate agency tomorrow."

Arch said, "Ah, yes, 'best waterfront river view on the East Side,' he claims. I'll believe it when I see it. After the way those pissants at the River Club acted."

Henninger whipped a card case out his coat pocket and produced a thick cream-colored personal card. "If you're interested in something on the river, give me call. I'm on the board of the East River Yacht Club. We have three excellent apartments that are about to go on the market."

Arch fumbled for his wallet and let it drop to the table. Loose bills fanned out. Connie scooped them back into wallet, but not before Henninger saw a thick sheaf of twenties, tens, and fives. She covered the check and slipped the wallet back into Arch's breast pocket. "Thank you for the offer of the port," she said, "but as you can see, he's had more than enough."

"Nonsense, I'll not be treated as a child." Arch wobbled to his feet. Connie grabbed an arm and led him to the front door. Henninger lit a smoke and watched them until Daphne put a hand on his shoulder and whispered something to him.

I settled up and left.

Chapter Thirty-One

Connie and Arch were waiting in my rooms at the Chelsea. Connie was in the chair by the open window and she'd propped open the door. It had cooled off by then. The sounds of the cars on Twenty-Third Street and a breeze with hardly any exhaust fumes came in past the curtains. Connie was frowning, thinking about something and looking worried. Arch was angry, pacing the room. He'd taken off his coat and loosened his tie. "Christ almighty, Henninger is the kind of rich arrogant asshole that gives rich arrogant assholes a bad name." Figure he'd been talking like that from the moment they got in the cab. I hoped he was running out of steam.

"Simmer down," I said. "He's the mark. You can't play him if you let him know what you think."

Arch shook his head, trying to clear his mind. "Now's not the time."

"Daphne called it. She said if I wore the short tight skirt, he wouldn't take his eyes off me."

"Neither did any other guy in the place, but that was the easy part. We knew he'd glom onto you. Did he buy Arch?"

He nodded. "Oh, yes. I caught the look on his face when I spilled the wallet. If he didn't see me as a mark before then, that did the trick. To him I'm a rich, sloppy drunk, careless with cash. The question now is, how long do we wait before I call him?"

Connie said, "Daphne will tell us. He's back at her place now, right? She knows him better than we do. We follow her lead."

They agreed. Arch picked up his hat, still a little angry. "Just so you know, I borrowed your car and used it to bring some bedding back to the bar. With everything that's been going on, and the cash that's still in the safe and the private stock we've secreted in the cellar, I'm thinking it's not a bad idea to have someone there overnight. I also noticed that you were storing some unusual items in your boot."

"What items?" Connie said.

"The tear gas grenades. From Newark. You remember, I told you about it."

After Arch left and we were undressing, she said, "This is going to be a long night for him."

I knew what she meant but didn't say anything, just watched as she toed off her shoes and took off her skirt and blouse. "He's falling for Daphne a little." She gave me a look, saw the way I was smiling. "You know what I mean. Sure, he wants to go to bed with her. What man wouldn't? But she's getting to him, too, and he knows what's happening over at her place right now with her and Harold and it's making him crazy. That's really why he's so mad."

"If Henninger wasn't in the mood before he saw you, he sure is now."

"That's exactly what Daphne said. And it looks like he isn't the only one."

She pulled her slip over her head. I massaged her shoulders as she folded it into the bureau. She grabbed my hands to stop me and rubbed her cheek against my knuckles. "What are we getting ourselves into? And why? We don't need the money."

"If guys are going to come in and bust up the place every week, we need the money."

"Don't joke, you know what I mean."

"Yes, I do and I'm not joking. I don't know what we've got ourselves into either, not with Daphne and her fatassed boyfriend and not with goddamn Nazis thugs." I pulled down the blanket and got into bed. Connie continued to undress, taking her time. She turned out all of the lights except the little table lamp by the bathroom and slid in beside me.

"And how did you feel this evening, with all those eyes on you in the Parisiene?"

"It wasn't like it is when we're out. If you and I go out for an evening, you're going to wear one of your really good suits, fresh shirt, shoes shined, maybe even comb your hair. I've got to keep up my side."

"Baby, when you wear one of those French outfits, I could be naked and nobody'd notice."

"Hah." She straddled my stomach and grabbed two handfuls of my hair. "You say that but we both know it's not true. But, how did I feel tonight?

I don't know, I was uncomfortable. That's the first thing. I was acting and that's not something I know how to do, so I was sure everybody could see how phony I was. Daphne told me a couple of tricks. How to hold my head up and to be careful exactly where I look. She said to pay attention to Arch. Make sure every man in the room knew I was with him, but to be careful when I stepped in, so I didn't look like I was bossing him around."

"The business with the wallet and paying the bill."

"Right. As soon as Arch said the word 'waterfront,' and Harold produced that card, I was trying to get us out."

"Daphne will tell us whether or not Henninger bought it."

"Yeah," she said and paused. I could tell she was still thinking about whatever was really bothering her. After a few seconds, she looked at me. "How did you feel when I was slinking through that place and everybody was watching my bottom?"

"I didn't like it a damn bit." *Why lie?* "I like it fine when you doll yourself up and we're out together and other people notice. That happened before you went to France, you know. It's not just the *couture*. No, what bothered me was all those geezers with teenage girls who could be their granddaughters. Not that I haven't seen that before. Hell, we get older guys and younger girls in Jimmy's Place every night. It's normal, but I haven't seen that many rich old guys in one place acting like they owned those girls. That's what bothered me."

"Seeing me with Arch didn't bother you?" She smiled, knowing she was needling me.

"Maybe a little at first, but then I remembered both of you were acting. I'll tell you one other thing that bothered me a hell of a lot more. Henninger."

She shivered and wrapped her arms around me and muttered into my neck, "Yeah, me too."

I stroked her back, pulled her closer. "I saw exactly what he wanted when he stared at you, and I think he's so used to getting anything and anyone he wants that we're going to have to be careful. He's gonna try to get you alone, and since he's the mark, we've got to string him along. We don't do anything to frighten him. But if what Daphne suspects is right and he's up to something crooked, then it may come to pass that I'll be able to show him what I think of him."

"You're serious."

"Sure I am. But business first." I whispered slowly, "Think how good it would feel to steal him blind."

I felt her shiver as she reached down and grabbed me. "Oh, yes…"

The thought of money does that to her.

Chapter Thirty-Two

Late Sunday morning, I found a note on the door from Bernard and David telling me to come up to their workroom on four. Connie was still asleep, so I put on my brace and yesterday's clothes, found a pistol, and walked over to the bar. I let myself in through the gate at the backdoor, went inside, and smelled coffee. I checked the cellar and saw that Arch had cleared space for a blue striped mattress on one of the long tables. No sign he'd used it. I climbed the stairs to my office and found Arch behind the desk with a cup of coffee, a snifter of cognac, and the bottle of hundred-year-old Croizet. Looked like he hadn't slept much.

"Quiet night," he said. "Curious isn't it, at my advanced age, I've become overly cautious, but it's god's honest truth that I've never had this much money at one time and now I'm frightened that someone's going to take it from me. Go figure. And when is that counterfeiter of yours—what's his name, Bik, Bock?"

"Beck. Petey Beck."

"Right. When is he going to provide the papers I need to get a safety deposit box?"

"Been so busy with everything else, I forgot about him. I'll call him tomorrow. Is there more coffee in the kitchen? Let's make breakfast."

Arch leaned back, looking sheepish. "You do it. I, uh…" He stammered, "Daphne said he might leave this early on a Sunday," 'he' being Henninger, "and she's going to call as soon as he does. I told her I'd be here."

Yeah, it had been a rough night for him. Figure he'd been here alone thinking about Harold and Daphne together, Harold being hornier than usual after seeing Connie dolled up.

In the kitchen upstairs, I poured a cup and found a leftover baked potato and a chunk of short rib in the refrigerator. Hashed them together and put half of them in a little skillet over low heat. When they started to get the right shade of brown, I cracked a couple of eggs over them and let them set. While mine were cooking, I started a second skillet for Arch. When I finished eating, his were done. I put the plate on a tray and a dome over the plate and took it back down to my office. Figure Arch had been smelling it since I started cooking. When he saw it, he said, "Bless you, my son" and dug in.

"About last night, you had any more thoughts?"

He nodded. "It seems to me, given Henninger's reputation on Wall Street, that he is trying to set up some kind of dicey stock transaction. I don't know nearly enough about the market to guess what it might be, so for now, I'm going to remain the mysterious Mr. Middleford who's interested in waterfront real estate. You probably couldn't hear it from your perch in the bar last night, but when we were conversing, I put on borderline snotty rich aristo British accent."

He went into that voice. "If he enquires into my background, I'll tell him the Middleford family had one of those great gloomy gray houses out in the wild Ireland west. I roundly detested every day I had to spend there as a youth and repaired to London as soon as I could escape. The I.R.A. helpfully burned it down. I went to Sandhurst, served in His Majesty's Royal Engineers. I'll make Middleford's travels much like my own, in the Caribbean, the Orient and Austria, though the fortunate Mr. Middleford has done it in a style I couldn't afford. Most of that's close enough to the truth that I shouldn't have much trouble. Henninger's an anglophile but according to Daphne he hasn't visited in several years so he's not likely to press me on details."

"What's your plan, then?"

"If Daphne tells me he's bought the story, I call him tomorrow and tell him I'm interested in seeing an apartment at the Yacht Club. I'll just nibble. Tell him the money isn't a problem, I'm more concerned with finding the right place. I expect to pay handsomely but I won't pay a penny for something I don't really like. I'm thinking of settling down here, at least for a year or so, and take it from there. If he brings up this proposition Daphne thinks he's pitching to his well-heeled friends, I will be skeptical. He'll have to work to get me involved."

"Are you going to bring Connie?"

"No, she'd be a distraction. We want him paying attention to me."

"Good, I don't want her around the son of a bitch."

He took a sip of the cognac and his tone changed. He got serious. "Do you realize how lucky you are to have that woman? She is one in a million. If I were ten years younger, I'd do everything I could to take her, but I'm not and I won't. I will tell you that it felt fine last night to go into that cavern of thieves with her on my arm."

He smiled at the fresh memory. I couldn't blame him. "You're going to have to work to keep her," he said. "She only got the tiniest taste of Paris, and so she has to go back. Be ready to go with her or lose her."

What he said scared me because he was right. "She made me get a passport."

I walked back to the Chelsea and went up to David and Bernard's workrooms on four. The door was open. Connie was talking to the two guys. David said to me, "We've got another wig and a set of clothes. They're not what we talked about and they may not be what you need, but take a look anyway. Have a seat."

I got into the barber's chair and David raised it up. He showed me a blond wig that looked to be slicked down with pomade and did the same business of brushing back my hair and putting on a silk cap before he fitted the hairpiece. Bernard held up a pair of wide white floppy pants and a white sweater. "These came from a show called *Hell's Bells*. The juvenile who wore them said, 'Anyone for tennis.' That one didn't last too long, as I recall. What do you think, Connie?"

They both studied me while David got the rug squared away. Connie shook her head. "I don't know what to say. The gray wig and the old man makeup were completely realistic. With his dark complexion, the blond hair just looks phony."

"But do you recognize his face?"

"Of course."

"Would the people you're watching recognize him?"

David handed me a mirror. I said, "They'd recognize some idiot wearing a ridiculous disguise." Then I remembered something else. "I'll take it. The wig, not the other stuff."

They showed me a baggy suit and a bowtie that went with the gray wig and the metal crutch. At first, I was going to balk at the bowtie. I remembered from when I was a kid hearing Mr. Rothstein tell Lansky that short guys like him should always wear long neckties because bowties made them look even shorter. True or not, I never wore bowties and I never saw Lansky in one, either. Then I realized that was the point of a disguise. They said they could have everything ready by Monday. We talked money and I agreed to bring half of it over later that day.

Connie and I went back to my rooms on three. I was ready to settle down with the rest of the Sunday papers, but she found her purse and beret. "Is Arch in your office or did Daphne call?"

"He was waiting for her when I left."

She looked at her watch. It was about three. "We're supposed to go to her place this afternoon. Harold ought to be gone by now, but I'd better check with Arch first."

I found my hat and my stick. We walked over and went in through the front door so I could take another look at the painters' work. Connie went straight up to the office. The electrician's drawings were still on the bar. I looked them over again and tried to imagine the amber light in the Parisiene in my place. Somehow, it didn't seem right. As I was thinking on it, I heard the telephone ring in my office. Arch and Connie came back down a few minutes later. Smiling, excited.

Arch said, "I believe Mr. Middleford has attracted Mr. Henninger's attention."

"Daphne says he kept pressing her for details. Wanted to know everything she remembered about him."

"O.K., it's working. What next?"

Connie said, "We're going to her place. She's written down some things that Harold told her last night."

"Want me to come along?" Connie could see that I didn't mean it and said no, it'd be easier to get two in a cab.

After they left, I opened the safe and checked the supply of cash to settle up for the wigs. I took out what we'd agreed to and as I was putting the rest back, I saw the manila folder and the photographs of the four Nazi bastards that Turcot had left on Thursday. The grainy, blown-up enlargements of the guys' faces still didn't tell me much, but the other one, the one of the car and the storefronts, that made me curious. Where did Turcot say it was? Pearl Street. It must be down past the Brooklyn Bridge where Pearl angled and narrowed. Why not take a look? I didn't have anything better to do on a Sunday afternoon, and it was only a mile or so. I folded the picture in half and slipped it into my breast pocket.

Chapter Thirty-Three

I walked south on Seventh and Sixth down to Church Street and turned east on Fulton. It was a cloudy afternoon and traffic was light on the streets and sidewalks. Any other Sunday like that, Connie and I might have been walking the same route just to take the air on a mild afternoon. But I couldn't forget why I was there, so I kept an eye out for any big blond guys who happened by. I still couldn't concentrate as well as I needed to. Arch was right. Connie was going to go back to Paris. I tried not to think about it, but I knew it. She was from this little farm town in California, so she just didn't understand that now she didn't have to go everywhere and see everything. She was in New York. If something was worth seeing, it would come here. If it didn't come here, was it really that good? Probably not.

Paris had changed her. It wasn't just the clothes and the confidence they gave her. She'd seen a different way of living and she liked it. Hell, she loved it. And then everything that happened after she got back from Paris, that night of killing, all of it face to face, within arm's reach—five men shot, beaten and stabbed to death. She shot two of them, both trying to shoot her, and I hoped that her anger at what they'd done to her and tried to do to her had washed away the horror and guilt of that night. Maybe all of that, I realized as I walked, was another reason for her to get back to Paris. And when she went, what would I do?

Some time later as I got closer to Pearl Street, I looked up and saw the tracks of the El. When I got to Pearl, the street was just two narrow lanes and it felt narrower because of the steel uprights and the girders and train tracks overhead that kept most of the street in shadow. Beyond them, I could see the polished stone sides of one of the Wall Street buildings in the distance. On a Sunday, the street was empty of cars and people. I was alone.

There were "To Let" signs on maybe a third of the storefronts. The businesses were mostly wholesale commercial, not retail. Painters, plumbing supplies, sand and gravel, cleaners and solvents. The cobbled pavement was broken at the curbs and the sidewalk was cracked. I took the photograph out of my breast pocket and unfolded it. I needed to go farther down to get to the place where the four guys had been standing, just past a subway stop. Most of the windows I passed were clouded with dust. I reached the spot where the big car had been parked with the guys standing around it, and looked back up the street. The guy who took the picture must have been about half way to the intersection. What reason would four Nazi thugs have for being here?

I looked at the picture again. There were no other cars on the street. They could've parked anywhere. What were they closest to? There was a place selling ductwork, tubing, and pipe on one side of the street and a vacant storefront with whitewashed windows on the other. I walked the rest of the way down the block and back up, looking through windows. I didn't see anything that looked like it could've had anything to do with Fat Joe. No German names on any of the signs either.

But Fat Joe looked like he'd been rolled in that black stuff—asphalt. The sand and gravel place might deal in asphalt, too, if it had been open. It was one of the storefronts with a "To Let" sign in the window. I went up three steps to the front doors, cupped my hands against the afternoon sun, and tried to see inside. That's when I noticed the wire mesh in the pebbled glass panels on the doors, and the metal security shutters on the other side. I couldn't make out much else, just a counter with rows of shelves behind it. Stepped back onto the sidewalk and found the name of the place. Leyton and Sons Landscaping and Building Supplies. Established 1889. It didn't seem to me that dirt, gravel, and bricks would be much of a target for thieves, but the Leytons had done their best to see that nobody broke in and stole them.

Nobody paid any attention to me as I walked back to the Chelsea. When I got there, I found Bernard working on the alterations to the baggy corduroy suit I was going to wear with the gray wig. He wasn't finished but he wanted me to try it on.

As I was changing clothes, he said, "Connie tells me that you're trying to look like an absentminded professor who is really important to some hotshot lawyer, so he's being treated like visiting royalty and the hotel is rolling out the red carpet."

"That's the long and the short of it."

"And my part is to make sure that people who might have seen you in Jimmy's Place don't recognize you as that professor."

The pants were baggy at the knees and a couple inches too long, and the coat was starting to fray at the cuffs. I took my tie off and Bernard showed me how to tie a messy bow tie. Figure this guy I was pretending to be didn't care about a neat knot. Then it was back into the barber's chair for the wig and older-guy makeup.

"You'll want a pair of old brown shoes that need polishing to complete this creation," he said, and glued on the mustache. He fiddled with it and the wig for a time, and did something with a little sponge and makeup. Then he gave me the wire-rimmed glasses. When he finished, he lowered the chair and told me to take a look in the full-length mirror. I did.

"I'll be damned." With the bad suit, messy hair, and sloppy tie, I almost didn't recognize myself.

He gave me the crutch and helped me fit my forearm into the cuff. "You wear the brace on your right knee and carry your stick in your left hand, just like you should. So maybe you should try using this one with your right hand. It's probably unimportant but I'm thinking that if anybody thought he recognized you and he saw the crutch on the other side it would be another difference, even if he'd never thought about it."

I took a few steps with the metal stick on my right arm. The truth was that most times if I was simply walking or standing, I didn't need the stick, but if I was going down stairs or trying change direction and move quickly, my knee could buckle, even with the brace. The metal stick was about three inches too long to boot. It felt better when I switched it to my left hand, but I still felt clumsy with it. The more I thought about it, the less I liked it. I gave it back to Bernard.

"I'm not going to take it. Even if it's not the same, people who know me know that I use a stick. I'll pack mine in the trunk but this absentminded professor is going to be emptyhanded."

"You're probably right. Even the best actors can have trouble with a prop like this. They always overdo it and the audience recognizes that. If you can wait a few minutes, I'll finish the alterations on the suit and you can take it with you."

Connie and Arch got back around six. Since the Cruzon Grill wasn't open on Sunday, we went downstairs to El Quijote, the Spanish restaurant that was part of the hotel. Connie and I didn't really like the place. It was loud, gaudy and the food wasn't that good, but it was close and it was open, and Arch thought it was terrific. We took a booth.

Daphne told them that Harold bought Arch's act. "I asked her if she was sure that he didn't suspect a setup," Arch said. "And she swore he didn't, and she said they'd been together long enough that she knew when he was lying."

Connie said, "When we planned what we were going to do, all three of us agreed that when they got home Saturday night, Daphne wasn't going to say anything about us. She couldn't show any interest, since this old customer of hers made her uncomfortable."

"But Harold wouldn't shut up about us. He kept pressing for more details, mostly about the source of my wealth. He asked Daphne to call Polly and find out what she knew."

"What's next?"

"I'm going to call him late tomorrow and tell him about the wasted Sunday afternoon I spent with a realtor who showed me one overpriced crapulous river view apartment after another. I'm just about ready to chuck the whole damn thing."

Connie said, "So far, this is going just like we thought it would." She had a bright, sharp-eyed look, meaning she was really getting interested in what they were doing.

"It's almost enough to make one suspicious," Arch said.

Chapter Thirty-Four

Monday morning, I met Frenchy and Marie Therese and the electrician at nine. He brought three different light fixtures and had to know which kind we wanted. I left that to Marie Therese. Frenchy said he was still trying to find an upholsterer who'd do what we needed. While we were talking, I heard the telephone in my office ring and gimped up the stairs. Most times when I do that, I take so long they hang up before I get there. When it kept ringing, I figured I knew who it was. Turcot.

The Bureau man sounded pissed that he'd had to wait for me. "Listen," he said, "everything's ready, or almost ready. I need one more supervisor to sign off on this. He'll do it later this afternoon, and I'll have the papers you need to sign ready for you tomorrow."

"Tomorrow's going to be really busy here. I've got four guys lined up to finish repairing this place so we can reopen this weekend. You can bring them here if you want, but I won't have time to look them over before Wednesday, and I'm not going to sign anything I haven't read. You say all this is part of your routine but it isn't part of mine. If you want me to do this, don't push me." Like I was going to sign anything.

Silence, then, "All right. I suppose one day doesn't matter at this point."

He hung up. I brought a cup of coffee down from the kitchen and settled with the newspapers.

There wasn't much to say about Hauptmann. Bruno had spent a quiet weekend. Slept well, ate well with paper utensils. They cut his meat for him in the kitchen. New Jersey was still working on indictments and nobody had anything to say about what the wood expert was up to. The big local story was a riot down on the East Side at the Academy of Music, between anti-Fascists and music lovers who supported the National Fascist Militia Band, "musical ambassadors of good will." More than 8,000 people had crowded the intersections. They'd been protesting for three days and New York's Finest were ready. When things got dicey, like they did in Newark, a hundred cops waded into the crowd and had at them with billy clubs, and 75 mounted cops charged the sidewalks. As the Times put it, they "threw the belligerents into a panic."

In Germany, Herr Hitler drove through 60 miles of double columns of Storm Troopers, past triumphal arches decorated with harvest symbols to the city of Bueckeburg to celebrate the second anniversary of the National Socialist Thanksgiving. I wondered if the Storm Troopers had anything to do with the SS guy that Turcot was looking for. Hitler told a crowd of 700,000 peasants and city folk, "In our peasantry, we recognize a healthy contrary pole to intellectual urbanism. A nation of professors, State servants, scholars and the like cannot exist, if for no other reason than because the natural capacity to come to a decision of essential strength will grow weaker and weaker. So long, therefore, as Jewish intellectualism poisoned German life, there was no safety for peasant and worker."

Frenchy knocked on the door and told me that the glazier was there with new shelves. The electrician had left to get the fixtures Marie Therese chose. The glazier said he could work with the electrician. They wouldn't get in each other's way, and he had everything on his truck. I told him to go ahead. Frenchy said he needed to use the telephone in the office to call a couple of guys about the upholstery, so I took my papers upstairs to the kitchen and had them make me a sandwich. I sat at the little corner table where Connie and I ate on Friday night and stayed out of the way while they got ready for the dinner crowd.

By the middle of the afternoon, the glazier had replaced the glass shelves and two more mirrors behind the bar. The electrician said he could have most of the fixtures ready by that evening, the ones behind the bar and the hidden lights that would make the ceiling look higher. He could do the work he'd mentioned in the hall and the bathrooms on Tuesday. Then Frenchy said he'd found an upholstery guy who said he'd come by when he'd finished work on the job at hand, sometime after six or first thing tomorrow.

"Another one of those," I said, and Frenchy said, no, he knew this guy and if he said he'd come by, he would. Yeah, yeah, sure.

But the guy came through. The glazier had left and the electrician was screwing in the bulbs when a tall guy knocked on the front door and asked for Frenchy. The electrician was showing me the new switches he'd installed behind the bar that gave us more control over the level of light in four places, the coat room and entrance, behind the bar, the booths, and the hallway to the bathrooms. There was a separate switch for the hidden lights and when he turned it on, it really did make the ceiling look taller. The room wasn't brighter—nobody wanted that—but it wasn't quite as subterranean as it always had been.

Frenchy's tall upholstery guy made measurements and said he could bring some fabric samples by the next day. He gave me some ballpark numbers that I could live with and said if we chose something that was in stock, he might be able to replace all of the booths by Friday. If I wanted to grease the skids with a deposit, he'd call some guys and have them there in the morning. I looked at Frenchy. Frenchy nodded. I gave the guy a twenty.

Connie and Arch were knocked out by the new lights when they came in. Frenchy, Marie Therese and I had been replacing the bottles and glasses we'd put away, and the place was starting to look like a real bar again. When we'd finished Frenchy and Marie Therese went home. Me and Arch and Connie went to my office to call Henninger.

Arch sat behind my desk and dialed the number on the card Daphne gave him. He held the earpiece so Connie and I could hear.

A man answered. "East River Yacht Club."

"Henninger. Harold Henninger," he barked, using his loud British voice.

"May I say who's calling?"

"This is Archibald Middleford."

When Henninger picked up, Arch started talking fast. "Yes, Henninger, this is Archibald Middleford. We spoke briefly the other evening at that ridiculous French place, and I've got to tell you that I wasted two days wandering about with a young man who doesn't know his arse from a hole in his head when it comes to proper accommodations. No matter what I told him about my requirements, he insisted upon dragging me to one unsuitable place after another. I tell you, man, I'm ready to give this up as a bad idea, but my young lady is insistent and says that your club might be just what we're looking for. What say I pop 'round tomorrow and you can give me a tour?"

Henninger tried to answer but Arch didn't give him time. "Shall we meet around six? Perhaps bend an elbow. I'll see you then," and hung up.

Connie and I looked at each other. She was as confused as I was. "What the hell are you doing?"

He smiled and talked in his real voice. "Daphne and I have discussed this at length. She says that everyone treats Henninger as if he were God's gift to Wall Street. They bow and scrape and kiss the ring. When he meets a man who doesn't, he notices him.

"Now, if you will excuse me, Daphne and I need to fine tune my performance tomorrow." He kept a straight face while he said it.

Arch left. Connie went downstairs to look at the new lights. I called Detective Ellis. I didn't expect him to be in and he wasn't. I left my name and said he knew what it was about. He showed up a few hours later, carrying a bundle wrapped in brown paper and twine under his arm. He started to say something but did a doubletake when he saw the new lights.

"What the hell'd you do?"

I went behind the bar, scooped ice into a short glass, filled it with the good gin, and slid it across to the detective.

Connie said, "The magic of professional lighting."

Ellis nodded and drank. "Dresses up the joint."

I reached for the package on the bar. He put his hand on it. "I need more. Sallie wouldn't go for anything less than three and it was hard to get him down to that."

This was about what I'd expected. Figure Ellis and Sallie knew they could shake me down for more than two hundred and put their heads together to come up with a number. I'd been thinking four. I shook my head and said, "You know, for what we've got in mind, we can do it without this." I looked at Connie. So did Ellis.

She didn't know what was in the package or what I was talking about but she nodded and said, "I didn't think we needed it in the first place."

"I hate to lose two hundred dollars but I'm not going to throw good money after bad."

"Now, wait a goddamn minute, Quinn. We had an agreement."

After three more good gins, we settled on two-fifty.

When we got back to the Chelsea, Connie ripped into the package and spread the contents on the bed. "What the hell?"

I explained.

Chapter Thirty-Five

Late Tuesday morning, Arch woke up in Daphne Prewitt's bed. Andrew the cat was scratching at the door. He, Arch, stretched and smiled. It had been one of the most pleasant and exciting nights of his life. But not what he'd expected it to be. After he left Connie and me, he walked down to Gay Street. When Daphne opened the front door, he saw that she was wearing the peach-colored silk robe she'd had on the first time he met her there. Now, it was so tightly belted that the peaks of her nipples were obvious. "We both knew what she was doing," he told me one night, a year later. "The woman understands how to display the merchandise, and she has excellent merchandise." Her blonde hair was loose around her face and her lipstick was a darker shade of red than he remembered. And she was wearing a different perfume, "more redolent of the musky Orient."

Without asking, she poured two snifters of Harold's best cognac. Not as good as the Croizet, but worth a taste. She sat on the loveseat with a table lamp angled beside her to highlight her hair and breasts. Leaned back, holding the glass in two hands, and crossed her legs at the ankle. He noticed her high-heeled slippers, and how polished everything looked and smelled, the coffee table, the mantle, even the ashtray. The last time he'd been in her place, he figured she kept it neat because that's the way Henninger liked it. But now it wasn't just neat, it shone. Maybe Daphne had decided to seal the deal.

She said, "Since Harold brought up the East River Yacht Club at the restaurant Saturday night, I asked him about it. He tried acting off-hand, he does that when he's lying. 'I never told you I kept a little apartment there? I'm sure I did, but if I didn't, it's because I use it so seldom I tend to forget about it.' Then he started asking more questions about you. He wanted all the details of what you wanted to do in bed, how much you drank, if I'd seen you use cocaine or heroin."

"What did you tell him?"

"With the drugs, I thought it was best to stick with what I know. I said I'd never seen you use any or talk about them so I assume you didn't. Every time I saw you, you'd had too much to drink. But then, that's the case for most of the guys who come to Polly's. For sex, I made you a spanker, usually just the hands but very very hard with the hands. Sometimes the belt. No whips."

"No belt either but go on, I'm fascinated."

"He asked again about your money, and I said what you told me to. You always seemed to have more than you needed and spent it freely."

"Do you think there's any chance he'll talk to Polly?"

She shook her head. "I heard from one of the girls they had a falling out when I left. I assume it was over me but I may be flattering myself. You think he has another girl at the Yacht Club and I'm sure that's true. As long as I've been living here, I've seen evidence that there are other women, but Harold wouldn't want to embarrass me by bringing them up, just like he would never bring me up with his wife."

"Did he say anything about his obvious attraction to Connie?"

"No, he does that all the time. He did it when he went to Polly's. He'd be chatting up one girl and obviously be interested in her but if another girl came in and he thought she'd be better, he'd just get up and walk away from the first girl. Doesn't do much for a girl's self-esteem, I can tell you that."

"Did he ever do it to you?"

"Do you think I'd be here if he did?"

"I take your point. What else?"

"He kept bringing the subject back to your money and wanting to know how you got it, and I stuck to the things we talked about. You traveled extensively and spent a lot of time in Cuba and the Philippines, and somehow you managed to survive the Crash without mussing your hair. That impressed him."

"Good."

"What are you going to do when you see him tomorrow?"

Arch said, "Since this East River club is so new, I'm assuming it will in good shape, so I'll be able to tell him I'm more impressed with it than with any of the other places I've seen. I'll say I'm ready to sign but I'll delay things by bringing up questions of timing—when I could move in, when will they need a down payment or good-faith money, all that. Without putting it in so many words, I'll try to make Henninger think that I believe he'd make a good neighbor. What will he say if I propose that we meet for lunch or drinks later this week? Will that be too much or should I let him make that move?"

"Let Harold do it. If he's serious about it, he'll suggest a day and a place. If he's not, he'll say something like 'We must get together sometime soon.' And if he says something about bringing Connie along, then he's more interested in her than you, and he won't tell me about it."

"And were that to happen, he'd try to separate her from me and ask her out."

She smiled over the brandy snifter. "Of course, she's his type."

"What type is that?"

"Don't try to kid a kidder," she said. "Young, pretty, put together—God, those tits, I should have those tits—the glossy hair, and the clothes! Given a chance, Harold will put the move on her, all right."

"We don't want her there anyway. She's too big a distraction."

"What are you going to do if Harold asks you to invest in his project?"

"Express mild interest and try to change the subject. We want him to have to work to get me involved. Can't make it too easy for him, and without saying too much, I want to let him know that I'm nouveau riche. I'll admit that I don't know that much about the society world he's lived in all his life. He'll see right through me if I try to pass myself off as one of those yacht people. I don't want to be part of that world, either. I'm just a guy whose ship finally came in and I'm enjoying it. That ought to make me a better mark."

He sipped Henninger's cognac. Definitely not up to the Croizet. "The problem here is that we're still not sure exactly what the man is up to. It would be much easier to come up with a good plan if we knew what he's after."

"I think Harold's looking for excitement. He wants to put something over on the men he's worked with. One night in bed, he said that he hopes it's not too late to be a pirate. And that scares me. Harold thinks he's the smartest man on Wall Street. If he told me that once, he's told me that a thousand times. I know that whatever he had me doing before, that was shady and maybe if they'd found out he was involved with it, he'd have gotten a fine or something. But if he's planning something now that's really serious, something they put people in jail for, then he'll make sure that somebody else is holding the bag."

"And that would be the end of this little arrangement."

Daphne chewed a thumb knuckle and nodded.

"But maybe that's what you want."

Daphne shook her head too quickly.

Arch said, "I think you want to get out of the life you're living here, the life you've been living ever since you were in Polly's. Men have been coming after you since you were a teenager, maybe younger. You have the look of one of those girls who understood how to work on men before she knew what she had."

"And plenty of men have known how to work on me." She was serious.

"For a time, you thought that this arrangement was better because you didn't have to put up with the worst of Polly's customers."

"You better believe that's true, buster."

"And even though Harold says he will buy you anything you want, he's still in control."

"I just want a little nest egg so that I can buy a—"

"A nice little dress shop… C'mon, don't kid a kidder. You want more than that, a lot more than that. You want enough so you don't have to worry about money because you can buy whatever you want and not have to depend on Henninger or any other man."

Her eyes got wider and he could tell he had it right about her. "If you want to get it from Harold, you're going to have to take it."

Daphne put down her snifter, leaned forward. "And what do you want, Mr. Middleford?"

"I want to go upstairs and fuck."

Her laugh was loud, short, and sharp.

"I've wanted to ever since the first night I saw you in Jimmy's, and I've thought about you more than I should ever since. You're one of the most alluring women I've ever met, and I'd like to explore every inch of your body. The few occasions when I have had the time and circumstance to take my leisure and enjoy a girl to the fullest—those moments have been bouts of pleasure beyond my powers of description, and I believe the ladies would say the same. I relive them regularly."

Daphne stood and said, "I like a man who knows what he wants." She let the robe fall.

•••

"Jimmy, she was everything I'd imagined. Blonde and blonde, oh, yes, uplifted nipples of the most delightful rosy pink, thighs long and taut as she strolled away in those heels and I followed her up the stairs. A posterior kissed by the gods."

"And when you got to the bedroom?" I asked.

"When we got to the bedroom, she waited until I was right behind her and bent over and pulled down the covers. I noticed that she'd changed the sheets. After that, well, a gentleman never kisses and tells but I'm no gentleman. All the commercial sex I've had was fast, cheap, and unsatisfying, and never with a woman at her level of professionalism, so I cannot say how much of what she did was an act and how much was real enjoyment on her part, but she is imaginative and she can coax a man to feats of endurance of which he did not think he was capable."

I had to smile "'bouts of pleasure beyond my powers of description?' 'kissed by the gods?'"

The soup strainer twitched. "Have you ever known me to exaggerate?"

Chapter Thirty-Six

Around noon on Tuesday, we brought Connie's big steamer trunk down from her room on the fifth floor. I loaded up the extra clothes I'd bought from Bernard and put in a couple of my suits and shoes and books to make it feel heavy enough. I didn't want a bellhop noticing an obviously empty trunk. Connie packed a regular suitcase. The professor's corduroy suit and wig were in my office. We'd leave for the Cunard-White Star pier from there. When we got over to Jimmy's Place, we found that the electrician and Frenchy's tall upholsterer were already there. Marie Therese showed us the fabric she'd picked out for the booths. It was almost the same shade of green as the awning, which still hadn't been replaced. Connie said she loved it. I asked how much it cost.

While they hashed that out, I went down to the basement. The mattress Arch had brought was still on the table. It was covered with tightly tucked sheets and a blanket. Either Arch had got up early or he'd spent the night at Daphne's "fine tuning" his upcoming performance. I wished him luck. Then I remembered why he had the mattress there. His cash was still in the safe because Petey Beck hadn't come up with the counterfeit papers we needed for the deposit box leases. The bastard had stiffed us for more than a week, and right then, he became the target for all the frustration and anger that had been piling up since before they killed Fat Joe. Here was something I could fix. I checked my suit. It was a decent Finchley double-breasted. The tie was acceptable. I decided on a light topcoat to make myself look wider, dropped the .32 automatic in the pocket, and found my hat. You want to look your best when you're going to strongarm a cheap chiseler. On the way out, I told Connie and Marie Therese I'd be back. Didn't say anything else. Caught a cab down to Beekman Street.

I still couldn't remember the name of the printing company Beck worked for, but I recognized the building. Inside, I found an empty lobby with a receptionist's desk, and closed doors that probably led to offices. I could hear the thump and clank of heavy machinery somewhere else in the building and I could feel it through the floor. It didn't figure that Beck rated an office, and I doubted he worked a press, so I followed a hall to a set of stairs and went up to the second floor. The stairs led to a wide bullpen with about twenty guys on tall chairs bent over drafting tables. A big guy in shirtsleeves and a tie sat at a desk facing the drafting tables. Make him the supervisor. Petey was in the second row. I slipped the pistol out of my pocket and held it at my side. He didn't notice me when I walked over and stood beside him.

I kept my voice flat, expression hard. "Where are my papers?"

His head snapped up and his pen skittered across whatever he was working on.

"Christ, Quinn, what'd'ya doing sneaking up on a guy." That got the attention of the men working close to us and the supervisor. He got up from his desk and hustled toward me. When Beck saw the pistol, he jumped off his stool and backed away until he bumped into a cluttered cabinet.

I didn't raise my voice. "If you have the papers here, give them to me. If they're not here, we're going to get them. Now."

The supervisor yelled, "Hey, you, what the hell're you doing here."

I pointed the tip of my stick at him and said, "Back off," still in a level voice but louder. He kept coming toward me. I lowered the cane and raised the pistol. He stopped.

All the other guys at drafting tables were craning their necks to look at us. Beck's head swiveled around and he said, "It's o.k. This is nothing, just some private business." I cut my eyes between him and the supervisor. Sweat broke out in heavy drops on Beck's forehead and dripped onto his thick glasses. There was a moment when I thought he was going to run and turned the pistol toward him. The supervisor didn't move.

"The papers, where are they?"

"They're here. I've got them right here." He turned around and yanked open cabinet drawers and made a mess pulling things out. When he turned back around he had a business envelope in his hand. I put the pistol back in my pocket and took it from him. Inside there were three smaller envelopes that had been sliced open. Inside them were three bills from Consolidated Edison addressed to James Doyle, Paul Martin, and Dylan

O'Doyle. I didn't remember the addresses on the operator's licenses but these looked right.

As I turned to leave, Beck grabbed my sleeve and hissed, "Where's the rest of my money?"

By then, nobody else in the place was working. They were staring at us until I stared back. Then their heads dropped back behind the drafting tables. The supervisor stood there looking angry and didn't do anything.

"We're square."

I took a cab back to the bar and found two of the upholsterer's guys stripping the old padding and fabric out of the booths. No sign of their boss. The electrician was working on the hall and bathroom lights. Said he'd be finished by five. Connie said the Bureau man had called. No message.

Chapter Thirty-Seven

Late Tuesday afternoon, Frenchy loaded the smaller hand truck onto his flatbed and drove it around in front of the Chelsea. He double parked and brought the hand truck up to my room. We used it to move Connie's steamer trunk and suitcase down to the lobby and onto his truck. Then we took it back to the loading area behind the bar and locked it up. Inside, Marie Therese was keeping an eye on the upholsterers. There were two of them, neither of them the tall guy that Frenchy knew. All of the booths had been stripped down to bare wood and none of the padding had been put in.

I wanted to check on them but the electrician was waiting for me. He showed me the new lights in the hall and bathrooms and handed me his bill. I told him I'd write a check. He said he'd rather have cash. I went up to the office to get it out of the safe and found that Connie had our account books spread out on the desk.

"He already told me he wanted cash," she said. "How much is it?"

I gave her the bill. She read it and shrugged. Could've been worse. She counted out the money from the box. "Make sure he signs your copy."

He did, then wrote "paid in full" and asked when I would be reopening. He'd been telling his wife about this great place and he wanted her to see what he'd done. I fished a card out of my vest pocket.

"Reopening depends on these guys," meaning the upholsterers. "I'm hoping for Friday but call first. Marie Therese, what do you think? Friday?"

"I don't know." She looked over at Frenchy. He was frowning, this was supposed to be his guy. She said, "The one who's in charge said he had to go to check on another job. That was before lunch. Haven't seen him since."

Needs an advance to get started and then he disappears. Just like Petey Beck. "Frenchy, I'm going to be in the office the rest of the afternoon. Let me know as soon as this joker gets back and don't let him leave."

A little before five, Connie picked up the earpiece of the telephone and dialed the McAlpin Hotel. I was next to her.

"Hotel McAlpin switchboard. How may I direct your call?"

"Concierge."

A few seconds later. "Concierge. This is Mr. Reeves."

"Mr. Reeves, this is Mrs. Witherspoon." She was using her boss woman's voice. "I'm calling to make sure that all is in order for Professor Patterson's arrival this evening and his stay in the Herald Suite."

"One moment… I'm afraid I don't see—"

"You're to send a car to meet the *Olympic* when it berths at the Cunard-White Star pier this evening. If you cannot confirm that, I must speak to your supervisor immediately."

"Please, Mrs. Witherspoon, I just need to find, yes, here it is. Yes, the Herald Suite in the four-room configuration and I see we have a second reservation on the women's floor for Mr. Patterson's secretary—"

"That's *Professor* Patterson, and I believe his secretary, Miss DeMille requested a suite herself." Connie winked at me. She was having a terrific time.

"I don't see that here but I'm sure it can be arranged."

"Yes, it certainly can be arranged, you'll see to that, I'm sure, and now about the car."

"Oh, yes, I see *Olympic* is to arrive at eight. The driver will be there, you can be sure of that."

"Of course I can. I've checked with the White Star Line. They expect deboarding to begin around eight-thirty. If anything goes wrong, you can be sure that your manager, Mr. Woelfe, will hear about it."

She cradled the earpiece, smiling.

"Mr. Woelfe? Is that really the manager?" The way she said the name, it was something between "waffle" and "woeful."

"Oh yes, I looked it up. Are you ready to eat? I'm starving."

I hadn't been hungry until she said that, but it was enough.

"Phillippe's working tonight. I'll go to the kitchen and see what he can put together for us. And take a look at this. What do you think of Miss DeMille's outfit?"

When she stood, I saw that she was wearing a severe brown blouse that buttoned up to her throat and black skirt that came down to her ankles. She put on a black jacket, a pair of round glasses with black frames, and some kind of soft black hat that covered her ears and most of her hair.

"Isn't it hideous," she said. "It's almost as bad as that damned black gunny sack Mrs. Pennyweight made me wear. I've also got an umbrella. David and Bernard's collection is wonderful."

"It's pretty bad, all right, and nobody's going to recognize you."

"That's the idea." She took off the jacket and unbuttoned the collar of the blouse before she went upstairs.

My corduroy professor's outfit was in a suit bag, but I didn't want to put it on until I had to. Instead, I took the gun cleaning kit from the safe, and got the .25 automatic that Connie kept in the desk drawer. It was a Browning that fit easily in a vest pocket or a small handbag. I couldn't remember the last time it had been fired, so I took it apart and cleaned and oiled it. I took six bullets out of the clip, wiped them with the rag and reloaded the clip. I was about to do the same with the Walther I'd been carrying when I heard something loud down in the bar. Looked through the Venetian blinds and there was the tall upholsterer. Frenchy had pushed him up against a wall and was yelling in his face. I couldn't hear what he was saying, but I knew what he was doing.

I took a couple of minutes to reassemble the pistols and put hers back in the drawer before I went downstairs. I tried not to look angry, just not to be screwed with. The tall upholsterer was twisting his fedora. He kept looking at Frenchy and then at me and then at my stick like he didn't know who he should be talking to.

"Mr. Quinn, I've got to apologize, I didn't really know who you was and how important this is to you. I will have a full crew here first thing tomorrow. This was just a misunderstanding on my part. Now that Frenchy's explained everything, and I mean I should've known, but I promise you we will finish by Friday morning, maybe Thursday."

I didn't say anything, just looked directly at Frenchy until the tall guy said, "Friday, I promise. You'll be open for the weekend."

As I went back up the stairs, I could hear the guy still pleading with Frenchy.

Connie had a couple of Phillippe's hamburgers on French bread, more salad with that good gray dressing and a pot of coffee. We dug in. Between bites, she asked what had been going on downstairs.

"Frenchy told his upholsterer who I am."

"Did he do the big-time gangster routine? You have personally killed a dozen men, bodies buried under the basement, and you know where this guy lives?"

I nodded. Frenchy can be convincing. I do have a reputation and I'm not afraid to use it. But the truth is that everything I'd been doing that day, coming down hard on Petey Beck and then with the upholsterer, all that was because I was confused about everything that had been happening since Fat Joe was killed. And to top it off, I was about to do something that made less and less sense as I thought about it. Connie and I had talked for more than an hour late last night and into this morning, not arguing just trying to come up with something else that might work better.

"What we're about to do is nuts," I said.

"Probably, but we have to do it. Right now, getting this place open again is more important to you than finding who killed Fat Joe, but you've got to do something about him. We all do. Yes, he was a son of a bitch but he was one of us."

"And for now, we can figure that the four guys who busted up the place are the same guys who killed Fat Joe. The Bureau man says they're Nazis and he says that the McAlpin has been full of Nazis since the Great War, and Dr. Griebl has an office there, so there's a chance that if I look around, I may learn something about what's going on and who they are."

She grinned. "It almost sounds reasonable when you say it like that. And there's something else. I know you think you've got the Bureau man dancing to your tune, but he's smart and he's persistent. Once he gets you to sign something, he's got you where he wants you."

"Hell will freeze over before I sign anything. I'm worried that I'm going to be wasting my time and money at the McAlpin when I should be here."

Connie said, "Don't worry. Frenchy and Marie Therese can take care of the rest of everything we need to reopen. We go to the McAlpin for a few days, find out what we can, and you stay out of trouble."

Chapter Thirty-eight

While we were getting ready for the McAlpin, Arch was on the receiving end of a sales pitch for the East River Yacht Club from Harold Henninger. He'd told Henninger he'd be there at six. Showed up at the Sutton Place building late, just before seven. When he told the doorman that Mr. Middleford was there to meet Mr. Henninger, the doorman touched his cap and said, "Yes, sir, we've been waiting you. I believe Mr. Henninger is in the Club Room. Through the lobby and up the stairs to your right."

As lobbies go, the River Club's was large. It was carpeted with two elevators, the doorman's desk and a wall full of mailboxes. Straight ahead was a hallway. To the right, three steps led up to the Club Room. As he expected, it was wood-paneled with paintings of boats on the walls. Most of the light in the murky room came from the little electric bulbs over the paintings. Henninger was sitting with a group of men when he saw Arch. He downed his drink and left them. Even in the dim light, Arch got the idea the guys were happy to see him go.

"Glad you could make it, Middleford. Let me buy you a drink." He turned and held up two fingers to the bartender. "Did'ya have any trouble finding this pile of bricks? No? Good. Here, cut the dust."

Arch made sure to splash a bit of the whiskey as he took the glass. Henninger didn't notice.

"As I recall, the other night you said you'd taken a look at the River Club. Didn't fancy it. Good man."

"Fine view, all right, but who'd want to live with that lot of tight-assed snobs?"

"Certainly not me. I could buy and sell half of 'em but they'd never let me in. Here, let me show you the dock."

They walked to the far end of the bar. Wide windows and glass doors opened onto the terrace and a wide wooden dock. Henninger opened the doors and they walked out. In the dusk he couldn't tell how many boats he was looking at, but there were a lot of them, sleek wooden motor boats and bigger ones with tall masts, bumping against their moorings when a commercial boat rumbled past.

"My *Golden Mean*'s over there," Henninger said as he struggled to light a cigarette in the wind. "You can't really see her from here. That's Welfare Island in front of us and the Queensboro Bridge over there. Not much of a view from here but to be this close to the water and to be able to get out into the harbor so easily—that's the ticket."

"If you say so, what's the rest of the place like?"

They went back inside and Henninger led him through the formal dining room, the café, the pool, the tennis courts, the baths, the saunas, the ballroom. The place had all the amenities you'd expect of one that catered to men who had a lot more money than they needed and wanted to spend it on themselves. Being only a year old, it still smelled of fresh carpets, paint and polish. Arch was carefully disinterested.

"We have a full staff, of course, 24-hour service, but one doesn't want too many of them around upon occasion. That's why we have self-service elevators with automatic floor leveling. Not need to worry about stumbling over a threshold or plummeting down an empty shaft if one should be in his cups," accompanied by a hearty chuckle.

"There are some model apartments but let me show you mine."

"Why not?"

They took a floor-leveling elevator to one of the upper floors. It opened onto a short hall that led to two longer halls. Henninger led the way to a door that he opened without a key. *Doesn't keep his apartment locked? How can we use that?*

For a New York apartment, it was something Arch had never seen on this side of a movie screen. The room was wide and high-ceilinged. Polished parquet floor, new and unscratched. A few over-sized sofas and armchairs. Ornate lighted cabinet serving as a bar. Curtains opened on a glass wall and terrace. Henninger splashed whiskey into two glasses and motioned Arch to one of the armchairs.

"I think this is what I've been looking for," Arch said as he took the drink.

Henninger collapsed into a chair. "Really? I'd got the idea just now that you weren't taken by our little establishment."

Arch sighed, to give what he said next the proper emotion. "To be honest, Henninger, the idea of buying a place, here or anywhere really, is my final admission that the wild days are over. I'm finally settling down, like everyone's been telling me for years. I'm going to become… respectable, God I hate that word."

Henninger's eyes narrowed. *Maybe he bought it*, Arch thought. "You may be misjudging us, Middleford. Speaking for myself and several other members that I know well, we are not entirely respectable and we never will be. What line of business were you in?"

"Spent most of my time in India and the Orient. Toward the end, I invested heavily in jute, of all things. We did so much better than we'd hoped that I saw the writing on the wall. I didn't completely trust my partners. They were ready to invest everything we'd made in the emerald trade with the King of Afghanistan. I took my share, and a bit more if you must know, and bid them goodbye. They were not pleased."

Arch stood and walked to the windows overlooking the river. Henninger followed and clapped a meaty paw on Arch's shoulder. "You'll fit in here just fine, Middleford. In fact, I'm putting together a small investment opportunity that might be just the thing to keep you from sliding into respectability. Think you might be interested?"'

Arch shrugged away from the man's mitt and made a dismissive wave. "First, can you arrange a meeting with the management or the membership committee, if that's how things are done, and we'll get the damned process started."

"Of course. Let's say tomorrow at eleven. Afterward we can have lunch."

Arch tapped his glass with Henninger's. "Excellent idea. My treat."

Chapter Thirty-Nine

Professor Patterson put on his ugly corduroy suit and bow tie. Connie helped me with the wig, mustache, and make-up. When I was done, she called down to the bar and told Marie Therese to come to the office. When Marie Therese saw me, she had the same startled reaction that Connie had. Figure if I could fool somebody who knew me as well as she did, I might be able to pull this off.

Frenchy drove us over to the White Star pier a little after eight. It was dark by then and traffic was heavy with cars and taxis jockeying for space near the big arch in the middle of the row of piers. Frenchy got close enough to hail a stevedore. They haggled over the price, Frenchy making it clear we did not want the trunk to be moved onto the ship. Just put it right inside the big doors. We could see the smokestacks and the lights of the massive ship as it turned toward the dock.

At first, I imagined everybody was looking at me funny. They weren't, but I still felt naked standing there without my stick. As long as I had the brace properly strapped on, I could stand and walk fine, but that was all I could do. I had my knucks in my pocket and the Walther in the steamer trunk. After Frenchy left, Connie walked around inside the terminal. I stayed with the bags. The most convenient part of the parking area in front of the piers was reserved for hired cars. A few were waiting there and over the next half hour, it filled up. Liveried drivers got out of their cars and gathered at one side where they smoked and talked. As we waited, the sounds of the ship coming in to dock got louder—men yelling, tugboat engines, whistles, horns. A few minutes after that, the drivers all seemed to know that passengers were about to start coming out because they produced printed signs and little chalk boards with names on them.

Connie came up beside me and said in a low voice. "The McAlpin driver is here, but we don't want to be first."

When the crowd got thicker, I found another stevedore who put the trunk on a cart and out we went. Connie hurried ahead and raised her umbrella to the driver holding our sign. His car was a long Buick with a rack on the back big enough for a couple of steamer trunks. He unfolded it, loaded the trunk and suitcase, then held the door open for me. You could've put six people in the back seat.

He maneuvered the big car smartly out the parking area and said refreshments were available in the bar. There was a snazzy looking wooden cabinet behind him between the jump seats. I might've tried it but I'd have to crawl across the floorboard. I just sat there and kept messing with the glasses that felt strange on my face until Connie told me to stop it. The drive took about fifteen minutes and somehow the familiar streets looked different from the back seat of a limousine, and that's when I realized how ridiculous this whole idea was. I was on a fool's errand.

The driver stopped at the main entrance on Thirty-Fourth Street. The bellhops recognized the hotel's car and had the trunk and Connie's suitcase loaded onto a cart as we were getting out. The driver tipped his hat and said, "Have a pleasant stay, Professor Patterson." I slipped him a buck. The bellman tipped his hat, too, and told us to follow him. We went down a long wide marble hall lined with potted palms and such to the lobby. The last time I'd been in that hall, a week ago following Dr. Griebl, I thought I'd been there before. Now I remembered what it was, not specifically, but I was sure that Rothstein had played a big card game there, one of those that went on for more than a day. I was nine or ten, probably. It was a crowded room, like all of them, thick with cigar smoke, alcohol, and sweaty bodies. In games like that, there was never a chair for me. If any of the men who were watching the game wanted a seat, they took mine. I tried to find corners with enough light that I could read the funny pages. I was supposed to stay small, keep to the edge of the room, out of the way. Until A. R. called me. Then, I'd spring up and snake my way to the table as fast as I could. Don't make A. R. frown and say, 'Where is that damn kid.' The memory made my stomach churn.

The bellman led us away from the main registration desks to one without a sign that had two big leather chairs facing it. The guy at the desk stood quickly and buttoned his coat when he saw the bellman approaching.

"I trust you had a pleasant crossing, Professor Patterson. I'm Mr. Reeves, please have a seat." An older guy, balding and not trying to hide it. He had one of those smooth voices that made you think nothing was ever too much for him to handle. "If you need anything while you're with us, don't hesitate to call. I'm sure that I or any of the concierges can assist you. Now, if you'd please sign this." He slid a registration card across the desk and handed me a fountain pen.

As I started to sign, I realized that I didn't know what my first name was supposed to be so I just scrawled something short and then a messy Patterson. "Does my secretary need to register, or will this do for both of us?"

He noticed Connie. "Yes, Miss DeMille, I have your key, too, but could you stop by the ladies' reception room up on the mezzanine at your convenience and let them know that I've checked you in? You'll also find the ladies' restaurant and library on the mezzanine. Your room—I see it's a suite—is on the ladies' floor. That's number six.

"Professor, your suite is on the seventh floor. Here's your key, A-717. During the busiest hours, there may be long waits for elevators, but Miss DeMille can use the stairs without too much difficulty."

He snapped his fingers and another bellboy appeared. He gave the kid Connie's key and said, "Take Miss DeMille's bag to room A-625." They headed across the lobby.

"Now, Professor Patterson, I understand that you'll be working with a legal firm on an important matter. We've taken the liberty of placing a typewriter and a separate telephone line in one of your rooms. If you need anything else… well, you know. The gentlemen's floor is the twenty-second. It has a bar and there's a gentlemen's lounge on the twenty-third. If you haven't eaten, there's another restaurant on this side of the lobby."

I nodded and followed the bellhop with the trunk. That time of night, the lobby didn't look to me to be too busy. Guys drinking and smoking and reading newspapers in comfortable-looking stuffed chairs. We walked past them to the elevators where I'd seen Dr. Griebl. Seemed like a lot longer than a week. On the way, I dropped a couple of pennies in the coffee can at a newsstand for the late edition of the *Times*. The area in front of the elevators wasn't crowded. When the car arrived, the bellhop told the operator seven.

The hotel was really three towers with air shafts between them. My suite was in the central tower, at the end of the hall, overlooking Broadway.

The halls seemed dim and narrow, but I was comparing them to the Chelsea, or maybe I remembered the long day and night with Rothstein. When we got to 717, the bellhop opened the door and asked me where I wanted the trunk, bedroom or there in the parlor. I said bedroom and got rid of another buck. Yeah, I was overtipping but it figured I'd be asking for some favors and I wanted the staff to spread the word. The bedroom had a double bed, a good radio, and a dresser beside a massive wardrobe. There was another radio in the parlor. Both rooms had wide windows with blinds and heavy curtains. Two sofas, four armchairs, two tables. A connecting door opened to one office, and another connecting door from it led to the second office. As promised, there was a typewriter, a stack of Hotel McAlpin stationery and another of plain typing paper, carbon paper, manila folders, and pads of lined paper.

I called the hotel operator and asked for room 616. Connie didn't answer. Figure she'd decided to look around. After all, that was the idea. We were both going to look for Dr. Griebl, the Nazi thugs, and anyone else we recognized in this "nest of spies." I was planning to do a little more than that. Among the items I'd bought from retired Detective First Bob Sallie, now the McAlpin boss house dick, was a list of all the businesses that were based in the hotel, and a copy of a pass key. It wouldn't open every door but it would get me through most of them. But not just then. I picked up my newspaper and took the elevator up to the Twenty-Second floor.

When the doors opened, I could hear a bar down a hall to my left. Walking toward it, I passed a pair of wide glass doors with a sign that said it was The Army & Navy Club. The place was closed but I could see that it was a comfortable-looking lounge with more of the overstuffed leather armchairs, tables, and what appeared to be a small bar at the back. Sign on the door listed the buffet hours and said it was for officers and members of the diplomatic corps only. What had Turcot said? Griebl was trying to get something from an Army officer about Fort Totten? Maybe worth looking into.

The gentlemen's bar had a vaulted blue ceiling and boxy chandeliers. The marble floor had a wildly colorful pattern. A right-angle bar took up almost a quarter of the room. It was made of scarred walnut, in need of refinishing. Behind it, there was room for five bartenders to work. That Tuesday night, all of them were busy. It was a much nicer place than the one down in the basement by the Marine Grill. Livelier, too. Most of the tables were filled. The bar babble sounded friendly, and there was not much room at the brass rail. I slipped in beside two guys who were discussing the Cardinals' chances in the Series and hailed the closest bartender. Double Teeling on ice. This bar had it. When he brought the drink, he asked if I was staying at the hotel. I showed him my key. He noted the room number on the check and I slid another dollar across the bar. That was about as much as the whiskey cost. "Keep it," I said. "I'm going to find a table. Bring me another one in about twenty minutes."

"Sure. Thank you, Mr...?"

"Patterson."

As I crossed the room, I tried to see if anybody was paying extra attention to me. Nobody was. I guess the disguise was working. I was another short, middle-aged guy in a bad suit who looked like he was from out of town, like every other guy there. I sat where I could see most of the bar, opened the paper and tried to look like I was reading as I focused on individual faces. No Griebl, no blond thugs. The Teeling was excellent. I started with the Lindbergh news on the front page.

New Jersey authorities said they were planning to charge Hauptmann with murder and kidnapping, for the crimes he committed there, before the New York indicted him on extortion, based on the ransom paid in the city. Part of the decision depended on what the wood expert found out. But as long as New York had him, Representative Samuel Dickstein was trying to find a connection between Hauptmann and Nazi propaganda. And while all of that was going on, three middle-aged women jumped over a fence that surrounded the Morrow estate in New Jersey where Lindbergh and his family were staying. The gals were immediately set upon by Thor, the 200-pound police dog Col. Lindbergh bought to protect his young second son, Jon. A gateman rescued the ladies but not before Thor had shredded their clothes.

I was down to melting ice when the bartender appeared with another drink. "Here you go, Mr. Patterson. How long do you plan to be with us."

"Three or four days. Not sure."

"I'm Terrence. I'll be on this shift for the rest of the week. If you need anything, just ask."

A few minutes later, I was about to fold up my paper and take a look at the rest of the floor when two guys in black suits walked in, having a serious conversation. They went straight to a table near the bar, talking all the while. I knew one of them and thought I knew the other. Terrence ducked under the bar, hustled straight to their table, and took an order. He brought back two glasses of dark liquor. The two men continued talking. Actually, the shorter of the two was doing all the talking. The other one was listening and it looked like he didn't care for what he was hearing.

The listener was Bob Sallie, number one house dick. It had probably been six or seven years since I'd delivered an envelope to him. He'd been on Rothstein's payroll and Lansky and Charlie Luciano had fairly regular dealings with him after Rothstein was killed. He was a big guy, big the way a lot of cops are big, and he'd earned a reputation as a man who understood departmental politics down to the smallest detail and knew how to play them. That's why he'd been able to retire early and take a cushy job at the McAlpin.

The second guy was Romeo Forlini, the forger who was in on a big job with Petey Beck, or so Petey claimed. I'd seen Forlini a few times with Rothstein when I first went to work for him. At the time, Forlini was hawking Liberty Bonds. The guy I remembered from twelve, thirteen years ago looked a lot like the guy sitting with Sallie. Black, receding hair, talked with his hands, big schnoz, kind of pop-eyed. The more I looked, the more I was sure it was him. What did that mean? Figure Forlini was hoping to run some kind of con operation in the hotel and was negotiating the size of Sallie's cut. But if that's what it was, he wasn't getting anywhere. Sallie wasn't buying.

I left as the bar started emptying.

Chapter Forty

"CALL ME"

That was the note folded in my door. I told the hotel operator to get me room 616. Connie answered on the first ring. When I heard the click of the operator disconnecting, I said I was back. Connie hung up without saying anything. I unlocked the door, and she came in a few minutes later. It was about two in the morning.

She'd left her hat in her room but was still wearing Miss DeMille's heavy outfit that covered everything from her chin to her feet. She shrugged off the jacket and started unbuttoning the blouse as soon as I locked the door. "These clothes are stifling. I don't know how long I can wear these awful things."

She unbuttoned her cuffs, toed off her clunky shoes, and threw the blouse on a chair. The long skirt came next. She sat on the sofa, rolled down her woolen stockings and wiggled her toes. "Oh, that's better." She was wearing one of her good silk slips under Miss DeMille's costume. She looked great in it. After a time, she got up and went through the office rooms.

I said, "Help me with this damn wig. I don't want to mess it up. What's your room like?"

"It's a suite, not as nice as this. Show me the bedroom."

"Right this way."

She pulled open the curtains and raised the blinds to look down on Broadway. Then she examined the bathroom. I shed the Professor's corduroy jacket and bowtie. She told me to sit, then loosened the straps and tabs that tightened the wig, and put it and the silk cap carefully on the dresser. Then she dug her fingers into the muscles at the back of my neck and rendered me speechless.

"What'd you do after you checked in?" I said when I regained the ability to talk.

"I explored the women's floor, but I couldn't tell much. The receptionist said they start serving breakfast at six, but it's not crowded that early. She recommended the French toast and said they're serious about not allowing men on the floor. When I explained that I was working with a gentleman who was also a hotel guest, she said you'd need permission and an escort to come onto the floor."

"But nobody minds your coming here." I tried to pull at one corner of the mustache.

"Don't do that. It looks fine and I'm not sure we could get it back on. What did you do?"

"Went to the men's lounge and saw something I wasn't expecting."

"Yeah?"

"I told you about getting the pass key and the other items from the guy who's the house detective here, Bob Sallie, retired cop."

"On Rothstein's payroll."

"Right, known as a man you can work with if you approach him the right way. He came into the men's lounge tonight, and he was with Romeo Forlini."

"Who's he? I know that name but I can't place it."

"The first time I talked to Petey Beck about creating the phony documents for us, he said he was about to throw in on some big deal that Forlini was putting together. He didn't say what it was but Forlini has been in the hot paper business for years, back to the days of the Liberty Bonds. Rothstein was stealing and reselling legit bonds. Forlini had two cons. First, he'd figured a way to turn a real five-dollar bond of, say, General Motors stock into a seventy-five-dollar bond. He also made his own stock certificates, phony bonds that he forged and sold as the real thing. He spent some time in the federal pen in Atlanta back in the Twenties, and there was talk that he was pardoned by President Hoover, or that he turned down a pardon because he'd've had to leave the country, I don't remember the details if I ever knew them. The point is, even though I couldn't hear what they were saying, it looked to me like Forlini was trying to talk Sallie into something and Sallie was turning him down flat."

"Do you think it has anything to do with us?"

"I can't see how."

"Did they recognize you?"

"No, even without Professor Patterson, I don't think they'd remember what I looked like. I only saw Forlini once or twice, and to Sallie, I was just A. R.'s boy and I almost never dealt with him directly."

While I took off my shoes and trousers, she pulled down the heavy cover on the bed and crawled in. I unstrapped my brace and rubbed my knee. It was stiff because I'd overtightened the straps, and without my stick, I'd been putting more weight on it. The knee caught when I stood up, and I had to grab the edge of the dresser. Connie noticed. "How bad is it? Do you need the stick?"

"I think I'm all right, but I'm going to have to be careful tomorrow. I want to see as much of this place as I can, but I can't walk too far without sitting."

I slid into bed beside her. As soon as my head rested on the pillow, memories of the day rose up and exhausted me. Dealing with the electrician and the upholsterer, going downtown to have it out with Petey Beck, meeting the hotel car at the pier. And finally seeing Bob Sallie and Romeo Forlini together. I was going to say something more about that, but when I rolled over to tell her, she was already asleep.

Connie was gone when I woke up about eight o'clock Wednesday morning. That was early for me but then, ever since the Nazi thugs busted up my place, my normal sleep schedule had been shot. When we were working, most nights Connie and I would go to bed around three in the morning, and get up sometime in the afternoon, one of us usually an hour or so before the other, depending on what each of us had to do that day. That morning at the McAlpin, Connie had left a note on the dresser. BREAKFAST IN THE MEZZANINE CAFE 9:00.

I washed up, shaved, and put on a fresh shirt. Another sloppy bow tie, then the silk cap and the gray wig. I took time to get the brace right, not too tight, and finally, Professor's Patterson's baggy corduroys and glasses. When I saw my reflection in the mirror, I had to shake my head, I looked so awful. I gathered some of the office supplies the hotel had provided, and rode the elevator down the Mezzanine.

The café was packed and noisy, almost all men, so I spotted Connie straightaway. They'd given her probably the worst two-top in the place. I made my way through tightly packed tables, and found her finishing her French toast. I sat and poured a cup of coffee from the carafe on the table.

Connie said, "What are we—" and stopped when a waiter showed up. I ordered two scrambled, rye toast and salami. They didn't have any salami. Made it sausage.

When he left, Connie said," What are we going to do today?" Kept her voice low enough that the guys closest to us couldn't hear her.

"I want to get an idea of what goes on in this place. Several businesses have offices here, mostly on the lower floors. Griebl's office is B-477. Figure that's the central tower. We want to see that first. Then I'm thinking we should each take a floor and walk the halls looking for anything that seems out of place for a big hotel."

"What do you mean by that?"

"I don't know. Whatever strikes you as unusual. I've got a couple of lined pads and manila folders. If nothing else, we look like we're doing some kind of legitimate business, not just loitering around the joint."

She nodded. "I can't go to any of the men's floors, and you can't go on the sixth, and the sixteenth is called the 'sleepy sixteenth' because it's reserved for guys who work the night shift, and they keep it quiet during the day."

The waiter brought my breakfast.

Connie said, "I think one of us should go back to the bar to see how Marie Therese is doing. After the way Frenchy braced the upholsterer, I doubt he'd try to pull anything, but I want to be sure everything is right before we try to reopen."

"Agreed."

"And it doesn't make any sense for Professor Patterson to go back. I can catch a cab this afternoon and be back in a couple of hours."

"O.K." I signed the check. "I'll go up the men's floor, take a look at the baths and the rooftop lounge, and work my way down. You start here on the Mezzanine and go up. We'll get room service around noon."

She straightened her big soft hat and left. I took the stairs down to the lobby and bought two or three papers. Instead of going up to the top of the building, I told the elevator operator to let me off at the fourth floor where I found Griebl's office. The sign on the pebbled glass door read: Dr. Ignatz Griebl—By Appointment Only. It looked to be a large office. The two doors on either side had smaller signs reading Please Use Main Entrance with arrows pointing to the first door. There were other offices on that corridor, none of them open. I checked to be sure there was nobody else around and tried the passkey. It didn't work.

After that, I went up to the top floors and followed the plan. I walked slowly through each wing, acting like I didn't know exactly what I was doing. A few bellboys and most managers asked if I needed help, and I told them the truth. No, I don't need any help, I'm here on business and I'm having a look around. I took the stairs from one floor to the one below it, leaning heavily on the handrail and moving slow. As the morning went on, traffic in the halls picked up. More maids cleaning rooms, meal deliveries on covered rolling carts, residents hurrying off to work, bellboys mostly empty-handed but several carrying telegrams on small trays. Whenever the strain got to my knee, I'd find a place to sit and make useless notes of what I'd seen on a lined pad. By lunchtime, I was exhausted and I felt like I'd accomplished nothing. It was the same with Connie. Neither of us saw Griebl or the woman who got handsy with him under the table or any of the blond Nazi thugs.

After a quick lunch, she went to her room and changed into regular clothes, not Miss DeMille's sack and none of her traffic-stopping Paris outfits either, and took a cab back to Jimmy's Place. I checked all of the eating spots and lounges from the Marine Grill in the basement to the men's lounge on the twenty-third floor. There were about a dozen of them, including the Army & Navy Club. I saw a few blond guys, but none of them were the ones I was looking for. I went by Griebl's office three times. There was some activity in the other offices on that floor, but no sign of anything in his. By four o'clock I decided I was tired of wasting my time and my knee was throbbing, so I went back to my room, took off the wig, unstrapped the brace and found dance music on the radio. Then I settled down to read the latest Hauptmann news.

Most of it concerned who was going to put him on trial first, New Jersey or New York. Since the ransom had been paid in the Bronx, the D.A. there was ready to file extortion charges, but the governor of New Jersey announced that they had enough evidence to charge Hauptmann with kidnapping and murder within a couple of weeks. Who was going to go first?

Another item down at the bottom of the first page caught my attention. The headline read: ***Thief Terrifies the People of Bridgeport By Stealing 20 Pounds of High Explosives.***

The story said that somebody broke into the Remington Arms U.M.C. munitions plant by sawing off a lock. He stole twenty pounds of something called "polnol, the most powerful and dangerous explosive known." One pound was as powerful as a ton of black powder, and the stuff that had been stolen could demolish several city blocks. It was packed in pea green boxes with black rubber caps. The boxes were covered with oilcloth. In its pure form, the stuff was so touchy that any disturbance would set it off. This batch had been mixed with a stabilizer that made it almost as safe as dynamite or T.N.T.

When Connie got back, she said we were almost ready to reopen. The reupholstered booths weren't exactly what he'd described but they were better than they'd been before. I'd be happy with them. But the important news was about the Bureau man, Leo Turcot. He'd called once and come by looking for me. Frenchy told him I was trying to find a particular piece of neon lighting that was going to be behind the bar. Frenchy would have me call him as soon as I got back. "He was pretty steamed, Frenchy said."

"It figures. Why don't you put on your ugly Miss DeMille clothes and I'll take you to dinner at the fancy French place downstairs."

She wrinkled her nose. "I'm not really in the mood for fancy French. Let's get room service so I don't have to change clothes. I'll hide in the bedroom when he brings it."

We were supposed to be wandering around the hotel, but I couldn't disagree with her. I called and ordered the Broiled Guinea Hen with Banana, Sole Bonne Femme, two Baked Potatoes, and Spinach, and a bottle of burgundy. I don't remember what any of it tasted like. Connie said that Phillipe had spoiled us and she was right. After the meal, we talked about what we'd done that day and how little we'd accomplished.

"Let's give it one more round," I said.

"All right, I'll put the damn clothes back on, and I'll mess up the bed, so we don't scandalize the maid. See you back here later. What about you?"

"The same, but I'm going to try the bellboy uniform and the blond wig."

The bellboy uniform was part of the package I'd got from Sallie. The wig was from David and Bernard. By itself, I thought it was maybe the most obvious wig I'd ever seen, but under a bellboy's round cap, it looked all right. The uniform was dark gray with three rows of brass buttons and a black stripe down the side of the pants. Most of the bellboys being kids and teenagers, the fit was as good as it needed to be. Connie helped me unpeel the Professor's mustache and put on the wig before she went back to her room.

I checked myself in the mirror and squared my shoulders. Now I wasn't Professor Patterson who shuffled around, I was an energetic kid who moved quickly and with purpose. First, I went back by Griebl's office just to be sure nothing was going on there at night. It was as quiet as it had been all day. I walked through the halls I'd missed earlier. That time of night, nothing was going on. I stayed away from the public rooms where I might come across a manager who'd want me to do something. Not that it mattered. My evening rounds were as pointless as the rest of the day.

That was about to change.

Chapter Forty-One

On Wednesday, Arch went back to the East River Yacht Club. The doorman said, "Good morning, Mr. Middleford. Mr. Henninger asked that I tell our General Manager, Mr. Kingman when you arrived. If you'd like, you can go directly to his office. It's the first door on your left down the hall. I'll let him know you're here."

Curious, Arch thought. This isn't the man who was on duty last night and he knows who I am on sight.

As Arch walked down the hall, a man in a good suit stepped out of an office and extended his hand. "Mr. Middleford, I'm Miles Kingman. Good to see you." He was comfortably plump with one of those drawling Brit accents that set Arch's teeth on edge. He ignored the hand. Kingman withdrew it and continued without missing a beat, "Mr. Henninger told me he has shown you around but I'm sure you still have some questions."

"Can you show me the apartments that are available now?"

"Of course, just a moment, let me get the keys."

Arch followed him into his office. A younger man was typing at the secretary's desk. Kingman went past him into a larger office and reappeared a moment later. "Edward," he said to the young man, "I'll be showing Mr. Middleford 311, 405 and 556. Have the floorplans ready for him to examine when we've seen the units."

Edward nodded without looking up from his work. In the elevator Kingman continued his pitch—these are among our best apartments, I'm surprised they haven't been snatched up, actually one of them was but the buyer ran into some unexpected headwinds. Arch nodded and said yes when he was expected to.

All of the apartments were laid out on the same lines as Henninger's, but they weren't as large and the ceilings were lower. After they'd been through them, Arch said he'd take the two-bedroom. Kingman, an experienced salesman who knew when to shut up and get a signature on a contract, led the way back to his office. He told Edward to stop what he was doing and draw up a contract on 405. He ushered Arch into his office and said there were a few details they needed to go over. Arch endured about twenty minutes of the club's rules, initiation fees, and the like before Henninger banged open the door without knocking.

"We're going to be neighbors then, Excellent! Let's celebrate."

Kingman started to protest until Arch told him to finish drafting the papers. He'd want his lawyers—damn their eyes—to go over them, of course, but he'd come back to pick them up later that afternoon, and he'd be happy to leave an "earnest money" deposit if that would grease the gears. Kingman wanted a signature but he knew better than to argue when Henninger said that would be fine, and besides, he was hungry.

"Remember, this one is on me," Arch said. "Have you been to Keen's lately?"

Henninger beamed.

His Caddy and driver were waiting in front of the building. It took about twenty minutes to reach the restaurant. As they got out of the car, Henniger said to the driver, "We'll probably be a couple of hours."

The driver said, "Tell them I'll be in the usual lot."

Henninger ignored the crowd that was gathered around the front door and went straight inside where another crowd of men waiting for tables was even thicker. As soon as the maître 'd saw him, he snapped his fingers and beckoned them forward. The crowd parted. Henninger said, "Is the smaller room available?"

"Of course, sir. Right this way. Will you need menus?"

Henninger shook his head and they followed a waiter through the tables in the main room with the ceiling of clay pipes to a set of stairs at the back. They went up to the second floor, then down a short hall to a dark paneled room with heavy velvet drapes over the window, and a six-top covered by a white tablecloth.

Harold said, "I'll have a Manhattan. What about you, Middleford?"

"Jameson."

The waiter hurried away.

Henninger said, "I love this place but if you want to have any kind of private conversation, it's impossible in any of the larger rooms. Of course, I know most of the men here so we'd be constantly interrupted, and anyone close to us would be listening in hoping to pick up a 'hot tip,' as if I deal in such things these days."

"You have a big reputation on Wall Street, do you?"

Henninger chuckled. "It's wildly overstated but the truth is I have something of a gift for predicting trends and I've been lucky."

The waiter returned with their drinks. Henninger slurped down half of his Manhattan and said, "Another before we order." He looked at Arch. "You?"

Arch shook his head. After the waiter left, he said, "I've asked around about you and from what I've heard, it's more than luck."

Henninger tried to look modest. "I've been on the Street a long time. I know something of how it works, and so it's mostly a matter of recognizing the right moment to take the right risk. For example, how did you so quickly decide to join the East River Club. Have you lost your fear of respectability?"

Arch shook his head. "I keep telling myself that this is the right thing to do. It makes sense financially, and it's exactly what Constance wants. It's time to listen to my head, not my heart. I'm sure any sensible businessman would agree."

"I do agree but I think you're wrong to assume that you don't have to listen to your heart anymore. In fact, I think it's unhealthy to deny a vital part of your personality just because you're becoming older."

He found a cigarette and took his time lighting it before he went on. "I believe I mentioned that I'm involved with an enterprise that might interest you. Tomorrow, I'm meeting with my partners, my possible partners I should say. Let's have drinks later this week. I'll be able to tell you more then. Whether you say yes or no, I'm sure you'll be intrigued."

The waiter returned with Henninger's drink. "We'd best order, then. I suppose you're going to have the mutton?"

The joint was famous for its mutton chop. Arch said, "No. I've had so much bad mutton that I've lost all taste for it. I'll have the T-bone and the sautéed spinach."

"Good man. I'll have the same and what do you say we start off with some clams?"

Chapter Forty-Two

Professor Patterson and Mrs. DeMille spent Thursday wandering through the Hotel McAlpin, and we didn't do any better than we'd done the day before. After another room service lunch, Connie was so fed up, she changed into street clothes and said she was going back to Jimmy's Place, "to do something productive."

"Before I left yesterday, Frenchy and Marie Therese and I talked it over. We don't see any reason that we can't reopen on Friday. But you've got to be there. The regulars will ask too many questions if you're not." She was right. "Do you really think you're going to find anything here?"

"I saw Forlini and Sallie together."

"And what does that mean? Nothing. Admit it, Jimmy, this was a long shot and it didn't pay off."

I tried to find a way to disagree with her. "All right, let's say this. You three make sure that everything really is ready, then put a sign on the door saying that the Grand Reopening is tomorrow at five. I'll take one more crack at my longshot this afternoon and tonight. I don't come up with anything, we check out tomorrow. Dammit."

She grabbed Professor Patterson and gave him a long kiss. "You've got to get rid of this stupid mustache. It itches and tickles."

"Don't I know it."

She left and I went back to checking the bars, lounges, and restaurants for blond thugs. I kept at it until four o'clock when I decided it made more sense to wait where it was likely that they'd come past me. I found an armchair in the lobby near the elevators and pretended to read my papers. As the afternoon foot traffic picked up, I scanned the crowd, paying extra attention for beefy blond thugs. I didn't see any, but I did see Kate Moog, Dr. Griebl's big blonde girlfriend with the friendly hands. Finally.

She wore a steel gray suit with a tight skirt and jacket, a silk blouse with a high stiff collar, and a small hat pinned to her hair. She carried a large flat purse tucked under her right arm as she strode toward the elevators, not paying attention to anyone around her. I stood when she went past and maneuvered through the crowd to stay right behind her. One elevator was closing when we reached the cars. Two were opening. People hurried toward them. I stayed close. As the car filled, people called out floors to the operator. She said "Four."

She was the first person off at four. I followed and saw her opening her bag and reaching for her keys as she walked down the hall. By then, there was considerable activity in the other offices. She unlocked the door to B-477, Griebl's office, and went inside. I strolled down the hall slowly like I wasn't sure what I was looking for. I didn't have to wait long. A few seconds later, she came back out of the office with a long white cardboard tube under her arm. She carefully locked the door, and still moving quick, she went back to the elevators but walked past them to the next wing of rooms. I stayed several yards behind and saw her reaching into her bag again. She went all the way down the hall to the big suite at the end, overlooking Broadway and Sixth Avenue. It was A-417, three floors directly below mine. She unlocked the door and went inside. This time she didn't come right back out.

I worried over how to play it, and decided it was enough for now to know that there was another room involved. I went back down to the lobby, found a chair, and waited. Less than an hour later, Mrs. Moog got off an elevator and walked across the lobby to the Thirty-Fourth Street doors. No long white cardboard tube. I went back up to the fourth floor and down the hall to the second suite. I turned around right away. A pair of maids had a cleaning cart by the open door.

I went back to my rooms and tried to figure my next move. I guess it shows just how poorly planned this whole business was that when it panned out and I discovered that something really was going on there, I didn't know what to do with it. It made no sense to worry over it until I knew what was in the room.

It was full dark by seven. I took off the Professor Patterson wig, mustache, and suit, and put on the bellboy uniform. Again, with the change of clothes I felt like I could do more than the Professor could. What did I need to take with me? I thought about the pistol, but no, I had my knucks.

I found the little pad I used for new words and a small flash lamp that would fit in a pocket. With my blond wig and my little round cap in place, I set off, using the stairs to go down three floors to the fourth. My heart was really starting to hammer then, and I remembered what I always told myself when I got in one of these situations. Don't hurry, don't hesitate. Easy to say.

The maids had finished and there was no one in the hall as I walked to A-417. I knocked on the door and wondered what I'd say if someone opened it. I waited what felt like a full minute, took a deep breath, and fumbled for the pass key, the one that would not open Griebl's office. It was stiff going into the lock and wouldn't turn. But it didn't feel like it had in the office door. I jiggled the key, turned it again slowly, and the lock clicked open. I slipped through the door and closed it behind me. Being in a place I wasn't supposed to be had me jazzed. I forced myself to breathe normally and wiped my sweating hands on my jacket. Calm down, Jimmy. Take it easy. After all, what's a little breaking and entering compared to some of the stuff you've done recently? But, think about it. What are you going to do if somebody comes in?

The maids had left the curtains and blinds open and enough light came in from the street that my eyes adjusted in seconds. The layout of the parlor was the same as mine. Coffee table, sofa, chairs, table, radio. There was a large sheet of white paper on the table by the window. It was weighted down at the corners by ashtrays. I couldn't tell what it was. A drink service was on the coffee table. Glasses, a carafe of water and Griebl's favorite schnapps.

The door to the bedroom was on the left. It was open. Again, the layout was the same as mine. Double bed, low dresser next to a tall massive wardrobe. I took out my flash lamp and checked the inside of the wardrobe. Nothing. Nothing under the bed. There wasn't room for anything. I looked into the bathroom. No personal items there either. I went back to the parlor and tried the door at the other side. Locked. Griebl didn't need the extra room I had. I shined my lamp on the paper on the table. It took me a few seconds to realize it was a map. The lines and lettering were blue, and they were so thin and pale I couldn't make anything of them in the faint light.

I turned it off and had to wait for my night vision to come back. There were three drawers in the table. Empty. I went back into the bedroom and checked the drawers in the dresser. Empty. I was back in the parlor when

I heard the scratching sound of a key in the lock. I went straight back into the bedroom. With my back to the dresser, I put my hands flat on the surface and pushed up with my arms as I jumped and sat on it. Then I twisted and stood and reached up to grab the edge of the crown molding that lined the top of the heavy bureau. If this idea was going to go bad, it would be here. The molding held as I pulled myself up till my shoulders were over the lip, but my weight was enough to tilt the bureau toward the dresser. It hit the dresser with a loud *thunk*, then rocked back. I struggled to shift both hands so I could push myself farther up until I bent at the waist, twisted, and scooted my legs over. Anybody much taller than me wouldn't have had room between the ceiling and the top of the bureau, and if I hadn't spent years wrestling kegs and cases, I wouldn't have been strong enough to pull myself on top of it.

I didn't know how much noise I'd made. I held my breath when the lights went on in the parlor, and I heard sounds of someone moving around. As soon as I took a breath I had to grab my nose to stifle a sneeze. Nobody had dusted the top of that bureau since the day they put it in the room. The light from the parlor came in through the open door. I raised my head far enough to look over the top of the molding. All I could see was a narrow strip of the parlor floor on the other side of the open door.

The person in the other room sounded like he sat, opened a bottle, and poured a drink. Then he stood and moved around. When I heard him coming toward the bedroom, I lowered my head. He went into the bathroom, unbuttoned, and, with a contented sigh, had a long piss. When he finished, he did not wash his hands. Had to be Griebl, but I couldn't risk raising my head. If I could see him, he could see me.

For the next seventy-seven minutes—I checked my watch—we waited.

He drank several glasses of something. Figure it was schnapps not water. Moved around restlessly. Came back into the bathroom and turned on a light. Combed his hair, I think. Went back into the parlor. When I heard footsteps moving away, I raised my head. Still couldn't see anything useful in the parlor. He'd left the bathroom light on. I could see a bit of the tile floor and part of the sink. My looking around ended with a sharp rap on the door. I heard Griebl hurry to it.

He opened the door and clicked his heels. "Herr Oberführer."

A man walked in and I thought I heard him sitting in an armchair. "Relax, Griebl. What have you got to drink?"

"Schnapps."

"Swill. Call room service. Get me a bottle of whiskey." It was Franz Voss.

I heard the snap of a cigarette lighter. "And a bucket of ice cubes , not crushed." He was abrupt, impatient.

"Of course, I'm sorry, Herr Oberführer. I'll see to it right away."

Griebl picked up the telephone and ordered the booze. The answer he got didn't please him and he swore at the guy. Demanded to talk to his boss and raised his voice, almost yelling. He hung up the telephone and said to Voss, "These Americans, they can't do anything right. No discipline. I will have to speak to Katherina. I specifically told her to prepare both schnapps and whiskey. This is not the first time she has failed to follow orders properly."

"Just get the bottle." Voss sounded like he really wanted that drink. "Now what's so important that I had to come back here?"

"I think you will be pleased. We have the maps of Fort Totten. We know precisely where the new anti-aircraft guns are going to be positioned." Griebl was a schoolboy hoping to get a smile from his teacher.

Voss mumbled something I couldn't hear.

The doctor said, "No, you don't understand, we have the full set of maps."

They went back and forth like that for a while, Griebl trying to make the maps sound important and Voss not being impressed. They were still talking when room service knocked on the door. Griebl lit into the kid, wanting to know why it took so long. Sounded like the kid didn't get a tip.

Voss snapped, "Give me the damn bottle," and something about the way he said it let me know he was drunk. Not completely drunk, but on the way. He'd had a couple and was overdue for more. I heard the sounds of two cubes rattling into a glass and a cork being pulled. I doubted that Voss was taking a moment to enjoy the sight of pale whiskey and melting ice commingling. By the sound of it, he knocked the first one back and poured another. This was not the sharp, witty man in Savile Row. I'd never met this one.

"What you have accomplished here is estimable, and the Party appreciates it. Your work has been recognized and now," he paused for a long moment to keep Griebl on edge, "they want to debrief you in Germany. Yes, you and Mrs. Moog are going home. You'll have to think of something to tell your wife. We have tickets for you on the *Europa* to Bremerhaven. You'll meet with Admiral Canaris in Berlin."

"This is such an honor, I don't know what to say, but… but… we're just getting started."

"Events have forced our hand. The Hauptmann arrest changes everything. It is a huge setback and I must tell you, it did not come as a surprise to the Party. The Lindbergh matter has been discussed at the highest levels. We understood that when his child was taken, it made him even more important as a potential ally. He was already a hero and now he had experienced a tragedy beyond comprehension. We agreed that if anyone were apprehended, it would probably be an American gangster, hopefully a Jew gangster. We never dreamed it would be a German national. Nothing could be more damaging to our cause. I know Colonel Lindbergh. We spent almost an hour in conversation at the Embassy. I realized then he could become one of us. He could easily be brought over to our side. He already has a deep mistrust of the Jew, and he has been impressed with the progress Germany has made with our recovery. But as long as he and the Americans identify the kidnapper as a German, we can do nothing."

Voss stood, poured another drink and, by the sound of it, walked around the parlor as he spoke. "We need to take a different, more dramatic approach. Every day that we wait, the situation gets worse and so we must do something now. Something so dramatic, so shocking, so violent that they will forget about Hauptmann. And I have that something." He was quiet for a moment, like he was thinking. Then louder, "It worked at the Reichstag and it will work here, I know it."

Griebl said, "What are you talking about?"

Under his breath, so low I could barely hear him, Voss said, "Bruder was about to tell that damned Bureau man Turcot."

"What?" Griebl missed it. Voss mumbled something.

"I'm sorry, I didn't get that. Has your idea been approved?"

Voss ignored him. After a time, he said, "See me tomorrow. I'll give you the tickets."

They talked for another few minutes. It wasn't important enough for me to remember. It sounded like the meeting ended with a hearty handshake, and Griebl clicking his heels again as Voss left. As soon as he was gone, Griebl picked up the telephone and had the hotel operator dial an outside number. When the other end picked up, he said, "Zusa Muschi, I have wonderful news. Get ready. I'll see you soon."

He hung up and said something to himself in German. Sounded like he was smiling. He knocked back another shot of Schnapps, peed again, and left. I checked my watch and made myself wait five minutes before I moved. When I did, I found that my legs were stiff from being bent in one position for more than two hours. I swung them over the crown molding, and pushed and scooted until my hips were over the edge and I could drop to the dresser. I was half way to the door when I stopped and looked back at the parlor. Griebl had taken the bottle of Schnapps. He left the whiskey and the maps. I took the maps.

Chapter Forty-Three

"What happened to you!"

It was almost midnight. I'd let myself into the suite and Connie was horrified by what she saw.

"What?"

"You're filthy. What have you been doing?"

I saw myself in the mirror on the bedroom door. She was right. The bellboy's uniform was solid gray with dust. More dust and cobwebs on the round cap and wig, dirt on my face. She said, "Take those clothes off in the bathroom. Leave them on the floor. I'll sponge the worst of it off while you take a shower."

"I've been in Griebl's room. I need to write down what I heard while it's fresh."

"After the shower."

"All right. Here, take this."

"What is it?"

"Maps. Call room service. I'm starving."

I felt better after the shower, and I felt even better when I got dressed in my own clothes. No more Professor Patterson. For the moment. The food arrived while I was cleaning up. Over ham sandwiches and potato salad, I told her what had happened from the moment I saw Mrs. Moog. I wrote rough notes as I spoke. Connie's questions helped me with the details I left out. "And he didn't wash his hands."

"That doesn't surprise me, and this Franz Voss, do I know him?"

"You've probably seen him but I don't recall introducing you. Mid-thirties. White hair, not blond. Always dresses well."

Connie said, "I think I know who you're talking about. He's not very tall."

"Right. He usually drops in early for one or two quick ones. Likes to talk. Came to the place before I owned it. If what Turcot says is right, he's the guy who's in charge."

"He ordered those thugs to kill Fat Joe."

"Right."

She thought about that for a few moments. Then, "What are these maps?"

"That's what Griebl has been working on. Turcot said something about a 'honey trap,' where Mrs. Moog or some other fetching fraulein gets frisky with an officer in the service and then gets him to divulge secrets while they're in the sack."

"What are you going to do with all this?"

"I'm not sure. I want two things. First, Turcot off my back, and to do that, I've got to give him something. He's pretty steamed that I disappeared, so he'll show up tomorrow. We'll start with the maps and work from there. Second, I have to be absolutely certain I know who killed Fat Joe. Are we sure it's those four Nazi thugs? Turcot can help me with that."

"Then we're finished here?" she said. I nodded. "Let's go home, Jimmy. As quick as we can. I'm sick of this place. Let's just throw everything in the steamer trunk and have them bring their Buick around."

"No." She was about to object until I said, "Yes, we're going to leave tonight, but we'll do it right. Miss DeMille is going to call the front desk and tell them that Professor Patterson has been called away. The deposit we put down is more than enough to cover the charges. They should prepare a bill and return the rest of our deposit in cash. They won't be able to do that tonight but tell them someone from the lawyer's office will come around tomorrow to pick it up. We don't need the car service, a cab will be fine. Send bellboys to our rooms to collect the bags."

"Why go to all that trouble?"

"Because from the beginning, I wanted to be leave nothing to connect you and me to this hotel. Sure, Ellis knows I got the pass key and the bellboy's uniform from Sallie, but he hates Turcot. Wouldn't give him the time of day if he was under a court order. But Turcot's going to want to know how I got the maps and the rest. Figure it's not hard for the Bureau to take a look at hotel records. They're not going to find my name anywhere and they're not going to find anybody who comes close to matching our descriptions. All they know is that Professor Patterson and Miss DeMille came in from the White Star pier. Charged some meals and drinks. Made no outside telephone calls. Left in a cab. We take a short ride to Penn Station. Change cabs there. If he looks hard enough, he'll suspect it's me but he won't be able to prove it."

Connie leaned back in her chair and gave me a cool look. "You really did think this through."

"I had to. I'm scared of Turcot and the Bureau."

We followed the plan. She called the desk. We put on our Professor Patterson and Miss DeMille duds. Told the bellman out front to have the cab take us a block to Penn Station. Then we caught another one to the Chelsea. We were in bed at three o'clock Friday morning. Getting back to our normal schedule.

I was up by noon and took the Professor Patterson and Miss DeMille clothes back to David and Bernard. Without asking for any details about what we'd done, they wanted to know how well the costumes worked. All I could say was that nobody seemed to question who we were, and I didn't notice anybody looking at the wig like they suspected it was a wig. And Connie hated the Miss DeMille dress. They agreed that it was a crime that a young woman like her ever had to wear such things.

Over a quick breakfast at a diner, I read the Hauptmann news in the papers. The New York cops finally got their hands on Bruno's official criminal record in Germany. It was short but it showed that Hauptmann had some experience.

March 22, 1919, he was charged with burglary, theft, and receiving stolen goods. Guilty on five charges. Sentenced to two years, six months, one week.

March 26, 1919, charged with armed hold-up. Sentenced to two years, six months. Paroled March 30, 1923.

June 12, 1923, arrested on three burglary charges. Escaped June 20.

Give him high marks for effort, but he sure wasn't very good at what he chose to do.

I was walking down Twenty-Second Street and had almost reached the new green canvas awning when a car door opened in front of me and

Leo Turcot got out, hat jammed tight on his head. "Dammit, Quinn, where have you been?" He tried to block the sidewalk. I walked past him.

"Let's talk about that, but first I need to take a look at this. Looks like they did a pretty good job. What do you think?" The new canvas awning may not have been the exact shade of green as the old one, but it was close. And when you looked from it to the top of the stoop and the awning over the door to the Cruzon Grill, you couldn't tell any difference. The white lettering was the same on both of them. If the Bureau man had an opinion, he kept it to himself.

I unlocked the front door, relocked it behind Turcot, and switched on the lights. At first, I couldn't tell much. I went behind the bar and hit those switches and started to see just what they'd done with the new lights. "This is nice, isn't it?" It looked like the electrician had done something more near the ceiling, or maybe I wasn't remembering it right. The ceiling really did look higher, without brightening the room. From behind the bar, it looked larger, more inviting. "There are switches there in the hall in back, turn those on," I said to Turcot, and went around to sit in one of the booths. Looked just as good from there.

The Bureau man stomped over to me acting like he was ready to bite nails in half. I raised a hand. "Don't say anything. You think I've been avoiding you, but I had to get this done before we could reopen. I've been trying to help you in my own way. Here," I held up the rolled maps. "Let's go to my office."

I sat behind my desk. He stayed standing and pacing, trying to make me look up at him. That didn't matter. I moved the lamp, radio, and telephone to the edges of the desk and used them to hold down three corners of the maps. "A couple of weeks ago, you told me that Griebl and his girlfriend Mrs. Moog were setting a 'honey trap' for a General at Fort Totten. Something to do with the placement of anti-aircraft guns. Looks like it worked. Griebl had these maps."

Turcot moved the desk lamp to throw more light on the faint blue lines of the map. He let the first map roll itself up and examined the one beneath it. There were four of them. The markings on all of them were so thin and light I couldn't make out anything.

"How did you get these?"

I ignored that one for the moment. "Griebl called the man he was showing them to 'oberführer.' What does that mean?"

"It's a rank, an important rank in the SS. What's going on? How did you get these?"

"Somebody left them lying around. I thought you might be interested."

Turcot said, "I'm interested, all right. I had these maps drawn up, and I made sure that the General had access to them. Now how did you get them?"

"Let's just say that Dr. Griebl can be careless at times."

"No more screwing around, Quinn. What's going on?"

I shook my head. "Now it's your turn. Who killed Fat Joe and how do I find them?"

"We can continue this conversation at headquarters."

"With my lawyer, Dixie Davis." Dixie might not have been the best mob mouthpiece in the city but he had one of the biggest reputations. He wasn't exactly my lawyer, either, but I knew how to get in touch with him. And his name was enough to make Turcot think twice.

"Look," I said, "I'm not trying to be a tough guy here. Like I told you, I've been working on this on my own, and I've found a few things that will interest you. But you're going to help me."

"Tell me how you got this"

"Not now. Maybe later."

"Who's the oberführer?"

"I didn't see him." Only a small lie.

"Where were you?"

I shook my head. "Who killed Fat Joe?" I opened my desk drawer and took out the photographs of the guys Turcot had fingered. "Tell me more about them. What are they doing? Where do they live. Why do you think they killed Fat Joe? I want everything you've got about these guys, before I give you anything else. And there is more. This oberführer guy thinks the Fort Totten business is peanuts. He wants to do something bigger."

"Dammit, you can't hold out on me with something like that. What is it?"

"I don't know, but I can find out." Another small lie.

He said that wasn't enough.

I tapped the photographs.

He sat heavily, not trying to hide his frustration. "We don't know much more. Ever since they caught Hauptmann, all of our manpower has been transferred to the Lindbergh business. Even cursory surveillance is impossible. I can give you their background with the Silver Legion. I can tell you where and when they're likely to run into organized opposition from the Jewish groups, but from what happened in Newark, you and Lansky don't need any help with that."

"You took these pictures down on Pearl Street. You must have known they were going to be there. How?"

"Josef Bruder told us he was meeting them."

"And you were there to take the pictures. One of those guys or this oberführer must have made you."

"Made us?"

"Recognized you as Bureau men."

He shook his head. "Not possible." He didn't look like it was not possible.

I shrugged. "Do you have addresses for these guys? Places of employment?"

"Some of that, yes."

"Give it to me and I'll tell you everything else I know."

Chapter Forty-Four

Friday afternoon, a little after three, Arch Malloy and Daphne Prewitt were naked, sweaty, and smiling in her bed. Andrew the cat scratched at the door. Daphne rolled over onto one elbow and looked down at Arch. "What are you thinking?"

"Do you want the truth or do you want to hear what most men probably say to you in this situation?"

She frowned, then looked thoughtful. "I'll know if you lie."

"Of course you will. I was thinking that just now, before we got into bed, half of me wanted to slowly strip your clothes off and examine every square inch of that extraordinary body, and the other half was absolutely terrified, as I almost always am in this situation if I admit it. Terrified that I will not live up to my fantasy of myself. And now, after I've gotten over the fearful part and we've finished so wonderfully, I find that I'm still unsure. I'm wondering if you are one of the great actresses of our time or if you really enjoyed the last hour as much as you seemed to. I suspect it's a combination, maybe sixty-forty if I'm lucky."

For a long moment she stared at him and he could tell she was thinking about what he'd said. Then she laughed, and she kept laughing until she rolled to the other side of the bed and was crying. Not what Arch had been hoping for. So much for honesty. He tried to pat her shoulder but that was useless. The sobs subsided, then she slipped out of bed and into the bathroom, not letting him see her face. He heard water running. When she came out, she was smiling and her eyes were clear. She got back into bed, pulled the sheet up, and moved over next to him again, still on her elbow.

"I didn't mean for that to happen. Sixty-forty is about right, and that doesn't happen very often. Almost never, really. Now, what have you and Harold been up to?"

"I told you about lunch at Keen's. This morning I was over at the Yacht Club—what a ridiculous name—collecting the papers that I'm supposed to be taking to my lawyers. Apparently, Harold had asked to be notified when I showed up. He called the manager's office and told me to come up to his apartment when I was finished. We sat on his terrace and he broke out a bottle of godawful sweet sauterne."

"He loves that stuff. I can't stand it." Daphne moved closer, letting the sheet slip down so her breasts were inches from his face.

Arch cleared his throat and went on. "In the most general of terms, he told me that he has organized a 'slightly piratical investment opportunity.' He said that he was able to do this because he has such a solid reputation on the Street. Men know they can trust him. That's also why he can't really take part himself. He's simply too famous. Did you ever notice that whenever Henninger is trying to sound modest, the way he speaks changes. His voice sounds, I don't know, even more dishonest that it usually does."

"Oh, yes. It's usually right after he says something like, 'if I do say so myself' or 'to be completely honest.'"

"Precisely. He said that anything he does attracts notice and this enterprise is not the sort of thing one wants bruited about publicly. It must be handled *sotto voce*. He's invited about fifty likeminded men to join in. He said he needs no commitment from me, but if I decide I'm interested, he'll make room for me."

"What did you say?"

"I said, when you put it that way, sure, I'm in. But how much money are you talking about? A hundred? Ten thousand? He said whatever I wanted. Then I asked him about the risk. If it's slightly piratical, there's a catch somewhere."

"I'll bet he told you there was no risk, just like he told me with the 'instruments.'"

Arch said, "Not exactly. He said that yes there were some risks, but it was easy for an experienced investor to get around them. I told him I'm not an experienced investor and he said not to worry, he'd tell me everything I needed to know."

Daphne moved closer to Arch, her head on his shoulder, one arm over his chest. "He's planning it for next Wednesday night at the Rainbow Room," she said. "He wants me to be there."

"What's the Rainbow Room?"

"A nightclub. It opened a couple of days ago on top of Rockefeller Center. He's arranged to have it for the evening."

"Really? What else?"

"Just that he's seeing some important people and he wants me to act as hostess, looking my best. It's happened before, usually at cocktail parties or smokers, that sort of thing. He'll tell me which of the guests I need to be sure to speak to, meaning to flirt with and flatter. He wants me to bring a thousand dollars in cash. He said that if the action isn't moving quickly enough, he'll give me a sign and tell me what to bid on."

"*Bid?* Is it an auction then?"

"I don't know, but…" She started twisting her finger in the gray hair on his chest, and said in a softer voice, "I'm afraid he's getting ready to leave me. I've suspected it for months, but now I know. I've seen the signs. He hasn't been here in four nights. He's acting different. It's that blonde you told me about, the one the bartender mentioned. Or maybe it's somebody else, I don't know and it doesn't matter, what matters is that he's about to leave. There's somebody younger, prettier, with better tits. I knew it would come someday and I told myself I wouldn't get emotional about it, goddammit, and now look at me. Jeez, who turned on the waterworks."

Arch tried not to pay attention to what she was doing and to think about what she'd said. "You've suspected it for months. Then, that first night you came into Jimmy's Place, back in September, you weren't just worried about this scheme Harold's cooked up, you were also thinking it was time for you to making plans for yourself."

"That makes me sound so calculating."

"No, realistic." He didn't say anything else while he thought about what she'd said. Then, "You know this could work to our advantage."

"What do you mean?"

"Haven't you been trying to find a way to make a clean break? To take the money that you've earned since you moved here and leave?"

"Yes, but it was always something that was going to happen some time in the future, not right away." Her hand moved down to his stomach, and she rubbed his thigh with hers.

"Well, it is happening now." Arch cleared his throat again. "Next Wednesday. Can you clean out your bank account by then? Move it to another bank without Henninger knowing about it."

She stared at Arch, looking confused. "I haven't really thought about that. I mean, I guess I could. Harold co-signed account, but I have forged his signature when he told me to sign something for him. And other times when I'm paying bills, but I don't know. It wasn't supposed to happen like this." Her hand moved farther down. "Do we have to talk about this now?"

Arch said, "Absolutely not," and rolled her over onto her back.

Chapter Forty-Five

The Grand Reopening was supposed to be at five on Friday afternoon, but by four, about a dozen regulars were outside, so we unlocked the door. Franz Voss was one of them. I can't say that I was expecting to see him, but it didn't surprise me. I got the Teeling from the top shelf and found two solid cubes in the freezer. Put a napkin under the glass and said, "Welcome back. If you've got time, stick around. We'll talk."

I didn't need to ask the other regulars what they wanted, either. The bar filled quickly. Frenchy and Marie Therese took the tables. Connie worked the booths. Nobody had anything bad to say about the new booths and lighting. One guy actually asked me if we'd raised the ceiling. When everybody had a glass in front of him or her, I made it back to the end of the bar where Voss was perched on a new stool.

"Have they made any progress on finding the men who killed Fat Joe?" he asked.

"No. A detective named Ellis is in charge. I've seen him a couple of times and he says they've got nothing new."

"Any suspects?"

"I asked him that and he said no."

Voss shook his head. "With something like this, if they don't have someone within the first forty-eight hours, it's usually over."

"And since Fat Joe liked to make people mad at him, it's hard to narrow the field. I got the idea they're not busting their asses over this one. It pisses me off but I understand it. What have you been doing?"

"Right now, I have several projects at different stages of completion, and I'm at that point where I always think I'm working on the wrong thing. If I'm spending time on finalizing the stock transfers, I should be making the travel arrangements for employees who have to go overseas, and then there's a meeting coming up and I'm not prepared for it. But I will always make time for this place. You really do have the best bar in New York, and as someone who has done his share of traveling and drinking, I can say it is one of the best in North America or Europe."

"It's always good to hear something like that." *What was he up to?*

Voss tapped his empty glass. I poured his second. He stayed for two more rounds but we got busier and I didn't have time to talk to him again.

Arch came in around eight, with the slaphappy grin of a man who'd had a pleasant afternoon. He put on his apron and said, "I have news." It was so busy for the rest of the night that we didn't have time to talk until the crowd thinned around one in the morning. By then, the five of us were so tired that we made it Last Call and closed the place even though we could've stayed open for another hour or two. We cleaned up, got drinks, and sat at one of the six-tops.

Connie said to me, "Turcot called the office line while I was doing the first count. He left a message for you." She handed me a scrap of paper. "He wants you to meet him tomorrow." She'd written *Pearl St. 3pm*. Maybe he'd found something.

We congratulated ourselves on having such a successful reopening. Since I hadn't told Frenchy and Marie Therese in detail why I'd been gone, I explained what Connie and I had been up to at the McAlpin. But when I got to the part about Franz Voss, I got blank reactions. It looked like I was the only one of us who knew him. Marie Therese, Frenchy, and Arch said they recognized the guy I'd been talking to earlier, but they didn't know his name.

"Franz Voss first started coming in not long after I bought the place. Usually drops by midafternoon, early evening, but sometimes it'll be a year or more between visits. I've seen him maybe a dozen times. He always has a couple of Teelings with two large ice cubes. We talk about this and that. He knew Fat Joe and he acted like he was surprised and sad when I told him Fat Joe was dead. Sure convinced me, anyway. If what the Bureau man said is right," I said, "he's the guy that ordered the Nazi thugs to kill Fat Joe."

Arch said, "What are we going to do about it?"

"I've got some ideas, but first I have to find them."

"Maybe we should thank them," Marie Therese said. "The bar looked good after the first redecorating we did, but this is like it's completely new.

Everybody was talking about it. I think we're going to be doing much better business from now on, and that means we're going to need more help."

"You've got some people in mind, don't you."

"I wouldn't have brought it up if I didn't."

Arch said, "I've been busy with Miss Pruitt—"

"I'll just bet you have," Frenchy interrupted.

Arch ignored him. "I don't need to go into that now. What Jimmy says about this man Voss worries me. If I understand it, Voss and this group of thugs are now planning to do something big, and Voss makes a point of coming here where he can talk to Jimmy. It seems logical that if he ordered them to kill Fat Joe, he also ordered them to vandalize our place. Agreed?"

All of us nodded. Why hadn't I thought of that?

Arch went on. "It bothers me that he is so interested in this place, and because of that, I'm going to continue to sleep here."

About noon on Saturday, I let myself in the backdoor and found Arch sitting up on his bed and rubbing his eyes. I told him that Vittorio's guys were working in the kitchen. I'd have them send coffee and breakfast for two to my office. He found his shaving kit and stumbled upstairs to the bathroom.

My count of Friday's take matched Connie's. It was the best Friday we'd had in a long time. We'd need more of them to cover the cost of remodeling and adding another waitress or two. That's when I realized that none of us had really taken on any more work after Fat Joe was killed. Since Repeal, we didn't need anybody checking for alcohol control or federal agents at the door. Lately we hadn't had any large belligerent drunks that needed to be kicked out. They'd all been medium or small belligerents. No, I'd been paying Fat Joe to sit on his butt, drink a lot of free beer, and complain whenever he was asked to do any work. But none of that mattered. He'd been one of us.

Over a breakfast of spinach omelets, Arch told me what had been going on with Henninger and Daphne. When he finished, neither of us knew what to make of it.

"Got any ideas about this piratical investment deal? Sounds fishy to me."

"It does have a certain stench, and for the life of me, I cannot understand how this ridiculous blowhard has earned such a reputation as a Wall Street genius. Admittedly, I did not know him when he was young and hungry but now, he is just a blubbery lecher who drinks too much and is looking for something to occupy his time. I wouldn't trust him with a nickel."

"What are you planning to do?"

"I'll go his little soirée to see what it is, and then I imagine that Archibald Middleford will find a reason to decline to join the East River Yacht Club and vanish into the aether. If Henninger really is planning to leave Daphne, I'll try to help her sell the house on Gay Street. If it can be done without Henninger's signature, or with his forged signature, I'll take ten percent of whatever Daphne manages to shake loose."

He finished his coffee. "But the truth is, I'd rather help with what you're doing. Remember, I worked for those kraut bastards. I'm game for anything that screws them over."

I opened my desk drawer and took out the pictures that the Bureau man left. "I guess I should have shown you these before. You recognize any of these guys? According to the Bureau man, this one is Florian Hoffmeister. He's the guy who was at the bar with me the night they hit us. I think the other three were with him but I didn't get a look at them."

Arch went through the photographs carefully, taking his time, looking at each of them repeatedly. He turned one of the pictures around and said, "I am ninety percent certain that this man used to come into the warehouse where I worked for the bastards."

I remembered the warehouse. Another bunch of young Nazi thugs tried to torture and kill me there. "That was two years ago."

"So it was. Still, if I find myself in that neighborhood, I'll take a look around. As the book of Proverbs tells us, a dog always goes back to its own vomit."

Chapter Forty-Six

A little bit of rain had been falling when I left the Chelsea at noon. It was coming down harder when I left Arch, so I caught a cab down to Pearl Street. It was as deserted as it had been when I was there almost a week ago. I turned up my collar and tugged the brim of my hat as I walked under the El tracks. A black Ford four-door, several years old, was in the same spot where the Nazi thugs had parked their car. Turcot was standing beside it.

"I've got something for you," he said, kind of flat, like there was something else he'd rather be doing. "But first I need to know more about the source of your information, specifically anything you can tell me about this oberführer."

I leaned heavily on my stick and acted like I was debating with myself how much to tell him. Actually, I'd figured this demand was coming and knew how I wanted to handle it. "I can tell you a lot about him, including his name. What have you got for me?"

He hooked a thumb over his shoulder, pointing at the storefront behind him. Leyton and Sons Landscaping and Building Supplies. Established 1889. "That's where they did it."

We walked up three steps to the front doors. They were unlocked and the metal security shutters had been raised. I wondered how Turcot had managed that. Did he convince his boss to get a warrant, or had he decided to do this his own way? Inside, I shook the water off my hat. The place was as dusty as it appeared from the street. There was no sign that any business had been done there for some time. A few racks and display tables that seemed to be meant to hold tools were empty, and it had a stale chemical smell of dirt, asphalt, and paint. Turcot walked past the counter and through another set of double doors. They led to an empty unpaved yard bordered by a ten-foot wooden fence. There was a gate in the fence on a street that paralleled Pearl, and tire tracks on the hard-packed dirt that was turning to mud. A wooden garage had been built against the building. Turcot pulled the wide doors open, letting in weak gray light. He was right. This is where it happened.

Parked inside, there was a half-ton pick-up with a round asphalt mixer about three feet wide mounted on the bed. Looked like it had been tilted to pour out the contents and whoever used it last hadn't cleaned it. Hard sheets and chunks of asphalt had dried on the lip and been spilled onto the truck bed. Four gallon-sized wooden buckets were black inside. But most of the dried asphalt was on the concrete floor in big patches. I moved closer to one of them and got down on my good knee to take a better look. I thought I could see a bit of dried blood mixed in with the asphalt, but I didn't really know what I was looking at.

Even so, I could imagine how it played out and it turned my stomach. Figure the four guys persuaded Fat Joe to come with them. Maybe they told him they were going to tap a keg of good kraut beer. Maybe they told him Voss wanted to see him. They get him into the garage. Voss is waiting for them. He tells the thugs that Fat Joe sold them out. They beat him nearly to death but leave him conscious. They've heated up the asphalt mixer and they dump buckets of the steaming stuff on him. He's rolling around on the floor, and they dump more of it. When they're done, they toss him into the trunk of their car and bring him to my place. Seemed like a lot of trouble to go to just to get rid of a guy.

As I was working through that, I realized that the timing was wrong and said to the Bureau man, "You called last night and left this address. That means you didn't search the place until yesterday."

"We had no reason to think this block was anything more than a rendezvous point. But when reconsidering the matter," *after I brought it up*, "we decided that a more thorough canvassing of the street might be fruitful."

I didn't buy it. "Tell me more about the four thugs."

He handed me a folded sheet of paper from his breast pocket. "I had my secretary type up their personal information from our files. Age, height, weight, hair color, eye color, last known address. It won't do you much good. We lost track of them after the riot at the Newark rally. They were living in two rooming houses, but they haven't been back. Now, what have you got for me?"

"No, one more thing first. When did you take the picture?"

"It was just over two weeks ago… a Thursday, I remember. Whatever the date was. That's unimportant. What else do you know?"

It wasn't unimportant. I was starting to put some pieces together.

"I overheard a conversation between Dr. Griebl and a man named Franz Voss." At the name, the Bureau man got more interested. "Griebl addressed him as 'oberführer.' Voss has been an on-and-off customer of mine for several years."

Turcot pulled out his leather notebook. "Describe him."

"Short to medium height, white hair. Thirty, forty. Nothing unusual about his features. Always dresses well. From the way he talks and the things he's said, he's educated, travels a lot. Says he has spent time in Germany but he's told me he doesn't support the Nazis."

"I'm familiar with all the important Nazis and their sympathizers. I'll check the files but I'm certain there's no Franz Voss. Are you sure that's his name?"

"I've never asked to see an i.d. if that's what you mean."

He muttered, "You'll need to look at some photographs."

"Voss told Griebl that him and Mrs. Moog are being sent back to Germany in two weeks. An Admiral…" I pulled out my notepad to be sure I had the name right, "Admiral Canaris wants to talk to them."

Turcot's head snapped up and his eyes got wide. Figure this Canaris must be a pretty big cheese. "Voss didn't act like he cared that much about your maps and the honey trap business. He said that Hauptmann being captured and being a kraut is bad for them, and so they need to do something that will take people's minds off him and make Americans like Germans again. He said he has that something."

"Did he say anything more about it?"

I shook my head. "No, but Fat Joe knew what it was."

"What do you mean?"

"Right before he left, Voss said 'Bruder was about to tell that damned Turcot.'"

The Bureau man smiled and muttered under his breath. "This will change their minds." He snapped the notebook shut and dropped it back into his pocket. "There have been some delays in getting authorization for your testimony before a grand jury but there won't be any trouble now, believe me."

I didn't understand why he kept talking about my doing anything with a grand jury. Did he really believe me when I said I'd do it? But the way it kept being delayed made me think that maybe he wasn't able to sell it to his boss. I wouldn't have believed there were Nazi spies in New York unless I'd seen them and heard them. Figure some of the big wheels at the Bureau of Investigation felt the same way, particularly when they were trying to sell everybody on how important they'd been in capturing Hauptmann when they really hadn't done a damn thing.

"Have you got anything else?" he asked.

I said no. He said, "I've got something for you, or rather for you to tell your friends Lansky and Sedway."

"Yeah?"

"The Silver Legion is going to have another rally. The posters haven't gone up yet but it's going to be Wednesday night in the Yorkville Lyceum."

In the cab heading back uptown, I tried to figure Turcot's game. How did it start? The Bureau man came into Jimmy's Place for the first time two weeks ago, the Saturday before last. The news about Hauptmann had just hit the radio and newspapers. He was waiting for me when I came in and watched me for an hour and a half while I read and wrote down words I didn't know. He already knew that I pick up work as a go-between for parties who like to keep their business private and he said he wasn't interested in that. To get me into his game, he gave me a few of the inside details about the case against Hauptmann and they all panned out. He may have been showing off but he wasn't wrong. And then—how did he put it?—he said that Jimmy's Place was going to be part of an important investigation.

I didn't know it, but he'd already recruited Fat Joe to rat on his pals in the Silver Legion, and they killed him the next day, late on Sunday. I found him on Monday morning. But he wasn't dead then and I didn't know who he was. Turcot showed up a few hours later. When I told him what happened, he said 'dammit, they know' and followed the ambulance to Bellevue. He came back that afternoon and said Fat Joe was dead. His real name was Josef Bruder and he had been a double agent. That's when he said Dr. Griebl was behind the whole business.

Sometime later that week, Tuesday or Wednesday, Griebl came in. I told him about Fat Joe. It seemed to rattle him and he left in a hurry.

Remembering that Turcot had mentioned the Nazis working out of the McAlpin Hotel, I followed Griebl there. Turcot saw me in the lobby. Told me that Fat Joe had been recruited into the Silver Legion and Turcot had offered him enough cash to rat them to the Bureau. Turcot knew Griebl had a new boss, a guy from the SS. He said I would help him and he warned me that they were going to come after me. Right on both counts, dammit. The thugs busted up my place the next night. The day after that, Thursday, Turcot came in again. Said they'd gone after me because I was an easier target than Nat Arno's gym. That's when he gave me the pictures. Then two days ago, he stopped me on the sidewalk and I told him part of what I heard at the McAlpin.

What was going on then? I worked on that all the way back to my office.

Chapter Forty-Seven

My cab got back to Jimmy's Place around five. Even with the rain, we had a decent crowd. I gave the hat check girl my raincoat and lid and went behind the bar with Frenchy. Ditched my suitcoat, put on my apron, rolled up my sleeves, and stayed busy for the next seven hours. But I couldn't stop thinking about everything that had gone on. In the odd moments when I could step back, I wrote in my notebook, trying to make sure I remembered things in the right order.

It started on Wednesday, September 19, when they brought Hauptmann into the Second Street Precinct House.

Thursday, somebody from the Bureau took a picture of the four Nazi thugs and their car down on Pearl Street.

Saturday, the Bureau man, Leo Turcot, showed up early and told me that my place would be part of an important investigation.

Then on Sunday, the 23rd, Rabbi Wise and Judge Perlman asked Lansky to bust up Nazi rallies but not kill anybody. That night, the Nazi thugs beat Fat Joe nearly to death and dumped his body on my front steps. Franz Voss, the oberführer, ordered it.

On Monday, Fat Joe died and Turcot started nosing around.

Tuesday, I drove the teargas grenades over to Newark where Nat Arno's sluggers went at it with some Nazi thugs. And maybe, since Turcot knew I was there, Griebl and Voss knew it, too, but I couldn't be sure about it.

Wednesday, I told Griebl about Fat Joe and followed Griebl to the McAlpin. Turcot was there and he dragooned me into the Nazi-hunting business.

On Thursday, said Nazis busted up my place.

From Friday to last Tuesday, I worked on getting the place back open. That night, I put on the Professor Patterson outfit and spent a couple of days in the McAlpin, where I learned it really was a nest of spies. What a screwy mess. Then toss in the business with Petey Beck and the false identification we needed for the safety deposit boxes, and Arch helping Daphne get out from under Henninger's thumb, and it added up to an even screwier mess.

I'd got that far when I noticed that I had a new customer who'd found space at the bar. Moe Sedway, last seen in Meyer Lansky's garage with NYPD teargas grenades. He asked for rye and whispered he needed a word. I poured his drink and told him wait in the hall by the men's room. After a moment, I nodded to Frenchy. Guys wanted to talk to me on the QT often enough that he understood what I needed. I ducked under the leaf in the bar and met Moe in the back.

Still almost whispering, he said, "Lansky needs the material you've been holding for him next Wednesday. The krauts are having another rally at the Lyceum in Yorkville. Nat Arno's sluggers will be there, but it'll be crawling with cops, so he don't want the grenades anywhere near the place until the rally happens."

"What time?"

"Around six."

"You talk to him face to face?" Knowing how Lansky didn't like to use the telephone.

"Yeah, he came by the garage." Good. He was in town.

Around midnight, my beat cops Mahan and Norris came in. We had the night deposit ready for the Corn Bank. Frenchy took it after we closed around two. When he got back, I asked everybody to stick around and pour a drink. I had something to tell them.

"Last night, the Bureau man called and said I should meet him down on Pearl Street. I did and I saw where they killed Fat Joe. It was in a garage behind an abandoned business. They left asphalt on the floor."

Looking at each other across the six-top, I could tell that it hit them as hard as it had hit me. Nobody said anything for a long time. Then Frenchy said, "I still don't get it. Why did they do that? With the asphalt?"

"Perhaps they were trying to tar and feather him," Arch said.

"Or maybe they just wanted to hurt him more after they'd beaten him so bad."

Connie said, "What about the guys who killed him and busted up our place? Did the Bureau man have anything about them?"

"I've got pictures of them, but they don't show you much. Turcot told me their names and this afternoon he gave me their last known addresses but he says they're not there anymore. I just wanted you to know that I haven't forgot about him."

We talked a while longer but everyone was beat and ready to leave. As Connie was putting on her raincoat, she asked Arch how Daphne was.

"She's worried. She suspects Henninger is about to take up with a younger woman."

"We talked about that this afternoon," Connie said. "If Harold's not coming over tomorrow, I'll see her for lunch." I didn't know they'd got to be so chummy.

We took a cab to the Chelsea. By the time we were back in the room, we were so exhausted it took all our energy to wash up and get rid of some of the smoke and alcohol smell before we collapsed in bed.

Chapter Forty-Eight

I woke up around one in the afternoon on Sunday and found that Connie was gone. That was unusual. Then I remembered she said something about meeting Daphne for lunch. That was unusual, too, but I didn't have time to think on it. I put on a fresh shirt and tie and yesterday's suit and stopped at the closest good diner for a late breakfast. When I reached for my wallet in my breast pocket, I found the piece of paper the Bureau man gave me, the personal information on the Nazi thugs. The addresses of the rooming houses where they'd lived were in Yorkville. Might be close to the Lyceum. That was something to check later. I had other business.

I took a cab up Central Park West to Meyer Lansky's apartment building. When the guy at the desk called to tell Lanksy I was there, he said, "An hour later and you'd've missed him. They're bringing his car around." Figure he was headed up to Boston where his wife and kids lived while his son's cerebral palsy was being treated.

When I got up to his door, it was open with two suitcases on the floor of the hall. I knocked anyway and went in.

Lansky said, "Make it quick, Jimmy. I'm on my way out." He was wearing a good suit, silk shirt and tie. His topcoat was neatly folded over the back of the sofa and his Cavanaugh was balanced on top of it.

"Moe came in last night. Told me you want the grenades in Yorkville Wednesday."

"Any problem?"

"No, it's just I've learned a few things recently that you ought to know. Turns out that some of the goddamn kraut Nazi bastards have been customers of mine. I saw one of them that day in Newark. Really just heard his voice, but it was him. A guy named Griebl, a doctor. He's in this Silver Legion, Silver Shirts, Silver Something, I don't know. Then four of his

215

kraut thugs come over and tear up my place. They sucker punched me and Frenchy and broke everything they could get their mitts on—furniture, mirrors, slashing the booths, and they tossed a teargas grenade in as they were leaving."

Lansky lit a cigarette and nodded.

"And I've got reason to think that they had a hand in killing Fat Joe, my bouncer. You might have heard about that."

"Yeah, but I didn't know there was anything more to it."

"When I was over in Newark, Nat told me they weren't supposed to kill anybody." I didn't want Lansky to know I'd overheard the rabbi and the judge telling him that. "But if those bastards are at the Lyceum rally, I'm going to do something… anything I can get away with."

"Don't bring a gun."

"Course not. I just don't want you to be surprised if things get out of hand."

He frowned. "Judge Perlman and Rabbi Weiss told us not to kill anybody and they also promised to see that we got a fair shake in the local press." By that he meant the Jewish papers. "But they've been giving us hell, anyway, calling us 'gangsters' and saying we've brought shame on our people and things like that."

His driver tapped on the door and picked up the suitcases. Lansky stubbed out his smoke and put on his topcoat and hat. Then he said what I knew he was going to say. "It still wouldn't look good if any of those Nazi bastards got clipped at the rally, but after it, as the rabbi might say, you have my blessing."

About the same time, as I was heading uptown and Connie and Daphne were having lunch, Arch Malloy was casing the warehouse where he worked when I met him. It was on the Lower East Side between the Brooklyn Bridge and the Manhattan Bridge, on a concrete wharf on the East River. That put it two or three miles south of the East River Yacht Club but it might as well have been in New Jersey. The smells of creosote and the Fulton Street Fish Market were strong and no matter what the weather was anywhere else in the city, it was always damp and a few degrees colder there. That Sunday afternoon, there was fog.

He had been a nightwatchman at the warehouse, actually three warehouses on that end of the wharf: 115, 117, and 120. Arch had kept an eye on the buildings by making rounds and punching a time clock in each one every hour. But from time to time, the owners would tell him to stay away from 115. When that happened, Arch saw thick necked thugs arriving in cars. They stayed for an hour or two or three, and after they left, he found empty schnapps and beer bottles on the floor. Sometimes they'd pull smaller crates and boxes off the shelves to sit on, and he'd have to straighten the place up. It never happened with the other warehouses, only 115.

That Sunday, the wharf looked like it was empty, but Arch figured that if the warehouses were still in business, somebody would be there. 115 was at the north end of the wharf near a short pier. He walked past the building to a narrow, shadowed area, not really an alley, between it and 117. He waited there for almost forty minutes until he heard the sound of a door opening. Seconds later, an older guy with a big ring of keys jingling on his belt shuffled past. Seconds later, he opened the door to 117. When it closed, Arch went back to the front of 115 and climbed the steps to the front door. He still had the keys he'd taken off the big ring two years before when, as he put it, "the kraut cocksuckers shitcanned me."

Inside, nothing had changed. The small office was lighted by a gooseneck lamp. He went through the office to a passageway with tall shelves on both sides that led to the loading dock. He found the switch for the overhead lights and saw that the place was clean. No crates out of place, no bottles on the floor. But the trashcan was still where it had been when he worked there, to the right of the double doors that rolled open for trucks. Arch went down the steps to street level and opened the lid. Oh, yes, there were the empty bottles. They were still using it for their dirty work.

As warehouses go, 115 was small but it was still too large for any kind of search of the shelves, should the krauts have hidden anything there, but Arch still made a circuit through the wide aisles between the shelves. He also checked the stairs and the door in back. They were clear and the door that opened onto steps to the pier was locked. He found nothing, but when he got back to the loading dock, he noticed a stack of pallets about three feet high that had been pushed against one wall. Whatever was on the pallets was loosely covered by a piece of gray oilcloth. Arch pulled it off and saw two metal boxes marked "Remington Arms U. M. C. Munitions Bridgeport, Connecticut" The top of each box was held closed with hinged clips. Arch unsnapped the clips and opened the box closest to him. Well, he tried to open it. At first, it wouldn't move.

He got his fingers under the edge of the lid and pulled harder. It popped open with a faint hiss because it had been sealed shut. The interior of the box was lined with rubber and there was a rubber gasket on the inside of the lid. Rubber-lined dividers separated the interior into twelve spaces. Each space held a rectangular stick designed to fit tightly inside. When Arch pulled one out, he saw that it was made of heavy waxed pea green paper or cardboard with a black rubber cap. On the side, it said "Polnol 1 Pound Net Remington Arms U.M.C. DANGEROUS"

Arch eased the stick back in the box more carefully than he'd taken it out. What was it doing here? In the army he'd handled enough explosives to know that by itself, the stuff probably wasn't dangerous. Still, he closed the box and the clips gingerly. He checked his watch then and saw that he'd been in the warehouse for more than an hour. He was about to put the oilcloth back over the boxes until he noticed that one of the clips on the second box was loose. He unsnapped that clip and had no trouble lifting the lid because the second box had been opened before. It was almost empty. Ten sticks of the stuff had been taken somewhere else.

The Majestic doorman hailed a cab and told the driver to take me across the Park to the Lyceum on East Eighty-Fifth Street. It was about four in the afternoon. We usually opened around five on Sundays, and Frenchy and Marie Therese had the day off, so I told the cabbie that I needed to see where the theater was. Didn't have to get out. Then, I wanted him to drive past two other addresses nearby. After that, downtown. As soon as we got over to the East Side and across Park Avenue, the neighborhood changed. We were in Yorkville, the German section. There were more people on the sidewalks and about half the signs were in German. Drug stores, laundries, apartment buildings. A normal neighborhood until you noticed the guys swaggering around with swastika armbands. As New York theaters go, the Lyceum was like most others. Began as a vaudeville house. Nothing remarkable about the façade. A moving picture with Bing Crosby was playing. It was near a corner next to the German-American Business League building.

Except for that evening in Newark, I didn't know what to expect from a Nazi rally, but given the neighborhood, it looked like Nat and his sluggers were going to have a tougher time of it. Could get interesting. The two rooming houses were up on Eighty-Seventh and Eighty-Ninth. We slowed to a crawl. I searched the faces of people on the sidewalk. There were a lot of blonds, but not the ones I was looking for. I told the cabbie to take me Jimmy's Place.

When I got there, I found Arch and Connie sitting at a two-top and talking seriously about something. They moved apart as soon as I opened the door.

As I locked the door behind me, I said, "What's going on?" trying not to sound like I was suspicious or jealous or worried.

Connie said, "It's Daphne. She's not sure she's doing the right thing getting Arch involved with Henninger. She's beginning to think she misjudged him."

"I can disabuse her of that misguided notion if she'll simply listen to me. I don't understand why she's getting cold feet at this stage of the game."

Disabuse? I'd have to look that one up.

Connie said, "No, like I was trying to tell you, it's more complicated than that. It's not just Harold, there's the question of her house. Can she sell it or not."

"We've talked about that," he said sounding exasperated, "and apparently we'll talk again."

Connie gave him one of her men-are-stupid looks and started wiping down the tables. Arch and I went behind the bar, hung up our coats and put on aprons. He lowered his voice. "I didn't want to say this in front of her, but I went back to the warehouse this afternoon and took a look around."

"Yeah?"

"Looks like the cocksucking kraut bastards have the makings for a bomb."

"What?" He told me about the explosives and I made him go over it again to be sure I understood what it meant.

"You said it was labelled polnol."

"I worked with all kinds of explosives and munitions in the army but I don't know this stuff."

"They stole it from the Remington Arms plant in Bridgeport on Tuesday. It was in the papers."

Right then, I knew this wasn't a game about 'honey traps" and rallies and tear gas anymore. Voss said he wanted something big to happen. I didn't know from explosives but it figured that ten pounds of polnol could blow up something big.

Then what the hell was I supposed to do?

Chapter Forty-Nine

Right before we closed up, Arch said he'd talked to Daphne on the telephone and he needed to see her, but that could wait until tomorrow. "I want to have a good look around in the alley and anyplace else close by where those kraut cocksuckers with their damn bomb might be lurking about. Then it'll be another night in the basement for me."

I told him Connie and I could clean up and he headed for the door. Connie did the rough count. I sent the last load of glasses up to the kitchen in the dumbwaiter, wiped down the tables and called the cab company. When Connie came back down, she asked why we weren't walking the way we usually did on a pleasant night.

"I'll explain when we get back to the Chelsea. Arch learned something today that could change things."

I could see that she wanted to know more but she didn't say anything until we were back at the hotel. I took off my coat and tie and shoes and poured a couple of short brandies. She stripped down to her silk slip and then put on a robe because she knew I was easily distracted.

"Arch went by the warehouse, the one the Germans own, where he was working before. I don't think you ever went there but you've heard us talk about it."

"Lower East Side on the river. Where the Germans tried to kill you."

"Arch says it looks like they still use it as a private place to drink and plan. While he was there, he found two boxes of an explosive called polnol, something that's more powerful than dynamite, a lot more powerful if the *Times* is to be believed. One of them was full. Ten one-pound pieces were missing from the other box. The Nazis are having another rally on Wednesday up in Yorkville. Nat Arno and his sluggers are going to be there and I'm bringing the tear gas again. Now, I don't know that this polnol has anything to do with the rally, but it could. I'm more worried that they're going to do something else to Jimmy's Place, finish the job they started a couple of weeks ago."

"You've got to tell the Bureau man."

"Sure, Ellis too, but it makes me angry and scared to be dealing with bombs. Trying to kill a lot of people because you're a Red or a Nazi, that's crazy."

"Says the man who's shot how many people?"

"I never shot anybody who wasn't trying to hurt me. Or you."

"Really, how about—"

"All right, it's not that simple but you know what I mean. I'm just saying that this worries me, and it means that Arch and me and you and, hell, even Daphne, I guess need to keep our eyes open and be even more careful than we've been."

She didn't say anything. Knocked back her brandy and still didn't say anything, thinking. Then, "Hell. If these guys have got their hands on ten pounds of this stuff, they could be planning to blow up anything."

She took off the robe, pulled her slip over her head and got under the covers. "How do you expect me to sleep after telling me something like that. Get in here."

I didn't need to be asked twice. At least one good thing was coming out of this day. I stripped off the rest of my clothes and joined her. "You know," I said, "this really doesn't mean—"

"Shut up, Jimmy."

First thing Monday morning, I found a telephone booth on Twenty-Third Street, sat down, and called the New York office of the Bureau of Investigation. Agent Turcot wasn't in, did I want to leave a message. I didn't want anybody else there to know my name, so I said, "Tell him to call about Franz Voss. Got that, *Call about Franz Voss*" and cradled the ear piece.

I walked over to the alley behind Jimmy's Place and let myself in through the back door. Arch met me there looking like he'd had a long night. I asked him how he was doing.

"The building's still standing. I heard nothing suspicious, and I felt like I was never really asleep. I tried to convince myself that we're overreacting."

"But it doesn't wash."

"No."

"Look, go home. Get some sleep in your bed."

"No, I need to see Daphne first."

"Sleep in her bed."

After he left, I tried to telephone Detective Ellis. He wasn't in either, but the other cops in his precinct house knew who I was, so I left a message for him to call me. I was going back over the numbers for the weekend when Connie came in. She was wearing another of her Paris outfits and a beret.

"In the three days since we reopened," I said, "we've been doing terrific business. I don't get it, the place doesn't look *that* much better."

"No, but if you go back and track the increase we've seen since we remodeled in January, the jump in the rate really isn't that large. It's been increasing steadily. Being closed for a few days, we created more demand. We'll continue to do good business through Christmas and New Year's Eve, like we do every year. Now, open the cash box and give me two hundred dollars."

"What do you need two hundred dollars for?"

"You'll know when the time comes."

Arch woke up around one o'clock. Daphne was next to him, her eyes open and staring. It took Arch a moment or two to relize what day it was and the warehouse and the polnol and what Connie said about Daphne's indecision. "I can't remember the last time I slept so soundly, probably the last time I was here. You see, I've been sleeping in the basement of Jimmy's Place."

"What?"

Arch didn't mention the extra cash and illegal alcohol we had stashed there. He said we were worried about the Nazi thugs coming back, which was true enough. Then he had to remind her that I was a known associate of Meyer Lansky and he suspected that was why the krauts were after me in the first place. There was more to it, he said, but he was not privy to the details.

"Connie told me that you're thinking of staying with Henninger. I thought we'd decided about that."

She moved closer and scratched her fingernails lightly through the hair on his chest. "I don't know, I've been having second thoughts and this may not make any sense because there have always been other women with

Harold but this is the first time I've been with anyone else since I moved into this house, and it bothers me to be, well, unfaithful. That may sound strange considering everything that I've done, but it's true."

"And I believe you. It's been what, two years? You must have some feelings for the man, but you're right to be concerned. He may or may not be serious about this other woman and we still don't know exactly what he is going to be up to on Wednesday night."

Arch rolled onto his side, ran a hand along her silky hip. "I really think you should not make any decision until we have a better understanding of it. Remember, that's the source of your concerns, the scheme he's been keeping from you. Until we know what he's planning, you should keep all of your options open."

She grabbed a handful of chest hair and pulled. "You're just saying that because you want me in bed."

Arch rolled her over and moved between her legs. "Of course I want you in bed. As often as you'll have me, but until we understand Henninger's game, I believe there's a chance that you could be hurt by it, personally and financially if he were to try to remove you from this house."

"He can't do that, he said it's mine." Her voice was hot with anger but uncertain.

"Then let me talk to him again. I can arrange a meeting, probably this afternoon, for him to give me a better explanation of his piratical opportunity." He edged forward, put his arms under her shoulders and pushed her until the pillow was comfortably under her head. "There's no reason to rush into anything."

She hitched around and reached down to stroke him, moving him into position. "When you put it that way, it makes sense," she said with a little smile that told Arch he was doing exactly what she wanted him to do.

Chapter Fifty

After he left Daphne, Arch went back to his apartment and showered off her perfumed bed. He doubted that Henninger would recognize the scent but he didn't want to make any mistakes at this stage of the game. He found a suit that would do and called Henninger.

"Middleford, good to hear from you. I was beginning to think that you'd abandoned us."

"Oh, no, quite the opposite. I've been thinking about your investment opportunity and I believe I'd like to participate. When can we discuss it more fully?"

"Are you free tonight? I can show you what I'm talking about, or part of it. Where are you?"

"Downtown. This time of evening, it will take me fifteen, twenty minutes to get to your place."

"No, meet me at Rockefeller Plaza, much as I hate to set foot in the place. There's an entrance on Forty-Ninth Street between Fifth and Sixth. Take the escalator and I'll meet you on the Mezzanine."

• • •

Arch got out of his cab and saw a small neon sign on a marquee, easy to miss, for the RAINBOW ROOM. It was above a revolving door set back from the sidewalk. Inside, there were polished stone floors and a set of escalators dead ahead. It took him up to a bright, crowded, high-ceilinged lobby. People were gathered by a bank of elevators. Henninger stepped away from them and waved. As Arch approached, he knew what was about to happen. Henninger clapped a heavy paw on his shoulders, hard enough to have buckled a knee if he hadn't been expecting it. Arch twisted out from under it so quickly that it startled Henninger, but he smiled immediately and said, "Careful there, big fellow, you don't know your own strength."

"Right this way," said the big fellow. They walked past the elevators to a part of the lobby that was separated from the rest by a large curtain and a guard. A few people, men in white tie and women in evening gowns, were waiting there. The guard motioned them away and pulled the curtain aside as Henninger got closer. A second set of elevators with shiny brass doors was on the other side of the curtain. They went to the closest open door and stepped inside. More shiny brass and mirrors.

"I've got to admit that these really are amazing," Henninger said as he pressed the single button and the doors closed. "They're express elevators and they're going to take us up to the sixty-fifth floor faster than you'll believe." He was right. Arch's ears popped midway through the trip that took less than a minute. The doors opened onto a small lobby. Henninger led Arch around a corner and down a hall to a wide room that looked like a Hollywood movie set.

It was two stories tall with floor-to-ceiling windows on three sides. In the middle was a sunken circular dancefloor with an intricate parquet pattern. Above it, a chandelier. Around it, white tablecloths on two-tops and eight-tops, a bandstand, some kind of grotesque pipe organ, raised seating areas at the corners bordered by curved railings, and beyond that, the New York night. The Park to the north, mostly dark. Empire State Building south, the upper floors lit like a candle, and a million electric lights all around below. Arch whistled through his teeth. Hell of a view, he said to himself. Before he could admire it properly, the maître 'd, a harried gent in tails, hurried over.

"Mr. Henninger, what can I do for you?"

"Is everything ready for Wednesday?"

"Of course. The kitchen has the order for a cold supper for eighty. The bar will be fully staffed, of course. What else? Your colleagues have not yet brought the display materials, but, as Mr. Forlini described it, the tables can be arranged on the dance floor. Or, if they bring the second demonstration, we can remove the tables on the lower level. That would almost double the available space."

Henninger took his silver cigarette case from his pocket, selected a smoke, and tapped it on the case to tamp down the tobacco. The maître 'd whipped out a lighter from his vest pocket. "We don't need to decide that now. I want to show my friend around a bit. Bring us a couple of Manhattans—no, make that three. There's a good man." The maître 'd hurried off.

Henninger strolled over to the big window facing south. "You know, until a few weeks ago, they were going to call this place 'Stratosphere.'"

"After the Cloud Club, no doubt."

Henninger's eyes narrowed. "You've been to the Cloud Club?"

Arch nodded, like it was nothing.

"What did you think of it?" Henninger testing him.

"Not much. It seemed to me that whoever decided to put an exclusive club up there on what, the sixty or sixty-first floor, he made some damned silly mistakes. First, once you're up that high with spectacular views, much like these, why do you choose windows that are little isosceles triangles from which no one can see shit? And then to top it off, probably because of those foolish windows, the roof leaks and there are buckets and puddles everywhere. The man who designed this place at least understood the utility and attraction of large windows. And Rainbow Room? A much better name, don't you think, compared to Cloud Club which sounds like the anteroom of Heaven which few of us are likely ever to visit."

Not being used to one of Arch's little digressions, as he calls them, Henninger was dumbfounded for several seconds. Arch went on, "Tell me a bit more about your piratical opportunity. I gather from the brief conversation you had just now that you're going to wine and dine a number of potential investors and then dazzle them with this mysterious offering."

"That's one way of putting it."

"Can you be more specific as to the nature of the goods?"

Henninger smiled. "Of course I could, but I don't want to spoil the fun for everyone."

That's when Arch understood what was going on. For Henninger, this was a game or a circus, and the point of it was for all eyes to be on the ringmaster. Henninger wanted attention.

The maître 'd returned with three wastes of good whiskey on a tray. Henninger drained one straightaway and plopped the cherry into the second glass. Arch took the third drink. Sounding worried, the maître 'd said, "You know we'll be opening at six, and we have a full house." He checked his watch.

Henninger waved him away and pulled out a chair at a four-top. "Sit, Middleford, sit." Arch sat.

"I must admit there is a bit of showmanship involved, but I mean it to set the stage, to establish the proper mood. You see, all of the men I've invited are so wealthy that what I'm proposing is a lark, not a serious investment. Think of it as an entertaining way to use a little of your money, like going to the track, but without the element of chance and the unwashed crowd."

"Go on, I'm intrigued."

Henninger made a production of lighting another cigarette and then eating the extra maraschino before he spoke. "As you can see from this setting, I'm putting together something out of the ordinary. This place is Jack Rockefeller's idea. He had his 'star-studded' opening last week and was lionized in the society pages. I've never had any use for the tight-assed old bastard, and I can tell you it took some tricky footwork to keep him from knowing that it's me who's taking the place over on Wednesday." Henninger chuckled at the thought. "That is going to make the entire evening so much more enjoyable. By the way, you will be bringing that enchanting young lady, won't you? The one you were with the other evening."

"She hasn't expressed much interest but now that I've seen this place and with what you describe, I'm sure she'll change her mind. I've been telling her that it was going to be a discussion of unusual investment opportunities and that did not interest her in the least. She knows even less about the stock market than I do."

Henninger put an elbow on the table, leaned closer to Arch, and dropped his voice. "Let me explain how banking and stock trading, in fact, the whole financial system in America works. This is the truth that you won't hear from anyone else.

"A few of us, say one or two thousand men, are lucky enough to be born at the right time to the right families. We go to the same schools, bed the same girls, marry the same women, and then we're placed in positions of responsibility. We learn how the economic systems operate, and we persuade the government to create new looser rules that allow us to make piles and piles of money. Everything works fine until we get greedy. Recently we got so greedy that the whole system almost collapsed. We came out of it well enough, of course, but everyone else took it on the chin. That makes the men in government feel like they've got to do something, so they try to put new limits on us. But they don't really understand the complexities of the system and so they ask us to help them with new rules. We complain but agree. After the rules are changed, we continue to complain. We still make money with the new limits but we don't make as much money. Then after enough time has passed and people have forgotten what happened, we persuade the government that the rules need to be loosened again. They change the rules the way we like and we make piles and piles of money. Then we get greedy… You follow?"

Impressed, Arch nodded.

"And finally, after amassing more than we can count, what do we do with it?"

Chapter Fifty-One

Mondays were always slow. This one was slower than most. We had six customers. Frenchy was polishing glasses behind the bar. Connie and Marie Therese were talking seriously about something at a two-top. I was at my table in back catching up on the Hauptmann news.

The New Jersey grand jury was about to convene and everybody was sure they'd indict Bruno on kidnapping and murder charges. In case that fell through, the Bronx grand jury was ready to charge him on illegal entry into the country, extortion, gold hoarding, and a Sullivan beef for the little automatic they found in his garage. If they convicted him on all of those, they could lock him up for the rest of his life. But that probably wouldn't happen because Jersey had two new eyewitnesses who could put Hauptmann near the Lindbergh house before the kidnapping.

Bruno still claimed that he was completely innocent. He'd decided on his story and nothing was going to make him change it.

The telephone in my office rang about eight o'clock. I gimped upstairs, and the phone kept ringing. I knew who it was.

The Bureau man said, "What do you have for me?"

"It looks like Voss's kraut thugs have ten sticks of an explosive called polnol."

"They've got a lot more than that." Sounding like it didn't mean anything. "They recruit construction workers, veterans, service members. They're interested in anyone who has access to weapons and explosives. They're setting up camps upstate where they have regular military 'training drills.' I wouldn't worry about that if I were you. Dr. Griebl is much more important, and he says he's ready to cooperate."

"You talked to him?"

"Oh, yes. I showed him what we've got on him—hard evidence he couldn't deny of the Fort Totten plan and others. Then he started to talk.

He's still lying, of course. They all do that. They think if they mix a little bit of truth with self-serving lies we won't be able to tell the difference."

"What did he say about Fat Joe?"

"He's still denying that. In fact, he says he's never been in your establishment. That will change after you talk to the grand jury."

I didn't say anything.

"The approval review will finish tomorrow. I'll bring the forms for your signature the day after."

"No, unless you're here to buy a drink, I don't want to be seen with you."

He laughed a little. "Certainly. I understand. It might not look so good with some of your friends. Don't worry. I can be discreet."

"What about Voss?"

"Dr. Griebl will give us Voss. That's the idea."

"What do you know about him?"

"I've seen his file. It's thin. No one even knew he was in the country. The important details are the SS connection and a rumor that he's related to Himmler."

"Himmler?"

"Heinrich Himmler, one of Hitler's top men, the Reichsführer of the SS. According to a note in his file, Voss was involved in planning the Reichstag fire, but we have no good evidence."

"If you didn't know he was in the country, you don't know where he is."

"No."

"Next time he comes in, I'll ask him."

"The next time he comes in, you call me immediately."

Before I could answer, there was a quick knock on my door. It was Arch. I told Turcot I'd call him back.

Arch sat and loosened his tie. "I've just had an interesting evening with Henninger. D'you know what the Rainbow Room is?"

"I saw something about it in the *Journal*. Tony night club in Rockefeller Center?"

"That's it, but to be precise, it's on top of Rockefeller Center. I just visited the place with Henninger. He has apparently rented it out this Wednesday. He's invited a group of his fellow capitalists to view a piratical investment opportunity. Have I told you about this?"

"No." Since that night at the Divan Parisiene restaurant when Arch and Connie met Henninger I'd been so involved with the Nazi business,

I hadn't been paying much attention to the details of what he was up to. Truth is, I figured all that Arch was really interested in was hitting the sheets with Daphne.

"Remember that when she first came here, she was looking for help because she thought Henninger was getting involved in another shady business deal. She wanted to make sure she had a way out if it went south. Henninger has bought my little deception completely. He thinks my name is Middleford and I have made such a killing in the jute market that I am rolling in dough and can afford to join this East River Yacht Club of his. He also thinks that I am interested in something that he's calling a 'piratical investment opportunity.' He's reeling potential investors in by not giving away any of the details until he has this unveiling on Wednesday at the Rainbow Room, high atop Rockefeller Center."

"And you're going to go. Is Daphne?"

"Oh yes, and he specifically asked if Connie would be joining me."

That got my back up, remembering the Parisiene. "Is she?"

"We haven't talked about it yet, but I imagine she will, to show support for Daphne."

"What are you going to do?"

"I don't think we can string Henninger along much longer. He's going to realize that something's not kosher. He's got another woman, younger than Daphne, so she can see the possibility that this relationship is close to an end. If that happens, she wants to walk away with as much cash as she can. Ideally then, she'd sell the house on Gay Street."

"Can she do that? I vaguely remember that she told me she'd have to have his signature to unload the place."

"She says she can forge it."

"Good luck to her then."

"Getting back to the more important subject," Arch said, "have you been in touch with the Bureau man?"

"That was him on the line when you came in. He says the polnol is not that big a deal. The Krauts try to recruit all kinds of guys who can get their hands on explosives and guns. After I told him about Griebl and Voss, he's going after the doctor. Says he's ready to sing before a grand jury."

"I thought you said Griebl and the Moog woman were on their way back to Germany."

I nodded. "Griebl's stringing Turcot along just like I am. Turcot says Griebl will give him Voss but the Bureau doesn't know where Voss is."

Neither one of us said anything for a time until Arch piped up. "Isn't this the damnedest mare's nest of a mess—no, two mare's nests of two messes. If there's any sense to be made, I cannot see it."

After we closed and Connie and I were back at the Chelsea, I told her what Arch said about her coming to Henninger's 'unveiling' at the Rainbow Room.

She said, "Daphne told me about it," sounding distracted, like she didn't want to talk about it. "She doesn't know any more than Arch does." She took off her clothes quickly and put on her robe.

"Are you going to go."

"I think I have to."

"That's going to make us short-handed Wednesday night. There's another Kraut rally up in Germantown."

"And you're providing the teargas? I don't like it, Jimmy. Why are you doing this, it's not your fight."

"It is my fight. There's a chance the guys who killed Fat Joe will be there."

Then she started to get mad. "Why do we keep coming back to Fat Joe? He was a fat, lazy, foulmouthed son of a bitch. He didn't give a damn about you or me or Jimmy's Place. It was where he got free beer and a paycheck he didn't earn. You don't owe him anything. Don't do anything for him that spoils what we have."

She went on like that for another five minutes until she had tears in her eyes and that made her mad at herself. "Goddammit, after everything we have been through in the last two years, you are not going to let him ruin it. We've got what we need, Jimmy. We're doing good business. We're legal—"

"Mostly legal."

She threw up her hands. "Yes, we're mostly legal and I shouldn't say anything about that. You're not going to change. If Lansky wants you to do something, you'll do it."

"And if Daphne wants you to do something, you'll do it?"

She shook her head, still angry, as angry as I'd ever seen her. "No, that's different. I'm going to go with Arch and I'm going to see Henninger but it's not what you think. It's nothing like what you think."

That night, I couldn't find a way to tell her it wasn't really about Fat Joe any more. Everything she said about him was right. But after they killed him, they attacked my place. I would not let the bastards get away with it.

Chapter Fifty-Two

There it was on the front page of the Tuesday *Times*:

FLEMINGTON, N.J., Oct 8.—The text of the indictment returned today against Bruno Richard Hauptmann follows:
Hunterdon County Court of Oyer and Terminer,
Hunterdon County.
The grand inquest for the State of New Jersey in and for the body of the County of Hunterdon, upon their respective oaths, present: That Bruno Richard Hauptmann, on the first day of March in the year of Our Lord, one thousand and nine hundred and thirty-two, at the Township of East Amwell, in the County of Hunterdon aforesaid and within the jurisdiction of this court, did unlawfully, willfully, feloniously, and of his malice aforethought, kill and murder Charles A. Lindbergh Jr., contrary to the form of the statutes in such case made and provided and against the peace of this State, the government and dignity of the same.
ANTHONY M. HAUCK Jr.
Prosecutor of the Pleas of Hunterdon County.

I was reading the paper at the corner table in the kitchen of the Cruzon Grill. It was before noon. I was having eggs with a sliced tomato and toast. The stilted legal language seemed like the right thing for my cranky, confused mood. I couldn't stop going over everything that had happened over the past weeks, and maybe the indictment marked the end of something for Hauptmann. I didn't know what that something was, but for me, it had begun that afternoon when they brought him in at the Second Precinct Station House.

After I finished, I walked over to the garage on Ninth Avenue. It was a cool day, good for walking, but I couldn't forget seeing that other garage where they'd killed Fat Joe and remembering how they'd torn my place up, so I kept one hand on the .32 in the pocket of my topcoat and paid close attention to every guy I saw. If anybody was interested in me, I didn't see him. When I got to the garage, I unlocked the trunk of the Ford. The box of grenades was still there. I checked the float on the fuel gauge. More than half full. I didn't need to worry about that. I had a lot of other items on my worry list. First, Connie. I didn't want her to have anything to do with Henninger. Beyond my jealousy, which I wasn't going to pretend to hide, everything I knew about the man struck me wrong. Nothing good could come from dealing with him.

I worried over that as I walked back to the bar. When I got there, I propped the front door open, even though it was early for business, and did the same with the back door just to move some fresh air into the place. I was emptying and cleaning the ashtrays when Moe Sedway rapped on the door and walked in. I told him to close the front door and lock it. I got the back door. While I was doing that, I made sure there was nobody on the stairs or in the basement. Even so, Moe and I talked at the bar and kept our voices down.

He said, "Nat Arno wants to be sure you're still driving the green Ford, right? He says the krauts always start their rallies by the river in Carl Schurz Park. They like to get ready by playing some oom-pah music and drinking beer. Around six they'll march over to the theater on Eighty-Fifth. Most of them will be cockeyed from the beer by then. Nat wants you should park near the I.R.T. El station at Second and Eighty-Sixth. His guys will find you there."

"What time?"

"Be there by five. And if there are any grenades left when this is over, ditch 'em."

Business picked up Tuesday night. Frenchy and I stayed busy enough behind the bar. Marie Therese and Connie handled the tables and booths. Arch came in around nine. He ducked under the pass-through and put on an apron. By then things had slowed down, so I told Frenchy and Marie Therese to take the rest of the night off. After they left, Arch said he needed to talk to me and Connie.

We kicked the last customers out around one. Connie took care of the count. I cleaned the tables and sent the dirty glasses up in the dumbwaiter. Arch ran the vacuum cleaner. When we finished, I poured drinks and we sat at a four-top.

Arch said, "Connie tells me that you have other business to take care of tomorrow evening and the details are confidential. You can't talk about it and I'm not asking you to." I nodded. "May I ask if it will it have anything to do with Fat Joe or the missing explosives?"

"I don't know. It could. I'm just a deliveryman."

Connie snorted. "In a pig's ass you're a deliveryman." Being around me had changed the way she talked. And the way she thought.

"If things play out right, I should be back here by eight, nine at the latest."

"That's when Connie and I and Daphne will be attending Henninger's affair at the Rainbow Room. Daphne and I have discussed this more fully, and she's talked to you about it," he said to Connie. She nodded.

Arch's voice changed. He looked serious and spoke slowly. "To use the common expression, she is caught on the horns of a dilemma. On one hand, she suspects that Harold is up to something that could get him and her and everyone involved into trouble. And she knows that if that's the case, then Henninger is so well connected he'll waltz away from it and leave everybody else holding the bag. On the other hand, if he were to catch her trying to run away from their relationship, he could make her life hell."

"So, being a practical woman," Connie said, "she wants to do nothing for now, or at least until she learns what he's up to tomorrow. And so we are going to follow her lead. We'll go to this Rainbow Room—"

"Which you want to see anyway."

"Which I want to see anyway. No matter what Henninger is selling, Arch won't be buying, and when it's over, we'll be able to talk things over with Daphne and help her decide what to do."

"You see, it couldn't be simpler," Arch said.

Chapter Fifty-Three

On Wednesday, the governors of New York and New Jersey agreed that they'd extradite Hauptmann PDQ, and they made sure everybody knew about it. Early on Tuesday afternoon, the New Jersey governor telephoned the New York governor to say he was going to sign the extradition papers within hours. Where should he send them? To my home in the city, said the New York governor. At four-thirty in Trenton, the Jersey governor gathered a few of his fellow bigwigs and the press photographers to take pictures of them as he signed the papers. Before five o'clock, the papers were in an automobile speeding north to the other governor's place on Park Avenue. He got them about seven. Camera men were on hand to take more pictures of more bigwigs as the other governor accepted the papers.

I spent the afternoon getting things set up at Jimmy's Place and went back to the Chelsea around four. I found a pair of khaki pants, work shirt, wool necktie, leather jacket, Keds, and my most battered fedora. I was tempted to slip the knucks into my pocket but nothing had changed from Newark. I could get locked up for a weapon like the knucks and I'd never see them again. My stick was legal and a lot more useful in most situations. I was ready to leave when I had another thought. Like the stick, money is useful in most situations. I found the lockbox in the closet and added some fives to my money clip. I had the pictures of the four Nazi thugs in my jacket pocket.

I drove slowly uptown in the afternoon East Side traffic. As I got closer to Yorkville, foot traffic on the sidewalks was thicker. More brown shirts, Sam Brown belts, and red swastika armbands. Lots of men drinking beer on the street, laughing, fooling around. It seemed almost like a Saturday or a holiday. When I got close to Carl Schurz Park, I could hear an amateur band playing. There were more cops than you'd expect to see in a neighborhood like that on a Wednesday evening, but not that many more, not nearly as many as I'd seen in Newark. I had to circle several blocks before I found a space on Eighty-Sixth close to Second where I could park. I checked my watch. Ten to five. Most of the pedestrians were walking east, toward the park. I locked the doors and went around to the back to make sure the grenades were still in the crate. I was crouched down looking in the trunk when I heard horns blowing nearby. A long black Cadillac was stopped in the street beside my front fender. A chauffeur hopped out and opened the back door on the other side of the car.

Franz Voss got out.

I stayed in a crouch and edged closer to the curb, trying to make sure he didn't see me. He might've if he'd turned in my direction but he held the door open and said something to someone in the back seat. The horns continued. Voss ignored them. When he finished talking, he went toward the front of the car, away from me, and then turned onto the sidewalk. I saw that he was carrying a large briefcase in one hand. It was made of red leather with an accordion bottom. Heavy, judging by the way he gripped it and flexed his arm as he walked. The horns were even louder by then, and the sound of them changed as more joined in. The chauffeur paid no attention to them as he got behind the wheel and pulled away slowly. The Cadillac had traveled a few yards and was even with Voss when it stopped again. The chorus of horns restarted, louder and angrier. The back door closest to me was thrown open and a big man got out. He yelled so loud I could hear it over the horns, "Don't forget tonight, cousin. You promised."

It was Harold Henninger.

I swear I felt the pavement shifting under my Keds.

When the Cadillac moved again, I locked the trunk and leaned on it for a time, because I was so damn confused by what I'd just seen that I couldn't think straight. It passed. *Don't try to figure it out now, you've got work to do.* I looked down the street and saw Voss heading west. I followed. He turned left at the next intersection, continued for a block until he reached the Lyceum Theater. Two long red banners with the black swastika in the white circle were hanging from the second floor on both sides of the doors. They hadn't been there on Sunday. A hand-lettered poster above the ticket window read "Triumph des Willens." An older man in shirtsleeves and armband, was standing in front of the ticket booth. He raised his hand in greeting when he saw Voss. Voss waved back and they shook hands.

I leaned on my stick and pretended to be interested in whatever the German-American Business League was selling. The two men continued to talk. After a time, Voss cracked open the briefcase and pulled out a round can of film about a foot and a half across. He handed it to the other man, and they walked inside. With Voss out of sight, I went back to my useless speculating. What did it mean that Voss and Henninger were cousins? Then I tried to tell myself that I was wrong. I'd only seen Henniger that one night at the Parisiene. This must be some another big guy in a rich man's car. But, no, it was him, alright, and Voss had promised to see him later that night. He must be on the guest list at the Rainbow Room, and that meant… What? Eventually I remembered I was not where I was supposed to be and I hurried back to my Ford. Nat Arno, Newark's Fighting Hebrew, was waiting for me.

He was wearing a short jacket and a blue American Legion garrison cap. "Where the hell've you been?" He sounded tight, nervous.

"Casing the theater where the rally's gonna be. Looks like they're showing a kraut movie."

By then the sidewalk was filled with people, mostly men, walking west and we could hear the band moving closer. Nat and I stood close to the back of the car with the trunk closed. We made sure there were no cops in sight. I lifted the trunk. Nat reached in, took a couple of grenades from the box and slipped them into his pockets. As he did, I saw that he had a sawed-off pool cue under his jacket. His lips hardly moved when he spoke. "The other guys're coming by one at a time. We've all got Legionnaire's caps."

"How many?"

"Three, Abie Bain and a couple of the guys from Newark, and no need for you to hang around. Longy wants us to take care of these bastards."

"Take a look at these." I gave him the photographs. "These four guys busted up my place and they're members some kraut outfit called the Silver Shirts or something. If you see 'em, give 'em the business as hard as you can."

Nat crammed the pictures into his pocket. He said he'd show them to the others at the theater and hurried away. I stayed by the car. It took more than thirty minutes for the Abie and the other two to get their grenades.

When I'd passed out the last of them, I found my work gloves in the trunk and gimped back to the theater. Maybe Connie was right and it wasn't my fight, but Voss was there, and I had to know what he was up to. A thick crowd in front of the theater was moving slowly toward the doors. Streetlights had come on by then. I couldn't see any of Nat's guys but there were a lot of Nazi armbands around me. The crowd stunk of beer breath and sweat, and I heard more German than English.

In a thick crowd like that, being short can make it easy to shoulder through if you keep moving and don't mind stomping on some feet and using a cane to your advantage. I got close enough to the ticket booth to see that they weren't charging admission but they were handing out tickets and tearing stubs. I didn't bother with that, just slipped in through the bottleneck at the lobby doors and kept going forward with the flow of the crowd.

As I saw when I drove past it on Sunday, the Lyceum was a medium-sized older theatre, five, maybe six hundred seats. Not one of the grand palaces, but it was large enough to have a balcony. Most of the guys around me went straight through the doors to the main floor seating. There were two sets of stairs on either side of those doors leading up to the balcony and projection booth. I went that way, climbing the worn carpet on the stairs. I stopped near the top and looked down at the lobby, hoping to see a face I knew, but there was nobody, not one of Nat's guys, no blonde thug, no Voss. *What the hell was Voss doing with Henninger?*

On the second floor there was a smaller lobby and bathrooms. The projection booth was halfway down behind a door with a small glass window. Three doorways led to the seats. Maybe a dozen guys were already sitting there. I gimped down the steps to the first row and looked down at the ground floor. It was filling up fast. There were two more of the long red Nazi banners flanking the stage, a lectern and microphone stand in the center in front of a faded curtain. I took a seat in the last row beside one of the doors and waited and thought about Voss and Henninger. The more I thought, the angrier and more scared I got. I'd known since they killed Fat Joe that this was going to come to a bad end for somebody. I didn't have any reason to think that about Arch and Daphne's business. But if the two things had something to do with each other, then everything I thought was wrong. That made me even more angry and scared.

I guess it took another twenty or thirty minutes for the balcony to fill. Toward the end, one of Nat's sluggers came down the aisle beside me and found a seat in the middle of the section. A few minutes later, we heard the scratchy sound of a needle being put on a phonograph record and then loud music that the krauts knew. They all stood up and started singing "Deutschland, Deutschland, **über** alles." While the music played, a guy walked out from one of the wings to the center of the stage where he gripped the sides of the lectern and tried to look big. He wore black jodhpurs, shiny black boots, silvery gray shirt, black necktie, red armband. I was too far away to make out his features but I could tell it wasn't Voss or Dr. Griebl or any of the blond thugs. Whoever he was, he got a round of applause when the music finished.

Then he started talking in German. He went on for a few minutes until somebody in the crowd downstairs, one of Nat's guys probably, yelled out, "Why're you talking German? This is America. Talk American when you're here." He was cut off by more yelling and what sounded like guys trying to shut him up. Things quieted down and the guy at the lectern continued in German. He gestured back toward the curtain and I guessed he was saying something about the moving picture we were about to see. While he was talking, there was a lot coming and going around me as the Krauts headed for the bathrooms to offload their beer. I got up myself, just to move around. It figured that once Nat's guys got going I wouldn't want to be stuck in a seat.

When it sounded like the speaker was coming to an end, he gestured toward the projection booth and said, "Music." The lights went down, and the curtain parted revealing a white screen. The projector came on and filled the screen with light. The guy who'd been speaking moved away. The needle hit another phonograph record and music that sounded like an orchestra with horns and strings filled the theater. The screen went gray and the words "Am 5. September 1934" appeared. More than a month ago.

The picture started in the cockpit of a big airplane looking through the windshield at fluffy white clouds below. Then the airplane went down through the clouds and came out over an old city. You could see the shadow of the plane passing over church steeples, narrow streets, and buildings. The plane, a three-engine job, landed at a field surrounded by excited men and women and children who raised their hands in the Nazi salute. Then the little guy with the Charlie Chaplin mustache and the oily slicked down hair came out of the plane in a big overcoat. As he looked at the crowd, his little arm went up in a swishy version of the salute they were giving to him. After that, he was standing in the back of an open car as it drove down roads with more crowds of happy people and tight rows of soldiers on both sides.

If the whole picture was on that one reel of film that Voss brought, it probably had another ten or fifteen minutes to go when Nat's sluggers went to work. Angry voices came up from below, and over the loud phonograph music, I could hear guys yelling and cursing and smacking each other. That got the ones around me in the balcony jazzed and most of them ran for the stairs to go down the ground floor. I gimped over to the back wall of the second-floor lobby where I was out of the way and slipped on the work gloves. The picture was still going on and the balcony had emptied out when there was a loud scratching sound as the phonograph needle was knocked across the record. Judging by the noise from downstairs, including police whistles, a full brawl had broken out on the main floor

I went over to the projection booth and tried to look through the little window in the door but it was too high. I put my ear to the door and could hear the grinding whir of the equipment and two angry voices. The voices stopped with a loud thud from inside the booth that made the door vibrate. I stepped back. Moments later, the door flew open and a man with a bloody face stumbled out and landed on his back. The floor of the booth was two steps up. A second man jumped down the steps and stood in the doorway. The first man scrambled to his feet and ran for the stairs. A second man reached for the door to pull it shut. It was the big blond Nazi thug, the same one who'd been sitting at my bar before he tried to tear up my place. He recognized me two seconds after I recognized him. That was all I needed. Well, almost all I needed.

We about ten feet apart. I brought the tip of the stick up, aimed it at the center of his body and rushed him. I knocked him back. His heel caught the step behind him and he landed on his ass. I kept pushing forward, lowered the tip and stabbed his crotch. When he curled up, I cracked the top of his blond head twice and drew blood. Without getting to his feet, he crawled back up the steps fast. I stayed right behind him into the booth and kept hitting him wherever I saw an opening. The last thing I wanted was for the big son of a bitch to get to his feet.

At first, I didn't take in any details of the booth other than the noisy projector and the light from it that was reflected onto the black walls and ceiling. The blond thug, stayed on his side, his hands covering his head. He kicked at me and that kept me back. He managed to roll onto his hands and knees and tried to crawl away from me but I got close enough to reverse the cane and hit the back of his head. That stunned him. I continued to hit him as hard and fast as I could until he collapsed flat on the floor. Then I hit him some more. Yes, I will hit a man when he's down if I think he'll get back up and hit me.

When he stopped moving, my heart was hammering and I was breathing so hard that I felt like I wasn't getting any air. Both knees went weak. I would've fallen if I hadn't seen the little rolling stool beside the projector. I collapsed on it. I don't know how long I sat there trying to calm down.

The noise of the projector was so loud that I couldn't tell anything about what was happening in the theater. When I looked around the little room, I saw that there were two projectors, a rack on one wall for the big cans of film, and another rack for the banged-up fiberboard containers with canvas straps they used to ship the reels. Voss's red briefcase was on that rack. Near the projectors was wooden table with a metal gizmo for splicing film bolted to the surface. The phonograph that had been playing the music was also on that table. The needle was ticking at the end of the record. When I thought I was able to stand, I got up and looked through the projector window down at the floor of the theater. Nobody was watching the moving picture. The fighting had moved up onto the stage and guys were getting knocked against the screen. Some guys with armbands were heading for the aisles but more of them were trying to duke it out with Nat's sluggers and they were not having a good time of it. It was the same thing that went on in Newark, a few experienced, motivated fighters against a bunch of half-drunk bullies.

On the screen, more smiling people were raising their arms in salute.

I went over to the rack and picked up the red briefcase. It was heavier than I thought it would be. I took it over to the table where I could see better and pulled the top open. First thing, I heard another whirring sound, faint under the sound of the projector. When I got the top all the way open, I saw the bomb.

Chapter Fifty-Four

I knew what bombs could do. I remembered the big one on Wall Street and years later, a guy tried to blow up the back gate of my place and got himself instead. But the only bombs I'd seen were in moving pictures. Those bombs were put together neatly and they looked scary. This one was messy but still scary. It took me a few moments to figure what it was and how it worked. The first thing I noticed, right on top, was a one-hour wind-up timer, the kind you could buy in the Kitchen Department at Macy's. Two insulated copper wires had been soldered to the timer. One was on the tip of the arrow that was turning, and one was on the zero on the body of the timer. It looked like about three minutes were left but it was hard to tell from the way the projector flashed, filling the booth with white light in the bright shots and turning it black in the dark ones.

The timer was near the top of the briefcase. Wadded up newspaper pages had been stuffed around it to keep it in place. I pulled them out carefully and got even more scared when I saw what was underneath. The timer sat on a tangled mess of copper wire with black insulation. Below it, on the bottom of the briefcase, there were two big square batteries wired together. Looked like they might be meant for a lantern. Six sticks of Arch's polnol were next to them. A smaller cylinder, about the size of a pencil was stuck into one of the sticks. The pencil had two thin wires coming out of it. I could see that one of those wires was soldered to the arrow of the timer. The second wire disappeared under the tangle of thicker wires. A third wire probably went from the zero on the timer to the other battery but that one disappeared into the tangle, too. It didn't take Thomas Edison to see that when the timer hit zero, the connection would be complete. The problem was that the briefcase was crammed with so much extra wire.

I studied the damn thing. What to do? Try to crank the arrow back? No, maybe that would set it off. Yank the wires loose? Leave it alone and run out of the theater? That's about as far as I'd got when I heard the blond thug getting to his feet. Without thinking, I twisted around and whipped the crook end of the stick at him. I didn't mean to catch him in the throat but I'm not sorry I did. He fell back, gurgling. I didn't have time for him and went back to the bomb.

The work gloves made my hands clumsy as I moved the timer to one side so I could get a better look at the connections. The guy who made it didn't try to be neat. He'd used a lot of wire and it was so bent and mashed together that I had to pull at the pieces gently to get them apart. The first thing was to make sure both terminals of the batteries were clear. The light in the booth still changed with each quick shot, going from near complete darkness to blinding white, then back to black. Neither was helpful.

After looking at it longer than I should, I realized that the wires connecting the pencil were thinner than the others. I started at one coming out of the pencil and pulled at it carefully to separate it from the other wires and pushed them away. I worked by feel during the times when I couldn't see into the briefcase. When a bright moment came, I tilted the case so I could see down to the battery. There it was. For a second or two I could see where the thin wire from the pencil was twisted around a battery terminal. Hoping that I wasn't about to blow myself up, I pressed down on the top of the battery with one hand and tugged on the wire with the other. It slipped through my fingers and the briefcase skidded on the table. That was the scariest moment when I thought it was going to blow up. After my breathing returned to normal, I pushed down on the battery again, wrapped the thin wire around my fingers, and pulled on it as hard as I could. It came loose.

I moved it to one side and bent it to keep it from swinging back inside the briefcase. Then I parted the tangled wires with both hands, trying to find the other connection. It was harder because all of the other wires were thicker and the same shade of black insulation. After more fumbling through the tangle, I separated the wire that ran from the zero on the timer to the battery terminal. Again, it took two tries to yank it loose, and just as I pulled it free, the timer hit zero with a cheerful chime that made me jump back. After my breathing returned to normal again, I realized that they were still fighting outside.

I probably should have taken time to think it through, but I knew there were cops in the theater and the last thing I wanted was to be caught in the projection booth with a bomb and a body. The moving picture was still going. When it lit up the booth, I did a quick check to make sure nothing of mine had come loose and opened the door, letting in more light from the balcony lobby and sound from downstairs where Nat's sluggers were still hard at work. I stepped out of the booth and found an empty balcony. Almost empty. A couple of guys with armbands were staggering toward the stairs but that was all. I caught a small sting of teargas but none of the grenades had gone off on the balcony level. I looked back at the blond thug face down on the floor. He wasn't gurgling. I turned the thumb lock on the inside of the door, and closed it.

Heading toward the stairs, I saw that my work gloves were stained with blood, and so was my stick. I stuffed the gloves in my jacket pocket. For the moment, I didn't worry about the stick. You couldn't really see the red blood on the black wood, just like you couldn't see it on the black asphalt they'd dumped on Fat Joe.

Down on the first floor, it looked like about half the krauts had made an early exit. A dozen cops were inside the theater breaking things up between the belligerents, but I didn't hang around long enough to tell any more than that. There couldn't be many more minutes on that reel of film and as soon as it was over, somebody would be breaking into the projection booth. It looked like the theater owner was in on Voss's operation. If he found the dead thug before the cops did, what would he do?

On the way back to my car on Eighty-Sixth, I walked at a slow pace. All around me, guys were running toward the Lyceum or away from it. What I'd done didn't really hit me until I was behind the wheel of the car. I was about to put the key in when a chill came over me and I felt like I was going to be sick. Something like that has happened every time I've had to kill a guy. This one wasn't as bad as the worst. When it passed, I started the car and drove carefully back downtown.

What was my next move?

Chapter Fifty-Five

I stashed the Ford at the garage and walked back to the Chelsea. On the way, I made a list of things I had to do. First, ditch the bloody gloves in a trash can. Then I went back to Henninger and Voss and what they were up to. That took more thought and right then, I had no ideas. I wanted to go to the Rainbow Room but I had no chance of getting in the way I was dressed.

It was close to nine o'clock when I got to my rooms. I bundled up the clothes I'd been wearing for the trash. Soap and water cleaned the stick. After I'd taken care of that, I had a long shower and tried to use that time with the water pelting down on me to clear my head so I could come up with a plan. It didn't work. After the shower, I found a clean white shirt and a black three-piece single-breasted, one of Arnold Constable's best. It was a few years old and fit like it had been made for me. Finished it all off with a green and gold silk tie, and comfortable black shoes. Checked myself in the mirror and saw that I was everything that a good looking young gatecrasher ought to be. Yes, less than an hour after I'd killed a man, I was cracking bad jokes to myself. That shows you how shallow I am, or it means that I was alive and the blond Nazi thug who killed Fat Joe and tore up my place wasn't. Either way, so be it.

When I went to my dresser to finish the ensemble with my favorite brass knucks, they weren't there. Now, there was no question that I'd left them anywhere else. If the knucks weren't in my pocket, they were in the tray on my dresser, and I remembered putting them there a few hours earlier when I couldn't take them to the Lyceum. If they weren't where I'd left them, then there was only one possibility. Connie took them.

Smart girl.

I went into the bar through the gate in the alley. As soon as I opened the back door, I could smell something from the Cruzon Grill and knew I had to eat before I did anything else. I went straight up the stairs to the kitchen and told one of the guys working the grill to fix whatever he had on hand and send it down to my office. Then I went down to the bar to see how Frenchy and Marie Therese were doing. For a Wednesday, business was fine, what I could expect it to be.

I was back in my office before the food arrived. I don't remember what it was. After I ate, I opened the safe and took out five hundred dollars. I put the bills in a Corn Bank deposit envelope. Then I reached into the back of the bottom shelf and took out the Walther .32. It wouldn't fit in my vest but it was short, thinner than a revolver, and, in a coat pocket, it didn't spoil the drape. I called Frenchy again and asked him to get a cab.

At Rockefeller Center, I found the door on Forty-Ninth Street that Arch told me about. Went up the escalator to the lobby and wandered around until I saw the curtain that separated the Rainbow Room elevators from the others. There was a "Closed for Private Party" sign in front of it and a good-sized guy with a clipboard. He noticed me and stood up from his stool as soon as I got close.

"Invitation only, sir. Are you on the list?"

"No, but I work for Mr. Middleford—he's on the list—and he asked me to bring him something. I need to go up." I tried not to sound like an uneducated thug.

"Sure you do." He'd heard that kind of story a hundred times.

"Do you know what's going on up there?"

"That's none of my business."

"It's some kind of investment presentation. Mr. Henninger didn't share many of the details with Mr. Middleford, and it's none of my business either, but" I slipped the Corn Bank deposit envelope out of my breast pocket and opened it far enough for the guard to see that it was a thick stack of cash with a twenty in front. "This is what Mr. Middleford asked me to bring to him. Hand it to him personally, he said. If you call the Rainbow Room and ask for Mr. Archibald Middleford and tell him that his assistant is here, he'll tell you to send me up."

The guard looked skeptical.

"If you don't call, it's your ass, not mine."

He understood my logic and found a telephone. After about fifteen nervous minutes, I stepped into the elevator.

Sixty-five floors later, the doors opened on a small dimly lit lobby that led to a T-intersection with a hallway, also dimly lit. I could see lights and hear people on my left. The longer part of the hallway went off to my right. I followed it to the signs for the restrooms and locked doors leading to a Gallery and another room. Past that, the hallway became a shallow ramp that led to another set of locked doors. I turned around and went back the other way. The hall ended at steps that led down to the Rainbow Room.

The joint was every bit as spectacular as Arch described. All that glass and outside, the city lights winking and sparkling below. Inside, they'd set up buffet tables at one end near an open bar. A six-piece jazz group was playing softly on a stage right below me. A hundred people, give or take, were standing and sitting, chatting and drinking on the round dance floor and the tables around it. The men came from the same crowd I'd seen at the Parisiene. Older wealthy guys with really attractive young women who were dolled to the nines. Some of the men were in tuxedos, some white tie, some suits—a few of those as good as mine.

Arch had been waiting at a table at the foot of the steps and came right up. "What's going on," he muttered, worried.

I scanned the crowd carefully, slowly, looking for Franz Voss. He wasn't there. Daphne was on the far side of the room, talking to a couple of white-haired gents and laughing at something one of them said. Henninger was off to the side, by one of the windows, leaning over Connie, one big paw on the window glass. The other paw held a drink of something yellow. He'd maneuvered her near a corner, away from other people. Even at that distance, I could see how stiffly she was holding herself. She was wearing the black version of the knock-out blue outfit she brought back from Paris and a dark pink beret. Looked terrific. Henninger had his mouth near her ear and was yakking away nonstop. I wanted to split his skull with my stick. Connie was looking for a way out when she saw Arch and me.

"I don't know what's going on and that's why I'm here. I told you about the Nazi rally in Yorkville." He nodded, looking more worried. "I was there. A few hours ago, I saw Franz Voss get out of Henninger's car. Henninger called him 'cousin.'"

Arch's eyebrows went straight up. "Sweet mother of Jesus."

"That's only half of it. Voss had a bomb."

"What?"

"The rally was in a theater where they were showing some kind of Nazi moving picture. The leader of the krauts who killed Fat Joe was planning to set it off in the projection booth. I took care of him and the bomb."

Connie said something that shut Henninger up, and headed toward us.

"Voss was going to sacrifice a few of his fellow Nazis and blame it on the Jews or the Reds," Arch said. "Build some sympathy for the cause, the same thing they did with the Reichstag fire."

I hadn't figured that, but then, the old guy is smarter about those things than I am. He said, "But you didn't finagle your way in just to tell me that."

"As Voss was leaving, Henninger told him that he expected to see him tonight, he said Voss had promised."

Connie grabbed my arm. "What the hell are you doing here?"

Arch said, "Let's find a bit of privacy, people are starting to notice us." We moved back into the corridor toward the elevators.

"At the kraut rally this afternoon, I saw Franz Voss getting out of Henninger's Cadillac. Henninger called him cousin and said that he'd see him tonight. To me that means he's coming here. And as I was just telling Arch, Voss brought a bomb to the rally. The thug who killed Fat Joe was supposed to set it off in a movie theater. I kept him from doing that."

That was a lot to take in all at once and for a moment, Connie didn't know what to say.

"Has Henninger told you what he's up to?"

Arch and Connie shook their heads. "We don't know yet."

"He was about to tell me when you came in," Connie said. "All will be revealed when he produces the merchandize at eleven."

I looked at my wristwatch. It was almost eleven.

"Wait a minute," Connie said. "Let's go back to the bomb. What kind of bomb are you talking about? More tear gas grenades?"

"I think it was some of the missing polnol Arch found."

"And how did you keep him from blowing it up?"

"We fought over it in the projection booth of a theater. The rally was in the theater. I used my stick. Look, this talk is not getting us anywhere. Let me find out if Voss is here. I want to take a walk around, get the feel of the joint." What I really wanted to know was where the back door was. "We've got a better shot at finding him if we move around."

Connie said, "That's your plan for just about everything, wander around until you see something."

"Worked at the McAlpin didn't it?"

"No, you said you waited by the elevators until Miss Happy Hands walked by. You could do the same here. He's got to use the elevator."

"These aren't the only ones, and besides, the show's about to start."

Arch said O.K. Connie nodded, unhappy. "If that fat son of a bitch touches my ass again, he's going to eat his teeth."

Arch headed for the stairs. I grabbed Connie and pulled her farther back into the hall and kissed her seriously. She kissed me back the same way.

"When this is over, I'll explain everything, I promise."

She gave me one of her difficult looks and said, "So will I, whether you like it or not."

Chapter Fifty-Six

Henninger cornered Arch and Connie as they crossed the dance floor. I moved away from them to the other side of the room and made my way to the buffet tables. Looked like they had a nice spread of cold seafood and shellfish and smoked fish, steak, cheeses, fruit, everything you could want. If Vittorio served that up at the Cruzon Grill, the place would be mobbed, but with this crowd, the talk was about how none of it really measured up. It was the older guys who complained the most and their women generally agreed. I noticed that a lot of the tables were littered with plates of uneaten food. But I wasn't there for that. There were long screens behind the buffet tables. I walked to the far end and went behind the screens hoping to find a door to the kitchen. It was there, and traffic in and out of it was thick.

I continued around the room, staying close to the glass windows. I got the idea that Henninger's guests were getting antsy. Figure he hadn't told them any more than he'd told Arch, and they weren't used to being strung along like this. I kept moving until I was back at the stairs that led to the elevators and the restrooms. I went into the hall and then down the smaller hall to the men's and women's rooms. That's where I found what I needed to see—the fire door to the stairwell.

When I got back to the Rainbow Room, they were clearing the buffet and rearranging the tables. The jazz band had left the stage and a guy was setting up a microphone on a stand. Before he'd finished, Henninger lumbered up onto the stage and pushed him away. He started talking into the microphone but you couldn't hear anything over the people who were still yakking. Henninger motioned for the guy to come back and snarled at him. I hurried down the steps and gimped to the other side of the room. By then, people were closing in on the stage and Henninger had the microphone working.

He thumped it with his fat finger. The sound was so loud it startled people who hadn't been paying attention. He said, "Gentlemen, friends, and those of you who aren't gentlemen," he paused to chuckle, "gather round."

They did, most of the men close to the stage, the young women behind them. Henninger said, "All our lives we've played by the rules," and that got a big laugh. "Well, you know what I mean. Perhaps I should have said that we've played within the rules most of the time. But haven't you wanted to go off the reservation just once? To say, the hell with them. We've all managed to find ways to enjoy what we've earned but I've always wanted more—to test the rules, to take what I wanted knowing there was no safety net beneath me. I've done it and I am going to offer you the chance to do it, too."

By then, he had them. They agreed with him and they wanted to know more. I moved to a two-top near the raised seating area at the far end of the room where I could see what was going on. Waiters pulled the tablecloths off the long buffet tables, getting them ready for something else. I saw movement away from the crowd. It was Franz Voss in a black tuxedo pulling out a chair to sit at another two-top. He was on my side of the room but much closer to the stage, close enough that he and Henninger waved to each other. Henninger went on.

"All our lives, we've worked within a system that limits, I might even say strangles our natural aggressive, acquisitive instincts. Dr. Freud has told us that repressing these natural urges is unnatural. I found a way to break free of those limits, and I acted on it." Having set the hook, he paused.

"Gentlemen, I cannot tell you what a thrill it was. If you look around at the tables that are being set up around this dance floor, you will see stock certificates—yes, the very pieces of paper that we buy and sell every day but almost never see or touch—for many of our largest corporations and some for smaller, obscure companies. These are, I promise you, absolutely legitimate. No phonies." He paused again to let that one sink in.

"Now, you all know who I am. You know my reputation. If I say these are real, they're real."

Somebody in the crowd yelled, "If HH says it's true, it's true, we all know that."

"I cannot tell you what they are worth today but you can find that out. I also cannot guarantee their provenance or tell you how they came into my possession, but you've read the headlines and you know the stories. For this reason or that, certificates go missing or are misplaced. Things happen, and as we all know, possession is nine tenths." He raised one hand and snapped his fingers. "The young ladies who are passing among you are handing out lists of the items I've been describing."

"If you were to try to redeem these at any of the larger brokerage houses in the city, you might face questions, but if you take them outside the city as I did in Scranton, Stockton, and Muncie, you will get cashier's checks."

He pulled the three checks out of his breast pocket and held them high.

The waitresses who'd been serving drinks were walking through the group and handing out printed pages. The men were snatching them out of their hands and you could tell how excited they were. They were eating up everything Henninger dished out. At the same time, three waiters in white coats were setting out the stock certificates he'd talked about. Looked like there were about twenty stacks of the things, mostly big square pieces of thick paper. From what I could see, they were printed with illustrations and lettering done in brightly colored inks, like delicate tattoos. The guys who were arranging them on the table were being bossed by Romeo Forlini, the best forger in town, or so he claimed.

That's when part of it became clear to me and I thought 'absolutely legitimate… no phonies,' my ass. They were all counterfeit. How could a hot paper grifter like Forlini fool one of the most successful financial experts in the city? Then the answer came to me. No, it wasn't Forlini. It was Voss. He hired Forlini to create fake stock certificates. Then he convinced Henninger that he had a source for real stock certificates that could be peddled for pennies on the dollar. Voss put the deal together. I looked over to his table and saw that he was smiling, happy with himself. Then he slid his chair out and bent down for several seconds. I could see that he was working with something close to the floor, before he stood. He put a folded napkin over the back of the chair and stepped forward to join the crowd. He took a list from one of the waitresses and spoke to the man next to him. He pointed to something on the list and they began a conversation.

Staying close to the windows, I made my way to Voss's empty chair. Pulled it out and sat. Still warm. I lifted the white tablecloth and saw the briefcase. For a second, the sight of it froze me. Then, without really thinking about what I was doing, I picked it up and took it to the other side of the screens that had been set up behind the tables. Now, you could reasonably ask, why the hell did he pick up something that probably had a bomb in it? Believe me, I've asked myself the same thing many times. With the first briefcase, the circumstances were so strange that my screwy reactions make some kind of sense. But with the second, no… you see something that's going to explode, you get away from it as fast and as far as you can.

I didn't do that and, as I try to remember that night, I think the biggest part of it was that if Voss wanted that briefcase under that two-top, I wanted it to be somewhere else. If he wanted it to blow up, I wanted it not to blow up. Maybe it's as simple as that. Maybe I just wanted to piss him off.

Henninger finished his pitch and the crowd started applauding. They were still at it when I came around the last screen and gimped toward the elevators. The damn briefcase was so heavy I leaned heavily on the stick as I climbed the stairs. I was so slow that Arch caught up with me at the top. Connie was with him. Nobody paid any attention to us.

Arch hissed, "What's going on?"

I motioned for them to follow me and didn't say anything until we were out of sight in the hallway. "There's a bomb in here."

"What?"

"This is just like the one at the rally. The bomb was in a briefcase. I took care of it."

"How?"

"I pulled at some wires."

"Then you don't know what you're doing."

"No."

Arch said, "Give it to me. I have some experience in these matters. Now let's go somewhere private."

I handed him the briefcase and said, "Men's room's this way."

We went past the elevators and turned at the next hallway. When we got to the women's room, Connie stopped us. She said, "Wait here," and went inside. A minute later, two young women slammed the door open and hurried out, looking mean.

One of them said, "Do you believe she did that?"

"No, she must be crazy."

We went in and Connie locked the door behind us. I would've asked her what she did but I didn't want to waste time.

Arch put the briefcase on the vanity counter. "Was there any problem opening the first briefcase?"

"What do you mean?" I could feel my heart beating faster, and I could tell that Connie's was, too. What the hell had I got us into?

Arch said, "Sometimes they're designed to blow up in your face when you open them."

"I didn't think of that. Just pulled it open." This one was the same design—accordion bottom, top opened like a book, simple strap and latch to keep it closed. Arch moved it under the best light. He pulled the strap loose and eased the top open a fraction of an inch. He bent down to look into the gap between the two halves. Nothing. When he opened it fully and saw the kitchen timer and tangle of wires, he laughed. "Holy Christ, what a mess! This is the worst excuse for a bomb any idiot has ever made."

Voss had set the timer for one hour. It had fifty-three minutes left. Connie looked into the case and frowned. "But is it going to go off?"

"There's batteries and polnol under all that stuff," I said.

Arch pulled out the wadded newspaper and moved the tangle of wires to one side to uncover the polnol. He pulled the pencil out of the explosive and said, "It's good now." He held up the pencil. "This is the detonator. As long as it's not hooked up to the polnol, we're safe. But let's be sure about that. Hold this."

He handed me the pencil and pulled out the polnol. There were four sticks, held together by black tape. I was a little surprised to see that they weren't really sticks when Arch pulled off the tape. The four pieces were flexible, like damp clay wrapped in heavy waxed paper.

Arch said, "Now the briefcase is harmless. Or almost harmless. If these batteries produce enough juice to activate the detonator, it will explode. It's more powerful than a firecracker, but not much. Still, I've seen detonators blow off fingers and mangle careless hands. Now, how the hell did this thing get here?"

"Voss. He slipped in while Henninger was giving his sales pitch. It figures he's behind all this. These stock certificates he's pushing, they're counterfeit. Guy named Romeo Forlini made them. He's here tonight, too."

Connie said, "You saw him at the McAlpin."

"Right. Remember Petey Beck, the guy who made up the phony utility bills for us? He said the reason he was late with them was because he was in on some big deal with Forlini. Looks like this one called for a lot of work."

"But I don't understand. What's the connection between Voss and Forlini?" Connie said.

"Correct me I get any of this wrong," Arch said, "but here's a possibility. We can assume that Voss arranged the rally this evening in Yorkville, and he hoped to blow up a theater filled with German-Americans, which he planned to pin on the Jews or the Reds. And now Voss has arranged with Henninger—"

"His cousin."

"Voss has arranged with his cousin Harold to gather a group of New York's most important capitalists atop Rockefeller Center and he'll blow them up, too. Don't you see, the real threat isn't the Nazis, it's the Jew communists. They hate all of us, and they're so well-organized and dangerous they can set off two bombs on one night."

I was trying to work my way through Arch's reasoning when Connie said, "Then what are we going to do about it?"

Arch said, "I can fix Henninger's wagon, but what about Voss?"

"I want to say that as long as we've disarmed his bomb, we don't have to worry about him anymore, but how many of these goddamn things does he have? And if he's got more of them, what else would he like to blow up?"

"Oh, hell, Jimmy's Place." Connie almost looked panicked at the thought. "Arch, where's the telephone?"

"At that big mirrored bar on the back wall."

"I'm going to call Marie Therese and tell her to close up and go home."

"Tell her to try to get in touch with Mahan and Norris. Say somebody threatened to put a bomb in the place."

Connie grabbed her handbag and dashed out.

I told Arch that for the moment, I'd like Voss to think that his bomb was still in working order. "Is there any way to do that?"

Arch looked around. There was a fat jar filled with something that smelled good and looked like wood chips on the counter. It fit into the space where the polnol had been. The briefcase wasn't nearly as heavy but it looked right.

"Now what do we do with this stuff?" Arch said, meaning the polnol. "Doesn't seem safe to leave lying about like this."

I picked up a stick and twisted it to see if it was as flexible as Arch said. It was. I looked over at the stalls and said, "Whaddayathink?"

Arch shrugged, took one of the sticks into a stall. Dropped it into the commode and flushed. "Good, but best not put them all down one crapper and clog it. Spread the wealth."

When we were finished, three flushes later, Arch said, "What are you planning?"

"Can you rig that detonator to go off when you open the briefcase?"

Chapter Fifty-Seven

When we got back to the Rainbow Room, Henninger's guests were mobbed in front of the three long tables with the phony stock certificates. Henninger was on the other side. Arch went straight into the crowd and bulled his way toward the front. I stayed at the top of the stairs until I saw Connie. She was back at the mirrored bar talking on a telephone. Good. Figure she'd reached Marie Therese. I scanned the crowd for Voss, but couldn't spot him. Maybe he'd taken a powder to be sure he wasn't caught by his own bomb. Hoped not. I carried the briefcase down the stairs to the dance floor. The old guys were jostling each other, trying to get a better look at Henninger's goods. He was standing behind the center table and holding up one of the certificates. Daphne was behind him. When she saw me, she gave a small nod. I walked back to Connie as she was hanging up. I could tell something was wrong.

"What is it?"

"They won't leave. Frenchy just made last call, but they're going to stay there. She said they'll try to telephone Mahan and Norris but if they can't get them, she and Frenchy will turn on all the lights and stay outside by the doors."

"Goddammit."

"There's no talking them out of it. She's—"

Daphne grabbed Connie's arm. "What's happening? These men are going out of their minds with the bidding."

"It's an auction, then?" I said.

"Harold says it's more successful than he ever imagined."

"Not for much longer."

Daphne looked confused. Connie said, "It's about to hit the fan."

"Tell me something," I said to Daphne. "Do you know Franz Voss?"

She wasn't expecting the question. "Of course. He's one of Harold's oldest friends. They're related by marriage through the German branch of the family. Why?"

"It's too complicated to explain right now, but all the stuff that's about to happen, he's behind it."

Before I could say any more, Arch's voice cut through the noise of the crowd. Figure he must have spent some time on the stage because when he wanted to, Arch could really project. "What's your game, Henninger? These are phonies. Look at the muddy engraving here and they've even misspelled *Chrysler*!"

The other men backed away from him, leaving Arch and Henninger facing each other across the center table. "From the moment you started telling me about this piratical enterprise of yours something seemed less than completely copasetic, and now I know what it is."

"That is a lie, sir, a damnable lie!" Henninger could thunder as loud as Arch and he looked to be genuinely offended. I guess he was. Voss and Forlini played him for a sucker and he still hadn't tumbled to it. "I stand behind every word I've said tonight and everything I've presented. I'd be a fool to try to trick any of these men."

While Arch and Henninger yammered away at each other, I tried to find Voss. I spotted him when he stepped out of the crowd of men and started walking around so he could see Arch's face. Until then, Voss had only had glimpses of the back of Arch's head, Voss being, like me, not tall enough to see over the others. He craned his neck as he moved, trying to keep his eyes on Arch and Henninger. I whispered "Hold this," and handed my stick to Connie. Then I moved as quick as I could through the tables, trying to get close to Voss but staying behind him. I didn't want him to know I was there. Not yet.

I was guessing that when he heard Arch's voice, he knew that he knew it from somewhere but couldn't identify it. Voss had ordered his thugs to tear up my place after Fat Joe betrayed him, but he had no reason to connect anything involving me or the bar to his business with Henninger. He wasn't worried about Arch queering his deal with the phony stocks because, in a few minutes, he intended to kill everyone in the Rainbow Room anyway. Voss didn't really care about Henninger's argument but he was curious. When I was right behind him, I put the briefcase on the floor, leaning it against his leg. He looked down and tried to step away from it until I pressed the little automatic into the small of his back.

"I believe you left this at your table," I said keeping my voice low. "Wouldn't want anybody to walk off with it, would you."

He stiffened when he felt the barrel of the pistol and heard my voice. Figure then he knew something had screwed up and he was trying to think of a way to fix it. He meant to sound calm when he spoke but his voice cracked at first. "Jimmy, I didn't expect to see you at a function like this."

He tried to turn around. I jabbed the muzzle into his back. "Don't do it, I'll put a bullet through your spine."

"Is this some kind of joke? You've got a reputation as a tough guy but this is going too far."

"Is it, oberführer?"

Long pause. Then, "What are you talking about?"

"Pick up the briefcase. We'll go back to your table and talk about it." I held the pistol against my side and stepped away. "After you."

He did what I said and we weren't face to face until we were sitting at the two-top. He glanced down at the little pistol. I kept it against my leg, pointed at his stomach, and I knew we couldn't stay like that for long. You don't pull a gun on a guy to threaten him or control him, you pull a gun a guy to shoot him. We both knew I would have a hard time talking my way out of it if I shot him in the Rainbow Room. At first, he smiled and tried to keep bluffing. Made a show of taking a cigarette from his case and lighting it. Sitting back and blowing smoke. "Now what was it you called me? Ober-something?"

"It's not gonna wash. I know about the Silver Legion thugs. What they did to Fat Joe in that garage down near Pearl Street. I know about you meeting Dr. Griebl in the McAlpin and sending him and his sweet patootie back to the Fatherland. I know about the bomb at the rally. I know you're wondering why you haven't heard anything about what happened there. I know that you hired Forlini to make up these bogus certificates. And I know that you planned for this little party to end with a bang. Did I leave anything out?"

He kept smiling and shook his head. "Jimmy, I'm sorry, I have no idea what any of that means. Why would you think that I had anything to do with Josef's death? If you suspect that I do, I'd be happy to accompany you to any police station to discuss it with the authorities."

I had to hand it to him. Like Bruno Hauptmann, he wasn't going to admit to anything. "And I don't know why you've got that gun. You're not going to shoot anyone in this place, but I don't care for your threats so I'll be leaving."

He smiled, stubbed out his smoke, and got up. So did I, and I picked up the briefcase and held it out to him. He backed away. "Take it or I will shoot you, to hell with whatever happens next." He took it.

Arch was still holding forth and judging by the sound of the guys around him, some of them bought what he was saying. Voices were getting louder and angrier. Connie must have been watching me. She caught up to us on the stairs and handed me my stick. Voss glanced back when he heard her. His hard expression didn't change. I stayed close behind him through the hall and into the small lobby at the elevators. He pressed the button, the door opened immediately.

Voss stepped into the car and pressed the button. As the doors started to slide shut, his face twisted and I could see how angry he really was. He swung the briefcase back, ready to toss it into the lobby. I raised the pistol and pointed it at his face. The doors closed. We heard the hum of the motors and cables and seconds later, I imagined that I heard a distant snap of something small exploding.

Maybe I didn't imagine it because Connie said, "What was that noise?"

"The detonator. Arch rewired it to go off if somebody jerked the top open."

"Did it kill him?"

I shook my head. "Might've hurt him, but probably just surprised him." Behind us, the sound of men's voices grew louder then went silent, and we heard Henninger. "That is a goddamn lie and I'll fight any man who says it's so."

Chapter Fifty-Eight

When Connie and I got back to the Rainbow Room, Henninger and Arch were trying to stare each other down. Arch told me later that after Connie, Voss, and me left, a few more of Henninger's pals noticed things they didn't like about the certificates, and Henninger came around to their side of the table to argue his point. He glared at Arch, and the clincher came when Arch took a deep breath and used his big voice to say, "I know that that man," pointing at a guy on the other side of the table, "that man is a convicted counterfeiter. His name is Romeo Forlini. Do you deny it?"

Forlini didn't say anything, but the way he looked around like he was trying to find something to hide behind let everybody know Arch had nailed it. The room went quiet until Henninger yelled out "That is a goddamn lie and I'll fight any man who says it's so."

Arch smiled. "It's the truth, you smug asshole."

Henninger's face went red. The men standing closest to them backed away to give them room. As he shrugged off his jacket, Henninger said, "You'll live to regret those words, Middleford," and took a standard fighter's stance, left arm up, right tucked in. He was half a foot taller than Arch and might have outweighed him by fifty pounds, but he'd fought in the ring at Yale. Arch had fought in alleys and barracks and trenches and bars and back rooms and dirt and mud.

Arch didn't bother with his suitcoat. Before the big man took a step, Arch went straight for him, moving faster than I'd ever seen. I can't tell you what he did because I was looking at his back, but Henninger screamed and backpedaled. Arch stayed with him and moved in close to work on Henninger's body. His punches were so fast and tight his arms were a blur. Henninger kept backing away. When a couple of his friends tried to move in to help him, he waved them off. Arch slipped right back in and hammered away at his belly. Henninger tried to get him in a clinch. That didn't work so he pushed him away. As Arch was coming back in, the big man tagged him with a right that landed near the top of Arch's head but didn't slow him down. Arch still worked the body, moving lower, below the belt. He landed one solid shot that doubled Henninger over and knocked the wind out of him. Arch went for the head, crooking his arm to catch Henninger's nose with his elbow. The nose erupted. Henninger howled and went down on his ass. A few of his friends jumped in and went after Arch.

I came behind them with my stick. Reversed it and smacked one guy on the back of his head with the crook end. It split his scalp but didn't really hurt him. Reversed the stick again and stabbed the guy beside him in the ribs. When he turned to me, I jabbed the tip up under his chin. The first guy came down on my back and all three of us wound up on the floor. One of them got an arm around my throat. He was trying to pull me up when he went limp and his weight pushed me down again. The other guy was grabbing at me when Connie stepped in and smacked him in the mouth with my knucks. She tagged the first guy, too, knocked him out.

While we were going at it, somebody knocked over one of the tables and the phony certificates that had been neatly stacked up went flying.

I got to my feet, looking to see if anybody else wanted to dance. Nobody did. They weren't used to punches being thrown so seriously. By then, Henninger was sitting on a chair with his head bent back. Daphne was beside him, holding a napkin pressed to his bloody face. He was fighting against her as he tried to stand. I suspect Arch's shot to his nose must've rattled his brain. He pulled the red-stained napkin away and tried to talk. He pointed at Arch. "I don't know what you think you're doing, but these certificates are absolutely genuine. My cousin Franz can explain everything. He showed me all the proof any man needs to see." He stood and looked around the room trying to find him. "Franz, where are you?"

Franz was nowhere to be seen. Neither was Forlini. Henninger's knees gave out and he collapsed into the chair again. The rest of his guests, the old gents and their girlfriends, seemed dazed, not sure what they should do now.

Arch came over to where we were standing. Except for a smear of blood on his sleeve, he looked fine. I had a little blood on my face. It wasn't mine, but my good Arnold Constable was ruined. Hell.

Connie said, "Let's get out of here. I'm worried about Marie Therese."

We headed toward the elevator, but Arch stopped. Connie saw he wasn't with us and turned around.

Arch was staring at Daphne. Her attention was still on Henninger. Arch took a step toward her. She looked up at him. He didn't say anything but you could tell how much he wanted her to come with us. Maybe she thought about it, but Henninger snuffled and she pressed the napkin to his nose.

Arch said, "We need to go," and the three of us headed for the elevators. By then, a lot of Henninger's pals had decided they'd seen enough and the little lobby was crowded. The men who recognized Arch as the guy who'd mixed it up with Henninger backed away from us. While we waited for the elevator car, I worried. Despite everything that had happened that day, nothing had been decided.

Chapter Fifty-Nine

We were the first ones out of the elevator and headed straight for the doors on Fifth Avenue to catch a downtown cab. I gave the cabbie the address for Jimmy's Place and said there was an extra buck in it for him if he was fast. He tried but the traffic around midnight was thick. The three of us in the back seat didn't say much at first. Arch's expression was grim, thinking about Daphne, but when he saw that I was looking at him, he shrugged it off and might've smiled. It was hard to tell behind the soup strainer. Connie was worried that there was a third bomb. For my part, I knew that Voss wasn't finished, especially after I'd stupidly told him that I knew so much about his business. He wasn't going to let that go and what was he going to do about it?

I turned to Connie. "Marie Therese said they were going to call the cops, tell them about a bomb threat?"

"She said they'd call the precinct. Usually if we telephone, they'll radio Mahan and Norris right away, but you never know if they get them."

I said to the cabbie, "Pull over at the next telephone booth you see."

"But you said—"

"Get me to a phone and there's another buck for you."

Two blocks later, he pulled to the curb. I got out, fed a nickel into the slot and called the precinct house. When the desk sergeant answered I said, "This is Jimmy Quinn. Did you get a call for Patrolmen Mahan and Norris about something going on at my place?"

The sergeant, a regular, said, "Hiya, Jimmy. Yeah, Marie Therese called. I told the radio desk."

"Do you know did they reach the car?"

"Lemme check, hold on."

Seemed like it took him an hour as I sat there in the booth.

"Jimmy, yeah, he got 'em but he can't say where they are or what they're doing."

I gimped back to the cab and told the cabbie to step on it again. When he was on Twenty-Second headed toward Jimmy's Place, I told him to hold down his speed and go on to the intersection. If Voss or one of his blond thugs was in the bar watching the narrow street, I didn't want him to see anything out of the ordinary, like a cab crawling past.

"None of the outside lights are on," Connie said. "Maybe they went home." She didn't believe it. And I could see through the little window in the front door that there was light inside. Most nights, we'd leave the light on under the awning, if we remembered. It was dark.

When we got out at Seventh, I pulled a fiver out of my money clip. Mr. Big Spender told the cabbie to keep the change. Made his night.

Arch said, "What now?"

"We wait fifteen minutes for Norris and Mahan."

"What if they're not here by then?" Said Connie.

"Then we'll decide what to do." I didn't know what that would be, and I was so angry and frustrated by my place being threatened again that I wasn't thinking as well as I needed to. When I get mad, I get stupid. Sometimes I remember that.

Twelve minutes later, headlights appeared at the far end of the street. As they got closer, we saw the red light and the POLICE sign on top of the car, and we hurried down to meet it. Mahan and Norris got out. When they saw three figures approaching, their hands went to their pistols.

"It's us," I said, not raising my voice.

Mahan waited until he saw my face before he relaxed. "What's going on, Jimmy? Radio said you had a bomb threat?" He looked at the dark doorway. "Close up early because of it?"

"It's hard to explain but I think that the same guys who tore the place up before may be coming back and I know they've got what they need to make a bomb. We weren't here when we found that out. Connie called Marie Therese and she said her and Frenchy would stay but turn on the outside lights. That's all we know."

Mahan looked at the dark steps going down to the front door and the faint light coming from behind it. He told Norris to get the flash lamps from the trunk and asked if I had my key. I told him I did. "We'll check your entrance and then inside. That o.k. with you?"

"Exactly what I need."

Mahan and Norris went first, playing their lights around the steps and the door. Broken glass glittered on the ground. Norris pointed his flash up at the light fixture under the awning. The big bulb was broken. Connie said, "It was fine this morning."

This was getting worse and worse. I eased the.32 out of my coat pocket and worked a round into the chamber. Palmed the little pistol against my leg. Mahan and Norris went down the steps to the door. Norris raised a fist to knock. I said, "See if it's open."

It was. They turned off their lamps and went in. I was close behind them. Light from the bar came through the open door. The cops moved carefully, slowly. I was impatient. At first, as we stepped past the coat room, everything looked normal. No customers. Light was coming from behind the bar and the hallway to the bathrooms. When we got into the main room I saw them. Voss, showing no sign that the detonator had hurt him, was standing at the bar with his back to it. Frenchy was behind the bar. I think he'd started to smile with relief when he saw Mahan and Norris. When he saw me, he cut his eyes to the right, and I knew where the trouble was.

Marie Therese was sitting in one of the banquette booths about halfway back. She was in the middle, flanked by two blond thugs that I recognized from the Bureau man's pictures. She looked scared. They looked like blond thugs. All three of them had their hands below the table.

Voss, sounding like he was my oldest pal, said, "I took a chance that you'd be coming back here, and now we can finish our talk. Would the officers care for anything to drink?"

Without thinking it through, I stepped over and stopped in front of the booth. I was deliberately slow, leaning on my stick. And I was not threatening a soul until I raised the automatic and shot the two blond thugs. The one on Marie Therese's right looked to be the more alert and sharper of the pair. I pointed the muzzle at the upper right part of his chest, away from her and pulled the trigger twice. Both rounds hit him. I rotated right and shot the other blond thug twice. Missed once, hit once. He brought his pistol up from under the table and I shot him again. He dropped it. I turned back to my left. The first thug was sitting there with his eyes wide and his mouth open in surprise. He didn't raise his hands but I heard a pistol clatter on the floor. It all happened in less than five seconds.

I turned back toward Mahan as he was drawing his pistol and I put mine on the floor. Stepped back and raised my hands in the air.

Marie Therese shoved the first blond thug hard. The numb one. He slid a few inches across the seat. She shoved him again and he fell out of the booth and onto his side. She scooted out and kicked him in the head. Voss yelled for her to stop and I saw that he was pointing an automatic at her. Frenchy pulled the hogleg he keeps on a nail under the bar and belted Voss across the temple with it. He fell to a knee. Mahan yelled for him to drop the gun. Frenchy yelled over Mahan, "They did something in the men's room." Arch bolted toward the back and found the third bomb. It was the same crude workmanship but two sticks of polnol in a cardboard box. Guess Voss didn't have another briefcase. Arch said it was harmless.

After that, things got busier and more confusing.

Chapter Sixty

Connie rushed over to Marie Therese. The two of them went to a smaller booth in the back. I asked Marie Therese if she needed anything and she said, "No, but I would like to kick that blond bastard again, and the other one."

Mahan told Norris to go back to their car and radio for more cops and an ambulance and to bring in their first-aid kit. I stopped Norris on his way out. "Get Ellis," I said so nobody else could hear it. I wanted to be sure there was at least one detective on hand that I could work with. First I needed to figure what Voss had done over the past couple of hours and why.

Voss had been surprised to see me at Henninger's. He had no way of knowing I'd be there so he couldn't have planned to do anything here in the bar. How much time had passed between his leaving the Rainbow Room and our leaving? Thirty minutes, forty-five? Less probably. But he had been planning to make a getaway before the bomb went off, so he had these two thugs waiting in a car nearby. Figure they're armed. A third bomb? Possible. How did it play out? Voss gets down to the lobby of Rockefeller Center. He's angry and confused. What the hell happened? He's been planning this operation for months. Two bombings in one night that will show the world Germany is not the enemy. You see, these well-organized Jew bastard Reds attacked patriotic German-Americans and successful capitalists. And then this short good looking saloon-keeper shows up and ruins everything. Where did he come from? How is he involved? Before Voss can do anything else, he has to know the answer to those questions. He orders his two thugs to take him to Jimmy's Place. They force their way in, and when we get there Frenchy is behind the bar, where Voss has ordered him to be. Marie Therese is between the two thugs who have guns pointed at her. Without thinking it through, I shoot them, and now here we are.

The two perforated thugs weren't bleeding that much but the second one was making bubbling sounds with each breath. Figure I hit a lung. Mahan collected their guns and took a quick look at the crude bomb. His first comment was, "Jeez, what a mess."

Then he looked around and said, "All right, who's gonna explain this?" The thug on the floor was still dazed. Foam flecked the corners of his mouth. Mahan turned to the second. "What have you got to say for yourself."

He looked at Voss, who shook his head and said, "*Sag Nichts.*" Figure that meant *Shut up.*

Arch said, "They're not going to talk, officer."

"You speak German, Arch?"

"A bit but I don't think it'll help."

"We'll see about that." Mahan went over to the bar and took Voss's pistol from Frenchy. Voss had taken a seat at a two-top. He was holding a pocket square to the red welt on his temple. "You, what's your name and what's your part in all this?"

Voss moved to reach into his breast pocket. Mahan brought up his service revolver. "Easy there."

Voss made a show of using his forefinger and thumb to pull out his wallet. "As you can see, officer," he made the word *officer* an insult, "I have diplomatic immunity. I demand that you contact the German Embassy immediately and arrange for my transportation."

That's what happened. Eventually. The second blond thug stayed clammed up. The first blond thug shivered. I don't think he could've talked if he'd wanted to. The ambulance arrived. The attendants patched up the gunshot wounds and took them to Bellevue. When Mahan questioned Marie Therese and Frenchy, they mostly told the truth. Said we'd telephoned and warned that there might be trouble. They made an early last call. As they were closing down, somebody knocked on the door and these three forced their way in. The blond thugs said they'd shoot Marie Therese if Frenchy tried anything.

While they were telling their story, Ellis showed up. It was the first time I'd seen him since he delivered the things I used at the McAlpin Hotel. He made Frenchy and Marie Therese go over it again from the beginning, and he wanted to know who was the guy at the two-top and what did he have to do with everything. Mahan said his name was Franz Voss and explained about the diplomatic immunity.

Ellis said, "Oh, shit," and he turned to me. What was my story?

That was a little harder to work through. "It's like this," I explained. "I crashed a swanky private party in the Rainbow Room, high atop Rockefeller Center."

"The hell you say," he yelled in my face. "It's too late and I'm too tired to listen to some bullshit story you're making up."

"It's true," Connie said, and something about the way she said it made him begin to believe me.

"Anyway, at this party, I struck up a conversation with a gent I met there, fellow named Henninger, and it turned out that we had a common acquaintance, Franz Voss. I said that Voss had been a customer of mine for years. This gent said that Franz Voss was involved with a group called the Silver Shirts, and they were thinking about doing the same thing to Jews in America that they were doing in Germany. I told him that some guys had torn up my place and I had reason to think they might be these Silver Shirts. He suggested I might want to be extra careful then, and that's what I did."

I doubt that he'd have bought a word of it, but Arch came over and said that if Ellis doubted me, he could contact Rockefeller Center and see if the name Archibald Middleford was on the guest list of the private function that was held there.

Ellis said, "Middleford?"

"A young lady is involved and I thought it best not to use my real name."

Ellis shook his head. He turned to Mahan, "And there's no question that the other two were threatening Marie Therese when Quinn shot them."

"None. We have their guns."

"Alright, then I'll go to Bellevue."

More cops arrived after that, including a couple who said they were from the bomb squad. They looked at the tangle of wires in the cardboard box and shook their heads and laughed. One of them said, "This is the worst fucking excuse for a bomb I've ever seen." While all that was going on, Voss sat at the two-top and smoked cigarettes and said nothing. Until three o'clock when two beefy thick-necked krauts and an older, white-haired man came in the front door without knocking. One of them flashed a badge or official identification at Mahan and said they were authorized to take this man with them. The older man glared at Voss. Voss leapt from his chair. He stood at attention, clicked his heels and bowed to the white-haired man. The white-haired man made an impatient gesture toward Voss and Voss hurried over to him. While Mahan and the two thick-necked krauts dickered over what was going to happen, the white-haired man dressed down Voss. I don't understand German but I could tell that the old guy was ripping him a new one. A few minutes later they left.

It seemed strange to me that they could just waltz in and waltz out with him, but Mahan said it wasn't. "I've dealt with these characters before, and they can do pretty much whatever the hell they want and we can't do shit about it. The brass has explained that we have to let them act like this so that our guys in foreign countries don't get bullied around."

"Yeah, but it's a hell of a way to run a railroad if you ask me."

By then, Mahan and Norris were the only two left. I said, "Gentlemen, thanks for everything you've done tonight. The bar is open."

"No thanks," Mahan said, "Paperwork's going to be a bastard on this one."

I slipped each of them a fistful of twenties on their way out.

After they left, Arch went down to the cellar and brought up the hundred-year-old Croizet Cognac. Connie and Marie Therese wanted wine. We sat at a six-top and filled each other in on everything else that had happened that day and before. The sun was rising before we finished. And when we did finish, I was exhausted, and it felt like nothing had been settled, nothing had been accomplished. They killed Fat Joe three weeks ago. Since then, I'd been chasing my tail. The rally in Newark, the Bureau man Turcot, the blond thugs vandalizing my place, the McAlpin Hotel, the bombs. I didn't understand these things. And I'd put a bullet hole in the wall that would have to be repaired, and one of the blond thugs had bled on my newly reupholstered banquette.

Chapter Sixty-One

The Burean man said, "They matched one rail of Hauptmann's ladder with the floorboards in his attic. Some of the nail holes even line up with the joists. They've known it for weeks but they're holding it back, probably until the trial."

"Most guys, you'd think something like that would be enough to make them confess, but with Bruno, I wouldn't bet on it."

It was about noon on Friday. Turcot had called that morning and said he needed to talk. I told him to come over before we opened. He was sitting at the bar. I was behind it. He looked as tired as I felt. Red eyes, tie loosely knotted, dried mustard on his lapel.

"Knowing how interested you are in the Lindbergh case, I thought you'd appreciate that detail, but what I really want to know is your version of what happened at the Lyceum Theater rally." He drained his vodka and rattled his ice. I made him another.

"All I know about Yorkville is what I read in the papers. A dust-up between your Silver Shirt guys and some Jews. What was it, four people arrested?" There'd been no mention of a body in the projection booth.

"Horse manure. Tell me what you know."

That's when it came to me. "You didn't get the authorization you needed to go after Dr. Griebl." I was his last shot at getting enough information to convince his bosses. He didn't say anything, his expression was enough.

He looked at his vodka for a second before he drank. Then, "We were too late. He should have been at the Lyceum, but something went wrong there. Even though Arno's men were heavily outnumbered, they disrupted everything."

Yeah, four trained fighters against a couple hundred overweight slobs who'd been swilling down beer all afternoon. Who'd've thought it?

"Now Voss has disappeared and the cooperation that the city police promised has dried up. And because of that, I can't get the manpower I need for an operation. I'm disappointed, of course, not for myself or my career but because the Germans are still at it. They know war is coming. They're already fighting it in secret, and we refuse to see it. Not everyone, though. You've seen it first hand with what they did to Josef Bruder and the rest of it, but you're not going to do anything."

I guess there was a lot I could've said then, but I couldn't risk letting him know what happened. If I gave him anything to bring back to his bosses, I'd find myself in front of a grand jury and that would ruin me. He downed his drink and left.

There had been nothing in the papers about a disturbance in the Rainbow Room, but then I didn't expect it. The papers had nothing to say about anything out of the ordinary at Jimmy's Place either. Natch. A few customers who lived on Twenty-Second Street mentioned that they'd seen some cop cars and an ambulance in front of the joint. Our story was a couple of drunk customers got into a fight and hurt each other. Nobody we knew. Later in the week, Mahan told me about the blond thugs I shot. The first night at Bellevue, they stayed dummied up on Ellis. Since then, one had been released. They wanted to keep the other one, the guy I hit in the lung. The first thug was charged with something like disturbing the peace and given a low bail. He took a powder. The same thing happened with the second one when he was released. I can't say I was surprised but it was still damned unsatisfactory.

Of all of us, though, Arch had the toughest time with the way things turned out.

"There was a moment there," he told me late one night over our third drink, "when I was spending my nights in her bed that I could imagine a future where we pooled my fortune with hers, which we had taken from that candyass Henninger, and the two of us decamped to parts unknown. But it's not going to happen because she has taken him in."

"What?"

"Oh, yes, word has spread quickly that Harold tried to fleece his friends with counterfeit stocks. No one will have anything to do with him. There's even a rumor that his wife will demand a divorce. For now, he's living in Daphne's little house, though I'm sure both of them are beginning to find it a bit cramped. I've been keeping an eye on them. Yesterday, after I saw him leave, I telephoned her. When she heard my voice, she lied and said that she couldn't talk because Harold was there. It was better that I not try to call her again. She'll get in touch with me as soon as it's safe."

He touched his glass to mine. "To the one that got away."

As for me, I still knew that I'd spent three weeks trying to accomplish something I couldn't define. Somebody killed Fat Joe, so I had to do something about it. I did do something but it didn't mean anything. At work, I tried to be amiable with the customers and interested in what they had to say, but it didn't wash. I wasn't fooling anybody, certainly not Connie. Even if I couldn't explain to her what was bothering me, she knew what it was, and she knew what to do for me.

On the afternoon of Thursday, October 18, we were in the Chelsea getting ready to go to work. Somebody knocked on the door and a voice said, "Delivery for Quinn." I didn't remember ordering anything and looked at Connie. The way she tried to act like she didn't know what it was told me that something was up.

"What's going on?"

"One way to find out," she said.

I opened the door and a guy in a nice suit wheeled in a big chest about four feet tall strapped to a handcart. He released the strap and handed me a clipboard with a receipt from Abercrombie & Fitch and said, "Sign here." I did. He eased the chest off the hand truck.

"What is it?"

Connie said, "Abercrombie & Fitch's finest gentleman's steamer trunk and a matching suitcase. I wish I'd had this for the first trip. It's much nicer than mine." It was covered in dark brown leather with brass studs. She undid two brass buckles on leather straps and the lock in the middle. Then she pulled it open, and it smelled even more expensive. One side was drawers for small stuff. On the other side, you could hang about six suits with room for shoes on the bottom. And there was the suitcase with more straps and buckles.

"It's for me, then?"

"You signed for it."

"You bought it."

"Yes, I bought it for you. I also bought two tickets on the *Ile de France*, leaving from Pier 57 at 11:00 on Saturday. If you don't want to come with me, I'm sure I can find someone who does."

"But what about—"

"I've talked this through with Marie Therese and Frenchy and Arch. They can take care of the place for six weeks."

I didn't need to think about it and I knew that if I hesitated, she'd get the wrong idea. I'd said no too many times when she suggested doing something that scared me. "What time do we need to leave?"

Chapter Sixty-Two

Having done this before and talked to other passengers on her ship, Connie knew the drill. You didn't get your friend with his flatbed truck to take you and your luggage to the pier. No, you contact a car service and they collect the heavy stuff a day early. That's what we did. On Friday, a couple of guys came to the Chelsea and picked up our big trunks, and on Saturday morning, one of their cars picked us up. Connie was wearing her favorite Paris outfit, a black jacket and trousers, something you didn't see on women that much, but it looked terrific on her. I had replaced my good Arnold Constable three-piece that got ruined in the Rainbow Room and I wore it with a light blue shirt with a white collar, and patterned silk tie. I looked almost as good as she did.

When the car got closer to Pier 57, my nerves tightened and I saw that the knuckles gripping my stick were pale. Connie noticed and grabbed my hand. "Don't worry, it's not going to be like the last time. Nobody's trying to kill us."

"That, I knew how to handle. This… this is something I've never done."

Funny thing. I was born within blocks of the West Side piers and I'd spent a fair amount of time near the docks, but I'd never set foot on a ship. Traffic got thicker as we approached Pier 57 and the big black side of the *Ile de France* appeared. The driver kept to the right and maneuvered toward a cop who waved him to a lane for hired cars that took us into a busy parking area. The driver got out and waved to a guy in a French Line uniform who had a wooden cart that looked like a wheelbarrow. I gave him our tickets. He put tags on the suitcases, tore the tags in half and gave my halves to me. I tipped him and the driver, and Connie led me into the huge dim building. We walked through the crowd to the stairs that went to the upper level. I knew it didn't make any sense but I couldn't help tensing up. The last time

I'd been there, a big bitch tried to kill Connie and me. That's why I had the .32 in my coat pocket. People were gathered around three doorways that led from the pier building to the ship. Connie led us past them to another doorway for first class. A guy in a French Line uniform with a lot of shiny buttons looked at the tickets and waved us through.

We went out of the building back into bright sunlight and a gangplank with handrails. I glanced down and saw that we were high above the dirty water and the ship's smokestacks towered over us. It was a short walk across to the ship but it felt a lot longer, and just as we stepped inside, the ship's steam horn went off. It was a loud, piercing sound that startled me. I'd been hearing the sound all my life but not that close. Another guy in an even more important-looking French Line uniform took our tickets and snapped his fingers for a bellboy. Before the kid led us into the ship, the French Line guy motioned for us to scrape our shoes on a wide bristled doormat.

Connie said, "They try to keep the dirt from the port out of the ship."

The more important-looking guy gave the bellboy our tickets and two keys. He led us through a crowded, high-ceilinged lobby where somebody else looked at our tickets. Then we went into a series of narrow corridors. We passed another bellboy going the other way who was tapping a set of chimes. Connie said, "He's telling guests that it's time to leave. Ship's about to sail." The kid took us to a set of elevators where we waited for a few minutes, and then rode up a couple of floors. More corridors, these wider, until we reached our room… no, our "suite de luxe," Connie said. And she was right. Except for the two single beds which we could work around, it was not bad. Sitting room, bedroom, bathroom, two good-sized windows that opened onto the top deck… no, the boat deck. Connie said we had a maid and valet who'd press my suits if needed.

Since our suitcases weren't there yet, Connie took me on a tour of the ship. It was bigger than the one she'd been on a few months before, and she really didn't know her way around, so we spent several hours wandering through it. By the end, I was completely confused and doubted I'd be able to find anything on my own. We'd just got started on it when the horn sounded again with a long blast. That meant we were pulling out of the dock in thirty minutes, according to Connie. She took us through the main rooms, the first-class dining room and the lounge, all several decks tall, and designed like the Rainbow Room with curves instead of right angles.

Once the tugs had moved the ship out of the dock and turned it toward the mouth of the harbor, we went up to the boat deck. Outside, it was cold and windy and sunny. Connie grabbed my arm and we moved to the side of the deck to get a good look. I was as close to the Statue of Liberty as I'd ever been. Another first. At about the same time, I noticed the vibration of the deck and the bass rumble of the engines, and something caused the ship to shudder. Connie grabbed the rail and I braced myself with my stick but that passed quickly.

Connie wrapped her arms around me and said, "You don't know how wonderful this is going to be. Trust me, you're gonna love it."

I hate it when anybody says "trust me," even Connie.

We went back into the ship. I made certain I could locate a few key places in relation to the elevators and stairs that led up to our room. When we got there, our suitcases had arrived. Connie said that she had to change clothes for dinner. Even though we were on a French Line ship, ladies in trousers were not allowed. I told her I was going to find a bar. There had to be someplace on this boat where a man could sit down and have a quiet drink. I picked up my copy of the *Times* and set off.

The Smoking Room was out, and the big Lounge was too crowded and too loud. It took almost half an hour and the advice of a steward to find what I was looking for, a nice little hole in the wall with a short bar, a dozen two-tops, club chairs, and no customers that early. The place had the proper amount of dim light, but there were a couple of tables with reading lights. The bottles on the shelves behind the bar were top quality. My kind of place.

The bartender, who'd been reading a newspaper, looked up and said, "*Oui, monsieur?*"

"*Remy Martin, s'il vous plait,*" I said, using up most of the French I'd learned, and put my key on the bar. He saw it was first class and poured a generous shot. I took it to one of the reading tables and opened the paper. Bruno Hauptmann had made it back to the front page, above the fold. They'd extradited him to New Jersey on Friday night. At 7:10, the Appellate Court denied his appeal against it, and by 8:40, he was crossing the George Washington Bridge and heading for a jail cell in Flemington, New Jersey. Looked like he'd be arraigned on the murder charge on Monday, and the trial would begin next month. The governor swore it would be fair. Trial of the Century and I'd be missing it. I thought about it over a sip of Remy. Then I heard a familiar voice.

"*Avez vous Teeling? Et de bons glaçons solides?*"

"*Oui, monsieur.*"

Voss, what the hell? Even with his back to me, I recognized the bone-white hair and the Savile Row suit, the Davies & Son. The bartender gave him the drink. He raised it to the light and said, "*J'aime lui donner juste quelques secondes pour refroidir—*"

"I give it a few seconds to cool to the proper temperature," I said. His back stiffened. I slipped the .32 out of my pocket and laid it on the table. Covered it with a section of the paper. "Two completely frozen cubes are all you need to chill the whiskey. Don't use cracked or shaved ice. Look close and you'll see the amber whiskey and the melting ice commingle in the glass."

Voss turned around and tried to smile when he saw me but he couldn't hide the anger and surprise as he stepped slowly to my two-top. I heard it in his tight voice. "I certainly didn't expect to see you here."

"Like a bad penny, right?"

"I am wondering how we find ourselves on the same ship. I cannot believe that it's a coincidence after you have involved yourself so forcefully in my recent affairs. I struggle to understand it."

He paused while he thought. "Turcot got to you, didn't he. He must have seen Josef with the others, and he used that to force you to cooperate with him. But that doesn't explain the rest of it." He sat, trying to look relaxed but he was strung tight.

"I'm going to Paris, and I guess you're heading back to the Fatherland. From the way the old guy with the glasses was dressing you down, I figure that your plan to set off two bombs on one night had not been approved, and your boss was really pissed off. Is that about right?"

He stared straight at me and his expression turned stony. "I know you work with Lansky and Arno, and that explains your presence in Newark and at the Lyceum. It was a mistake to trust those idiots with the briefcase. I shouldn't have hurried."

Hurried? Why did he hurry? Because of Hauptmann, because the guy who committed the Crime of the Century, was German.

"And it still makes no sense to me how you could have acquired this information or even why you would have been involved in the first place.

And how could the old man who works for you have been invited to Harold's auction."

I shouldn't have said anything. Should have let him wonder and worry about it for the rest of his life, but I couldn't. I leaned forward and said, "You made three big mistakes. First you killed Fat Joe. Second—"

"He betrayed us to Turcot, and they weren't supposed to kill him. He was to be beaten severely. I wanted him to live and become a warning to the others."

"Second, you dumped him in front of my place. That insulted me and then you insulted me again when you sent your thugs to tear it up."

"The idiots did that on their own."

"They were your idiots, just like Fat Joe was my idiot."

"Then we're even."

I shook my head. "Not nearly. But tell me something. I'm a decent judge of character, particularly when it comes to customers, and I genuinely believed that you enjoyed coming into Jimmy's Place—the Teeling and the conversation."

He sat straighter and his face brightened. "Oh, I did. For a time, it was one of my favorite places to visit. I made a point of seeing you every time I was in the city. But then it changed."

"What changed?"

"I learned that you worked with Rothstein and Lansky. I don't understand how an intelligent man like yourself can bring himself to associate with the Jews. I thought there might be hope for you until you said that you knew good Germans and bad Germans and good Jews and bad Jews. That kind of race treachery cannot be allowed."

His voice rose as he got more wound up and he hit the table with his fist. "How can you not understand *there are no good Jews!*"

The bartender's head snapped up and he turned to us.

"Then let me get this straight, because you hate Jews and because Hauptmann is making Germans look bad, you're willing to blow up a couple hundred people."

"A small price to pay when it comes to winning a war." He leaned back in his club chair, sipped his Teeling, and smiled.

"You're worse than your damn cousin."

Something about that insult got to him and he started to lunge across the two-top. He stopped when he saw the .32 pointed at his stomach and sat back down.

"You're not going to shoot me in this bar."

"Maybe not here but it's a big ship."

He laughed and tried not to believe me. "You can't shoot me on this ship."

"I've got six days."

It took five.

Author's Notes

The theft of polnol from the Remington Arms munitions plant on Oct. 1, 1934, was real. (I can find no other references to the substance anywhere, though I haven't searched diligently.)

Judge Perlman and Rabbi Wise arranged a meeting with Meyer Lanksy. The details that Jimmy recalls are consistent with other accounts, though some writers state that it happened several years later.

Meyer Lansky, Moe Sedway, Nat Arno, and Abie Bain were real early opponents of American Nazis.

The confrontation between Jewish fighters and American Nazis in Newark happened much as Jimmy describes it.

Leo Turcot is based on Leon Turrou. To paraphrase Stephen Hunter, I have tried to separate the real historical antecedent from my grossly fictionalized version of him. Turrou was one of the famous FBI agents who, like Eliot Ness and Melvin Purvis, eventually ran afoul of J. Edgar Hoover and left the Bureau. (In 1934, it was not yet the FBI; it was simply the Bureau of Investigation.)

The McAlpin Hotel, now the Herald Towers apartment building, was one of the headquarters for German espionage operations in the United States.

Dr. Ignatz Griebl and Kate Moog were involved in German espionage. The activities described here are similar to ones that occurred later in the 1930s.

The Rainbow Room opened on Oct. 3, 1934.

Romeo Forlini was arrested for selling forged and doctored stock certificates several times. He refused a pardon from President Herbert Hoover.

The details of the Hauptmann investigation as they were made public are presented in order. Though some conspiracy theorists have claimed that Hauptmann was partially or completely innocent, his guilt and Jimmy's assessment of his actions are indisputable.

To create Jimmy's New York of 1934, I depended on the contemporaneous work of Rian James, Martin Lewis, Berenice Abbott, Reginald Marsh, Lloyd Morris, John Dos Passos, Tony Sarg, Al Hirshfeld, Gordon Kahn, and John Sloan.

Sarah Gay and Florent Crayssac at the French Line Archives provided information, photographs, and film of the company's glamorous ocean liners.

Fearless beta-readers Tom Bergin, Kim Fahs, Jan Harrison, Carole Molder, Conni (no "e") Rivers, Nan Seamans, George Seminara, and Rachel Warren Ratliff provided helpful and much-needed criticism. I cannot thank them enough.

Finally, thanks to publishers Otto Penzler and Phil Garrett.

About the Author

Michael Mayo has reviewed films for numerous publications, including The Washington Post. He has worked extensively in radio and was co-host of the nationally syndicated Movie Show on Radio and Max and Mike On the Movies. Among his books are *American Murder*, *Videohound's Horror Show*, *War Movies*, and the *Jimmy Quinn* suspense novels.